Rachel Buchanan *knew*. She knew that Mayor Henry Lee Slater was after her granddaughter Sheila. Since she had discovered Sheila was meeting Slater in secret, Rachel had resolved to put a stop to it. She would expose him for what he was, to the citizens of Rio Del Palmos and to his wife. But Rachel underestimated the obsessive nature of Slater's desire.

BAD DESIRE

BAD DESIRE

Gary Devon

A SIGNET BOOK

SIGNET
Published by the Penguin Group
Penguin Books. USA Inc., 375 Hudson Street, New York,
New York 10014, U.S.A.
Penguin Books Ltd, 27 Wrights Lane, London W8 5TZ, England
Penguin Books Australia Ltd, Ringwood, Victoria, Australia
Penguin Books Canada Ltd, 10 Alcorn Avenue,
Toronto, Ontario, Canada M4V 3B2
Penguin Books (N.Z.) Ltd, 182-190 Wairau Road, Auckland 10, New Zealand

Penguin Books Ltd, Registered Offices: Harmondsworth, Middlesex, England

Published by Signet, an imprint of New American Library, a division of
Penguin Books USA Inc. This is an authorized reprint of a hardcover
edition published by Random House, Inc.

First Signet Printing, December, 1991
10 9 8 7 6 5 4 3 2 1

 REGISTERED TRADEMARK—MARCA REGISTRADIA

Grateful acknowledgment is made to the following for permission to reprint
previously published material:

CPP/BELWIN, INC., AND INTERNATIONAL MUSIC PUBLICATIONS: Excerpts from "Mood
Indigo" by Duke Ellington, Irving Mills, and Albany Bigard. Copyright 1931
(Renewed) by Mills Music, Inc. International copyright secured. Made in U.S.A.
All rights reserved. Rights throughout the British Commonwealth and the
Eastern Hemisphere are controlled by International Music Publications. Re-
printed by permission of CPP/Belwin, Inc., and International Music Publications.

HAL LEONARD PUBLISHING CORPORATION AND CHAMPION ENTERTAINMENT ORGANI-
ZATION: Excerpts from "Every Time You Go Away" by Daryl Hall. Copyright
© 1980 by Hot Cha Music and Six Continents Music Publishing Inc. All
rights controlled by Unichappell. International copyright secured. All rights
reserved. Rights throughout the world excluding the United States and
Canada are controlled by Champion Entertainment Organization, Inc.
Reprinted by permission of Hal Leonard Publishing Corporation and
Champion Entertainment Organization, Inc.

WARNER/CHAPPELL MUSIC, INC.: Excerpts from "When Your Lover Has Gone"
by E. A. Swan. Copyright 1931 (Renewed) by Warner Bros. Inc. All rights
reserved. Used by permission.

Printed in the United States of America

To my agent and friend,
FREYA MANSTON,
who made the deam come true

I want to express my appreciation to Phyllis Levy for her unwavering enthusiasm and support during the writing of this novel. Also, thanks to my editor, Susan Kamil, for her patience and understanding. But most of all, my gratitude to my wife, Deborah, for her love and loyalty, which go beyond these words.

PART ONE

1

HIS NAME WAS John Howard Beecham, but there was not a soul still alive who could have looked at him and sworn who he was, not mother or family or kin. Over the last few years he had had his face altered twice, the first time in Quebec and then more recently in Mexico City, both times thinking that he had enough money to quit this business and live in quiet seclusion. But money had a way of running through his fingers.

He had been a good-looking man who wanted to look ordinary, and for the most part he had what he wanted—at the age of forty-nine, he looked different than he had before and, also, years younger. He knew only the illusion was important. There were some things, of course, that couldn't be changed—his crow black eyes, for example, inherited from his grandmother who had been a full-blooded Creek Indian. He thought strangers remembered his eyes. Sometimes he felt it when they looked at him, and he had to keep telling himself that as long as he didn't get caught, it didn't matter. But it worried him excessively. An idle mind, his grandmother had scolded him, is the devil's playground.

Taking the southern route, he had come to California from Biloxi, Mississippi, where there were now two outstanding warrants for his arrest on charges of first-degree murder. The warrants had been issued several months apart for men of different names and descriptions, but Beecham knew who they were for. In the past ten years, he had murdered sixteen people, men and women alike.

It was 8:55 on a Monday morning when he arrived in Los Angeles, stepping down from the bus and walking straight through the station to the street. Beecham carried an oversized gym bag, nothing else. He wore a clean blue chambray work shirt rolled at the cuffs, sturdy khaki trousers with a military cut and brown calfskin Wellingtons. He looked like a common worker, someone, he thought, who would remain anonymous in the early crowd.

On the sidewalk, he experienced a moment's disorientation, but he wasted no time, setting out toward a red Avis sign a few blocks away. From Los Angeles, Beecham would have an hour's drive north, up the coastal highway to a town called Meridian. He would arrive there a day early, exactly as he wanted it. Still keeping a deliberate pace, he crossed the intersection, all but hidden in the flow of clerks and shop girls on their way to work.

A tropical front had moved in; for the third week in May, the weather was surprisingly hot and humid. Not much different, he thought, from New Orleans. But he paid it no mind. For Beecham, things were always pretty much the same.

The stores were beginning to open for the day; interior lights were coming on behind the large plate-glass windows facing the street. He passed the window of a jewelry store where a man was setting out watches, a dress boutique with its haughty manne-quins, a department store where multiples of the same product filled each separate section of window display. A shiver crept up his spine and sank into the roots of his hair. He stopped and looked behind him, always wary, checking to see if he had somehow been followed, but no one was rushing at him from behind; nothing unexpected had happened.

When he turned his head again, Beecham saw himself endlessly reflected in a wall of thin, wire-rimmed glasses, the kind his grandmother had worn before she died. It was as if something from his past reached for him. She could have been standing there, gazing at him a hundred times over. SEE BETTER! the sign said. SEE MORE! ALL SIZES & STYLES. YOUR CHOICE . . . $9.95. It occurred to him that glasses might be the last remaining touch needed to disguise his face. If he could find lenses of clear glass, they might soften the penetrating blackness of his eyes. He decided it was worth a try and entered the store.

TWO DAYS LATER, in the town of Meridian, the door of Delaney's Tap & Dine opened and a man came in. He was a medium-size man, rough-looking, dressed in faded work clothes that were clean but a little damp from the sweltering weather outside. He carried a folded newspaper under his arm and he wore thin, wire-rimmed glasses—the air conditioning in the room made the lenses fog. For a moment, he stood inside the door, his black eyes skittering behind the steamed ovals. Then he took the glasses off, wiped them on a handkerchief and reset them on the bridge of his nose.

It was minutes before four o'clock in the afternoon, the slow time of day at Delaney's. The bartender squinted at him and went back to working the daily crossword puzzle in the *L. A. Times*. At the

sound of the door closing, the few men at the bar
glanced over their shoulders, then returned to the
last inning of the Dodgers-Phillies game. Everything,
even the noise of the television set, seemed muted to
Beecham, like the distant buzz of a saw. He looked at
his watch. 3:56. Four minutes early.

The dining area, in the back half of the long
room, was deserted, and Beecham walked toward it.
At the end of the bar, where a waitress was counting
her tips, he ordered a pot of coffee and two cups
and paid her with a ten-dollar bill from his folding
money. "Keep it," he said, returning the other bills
to his pocket. "I'm meetin' somebody. See to it that
we're left alone."

It was a lot of money for a pot of coffee and the
waitress looked at the bill and then carefully looked
at him. She had seen him before. He had been at the
bar a couple of times yesterday, drinking a beer and
leaving and then coming back hours later, but he
wasn't from around here. "You'd better watch that
one," she had muttered to Charlie, the bartender.
"He's up to no good." There was something strange
about his face, and in his eyes there was a haunted,
empty look, like the eyes of a dead man. "He gives
me the creeps," she'd told Charlie.

The waitress put the money into her apron pocket
and went to the kitchen in the back. Beecham crossed
through the zigzag of tables and took a side booth so
he would face the front of the room. As soon as he
was seated, he put the newspaper down beside him,
near his hip, opened it, and removed the snub-nosed
.38 Special it had concealed. Taking a silencer from
his pants pocket, he attached it to the barrel with a
deft twist of his fingers; then he placed the .38 down
along his right thigh, within quick and easy access.

He shrugged to loosen his shoulders, trying to relax, and leaned back, watching the front door. The room was like a long tunnel; at the end of the shaded interior was the saloon's large front window, rippling with sunlight. Outside, along the sidewalk, dry palmetto fronds hung motionless in the heat, and across the street, beyond the rocky seawall, the Pacific looked like stressed metal.

The waitress brought his order on a cork-lined tray—two white cups on white saucers, the chrome pot of coffee, a creamer and a sugar dispenser. As she placed the cups and saucers on the table, she started to ask if there would be anything else, but he stopped her. He took her wrist in his hand and his grip was hard and cold like iron. "Just leave it," he said. It was as though something mechanical had closed on her flesh and she flushed and drew away from him, returning to her station behind the bar. Beecham did not make any movement to pour the coffee, but sat staring through his glasses at the front of the room.

Behind him, in the area of the rest rooms and the public telephone, a second man stood watching them. The waitress noticed him, but went on washing the beer glasses. It was as if he had wandered in here by mistake, she thought; he seemed out of place in this forgotten neighborhood bar. The back of the room was dim, his tanned face shadowed, yet he appeared comfortably sleek and handsome. Tall, in his forties, he wore a light summer raincoat, which was unbuttoned, showing glimpses of a white shirt and tie. The waitress had never seen him before.

He had his hands in his raincoat pockets as he approached the booth and he kept them there as he slid into the seat opposite the man in work clothes.

Neither of them spoke. For several seconds, they studied each other, coldly, without expression. Then the man wearing the glasses raised his hand from beneath the table, took the sugar dispenser and tipped it above the black Formica tabletop between them. The sugar gushed from the spout, the white grains bouncing and spreading in a wide mound. When half the jar was empty, he set it aside and with the flat of his hand, he spread the sugar into a thin, irregular coating on the black surface. With a blunt forefinger, he began to write in the sugar.

He wrote the first word and smoothed it out, the gawky letters vanishing under the swipe of his hand as soon as the word was completed. Then he wrote again, wiped the words out and drew his hand back, leaving the sugar surface flat and ready. The man in the raincoat watched this without any reaction, his deep-set eyes switching from the marks on the table to the man making them.

Again the two men looked at each other.

At last the other man's hands rose to the edge of the table, an aristocrat's hands with slender, uncalloused fingers. Beecham saw that the man's left hand sported a square diamond ring. With his right index finger, the man wrote in the sugar and after a moment, wiped out the two words. The diamond ring gleamed. He wrote and smoothed and wrote. Then he prepared the sugar for a reply.

And Beecham wrote NAME and again flattened the white crystals.

The man wearing the raincoat did not hesitate. RACHEL, he wrote and then added the rest of the name, BUCHANAN, and when he had wiped the sugar flat again, he spelled out where she lived.

Beecham nodded, the first time he had made any

such movement, and wrote WHEN and the other man wrote SAT. NIGHT, erased it and wrote, BEFORE 12.

There were other things that had to be understood and so it went on: first the man in the raincoat writing and wiping across the sugar and then the other man following suit, but always with fewer words, one or two at a time.

All at once, it was ending.

The dark-haired man in the raincoat wrote NOT THE GIRL and quickly smudged it out. Then, NO MISTAKES, and the words vanished.

He brushed his hands together, knocking a few white grains from his fingers. He pulled a pack of cigarettes from his shirt pocket, laid it in the midst of the sugar, stood and immediately left the dining room through the rear.

Underneath the clear wrapping on the cigarette pack was a small metal key. Beecham took the red pack in his hand, shook out a cigarette and set it on his lips. He put the pack in his shirt pocket. With his hands hidden, he quickly removed the silencer from the .38 Special, slipped the handgun under his belt inside his shirt and returned the silencer to his trouser pocket. Twisting the newspaper into a cone, he parted the pages until they made a pouch. Then using the side of his hand, he scraped the sugar off the table into the wedge of newspaper, leaving only a few thin white seams on the black Formica. He folded the top of the newspaper over so nothing would spill and clamped it under his arm.

With that done, he put the cigarette, unlit, in the ashtray and sat looking through the long interior, toward the palmettos outside and the passing cars and the ocean that never changed. Above the sun-streaked window hung a sign for ANCHOR STEAM BEER and a clock that Beecham watched, its second hand sweeping around and around. When five minutes had passed, he got up and went in the direction the first man had gone, toward the rest rooms in back, and never returned.

CANYON VALLEY DRIVE ran through the oldest residential section of Rio Del Palmos, California. The street dated from a time when parcels of land were sold in tracts of five or ten acres instead of the quarter-acre lots currently on the market. In the thirties, the Canyon Valley district had been favored by the owners and captains of fishing fleets, and by the prosperous doctors and merchants in town; now, although the houses were still imposing, the area was decidedly middle-class, abandoned by the wealthy for the northern hillside estates on the other side of the city. Surrounded by grassy foothills, it was a pleasant neighborhood of widely spaced houses. The streets were like paved country lanes, curving, rising and falling with the contours of the rolling terrain.

With no more noise than the soft throb of its exhaust, the dusty black Mustang rolled through a dip in the street, coasted up the opposing knoll and slipped from sight. It was five after six on Thursday morning, the darkness just now turning deep blue with the sunrise. Mailboxes stood at the ends of driveways like lonely sentinels. One, a rusty, tin mailbox, carried the number 522 and the name: R. BUCHANAN. The Mustang's brake lights flickered for a second as the small black car rolled by, tires grinding softly at the pavement. Another mailbox appeared and sank away, then another. At last the brake lights came on solidly—the Mustang turned into a neighbor's shrub-lined drive, slipped back and started its return, moving forward on the power of its idle.

When the white house belonging to the rusted mailbox again came into view, the Mustang stopped. The engine was shut off; the driver's window slid down. John Howard Beecham sat staring past the iron fence, across the ample front yard at the two-story stucco house in need of paint. Next to the mailbox, a driveway ran alongside the fenced yard through a porte cochere to the white garage in back. Even deeper in the backyard, the green painted roof of a small barn or shed could be glimpsed through the leafy trees.

Beecham studied the house in detail, placing the location of the doors and windows firmly in his memory. The age and Mediterranean style of the house told him little; by the arrangement of balconies and curtains and blinds, he tried to imagine it inside—a long parlor or living room running from front to back on the right side of the downstairs, on this side a large dining room and an equally large kitchen in back. Upstairs, some bedrooms and a bath. But it was only a guess. There could be other rooms somewhere downstairs. He estimated the distance to the closest neighbor to be about forty yards, the separate properties divided by a grove of what appeared to be wild lilacs. The high bushes created a natural shield. Perfect, he thought.

As he made his various calculations, a light came on in the rear of the house; a shaft of light spilled over the driveway. That's the kitchen, Beecham concluded. Seconds later, he noticed that lights were coming on in the other houses along the street. He started the car and drove down the winding road to wait.

At 7:30 that morning, a school bus lumbered past the old mailbox and stopped at the next driveway to board three children. At the same time, a red and brown station wagon emerged from the white garage, moved under the porte cochere and down the drive to the street, where it proceeded on in the direction of Rio Del Palmos. It was driven by a girl, still in her teens. An elderly woman occupied the seat beside her. Through the car windows it was possible to see that they were talking in a lively exchange, but their faces, marred by reflections and tree shadows, were visible only in flashes. As they passed the San Lucia Mission—a small historical chapel and cemetery where restoration work was being done—Beecham pulled out behind them.

In leaving the neighborhood, Canyon Valley Drive meandered through an uninhabited wooded area and became a frontage road, dropping toward the lush basin of Rio Del Palmos and eventually joining the interstate. The traffic through town was already moving at a brisk pace as the station wagon crossed the Rialto River Bridge and left the six-lane highway. The girl maneuvered through two traffic lights, made a right-hand turn and pulled into the high school parking lot. At the busy intersection, the Mustang drew to the curb.

Gathering her books, the girl left the station wagon, mingling with the scattered flow of students headed toward the turreted building. Okay, Beecham thought, that's the girl. Even at a distance, she was strikingly beautiful; tumbling about her shoulders, her blond hair glistened like a lovely gold cap.

On a flagpole in front of the school, two flags snapped out on the wind—an American flag and below it, another flag with a panther leaping through

a giant red *P*. Fluttering across the flag's top and
bottom ran the legend: HOME OF THE RIO DEL PALMOS
FIGHTING PANTHERS. Beecham's eyes took it in and
then returned to the station wagon. The elderly
woman, who had stayed behind, arranged herself
behind the steering wheel and drove out of the parking lot. And that's the woman, he thought, waiting
for her to pass before pulling out after her.

She stopped at Masterson's Flower Shop and came
out carrying a sprig of white flowers in a chilled
cellophane box. She went into a dress shop, which
according to its window specialized in weddings and
formal affairs. Beecham noted that she was gone for
less than ten minutes. With a plastic garment bag
over her arm, she came out still talking to the dress-
maker, who accompanied her as far as the sidewalk,
gossiping and saying good-bye. The woman drove to
the post office and went inside; minutes later, she
was back driving the station wagon. Everywhere she
received polite attention, and when she had gone,
the smiles on peoples' faces were tolerant, even kindly.
She was obviously well known, holding a certain standing among these people and commanding their
respect.

She was a vigorous woman of seventy or so, Beecham thought, and she looked like a New Englander
or a Quaker. She had that look about her—that look
of independence and thrift, of God-fearing self-
reliance. She carried herself erect; there was still a
spring in her step. Age had not diminished her in
any way that he could see. Her hair was dark silver,
going to white, and she wore it short, like a boy
badly in need of a haircut.

In the open-air market of a greenhouse on Quincy
Avenue, Beecham stood among flats of potted bego-

nias and watched as she approached the makeshift counter carrying a plastic tray of six tomato plants. "Young man," she said, loud enough to be heard distinctly, "could I speak to your father?"

The balding man behind the counter seemed a little frazzled. "You know Dad retired last year," he told her. "Rachel, you know that."

Beecham missed nothing. Appearing to sort through pots of begonias, he concentrated intently upon her, memorizing every small action and mannerism. Even the motion of her hand was printed indelibly in his mind. She said, "Then Jimmy Thompson, I'm ashamed of you. A dollar sixty-nine cents for six puny tomato plants. How much does your dirt cost nowadays, for pete's sake? I've never in my life paid more than fifty cents for a handful of plants, and that was too much. Does your father know what you've done to his prices?"

The man began to explain his rising costs, but it was no good. "All right, Rachel," he said, at last. "This time you can have them for seventy-five cents, but that's rock bottom." And then after she had paid him and with a mischievous glint of victory in her eyes, taken the plants to her car, Jim Thompson muttered to himself, "Feisty old Yankee broad." But he couldn't help smiling. Rachel Buchanan—as tough as ever—had been his sixth-grade teacher.

As soon as the station wagon drove away, Beecham left the market. Half an hour later, along the strip of motels flanking the interstate north of the city, he checked into the Tides Inn. He paid in cash and signed the registration card with a name that occurred to him as he stood at the counter: Jim Haskins of Beaumont, Texas.

At eleven-thirty that morning, he left the rented

room and drove twenty miles inland to the town of Morocco. It was exactly twelve noon when he entered the old Cypress Line train station, where a window fan stirred the damp heat and dust. A CLOSED sign hung lopsided in the ticket cage; the pewlike benches were deserted.

The room sounded hollow as Beecham made his way to the wall of metal lockers. From his pocket, he produced the small metal key, inserted it into the lock of locker number 28 and opened the six-inch-square door. The locker contained two Antonio y Cleopatra cigar boxes. Again, Beecham looked around him before he opened the lid of the box on top. It was filled level with used twenty-dollar bills—altogether there would be seventy-five hundred dollars, payment in full. He emptied the money into his gym bag, discarded the boxes and left the key in the slot.

Now would come the time that he hated, the two-day wait when his mind and the world fused into emptiness. There were still things he had to do, a few loose ends to take care of, but already he knew how it would happen. He could almost feel the minutes yielding, one into the next, impossible to stop now.

2

THERE WERE SIX of them, six young girls walking along side by side, rhythmically swaying their hips, and in their supple carelessness they were like thoroughbreds, long-legged and high-hipped, switching their tails. One of them ran up in front of the others and started walking backward, telling of some adventure, but Slater hardly looked at her. With his eyes hidden beneath the bill of his cap, only one girl among them held his gaze; only she had a kind of grandeur. She was like something he had left behind long ago.

She was a magnificent-looking ash blonde. He couldn't see her face—her head was turned—but he knew it. At seventeen, she was like ice cream, all the wonderful, cool, ripe colors: cherry and vanilla, peach and a smear of blueberry for her eyes. Thoughts that had lain dormant within him for years and years stirred once again.

In the light of the late afternoon, she was walking away and time seemed endless to him, elastic and slow. Her hips pumped softly, switching from side to side with the subtlest kick, her hips rising and falling and switching and then that tiny kick as if something very sweet were caught between her legs. On and on, pump and shift and then that little kick, pump and then kick, alternating to the movements of her straight sleek legs.

Her arm came up as she walked and settled around the girl next to her. She lowered her own head, drew the girl over close and whispered into her ear. Slater could almost feel her soft breath strike his cheek, imagined the small secret voice spilling into his ear, and the sensation of it ran up and down his body like a flame.

But time was passing, after all, and while he watched, she turned the corner. The shivery excitement washed through him; he was gripping the steering wheel harder than he knew. On his left hand, the square diamond ring gave off steely points of light. He forced himself to wait to the count of ten, careful, always careful, before he pulled away from the curb and went after them. Stopping at the intersection, he saw the girls trailing along together, drifting down the sidewalk. The traffic light was red; Slater made a right-hand turn, but before he could decide how to proceed, other cars were coming up behind him. He couldn't go slow enough to stay in back of her, so he speeded up, drove past without even glancing her way. At the corner he turned, went to the next intersection, whipped into a U-turn and came flying back.

The girls were gone. It was as if the late afternoon light had swallowed them. How could they disappear?

Halfway down the block, past the point where he had last seen them, he pulled into the alley, quickly backed out and resumed his search. The sun was going down; the sidewalks, lined with palms, were nearly deserted. Slater knew he shouldn't stay here. Every minute had its own risk. And yet, as he looked for her, all his other preoccupations left him.

They were coming out of Sweeney's, a café the juniors and seniors used as a hangout. Two of the girls sauntered out first, followed by the others, boys and girls straggling out together. And there she was—her proud head, the cascade of her tawny hair, the way her clothes clung to her as if she wore nothing underneath. Keeping his distance, Slater pulled to the curb.

She looked tall. It was only on those occasions when he stood close to her that he realized, all over again, that she wasn't. At about five six, she was a little taller than the other girls in her class, but she was so well proportioned, her body so lush and overripe, that she seemed to rob them of light. Now she draped her arms lazily behind her head, lifting her white-gold hair and fanning the back of her neck, and then letting her hair slide and uncoil through her fingers. His stomach tightened into a hard knot.

The boys were flirting with her, obviously paying court to her. One of them bounced a soccer ball against his forehead, keeping it alive in the air. Another, a good-looking kid about her age, put his arm around her and slipped his hand into the hip pocket of her jeans. Outwardly, she went on talking and laughing with the others, but her fingers came back behind her, closed on the boy's wrist and withdrew his hand.

Slater couldn't take his eyes off her.

There was a period of confusion when the boys separated themselves from the girls, saying so long, wandering out across the street, tossing the ball. But then, before anything else could happen, she, too, was breaking away from her friends, waving good-bye.

The old red and brown station wagon whisked by

Slater's side window. Rachel Buchanan. Slater glimpsed
her as she drove past and his face went pale and
hard with hate. He slid lower in the seat, his knees
rising on either side of the steering wheel.

He felt lacerated by her arrival. Now, even the air
stank of danger. She had been threatening to expose
him for several weeks now. She claimed she had
found something he had given the girl, that she
knew what he was trying to do. All he could think
about was seeing her dead. There's no other way, he
told himself. She'll go to the newspapers; the girl
had just turned seventeen. The scandal would anni-
hilate him. "She'll tell," he muttered to himself.
"*Goddamn her,* I know she will." She'd tell his wife
and destroy his marriage such as it was, ending all
his plans. No doubt about it: Rachel would smear
him with rumors that no amount of explaining would
ever erase.

Slater started the engine. I want this over with, he
thought. Just get it done. Then everything would go
on as planned.

The girl stepped over the gutter into the street.
Idling, the station wagon sat double-parked, waiting
for her. The girl reached for the door handle, and
as she grasped it, something rushed out of him. She
turned suddenly. It was as if he had called to her
and she had heard him. Her body twisted; she looked
over her shoulder, and the shape of her back changed,
the curves drawing in—the thrust of her breasts and
her buttocks held for a heartbeat in sheer volup-
tuous power. Her hand came up, touching her hair,
surreptitiously shading her eyes—she was looking
directly at him. With her glance, he lost all thought.

For as long as it lasted, his eyes burned over her.
The moment evaporated like a bubble. She slipped

into the station wagon and was gone. He watched
the red taillights shrink in the darkening air. Now,
there were five teenaged girls, careless and supple,
walking away from him but there was no longer any
excitement, no longer the magic.

He left Rio Del Palmos the way he had come, past
the turreted high school and its expansive lawn, glowing with dusk. He took back streets, driving down
the long, residential boulevards set at close intervals
with palm trees, all severely pruned and crowned
with tiny green shoots.

Minutes later, he caught the on ramp to the interstate and saw, up ahead, the rear of the brown and
red station wagon. His foot eased off the accelerator.
Through the wagon's back window, he could barely
make out the shape of Rachel's gray head, but he
could almost feel her flinty stare. With the sunset
hitting his windshield, he doubted that Rachel could
see him; still, he felt exposed. Once again he was in
the throes of conflict: hatred for the old woman
laced with tenderness for the girl.

He let the Jeep slide over into the right-hand lane,
eliminating the chance that Rachel might spot him
and gaining a better angle at the side of the car
where the girl was riding. Her window was rolled
down; wisps of her blond hair blew out, fluttering
against the red paint; her hand dangled playfully
against the wood-grained door.

Suddenly her fingers flicked out. Five. Then, very
fast, she flashed her fingers twice more. Ten. Fifteen.

She would meet him in fifteen minutes.

He took his foot off the accelerator, deliberately
losing speed, waiting for and then letting another
car fill the gap between them. He glanced down at
his speedometer, the needle twitching at forty-five.

He accelerated to fifty and held the Jeep there. After a quarter mile, the station wagon changed lanes, its right turn-signal blinking. A gust of noise and color flew past Slater on the left; another car was edging past him on his right.

The black Mustang seemed to gain on him in inches; he saw the dusty front fender, the side mirror, the door panel. He turned his head and looked at the driver and the driver looked at him. Slater saw the light spark off the wire-rimmed glasses, saw the man's strange, smooth face.

Chill after chill struck him; for a split second his foot hit the brakes. Instinctively, as if to avoid a sudden crash, he twisted the wheel, careening out into the far left-hand lane. The hired killer was the last person on earth he had expected to see.

He doesn't know me, Slater reminded himself. *I don't want him to know me.* Just do the job and get out. If he finds out who I am—I'll never get rid of him.

Damn, he thought. *Damn! Damn! Damn!*

The knot of traffic hurled on past, the Mustang with it. Slater fell back. *He saw me. I know he saw me.*

Now several cars back, he watched Rachel Buchanan's station wagon veer onto the Canyon Valley exit on a downward course. Moments later, the black Mustang followed it. Slater wiped the sweat from his brow. His foot pressed down. The raw, powerful sound of the Jeep opened up, roaring past the down ramp and the sinking black roof.

It was Thursday. Slater checked his watch. A quarter to six.

A maze of country roads crisscrossed the hills and valleys surrounding Rio Del Palmos and he knew them all. At the next exit, he left the interstate. When he stopped at the bottom of the grade, Slater was gripped by a seizure of fright, afraid to look behind him, expecting, against all logic, to see the dusty black Mustang materialize behind him. When he did look over his shoulder, nothing was there; no one was following him.

Off to his distant right lay the Pacific, but Slater turned away from it through the underpass, taking the two-lane blacktop called Old Sawmill Road. After a mile and a half, a ridge, strewn with boulders and wild brush, began to mount steadily upward on the far left side of the road. Four miles farther on, he turned in through a set of weathered gateposts, overgrown with honeysuckle. By maneuvering the Jeep around and backing into a stand of cedars, he was hidden from sight. Across the road, the rocky ridge stood at a height of thirty feet. In the valley on the far side of the ridge, the girl lived in the large stucco house with her grandmother.

They wouldn't have much time.

Shutting off the engine, Slater got out of the Jeep. He kept looking at his watch—in twelve minutes, he saw her at the top of the crest. Nimble as a young mountain cat, she came down the face of the ridge, following the old paths, grabbing a bush and swinging herself around and down. She dropped to the drainage ditch and came up, brushing her hands on the seat of her jeans; then she ran across the road, toward him.

Entering through the tangled gateway, she slowed to a walk. "I can't stay," she said, still out of breath. "Why were you following me? I thought you weren't going to do that anymore."

"I wanted to see you," he said.

"Why?" she said smiling at him but he could see she was tense. "Look, I just slipped away for a few minutes. I didn't tell her anything. I'll have to think of something to tell her."

The leg of her jeans caught on a bramble—she reached down to pick it off and her breasts plunged abundantly against the cloth of her blouse. There was nothing insubstantial or ephemeral about her. Since she was a child, he had always felt protective of her, but now she had grown up. And still she was so young.

"I brought you something," he said.

"I don't want you to give me things." She sounded exasperated with him. "I have to hide them. Don't you know what she'd do if she found out about this?"

How nervous she was and he wanted to calm her. Slater grinned. "What would she do?"

"I don't want to think about it."

Down the hollow distance of the road, they heard the sound of a motor traveling toward them at high speed. "It's coming this way," she said. He caught her hand and felt her trembling transfer to him like a warm vibration. Slater drew her back beside the Jeep, into the clearing among the cedars. Through the roadside foliage, they watched the silver car fly past.

Again she smiled at him, that smile that broke his heart.

"Well . . . ," she said, "what is it? Hurry up and give it to me." Her blue eyes, shot through with gold currents, looked up at him at a distance of inches.

Wrapped in white tissue paper, the parcel was no larger than his hand; he took it from his pocket and handed it to her.

"You shouldn't do this," she said, ripping away the thin layers of paper. He saw the nervous falseness enter her smile. She was fighting to hold in her excitement, her eyes, the soft flush in her cheeks, all of her suffused with it.

She tore the last shreds of the paper away, and in her hand, a small gold sea horse appeared. It was hardly an inch long, encrusted with tiny jewels. "Oh, my God," she moaned, under her breath. "Is this for real?"

"Of course it's real." He started to laugh. "Don't you know I'd give anything for just one of your kisses?"

The seconds were passing quickly; he knew their time would soon be over and yet he continued to look at her as long as he could. Only her face was before him, her eyes gazing at him, and what he was really saying to her with his eyes was inexpressible. Gently he placed his hands on her cheeks, framing her face, and then he kissed her. It was a chaste kiss like so many others he had given her and yet the little murmur she gave when their lips met was also the sound at the very center of his soul.

Her hand came up, tentatively, to touch his cheek and she returned his kiss. It was like a sacrament that passed between them. Her lips parted under his so that he tasted her warm, wet breath. For a moment, it was as if she were giving herself to him utterly—he could almost feel her ripeness enfold him. He wanted to take her in his arms even though he knew where it might lead, knew it was impossible. Then she drew away from him. "Whew," she said, blowing through her lips and fanning herself. "I can't stand it."

She turned as if to go and again looked at the jeweled sea horse. "I'm not so sure I should be taking this from you. Are you certain this is okay to do?"

Still dazzled by her, Slater said, "Of course, it is. When can I see you?"

"I don't know," she said, starting to back away.

"Try for Saturday afternoon," he said. "You know the place."

"No," she said. "I'll be getting ready for the prom on Saturday. I'm sorry; I really have to go."

"No, Sheila, come—"

The cedar boughs whipped round her as she fled toward home. After a moment, even they denied that she had been there; the boughs were standing motionless, very full and very green.

IT WAS ALMOST six-thirty when the Jeep shot down the interstate, still headed out of town. Turning under the high trestles of the Bay Court exit, he again drove inland—the highway quickly becoming a narrower, secondary road running beside a freshwater stream.

The valley was burnished with purple shadow that evening. The setting sun cast the fields and wooded foothills in a rich, warm chiaroscuro. Long tree shadows lay across the road like bars and the Jeep ran smoothly through them, the light beating against the windshield in deep flickers. Once this road had been featured on scenic maps; the countryside was scattered with remnants of that other time—a caved-in souvenir shack, a crumbling drive-in restaurant. Slater passed by filling stations without signs or pumps. Now they were enclosed by fences; the landscape had reverted to pasture. Grazing sheep and goats wandered through the forgotten buildings.

Fifteen miles from Rio Del Palmos stood the remains of an abandoned almond grove. Many of the trees were dead—blackened twigs exposed to the wind—the rest would bear some leaves, nothing more. At an opening in the barbed-wire fence, the Jeep turned in on an old grassy trail, followed it for a hundred yards and dropped from sight over a rise. What was left of the trail, on the backside of the slope, curved down to a stream that ran in the crease between hills.

The draw was badly overgrown. Among chaparral and a stand of ancient oaks lay an old homesteader's spread. Only three of the buildings still stood: the house, a barn beyond repair and the stable that Slater had converted to a garage. At the edge of the yard where the stream ran past, someone long ago had built a dam, creating a deep rock pool, edged with sun-bleached boulders.

After searching for nearly a year, Slater had discovered the place last summer during a long Sunday afternoon hike. He had been attracted to the rock pool and the blind privacy of the place. Using an assumed name, he had purchased the property from the absentee owner, who was living in Hawaii. The transaction had been arranged by telephone through a rural real estate agent, the check drawn on Slater's own secret account at a Vandalia bank. He came here when he could get away in the evenings or on weekends and worked at fixing up the old house. No one knew this place was his, not even his wife.

Skirting the dirt driveway, he pulled the Jeep around to the back and entered the stable by the new overhead door. Once inside, he hit the button to shut the door, and the gloom closed around him. It was like a place under the sea, the dwindling sunlight filtering through chinks in the siding. Next to him, in the dimness, sat a brightly polished, navy blue Cadillac Eldorado.

Slater got out of the Jeep and flipped on the single light bulb over the workbench, checking to see that the place hadn't been broken into. He always looked, first, against the wall under the old workbench, at the steamer trunk that had been his father's in the Korean War. Locked with a padlock and covered with cobwebs, the trunk contained nothing of value—only the little that remained of Slater's young life. There were no pictures in it, not even a picture postcard of the Peabody mine, and he sometimes wished there had been a few pictures left of his Ma and Dad. He had never opened it. The trunk was still the way he had packed it when he was nineteen, with his father's hard hat and his own, the carbide lanterns, the pickaxes and lunch pails and the borrowed books on chemistry and electrical engineering that Slater had poured over at night, trying to win a scholarship and improve his lot. It was in January when the morning crew hit methane gas, thirty men dead at twelve hundred feet, including Joseph Slater, his father. Ruled to be unsafe by the courts, the mine was sealed, his mother dead of heartbreak before the following spring. That's when Henry Lee Slater packed the trunk. He had taken it with him everywhere he had gone, storing it in depots and train stations, never wanting to open it. No one knew that it was always with him. It was a part of his life he found no reason to talk about.

Satisfied that nothing had been disturbed, Slater opened the back of the Eldorado, where a second set of clothes was laid out: a dark blue suit, a clean white shirt, a red silk tie, black oxfords, black socks.

He tossed his plain blue baseball cap into the Jeep and went through the tack room to the small bathroom, which had taken him three weekend afternoons to fix up. He flipped the light on, washed his hands and returned to the opened trunk of the car. Taking his wallet and some change from his pockets, he quickly undressed, stripping off his gray sweatshirt and faded blue jeans. Leaning against the massive fender, he removed his running shoes and athletic socks one foot at a time and replaced them with the black socks and shoes. He gathered the old clothes up in a bundle, dropped them into the back of the Jeep and locked it.

By the time he took up the finer clothes, his manner had begun to change. He dressed carefully, buttoning the small white buttons on his chest and wrists, lifting the pant legs off the floor and drawing them over the strong articulations of muscle, the fine black hair of his legs. He set the clasp on his waist, pulled the smooth zipper up, the belt already run through the loops, slipped into place in the buckle. Returning the wallet and change to his pockets, he picked up the red silk tie, and when he turned a second time toward the tiny bathroom, his stride was solemn and solid.

The bathroom mirror was lodged in a frame of hammered tin. He stood before it, looping the red tie around his neck, tying it and then folding the collar down, leaving only the knot visible in the immaculate white wedge at the hollow of his throat. Slater was critically aware of how he looked, wanting to give the impression of power and mystery when he spoke later this evening. He flipped off the bathroom light, took the suit jacket from the trunk of the Eldorado and slipped it on.

At forty-three, Henry Lee Slater was very much a man in his prime, a dark, good-looking man with gray eyes that were unfaltering. He credited his Irish ancestry for his full head of black hair, his good cheekbones, his bony Celtic nose and for the music he could bring to his voice. Now fully clothed, he had assumed the manner of a man armored in principle and authority, a man worthy of the prominent position he held in Rio Del Palmos.

He slammed the trunk lid shut and stood listening to the night outside. It was almost dark in the stable, the last scraps of light withering away. The overhead door cranked up and the glossy dark car backed out into the deep sunset.

NOT A TRACE of fog softened the cool May air that evening as Slater picked up the receiver from his car phone and dialed his home number. The maid answered. "Luisa," he said, "I'm running a little behind schedule. Let me talk to Mrs. Slater."

"Mrs. Slater is not here," the maid told him. "She says tell you Manuella Arturo have her baby. Very long, hard labor. Mrs. Slater goes, taking some clean things. She says you must go to meeting and she will come meet you there."

Slater thanked her and hung up. It wasn't the first time this sort of thing had happened. His wife had developed the annoying habit of rearranging her schedule at the last minute. Two years ago he'd found it infuriating when she raced out the door every time the church called, always in a hurry to take care of her strays; now it was little more than an irritation. He started the car and pulled away, feeling only an abiding ambivalence: as far as he was concerned the marriage had run its course long ago. But he had to keep his feelings secret, even from her. A man in politics could never lose sight of the necessity of having a good marriage.

Ten minutes later, he drove down the aisle of live
oaks to the country club. Straight ahead, far out over
the Pacific, beneath a towering bank of cloud, the
sun clung to the horizon, and the bright dying light
transformed the trees and the club's compound of
buildings into stark cutouts. At a distance, the steeply
shadowed landscape amazed the eye with its artifici-
ality. Everything, even a bird diving for its nest,
seemed sharpened to a painful edge.

At the parking lot entrance, he passed the large
glass-covered placard where coming events were listed.
Beneath the announcement for the Early Bird Golf
Tournament, he saw his name: 59TH ANNIVERSARY
CELEBRATION. MAYOR HENRY LEE SLATER, SPEAKER. The
lot was filled with parked cars. He drove among
them to the row nearest the clubhouse lodge and
parked in the space reserved for him.

The sun was about to go down. The light from the
infinite ocean space was so brilliant and cutting that
at first he didn't see her, couldn't differentiate her
presence from the shrubbery. As he stepped out of
the car, she came toward him, wearing a strapless,
emerald gown set about the shoulders with a shawl
of black satin. Tall and slender, she hovered on the
evening air like a fantastic luna moth. Faith Slater
was not a pretty woman, but she worked hard at
what God had given her. Other women always remarked how striking and elegant she was.

The silver bracelets clinked on her wrist as she
lifted her hand to his cheek, kissed him and said, "I'm
sorry about the mix-up. Mrs. Simms from church
called me and I felt I simply had to do something."

"I was running late myself," he told her. "There
was something I had to do." His hand settled comfortably on the small of her back, just above the jut

of her hips, maneuvering her toward the side door where they would enter and from where he would go to the podium. "Looks like quite a crowd."

"Yes," she said. "I pulled in just before you got here. I saw John and Nancy Herbert as they were going inside. They didn't see me, thank God. It saved me the embarrassment of explaining why we're both late. Anyway, you'll have a good audience. We'd better hurry . . ."

Faith went on talking, which was exactly what he wanted her to do, although he scarcely heard a word she said as he prepared himself to step before the large gathering of the club's exclusive membership. Ushering Faith before him, he opened the side door for her and then stepped into the darkened vestibule himself. One of the committee women met them. "Oh, good!" she said, "you're here." Then she rushed to signal the woman at the podium. Catching the signal, Mrs. Harriet Vance immediately launched into her final remarks. "And now it's my very great pleasure to introduce to you this evening a man who, in fact, needs no introduction, a man who has reshaped the nature of city government in Rio Del Palmos."

Faith brushed his lapels and told him to "give 'em hell," and Henry Lee Slater strode into the floodlights toward the podium.

Applause spread throughout the packed room. A few flashbulbs popped. A low rumbling chant began to gain definition: "SLA-TER, SLA-TER."

Joining in the applause, the guests of honor and the high-ranking committee women stood at their chairs on either side of the podium. Slater smiled and began to greet each of them, shaking their hands warmly. "Good evening," he said. "Good evening, Mrs. Vance, thank you for the kind words." And as he moved among them, going from one to the next, the memory of watching the girl walk away was fresh in him; the thought of seeing that tiny kick move through her hips quivered like a burning speck of poison in the depths of his mind.

3

SHEILA HAD A campaign button with his picture printed on it that she kept in the handkerchief drawer of her bureau. The button was several months old now—she had worn it pinned to her sweater at his rallies late last fall—but the picture was still a good likeness of him. In the evening, after the dishes were done and she sprawled across her bed listening to her cassette player and talking on the telephone, she sometimes pulled the drawer open, took out the button and looked into Henry Slater's eyes. To her, they were like the brooding eyes of a god.

She couldn't think of a time when she hadn't been in love with him; she still had all the things he had given her. She remembered coming to Rio Del Palmos to live with her grandmother and how he had walked across the street toward their parked car to welcome them. It was nearly dark, crickets chirping; they had been driving since ten o'clock that morning. He came up along the passenger side of the car and looked in through her open window. "Well, Rachel," he said, across the car's interior, "what have we here? Is this your new boarder?" Her grandmother said, yes, it was, all the way from Farley, Nevada. He had smiled and then he had spoken directly to her, a girl ten years old. "Hi," he said, "I'm Henry Lee Slater. We

live across the street. I'll bet your highness'd like to
stretch her legs. Here, let me help you out." He
opened the car door and offered his hand and his
hand was big and strong; it swallowed her fingers.
"What's your name?" he asked her and she told him
it was Sheila.

His after-shave smelled cool and fresh, she remembered, and he wore a white shirt and a dark
blue necktie. Pressed into its silky material was a tiny
gold clasp in the shape of an arrow. When her feet
were on the ground, Sheila pointed to it. "It's pretty,"
she said. He stooped to make himself not so much
taller than she was. "You mean this?" He laughed.
"I'll tell you what, you can just have it."

He undid the clasp while her grandmother stood
behind them protesting. "Henry, you shouldn't. Don't
give her that. You'll spoil her." But he placed the
tiny arrow in her hand and closed her fingers over
it. "There," he said, "now it's yours. A pretty girl like
you can have anything she wants."

After she and her grandmother had gone inside,
Sheila said, "He's a strong man, isn't he, Gramma?"

Lifting the last of their suitcases to take along
upstairs, Rachel looked at her and smiled. Then she
said something that had stuck in Sheila's mind ever
since. "Well, I don't know about that," her grandmother told her. "Henry's been a good neighbor.
But, Sheila, you shouldn't put much stock in him.
There's something about him I've never trusted. He's
a born salesman. Nobody loves to hear himself talk
as much as Henry Slater."

The next year the Slaters moved to the house in
the hills on the other side of town. Hidden away
with the other things he had given her, Sheila still
kept the little gold arrow.

But that was seven years ago.

Tonight through the network of bedroom telephones, the girls of Rio Del Palmos High were excitedly preparing for the Senior Prom, now barely two nights away. Sheila talked to Christy Bledsoe for nearly an hour trying to convince her that Jeremy Phalen was an acceptable prom date, even if he had waited till the very last minute to ask her. "But Christy, all of us junior girls are going with seniors. Look, if you're still really nervous about it, I'll talk to Denny and Tommy and you can go with us. Nobody'll know it's your sister's dress. Wear that silver necklace and earrings you wore to church that time. You'll be a smash."

"Wouldn't that be too casual?"

"With that formal?" Sheila advised her. "Are you kidding?"

Among the clutter of books and papers, the brooding eyes on the campaign button drilled into Sheila as she talked. "I know he wants to go out with you, Christy. He told me so."

Minutes later, she hung up the telephone and again stretched out across the bed, tapping the pencil against her teeth, half-heartedly attempting to begin her last book report of the semester:

A Thing of Beauty by A. J. Cronin is an interesting book but it took forever to read. I picked this book because I really liked The Citadel, which was on the reading list, and I wanted to try something else by Mr. Cronin, thinking it would be as good . . .

She rolled over on her side.
The way he kissed me—

On her nightstand, she kept a cluster of photographs in a variety of frames—the one she liked the best was a blown-up snapshot, showing her with her boyfriend, Denny Rivera, their arms thrown around each other. It had been taken on the fifty-yard line the night the Panthers won the semistate. Sheila was wearing her cheerleading outfit, Denny looked ragged, but triumphant; his jersey was torn and muddied, grease smudges under his eyes ... and yet, tonight, her thoughts kept straying back to the campaign button. For minutes at a time she managed to stop thinking about Henry Slater, then suddenly she was back again. *Why me?* she wondered. *Why me?* But Sheila loved meeting him in secret, loved the danger. What if someone saw us? She shivered.

Digging into her pocket, she pulled out the jewel-encrusted sea horse. He's so much smarter than I am, she kept thinking, and he's so powerful. Once more the feeling of unreality crept over her. This's unbelievable, Sheila thought. *He's married.*

She swung herself off the bed, took a miniature key from the drawer of her nightstand and went to her closet, leaving the door ajar for the light. Her dress shoes were stored in the original shoe boxes, neatly stacked on the floor. Dropping to her knees, she quickly and quietly set the boxes aside, exposing, behind them, an old leather-covered stationery box standing on end. Sheila took it up and leaned into the spill of light. A small metal hasp and lock held the lid snug. With a twist of the miniature key, the lock snapped open.

The shallow box contained gold bracelets and gold chains and earrings, gold and jewelled pendants, gold pins, one set with diamonds or rhinestones— she couldn't tell which. Some of the pieces were heavy for their size, she thought. He also had given her money from time to time, and Sheila kept it hidden here, the twenties, the five fifties, rolled very tight and held by a rubber band. "Buy yourself something pretty," he would say. She didn't take time to count it now, as she often did, with wonder. Tonight, she placed the sea horse among the other things, closed and locked the box and put it back, rearranging the camouflage of shoe boxes in front of it. I'd better find a new place, she thought, closing the closet door, before Gramma stumbles onto this one. She went back to her book report on the bed.

It was after eight-thirty when Denny Rivera called.

"Where've you been?" she asked him. She returned the campaign button to the handkerchief drawer and her homework to the nightstand. Then she said, softly, "Wait a minute."

Carrying the telephone in her left hand, Sheila walked out on the landing and listened for her grandmother's movements downstairs. She heard nothing out of the ordinary, went back into her bedroom and quietly shut the door.

"I can't," she whispered. "No, you know I can't. *Denny!* Not this close to the prom. You think I'm crazy? If I got caught, she'd ground me for sure. You know my Gramma!" Sheila brought a strand of her hair up through her lips and chewed it. Then with her fingers, she drew it away, wet, across her cheek. "Uh-hum," she murmured.

The cassette had finished its cycle. She flipped the switch to the radio, and music of a different tempo spilled from the cheap speakers. She smothered a laugh in her hand, her cheeks reddened and she looked back at the closed door as if expecting to find her grandmother there. "You know I do," she mur-

mured, and she took a few steps, swaying, dancing to
the music, watching herself in the vanity mirror.
"You're terrible."

Her whisper grew even more discreet. "I *can't.
Dennnee,* stop it! *Stop* it. I really can't . . . I've
already—" She checked herself and didn't finish.
She didn't say: I've already lied to my Gramma once
today. In the end, she told him, "Okay. Okay, I'll
try." She cupped her hand against the receiver so
that nothing she said would escape. "Wait for me . . .
you know. If I'm not there by ten-thirty, I can't
make it. Okay? Okay, I promise. Okay, bye."

At a quarter to ten, she heard her grandmother's
footsteps climbing the stairs. With her face washed,
her teeth brushed, wearing her nightgown, Sheila
drew the quilt up, nestled her head deeper into the
pillow and shut her eyes. She took long, slow breaths,
as if already sound asleep. On the black screen of
her eyelids, she could almost see her grandmother
mounting the wide tier of steps. Her hand, nowadays, always clasped the rail. Rachel was humming
some old tune as she reached the landing this evening. If she saw that Sheila was awake, she would
linger in her room, talking and saying good night, as
they usually did.

Lying very still, she listened as her grandmother
went into the bathroom across the hall where she
would change into her nightclothes—as she called
them; Sheila heard the water turned on, then off;
she heard the doorknob jangle, the click of the latch,
the yawning creak of the hinge as the bathroom
door opened.

With her eyes closed, Sheila sensed more than felt
her grandmother in the bedroom with her. She imagined Rachel hovering closely over her, inches from

her pillow. The clock on the nightstand was taken up. The striking mechanism chimed once, softly, as Rachel checked to see that the alarm was set.

Sheila took another slow, sleep-deep breath.

The slippered footsteps padded around the bed, a window was wrenched up, then the steps faded away altogether. Still, Sheila waited a few minutes longer before she opened her eyes and sat up. She looked at the clock—five after ten.

All the lights were out; the silence settled through the house like emptiness in a jar. From the large front bedroom, as if through a funnel, she heard her grandmother's mumblings and knew by heart the words that were always spoken: ". . . and lead us not into temptation, but deliver us from evil, for Thine is the kingdom, and the power and the glory. Forever and ever. Amen."

Through the two east windows, moonlight fell across Sheila's bed like silver rails. She stood away from the sheets, the hem of her nightgown falling about her ankles. As she passed through the moonlight her body glimmered through the sheer cloth. Reaching beneath the cushion on the old chaise, she grabbed her bathing suit—even in the dark, it gave off a faint scintillation.

Going into the shadows, she shed her nightgown and pulled on the black bathing suit, drawing the spaghetti straps over her shoulders. The suit fit her like a second skin, making her body feel smooth and power packed. Over it, she pulled on jeans and a denim shirt, her fingers rushing to close the zipper and the buttons. Again she looked at the bedside clock. Eight minutes had passed. 10:13. It didn't seem possible. I have to hurry, she thought.

Without making a sound, she bent to the vanity

mirror, uncapped her lipstick and applied red color
that looked black on her mouth. She ran a brush
through her hair, then took up the spritzer of cologne but instantly changed her mind and shoved
the glass vial into the pocket of her jeans. Even the
slightest scent might betray her in the dark. Sheila
lifted her canvas shoes, hugged them against her—a
thrill of fear and excitement ran through her.

On tiptoe, she edged up to the doorway of her
grandmother's bedroom. The raised doorsill pressed
firmly against the arch of her foot; through her hair,
a cool draft from the stairwell licked the back of her
neck. With the moon's sudden passage through clouds,
the light in the front bedroom waned, then bur-
geoned to a ghostly glow and shrank back to gray
again.

A corner of dull moonlight exposed the mono-
grammed *B* on the pillowcase; the carvings of the
headboard stood out in delicate, twisted tendrils. Gradually Sheila's eyesight adjusted to the shifting darkness; she saw her grandmother's sleeping face. She
went no farther into the room. In the stillness, she
could hear the slow progression of her grandmother's raspy breaths.

Feeling her way back across the landing, she started
down the carpeted stairs, trying to remember every
loose plank, stepping over the familiar stair that
creaked so loudly and then, halfway down, where
there was an audible weakness in the joists, sitting
down and sliding from step to step until she counted
four and stood upright again. The rooms downstairs
seemed to ebb with the changeable moonlight. Emerging through the gloom, Sheila sat on the last of the
stairs and slipped on her shoes.

The double front doors lay in a line almost di-

rectly beneath her grandmother's bed, so she retreated from them—went back through the house,
taking the cologne spritzer from her pocket. She
lifted her hair and sprayed the back of her neck
once and then sprayed once more inside the collar of
her shirt for good measure. Returning the vial to her
pocket, Sheila crept to the back door, looked over
her shoulder and grasped the doorknob.

When she drew the door open, the pane of glass
quivered, and she stepped outside, holding back a
deep sigh. The night rushed up around her, full of
tiny sounds. The glass shuddered softly a second
time when she pulled the door shut.

The sky was swept with dazzling stars. Mist thinned
and broke around the dark columns of trees. Sheila
leapt from the porch step to the grass and darted
around the corner of the house. Suddenly, she
stopped, her nerve endings tense with fright. She
had the overwhelming sensation that she had passed
someone close by, brushed by some breathing thing
in the dark. Her toes dug down, gripping at the
insides of her shoes. She looked back toward the
garden, searching the dark trellises and arbors. Leaves
stirred and grew quiet. *There's something I can't see.*
Rotating on her toes, Sheila turned, crept back to the
corner of the house and stepped out bravely into
the moonlight. She peered at the back porch, but the
door she had closed only moments before was still
shut, exactly as she had left it. Touched by the wind,
the pane of glass again shimmered in the door frame.
No one was there. This is silly, she told herself. I'm
imagining things.

She hurried down the side of the house to the
front yard, where street lamps burnished the lawn
with light. There was nothing to do but to cross

through it, and so she fled toward the far corner of the iron fence.

Behind her, in the garden, the figure in the rose arbor remained in darkness except for the transitory gleam of his wire-rimmed glasses. Beecham stood watching the girl as she ran through the moonlight. That was close, Beecham thought. Now that she had vanished, he moved out from under the canopy of vines. He wondered how long the girl would be gone, when she would come back, but he really didn't need to see any more. Tonight he had studied the interior of the house through its downstairs windows; he knew everything he needed to know.

Swinging up over the old iron fence, Sheila shrank into the dark crevice between the lilacs. A hand—she saw a boy's hand—reached for her, and Denny drew her into his arms. "The curtains," he whispered, "upstairs," and he looked toward the front of the house, all awash in shadows. "I saw something."

Catching her breath, Sheila looked in the same direction Denny was looking, but the upstairs windows only appeared dark to her and blank. "No," she told him, "it's nothing. She's asleep; I checked."

Denny was a year older than she was and several inches taller; his hair lay in dark rumpled curls. He touched her cheek with his hand, and her mouth was soft and slick when he kissed her. "They're waiting," he said, quietly, leading her through the crooked lilac branches toward a car that emerged from the shade of the roadside oaks, a gray Firebird idling at the curb with its lights out.

The charcoal-colored door swung open for them, the seat fell forward, and first Sheila and then Denny scrambled into the back of the car. "Hi, Mary," Sheila whispered and then to the driver, who had shifted gears, "Tommy, please, *please,* don't gun it. Don't wake her up. I think maybe she heard you last time."

Tommy Ames looked back over his shoulder and grinned at her. "Sheila," he said, "you worry too much." But he did as she asked him.

Invisible except for the streetlight glancing from its chrome, the gray Firebird moved smoothly into the night. Behind it, the air carried only a trace of the warbling in its mufflers.

When there was no sound at all left beating the air, the brown-spotted fingers let go and the part in the upstairs curtains fell to, as if weighted. That boy, Rachel thought. It was maddening—all this sneaking around. One minute she would think, I've got to put my foot down; the next she was torn with indecision. She knew that Denny Rivera was the least of her troubles; she wanted Sheila to be interested in some-one her own age. This wasn't the only time the girl had slipped away in the last few hours—Sheila had also disappeared before suppertime for almost half an hour and Rachel was certain she knew who she had gone to meet.

"I'm going to have to do it," she whispered to herself. "I said I would; now I have to." She crossed the dark landing and entered Sheila's bedroom. Reaching under the shade, she flipped on the bed-side lamp and tugged open the drawer of the night-stand. The key was still there, where it always was. Taking it firmly in her fingers, she went toward the shoe boxes in Sheila's closet, wondering what new bauble Henry Slater had given her this time.

I've got to do it, Rachel thought. She's my little girl—and he won't quit. He's still after her.

THE GRAY FIREBIRD rumbled through the country club parking lot, staunched its headlights and swung in beside the black and gold Trans Am. Doors flew open, dome lights blinked, doors slammed shut. A murmuring rose among the gathering of high school boys and their girlfriends—ten of them, juniors and seniors, congregated between their parked cars. Cans of cold beer were passed around; a joint was lit, burning a red point in the night. One of the boys streaked across the dun-colored grass to the privacy fence. Seconds later, the gate squealed open and the underlit, Olympic-size swimming pool glowed before them like an eerie green lagoon.

"That thing better be heated," Claudia Finney said.

"Trust me," said two of the boys simultaneously.

Zippers and buttons slipped undone. They were quickly pulling off their outer clothes. On Mary McPhearson's swimsuit, a sprig of blue sequins glittered. Twisting her hips, Lana Russo wiggled out of her bib-overalls, revealing a bikini of bright chrome yellow. Two of the couples ran off toward the pool.

"It looks radioactive," Claudia groaned.

"Just think," her boyfriend said, "tomorrow we'll be salamanders."

Denny was stripped to his trunks before Sheila had folded her jeans. "Go ahead," she told him. "I'll be just a minute."

In the carbon light, he looked lean and tough. "I'll wait," he said and stood looking at the pool.

"No, go on, Denny," she insisted. "Go ahead. I want you to. I'll come with Mary." Sheila smiled at him, her fingers motionless on the top button of her denim shirt.

"Oh, I get it," he said. "Another heart-to-heart." He backed away in the direction of the pool. Sheila went on, then, unbuttoning her shirt, watching until he had trotted from view. Slowly, she turned her head.

Across the thirty yards of asphalt, parked in a reserved space near the front of the clubhouse, she had seen Mr. Slater's dark blue Cadillac. Just looking at his car and knowing that he was in there drew her like a magnet. From inside the main building, she heard the muted throb of a band playing, and she felt oddly left out. It was impossible not to imagine him dancing with Mrs. Slater, holding her close in his arms. Sheila wanted to do something to let him know that she had been here, too. *I'll* surprise *you*, she thought.

But how?

Mary McPhearson interrupted her reverie. "Doolin's got the nerve, hasn't he?" she said. "Sneaking his old man's keys like this." The two of them were alone now between the Firebird and the Trans Am.

"Sheila, if we get caught, it's my ass."

"Me, too," Sheila said. "This's crazy. If it wasn't for Denny . . ." She shrugged. Peeling off her shirt, she laid it, along with her jeans, on the backseat of the Firebird.

Mary stood appraising her, shaking her head with appreciation. "I love that bathing suit on you. You always look so damned fabulous—it makes me sick." Mary handed her a towel, which Sheila knotted over the top of her bathing suit.

"You ready?"

"I think so," Sheila said.

They stepped over the curb, onto the grass. Again, Sheila looked back toward the Cadillac; she had a habit of playing with her necklace when she was preoccupied and now her hand trailed thoughtfully to her throat. My necklace, she thought. "Mary," she said, "I forgot to take off my necklace. You go ahead. I'll take it back to the car."

Mary waved and kept on walking.

If Sheila was going to do something, she knew she had only a minute or two to do it in before Denny would come looking for her. As Mary's plump shape disappeared inside the privacy fence, Sheila rushed across the parking lot and slipped in alongside the large polished fender of the Cadillac.

The late evening mist had condensed to dew; it stood in bright, glistening beads on the car's long surfaces. Sheila felt the urge to write something in it with her finger like a child. HI HENRY or even something more private, but she knew she shouldn't. She *couldn't*. She didn't want to cause him any trouble. When she came to the door handle, she stopped and touched it, rubbing the wet condensation between her fingers.

When the evening was over, the two of them would come out to the car. His wife would walk ahead of him; Mr. Slater would open the door for her on the passenger side and come around to the driver's door. And . . . then what? What could she do?

Something should be waiting for him.

Quickly, Sheila lifted the fine, gold chain from around her throat. She pulled it through the press of her fingers until she came to the clasp, which she undid with her fingernails. What would he think? Would he wonder whose it was? She carefully draped the unfastened necklace over his door handle. No, he would realize immediately who had put it there. He had given it to her, once, and now he would give it back to her again.

Turning and glancing at what she had done, Sheila ran across the asphalt with a feeling of elation. The knotted towel came loose and fell; she swooped down and snatched it up, suddenly in a hurry to join the others in the smoky green depths of the pool.

Against the dark flank of Slater's Cadillac, the thread of gold dangled in the moonlight, sparkling, catching and giving off slivers of brilliance, like the loveliest, the most delicate, the tenderest bait.

4

HENRY SLATER KEPT to his regular half-day routine on Saturday morning, stopping at the Beachcomber Cafe for a breakfast roll and coffee and arriving at the office shortly before nine. He knew that on this day nothing could seem even slightly out of the ordinary. He told himself he had nothing to fear, but fear continued to gnaw at him when it was least expected. All his senses were heightened and on the alert. Tonight, he thought. Tonight, it's over.

The glass door flashed around him as he strode into the secretarial lair, deserted this morning except for Abigail Giddings, his executive assistant, who was speaking on the telephone. Hard-working and efficient, she was a middle-aged woman who had been with him for the last eight years. Without lifting an eyelash, she held up a thin stack of messages as he headed toward the side door of his office.

The sixth-floor mayoral suite was like a pied-à-terre, spacious and austere; entering it always gave him a tremendous sense of power and well being. Windows ran floor to ceiling along two of the walls; his large desk was situated in the crossfire of natural light. From almost any angle, the view of the Pacific was immeasurable. This morning, looking out at the endless gray strata of ocean and sky, he felt as if he had arrived at the end of the world and this office was his home, his last good anchor. He shuffled through the messages, discarding most of them, slipped out of his suit jacket and hung it in the closet. Don't look at the time, he told himself. Just don't do it.

After he had forced himself to sit behind his desk, the morning began to go quickly. He took two calls, back-to-back, and then summarily answered with a note or a call the few remaining messages he'd kept. Abigail brought in the morning mail and pulled the files he asked for. She handed him his fourth cup of coffee from the kitchenette, then corrected her notes while he outlined in final draft the strategic details of his upcoming city council presentation. But Slater was no more aware of her and the world surrounding them than he had to be.

Everything seemed distorted and unreal. It was as though a great bell of glass had descended around him, and life reached him through its warp. All of his actions were conscious and mannered, focused outward, but his mind wandered inexorably back to the thought that an unknown murderer was waiting somewhere out in the streets. Only he knew of the malignancy about to visit their lives. Never before had Slater experienced such a commingling of dread and expectation. Tonight, he thought. After tonight, I'll be all right.

At a quarter to twelve, Abigail came to his office doorway to say she was on her way out. "Don't forget your umbrella," she told him. "It's going to rain." Slater nodded, smiling at her solicitude, told her to lock up and waved good-bye as she stepped from sight. Listening to the door close behind her, he rubbed his eyes with the tips of his fingers. The desk clock sat directly across from him. The second hand hummed in the stillness of the noon hour; the movement of each minute was like a slow, steely step. He couldn't keep his eyes from the clock's face.

At one that Saturday afternoon, he left City Hall. A terrible seizing-up of anxiety gripped him when he walked out on the sidewalk. *Where is he?* Slater thought. *He's around here somewhere, I can feel it.* But he saw no one he didn't know by name.

A PAVED ROAD called Condor Pass rose steeply into the northern rim of the city. The cliffs on the right had been left uncultivated, tangled with creepers and wildflowers; the other side fell straight to the rocky shore below. High in the hills, the Eldorado dipped over a knoll and turned onto an asphalt driveway that curved like a carriage drive among stately live oaks. Here, the immaculate yard sloped downward for fifty yards and vanished. Far below, the sparkling bay of Rio Del Palmos was revealed as if viewed from the wrong end of a spyglass—the tiny, white city glowing in the lap of green hills, the Pacific black as rumpled satin. At the end of the drive, in front of the shake-roofed house, Slater parked the Eldorado on bricks that were half a century old.

The Slater house was a large, sprawling, rambling ranch built into the side of a hilltop. Once it had been the love nest of an oil speculator from Wyoming, a man who had hobnobbed with Will Rogers and who then lost everything in a scandalous divorce. Slater got out of the car and walked up on the long veranda, which was always, even in the heat of day, as cool and shaded as a springhouse. Wicker rockers and tables were artfully strewn down its length; flowering vines grew up the roof posts.

He entered the house through one of the sets of French doors. No one was home. Many Saturdays he came in late, after Faith was gone, but he had never been so aware of this deep, midday silence. It was unnerving how perfectly still everything was now, as if it had been waiting for him, endlessly waiting. More and more, this empty house had become a reflection of his marriage. On those rare times when he thought about it, he found it strange that Faith could be so oblivious to his feelings.

The living room was large and classically proportioned. He made his way among the sofas and chairs, past the gleaming mahogany side pieces, trod over worn antique Chinese rugs, glimpsed himself in the huge, gilt-framed mirrors. The colors, the textures, all seemed to have aged together, as if from some masterful, loving lifelessness. It was not the air of indulgence that Slater found suffocating but the unyeilding sense of time standing still—of time spent wastefully and going to waste.

On a raised platform, the dining room sat like a separate pavilion inside the house—a Chippendale-style pagoda with its own silk roof. He took the one step up to cross through it and went down the hall.

As if suspended in midair, the master bedroom jutted out from the hillside at the end of the house. In the dressing room, he changed into khakis and an old sweatshirt. From the trouser pocket of his suit, along with the quarters and dimes, he brought out the necklace Sheila had left in the night to surprise him. Only a few more hours, he thought. Slater felt light-headed as he put the necklace into his pocket with his change. He took off his watch, put it into his pocket as well, and went back through the house, outside.

In the third bay of the garage, under a tarpaulin cover, sat a Jaguar XK 140. He untied and peeled off its cover. He had loved it since the moment he first saw it in a neighbor's garage. He had talked the man out of it immediately. A very precise machine, always, it seemed, a little out of tune, the roadster was an ancient dark scarlet with black fenders. Its sharklike hood, its primitive cockpit and tattered leather interior gave the car an air of impoverished elegance that he admired. All right, he thought, let's get you started.

Slater kicked the blocks from the tires and rolled the two-seater out into the sunlight. It positioned him ideally at the topmost crook of the drive. He wanted to know if he had been found out. If a dusty, black Mustang drove by on Condor Pass, he would see it at once. While he immersed himself in working on the car, Slater frequently lifted his head, wiped his hands on a rag and looked to the left, down the long shaded driveway to the main thoroughfare. He didn't know quite what he expected to see. He didn't actually believe that the killer would show up here, but he would've felt vulnerable working on the car anywhere else.

His sense of unreality persisted like a mild intoxication. The day reeled around him and away, irreversibly. Luisa came back in a taxi from her shopping. Half an hour later, Faith drove her car into the garage. She loitered beside him a few minutes, teasing him about the Jaguar. "Poor old accident," she said, breezily, "looking for a place to happen."

He grinned. "Oh, you think so?"

The Vietnamese gardener arrived with his basket of tools and attacked the hedge. At times during the afternoon, when the noise of a falling limb or the jarring screech of a neighbor's chainsaw startled him momentarily, Slater straightened and looked carefully about him, took his wristwatch from his pocket, checked the time and put it away, all as if in studied reflection.

At six-thirty, when he cranked the ignition, the dials in the cockpit stood upright, twitching, the engine drinking oil but ready for whatever he asked of it. Behind him, across the lawn, the automatic sprinklers came on with a repetitious chatter. Slater looked at the house, where the setting sun cast the windows bronze. He set the clutch, shifted gears and tore down the driveway for the road.

Hitting eighty-five, he banked into a tight curve, executed a flawless speed shift into second and flew out the other end as if from a slingshot. He pushed the Jaguar up to ninety, backed it down, then wound it up again.

The sun had fallen behind the hills, the moon stood in the indigo East and the curves of the road meandered like quicksilver toward the valley below. Approaching a bridge marker, Slater hit the brakes, cut the wheel. The roadster spun to the side, throwing up gravel, and whipped around as he jammed the stick into first, buried the gas pedal and rocketed back the way he had come. He hadn't felt such freedom since he was a boy.

Night was collapsing all along the western coast; he had no control, whatsoever, over what was going to happen.

*   *   *

DINNER THAT EVENING was at the Rod and Gun Club, a few miles north of Rio Del Palmos. On the way there, Faith turned to him and said, "Henry, let's not go, tonight. It's so lovely out. Why don't we drive up the coast like we used to. What's the name of that place you took me to?"

"The Fireside," Slater said.

"Yes, that's right," she said, smiling at him. "I wonder if it's still there? Remember that crazy band? Oh, come on, let's do it, Henry. Let's go on a real date again; we'll dance and drink beer and spend the night like we did before. No one needs to know where we are. You'll have a good time, darling; I promise you."

For a moment, as he drove, he seemed to consider it, but in the end he grinned and shook his head. "Faith," he said, keeping his eyes on the road, "we can't tonight. And besides ... we're not kids anymore."

She laughed and nestled closer to him. "Oh, shame on you," she chided, keeping the moment light. "We're not that old."

In the rustic lodge room of the club, they were seated at the table for twelve, among friends. The lofty, old hall was cozy and dim, the tables made intimate with trailing centerpieces of pine boughs and glimmering candles. Throughout the dinner courses—the chilled green tomato soup, the clams, the rack of lamb—Faith was aware, gradually, of her husband's preoccupation with the time.

At first, it seemed so inconsequential that she hardly gave it a second thought, but he kept doing it and in the most unobtrusive ways. Each time, the tilting of his watch was cloaked in a passing gesture, subtle and sly. What's he waiting for? she wondered. Otherwise, he seemed entirely himself, ebullient, charming, almost boyish in his desire to please. Still, it had a disquieting effect on her; almost against her will, Faith found herself keeping track of the time, too.

It was seven-thirty; it was ten past eight. Whenever he looked at his watch, Faith inevitably lifted her own watch to the edge of the tablecloth in her lap and again checked the time, but the position of the small gold hands meant nothing to her. What is it? she wondered. What's bothering him? Henry didn't seem to be particularly on edge. Was the evening moving too fast for him or was it impossibly slow? It can't be anything important, she finally decided. She would have known if it was, wouldn't she?

The relaxed conversation and laughter rippled around them. With a subdued clatter of plates, the waiters cleared the table; coffee and brandy were served. Against the protests of his wife, Deke Holloway told a joke about nuns and a parrot—the abrupt wave of laughter eddied away; on Faith's left, Bunny Cartwright praised the diving crew she'd hired on North Eleuthera; across the table from Henry, three of the men were baiting him to join in still another poker game, the "Saturday Night Massacre" Henry sometimes called it.

"All right," Claudie Murdock said, "we're in Kansas City and I'm in this game, straight poker, seven-card stud. Sixth card, two other guys still in the game, betting like hell, no end in sight. One's got a straight flush, nine, ten, Jack showing, could, conceivably, fill a royal. The other guy shows an ace and three deuces, have to figure he's got the fourth. I'm showing two ladies and I've got the other two in the hole. One card to go. The deuces bet fifty, the flush bumps him fifty. So, Henry, what would you do?"

Slater grinned. "I'd order some whiskey," he said and everyone started to laugh. Faith knew what the men were doing; she had listened to this talk before. Saturday night poker was a fiercely guarded tradition among the club's wealthier members and Henry rarely lost at poker. She was aware that he had a reputation as a savvy but unpredictable player. In the lull of after-dinner conversation, the men were dealing him speculative hands, asking how he would bet them, all designed to lure him into a game. When Faith had a chance, she whispered, "Henry, go ahead, if you want to. I've got lots of catching up to do with Jeannie and Fran."

He leaned back, expansively, put his arm around her and gave her a familiar hug. "All right, Claudie," he said, "you set it up, but no wild cards. Straight poker." Faith collected her purse, Henry drank the last red-gold dollop of his cognac and they stood, along with several of the others, who were also leaving the long table.

Except for her vague feeling of uneasiness this evening, she was happy trailing a step behind her husband. It was the order, the comfort of being married that lent stability to her life. She depended on it. Faith liked the confidence with which Henry moved through the crowd, calling everyone by name, a handshake here, a slap on the back there, a few effortless words of flattery or good-natured teasing, laughing companionably all around, then moving on, leading her through the rough tide of his admirers, while she twisted around in his wake, saying, "Hi, Fran, save me a place. Yes, thank you, order for me, same as always."

The crowd scattered at the dining hall entrance. Henry signed the check, passed it back to the maître d', then he winked at her and said, "This won't take long." As he turned to accompany the men to the locker room where the game would take place, Faith heard him say, "I'll sit in for an hour and that's all tonight."

It was then that Henry removed his watch, wound it with a twist of the tiny knob and returned the polished gold band to his wrist, all without appearing to notice the time. But Faith knew otherwise. When she leaned down to say good evening to the Kramers, who were still seated at their table, she, also, looked at her watch. It was twenty past nine.

Oh, stop it, she thought.

At ten-thirty, she saw him leave the locker room. In the lounge where she was sitting, the quartet had started up again after taking its second intermission. Fran Baudin, complaining of a cold, had gone home early; Faith had lost Jeannie Whitman in the crowd. The conversation around her had grown muted, rich with gossip. "Did you hear what happened to Carolyn MacRae last night?" "No—don't tell me." Faith tried to be polite, but was unable to concentrate on the tales of local intrigue. She excused herself and went to find her husband.

The outer regions of the lodge were deserted that evening as she made her way through the smoking room, then the trophy room with its walls of mounted antlers, and out through the music room, moving quickly around the silent Boesendorfer. The lodge's back entrance appeared at the end of the hall. Faith was headed toward it, past the dark, cavelike ballroom called The Cotillion, when a gust of wind blew from its vast interior, carrying with it flecks of confetti and a few tumbling curls of white and silver ribbon.

In the spindrift of debris, she saw something tightly crumpled and green. Money, she realized. It must've fallen out of someone's pocket. Hardly breaking her stride, she stooped to pick it up and saw—across the blackness of the dance floor—a service door swing open. In the sudden wedge of moonlight, the silhouette of a woman appeared for a moment before the door clapped to. Who was that? Faith wondered as she continued toward the lodge's back door, but from somewhere in the darkness behind her came the long, silvery echo of a laugh.

My God! That's Jeannie's laugh. *Jeannie Whitman.* Meeting someone! Quickly, Faith went outside and across the patio, hearing her heels strike the old clay tiles. She didn't see Henry anywhere.

The perfume of star jasmine hung on the air like scented beads and she could feel her linen dress relaxing with the night's dampness. Before her, the golf course stretched for a thousand moonlit yards, but out over the Pacific, the clouds were heavy and rolling and black. No stars shone there. Leaning forward against the stone balustrade, Faith closed her eyes and breathed in the warm air. One of those treacherous spring thunderstorms was blowing in, maybe the last before summer, she realized as she opened her eyes. Every few minutes, a blue-white flash of lightning ran jaggedly along the horizon, silent, ominous. "I don't like lightning," she murmured to herself.

Jeannie Whitman! My God, what gets into people? She has four children. Faith felt the beginnings of a profound loneliness settle over her. I don't understand how people can do that to themselves. To take her mind off it, she loosened the wadded money she'd found, smoothed it out and examined the two

ten-dollar bills in the moonlight. It was as if God had
put the money there to stop her so she would find
out the truth about her friend. What an odd twist of
events.

Folding the bills, she put them into the pocket of
her loose, pajama-like jacket. All right, Henry, she
wondered, biting her lips, Where did you go? She
lifted her head and looked back in the direction of
the ballroom. Someone—some man, undoubtedly—
had been waiting there in the dark for Jeannie. Henry
had come this way and vanished.

Shame on you, she scolded herself. You ought to
be ashamed of even thinking such a thing. Henry
and Jeannie? Don't be ridiculous.

She heard nothing but the eternal hiss of the Pacific. Then, as the currents of the night changed,
Faith sensed that someone else was standing farther
down the patio, beyond the honeysuckle that trespassed the stone railing of the balustrade. She tried
to see over the tumbling mass of flowers but all she
could make out was the motionless profile of a man,
facing the night. Is that Henry? she thought. Without making a sound, she lifted the vines aside to see
him more clearly.

A reading lamp inside the lodge had been left on;
the beam it sent across the patio was fine as mulled
cotton. It caught one of his shoulders and half of
Henry's face. Immediately, she went toward him.

His left hand was thrust in his trouser pocket, his
right hand held a cigarette. In the way he stood, in
the set of his head, Faith could see how intensely he
was gazing into the distance and she approached
him quietly. When he lifted the cigarette cupped in
his hand, she noticed how his fingers were webbed
with light, his lips cast red by the glow. A few steps

behind him, she stopped. "Hello, sailor," she said, lightheartedly, "want to dance? I think I'm free tonight."

It was as though her voice had struck him physically; she could feel his body go rigid as if to ward off a blow.

"Henry, what is it? Are you all right? What's going on . . ."

When he finally turned to look at her, his voice was calm, but flat. "Why're you always following me?" he said. "Can't I get a breath of air?"

Faith swallowed the dryness in her throat. "I don't always follow you. I hardly ever follow—"

"You're here, aren't you?"

"I was only going to ask if we were winning or losing at poker—but I will gladly leave you alone." She took a step to go, but all her instincts told her not to leave him like this. "What's the matter with you, anyway? What is it, Henry? Are you angry with *me*? You're certainly angry about something."

For several seconds he didn't speak. He stared at her, eyes flashing. She saw something in him then that she had never seen before and it chilled her. His eyes were a thousand years old, hard with hatred, the eyes of an old, old soul masquerading in his man's face. "Why are you staring at me like that?" Like the changing moonlight, in an instant, his expression seemed to her to dissolve, his face returning once again to that of the husband she knew. It's the night playing tricks on me, she thought.

"I hate these people," he said, quietly, "sometimes . . . *goddamn*, I hate them, I can't begin to tell you. We're all on our own out here, Faith."

He wasn't making sense to her but she dared not ask what he meant.

An abrupt snap of wind shook the panes in the lodge windows behind them and the first plump raindrops struck the awning above. They stood at the edge of the patio, facing each other, like cats. Rain rustled in the bougainvillaea, lightning cracked and the thunder rocked the tile floor beneath them; he stiffened and looked at the night.

"What's the matter, Henry," she said, softly, "afraid of the storm?" Never before had she wanted to sound so loving, so tender. "Something's going on, isn't it, my darling?"

Through the wet air, her hand went out until she was touching his sleeve. "You're so tense and keyed up; you've been looking at your watch every five minutes." Her fingers continued to search until finally she touched his hand; gently she closed her fingers on his. "What is it, Henry? I've had an awful feeling these last few weeks that you want to tell me something and you can't. It's something about you and me, isn't it?" She tried to smile, but her whole body shivered. "So tell me, Henry . . . just tell me this is all the silliest damned thing you've ever heard of."

He knew at once he had nearly revealed too much. "I swear to God, Faith—what are you talking about? There's a lot of things going on. I'm a little strung out. I'll be all right."

"So you really have nothing you want to tell me? Nothing at all?"

"No," he said. "Except I'm going back in there. I have to."

He turned his head to look at the rain.

She saw the back of his neck where the hair whorled into a thin dark fold and it all came flooding back to her, the apartment in Chicago, the roughneck boy she had loved so recklessly, the disgrace and humiliation when he lost everything. "In a minute," Faith said. "You can go in a minute. But first, is this something I've done?" She drew closer to him. "Or have you done something? Why won't you tell me? Have you fallen in love with someone else?"

It was unnerving how close she came to the truth. He remembered holding Sheila's face in his hands and her tentative, young kiss. There were moments when he thought how easy it would be to throw away everything he had worked for and escape with her.

But not this night.

His smile came easily. "Faith," he said. "Who would I fall in love with? Who, but you?"

Sudden relief swept through her. His face, close to hers, seemed pale but he was smiling; that great warm smile flowed toward her from his eyes, his mouth, the tilt of his head, from all the stretches of the whispering rain. "Oh, I love you so much," she told him. "I always will. Please don't scare me like this." She thought, Whatever it is, my darling, we'll get through it. Impetuously, she kissed him and clasped him to herself a long time, letting the kindling of her love come again as once, years ago, she had known it, trusting only in that, believing in it and wanting to believe, with all her heart, in him.

She felt him start to pull away and let him go. "Oh, I nearly forgot," she said. "Look." She held out the two ten-dollar bills from her pocket. "Look what I found."

He glanced at her outstretched hand and began to laugh. "Christ, Faith, it's just money. This goddamned place is practically carpeted in ten-dollar bills."

"Yes," she said, "I know. But these two are mine." *And so are you, my darling. So are you.*

Henry shrugged and then he put his arm around her shoulders. Moving her toward the door, he said, "You shouldn't stay out here in this rain. Go on in with the others; I won't be gone much longer." He opened the door for her and let her pass, and as she stepped inside, ahead of him, Slater looked down at his watch.

Now.

5

BEECHAM LAID THE room key on the dresser, took up his gym bag and stepped out to the sidewalk, shutting the door behind him. It was ten past eleven. With the wind whipping around him, he went through the hedgerow of rubbery jade plants and, again, studied the low, swarming clouds. The night smelled heavily of rain and electricity. He shoved the oversized bag onto the passenger seat and climbed in behind the wheel of the Mustang. Raindrops were beginning to pepper the windshield.

Driving toward Canyon Valley Drive, he remembered his own grandmother, who had raised him, and how she had talked to him and read him stories from the Bible. She told him there was a book in heaven and that everyone's name was written in that book and along with their names, a time was written— an hour, a minute—when each living thing would die. Beecham remembered her saying that nobody could tamper with that book or stop it or do anything about it, not even Satan himself—that we all lived until we died and that it was God's will. Beecham wondered if what he was doing wasn't something like keeping God's timetables. The thought of it made him smile.

The second hand swept past eleven-fifteen as he

staunched the car's headlights, pulled the black Mustang into the churchyard of the San Lucia Mission and parked between the construction trailer and a stack of lumber. He shut the motor off, unzipped the gym bag on the seat beside him and began to remove its contents. On top was the snubnosed .38 with the silencer attached. He set that out on the seat. Next was a denim field hand's coat and two flannel-wrapped parcels, which he placed on the shallow floorboard. Now that the rain had started, Beecham put on the hip-length denim coat. Then he took a navy blue sock cap from the bag and tugged it smoothly over his head. He pulled on a pair of thin latex gloves.

Once his hands were covered, he unwrapped the flannel from the two parcels: the first contained the working mechanism of a double-barreled shotgun sawed off to fourteen inches, an old LeFever Nitro Special, a beast of a gun still smelling faintly of oil and camphor. The second parcel held the stock, handmade of tubular steel; with a quick twist of a wing nut, he attached it to the back of the shotgun. Outside, lightning flared, but it was dark as a closet inside the car. He worked quickly, from memory. When the gun was assembled, he sat listening to the rain drum on the roof of the car and watching the lightning flash closer and closer. The storm was moving directly over him and settling in.

A third square of flannel, which remained in the bag, contained a twin silencer that Beecham had tooled himself, but the thunder made the silencer unnecessary tonight and he preferred to work without it. Fire would spurt from the shortened barrels of the shotgun, but the shot would be cleaner.

Assembled, the gun felt amazingly light; he swung

it up toward the passenger window, drawing the hammers back. His finger grazed the triggers and the hammers flew down, striking with a single empty clack.

He patted the two .00 bucks in his right denim pocket. They were three-inch, red-dot shells that he had loaded himself. He took the wire-rimmed glasses off and dropped them on the dashboard, squeezing the bridge of his nose with a pinch of his fingers. He returned the flannel pieces and the .38 Special to the bag and zipped it shut.

There was a strip of tape over the switch in the door. When he got out of the car, the ceiling dome light remained dark. He placed the shotgun inside his coat, snug under his left arm. Taking the gym bag, he closed the driver's door, locked it, then stashed the bag in the trunk, tugging briefly at the trunk's lid to make sure it was secure.

Beecham checked his watch. 11:23. The rain was falling harder now; his cap and coat were already wet with it. The lightning seemed to come in sheets and grow in intensity. Out over the Pacific, the storm was crossing the entire horizon like a volley of artillery fire. He set off on foot, following the short lane from the old chapel to the street and going across the street to the other side.

The Buchanan house was five houses away, and in the flashes of light from the low, rolling clouds he could see the outline of its tile roof through the wind-whipped trees. The curving lane was deserted at this hour; only the streetlights cast ghostly pools on the pavement. Most of the houses were completely dark, but Beecham stayed well off to the side of the road, the rainy wind rustling the grass around him.

When he was still a house away, he heard a car coming. Beecham looked back at the swell of head-lights and quickly hid in a grove of dwarf fruit trees that served as a property marker. The rain struck his face: a cold drop ran down his cheek and trickled over his lips. He waited among the crooked, drip-ping branches until the car sped by, its tires throw-ing up a fine spray. Then he continued on, feeling his stomach beginning to draw inward, a deep quick-ening of anticipation and tension.

He came to the corner of the old iron fence and stepped over it. Streetlight painted the front of the house, and a small outside light had been left on above the double front doors. The danger lay in the house's exposure to the street and he moved quickly across the yard into the shadow of the high eaves. The blowing rain lashed around him.

Again, he looked at his watch. 11:32. It had taken him nine minutes to get here. He would need less time than that to get back to the car. He immediately walked down along the side of the house and emerged in the woman's backyard flower garden, neatly laid out with brick walkways and trellises and arbors, all familiar to him now. The rain softened the snap of twigs under his feet.

Beecham paused to get his bearings. Through the latticework and the vegetation, he saw that a light was on in the kitchen, and that Rachel Buchanan was in there, moving about. Rain dripped from the eaves and rushed down the drainpipes. With the edge of his forefinger, he wiped the trickles of rain from his eyebrows.

In the next shard of lightning, the entire backyard spread before him. Beecham saw the screened-in back porch and inside that, the back entrance to the house. He headed toward it. A moment later, the scene collapsed into utter darkness except for the lighted kitchen window which seemed, like a photograph, to emerge from negative to reality before his eyes.

She was baking; Beecham saw the woman lift a large pan from the oven to the counter. No one else was in the room with her. He thought it odd that she was still awake and baking so late at night. But then he couldn't be bothered with the unexplained whims of an old woman.

The path was covered with leaves but there was gravel beneath them; he could feel the pebbles biting into the soles of his shoes. All of a sudden, she came to the window. It happened so quickly he could do nothing but stop dead still. She stepped up close to the glass and put her hand above her eyes, peering out into the night.

What's she doing? Can she see me?

He could have shot her then; the storm would've swallowed the noise of the gun. If he had brought the .38, he could have fired straight through the window with the absolute certainty of killing her, but he knew a shotgun modified like his LeFever was not reliable or even predictable at more than ten to twelve feet. And yet, even as he deliberated against it, the shotgun swung down into his hands. He broke the breech, dropped the shells into the chambers and snapped the barrels shut.

The old woman left the kitchen, hurrying toward the dining room in the front of the house.

Did she see me? Again, thunder cracked; again, the yard was flooded with pale, shimmering light. In the blackness that followed, he reached the screen door, opened it, and crossed to the back door, wiping the bottoms of his shoes on the bristly welcome mat. Wooden tubs and stacks of clay pots were neatly arranged along the wall. He stood, listening.

Carefully, he grasped the doorknob—it turned without sound, the brass catch drew back, the door opened. Noiselessly, Beecham stepped into the house, pressing the door shut behind him.

He listened for the woman's footsteps but all he heard was the noise of the storm outside. He inched forward, cautiously planting his weight, step after slow step, on the worn oak floor. He was in the long central hallway that ran to the front of the house, exactly as he had staged it in his mind. At the end of the corridor stood the double front doors, each with its oval glass, and the porch light left burning outside sent long pools into the hall. Near the front doors, the staircase curved up to solid darkness. But closest to him was the bright kitchen and through its open doorway, a wall of light angled across the hall.

Holding the shotgun cradled across his chest, Beecham edged up to the light from the kitchen, but he could see she hadn't returned. If she had seen him, she could have run outside, although there was no evidence of that. Or she could have a gun of her own.

Then he heard her, from another part of the house, heard her muffled voice. Too late to turn back now. Using only the pressure of his thumb, he drew the twin hammers back, slowly, methodically. Clickclick.

She was talking. She must be talking on the telephone, he realized. But there was something else, too. At first Beecham thought it was the rolling thunder. Then it dawned on him: a motor.

He heard voices. Laughter. Car doors slamming in the night.

The door that led to the porte cochere flew open and the girl, the incandescent blond girl rushed into the house in a pink formal gown. "Gramma! Gramma!" she called breathlessly. "Where are you, Gramma?"

The old woman came to the dining room doorway; she was smiling. "That was Liz Jaffe, telling me you were on your way. What's happened? Why'd you come home?" And there were other kids gathering behind the girl, two teenage girls and three boys, all formally dressed.

"We got *drenched*," the girl exclaimed, lifting the wet hem of her gown. "On the way to the car. I'll have to change; we all have to."

To Beecham, it felt as though time had speeded up; the kids were milling around, switching places before his eyes.

"Well, my goodness," the old woman said, "come in. Come in and close the door. Did you have a good time?"

Beecham stood riveted in the dark hallway, holding the shotgun poised against his chest. The kids were all talking at once; the girl ran to her grandmother, directly into his planned line of fire. ". . . a *great* time, Gramma!"

In the sugar the man had written, NOT THE GIRL, but the urge to go on lay inside Beecham like static. Slowly, he stepped backward.

"Oh, a really great time," the girl cried, vibrantly. "Will you help me, Gramma? I have to hurry."

I can't get off a shot. He took another backward step, the cheerful ruckus in the kitchen masking any small noise he made. He kept his eyes fixed on the bright doorway: if anyone stepped through it, he would kill them in an instant, no matter who it was. He heard the old woman say, "I just took some muffins out of the stove." Reaching back with his left hand, Beecham grasped the doorknob, turned it and steathily drew the door open. The rain had dripped on the floor, leaving a short trail of puddles around his feet.

Leave the door open, he thought, she'll think the wind blew it in. Still watching the kitchen, he backed out onto the screened-in porch. The door remained ajar. Holding the hammers firmly under his thumb, Beecham released them back into place.

All at once, he was outside, catching the screen door so that it fell to silently. He fled from the house, moving out through the rain, trotting along the wet lawns then across the street to the hidden Mustang.

It was infuriating. He expelled a long breath. Taking his bag from the trunk, he got inside the car. "Stupid!" he said, talking to himself. Dropping the shotgun on the seat beside him, he pulled the latex gloves from his hands. "Stupid, stupid bastard!" A dry, bitter taste coated his mouth. He felt sick to his stomach; he was consumed by rage. Beecham threw his dark soaked cap to the floorboard, pulled a T-shirt from his gym bag and wiped the rain from his face. "Before twelve," he muttered furiously. "You said, before twelve."

Keeping the .38 out and ready for any eventuality, he quickly unloaded the shotgun, dropping the shells, then the gun into the bag. There would be time later to clean and wrap them.

Okay, he thought, play it safe. Around midnight, patrolmen checked the construction site. He had to get away from here; then he would have to come back. Much later, three or four in the morning. He worried about leaving the car in the same place twice. He hated the thought of approaching the house on foot a second time. After she's asleep, he thought. And the girl would be there. That would make it ugly. Very ugly.

He tried to think it through. Noise that late at night bothered him. He would have to use the .38 with the silencer. Or a knife.

The Mustang tore from the churchyard onto the street, pointed back toward Rio Del Palmos. With the butt end of his hand, Beecham smacked the wheel again and again, unable to displace his frustration. "No way," he said, still talking to himself. "I couldn't kill 'em all."

The speedometer climbed to fifty-five, sixty.

"No fuckin' way."

Beyond the range of his watery headlights, thunder exploded and an erratic bolt of lightning struck a transformer. As the wipers switched across his line of vision, Beecham watched a high shower of sparks spew through the night and disappear.

"I've gotta go back," he said aloud, still mulling over it. And when he did it would be simpler to use the .38. But how would he do it? "No matter what," he told himself, "by tomorrow, I'm out of here."

As if cut by shears, the electrical cable snapped and swung downward with a faint whistle. With a deafening whack, the power line struck the Mustang.

Christ!

A hot blossom of light engulfed the car.

Beecham hit the brakes; the Mustang swerved; the tires blew, all four of them, instantaneously. Sparks drowned the windshield, blinding him. The crippled Mustang rocked forward a foot or two and stopped, still running but immobilized. The cable coiled down around the car, folding over the windshield, serpentine and deadly.

Beecham was shaking uncontrollably.

The stench of burning rubber filled the passenger compartment. The gauges began to hiss and smoke. His mind flew from one thought to the next without settling anywhere. He was unable to grasp what to do. *It's on fire!* he realized wildly. *Burning up!*

Without thinking, he grabbed the handle and opened the door. It swung out into the rain.

Then it sank in—what had he done? He stared, aghast, at the metal door handle. *My God!* Yet, he hadn't felt even the slightest shock. It must be okay, he thought. *I could have been dead.*

Afraid to move, Beecham tried to comprehend what had happened and decide what to do. Gingerly, he reached up and touched the metal surrounding the door. Again, he felt nothing. So something must have happened automatically, he thought, a breaker somewhere must have stopped the flow of electrical current.

He had to get out of there. With guns in the car, he knew he had to get away. A utility truck would certainly be on its way to start line repairs and when the Mustang was discovered, stranded in the middle of the street, the police would be called. Or a patrol car could show up while making its rounds. Beecham grasped the oversized bag and set it tightly under his left arm. He snatched up the snub-nosed .38 and pushed himself out of the car.

The instant his calfskin Wellington touched the pavement, sixty-four thousand volts of electricity flashed through his body, slamming him down. Everything in him snapped inward, tight, his vibrating finger seized down on the trigger and the .38 Special emptied its bullets.

When he hit the pavement, the voltage exited his body, blowing burning holes in his flesh—out the toes of his left foot that were fused to the asphalt, as if cemented there. His right foot hung twisted in the hinge of the opened door.

And the black storm moved on, rumbling over the once-prosperous neighborhood, over the hills and the rough pasture beyond, pounding swiftly off toward the distant dark mountains. In its wake, the moon reappeared; one by one the stars came out. On the ground, wreathed in black coils, the Mustang continued to hiss and smoke.

John Howard Beecham lay dead in the road, clutching the gun to his chest like a fiery summons.

6

SLATER HAD SLEPT so badly the night before, so fitfully, that he had the impression he hadn't slept at all. He remembered lying awake in bed, watching the clock's red numerals blink and change in the dark: 4:49, 4:50, 4:51. At daybreak, he pulled on his trousers and quietly left the bedroom, where Faith was still sleeping. He hurried down the hall to the front door, pulling it open and casting about for the Sunday newspaper. But the paper hadn't arrived yet. Telling himself he had to stop fighting against this anxiety, he lay down on one of the living room sofas to wait for the morning paper.

It's done, he thought. It's over with.

He took Sheila's necklace from his pocket, letting the thin gold chain uncoil through his fingers. Again he remembered her leaving it in the night for him to find. This was exactly the kind of thing he'd come to expect of her. The gold chain was fine and delicate, almost impossible to hold, like her hair. Lying there against the cushions, watching it slide and uncoil through his hands, Slater felt a senseless stab of fear. The danger of possessing her was now enormous and visceral—it seduced him and terrified him simultaneously. I think about you all the time, day and night. It never stops. When he returned the necklace to his pocket, he noticed how cold and lifeless his fingers were.

He knew that Sheila had to be devastated, but until he could act officially, there was nothing he could do to comfort her. Causing her pain had never been part of his plan, but it was unavoidable. Try to relax, he told himself. The paper would arrive; the phone would ring; word of Rachel's death would reach him in due course.

Hours later, it seemed, after the sun was clearly up and the birds were chirping outside, when at last he felt himself dropping toward the sleep he needed, Faith was talking to him, waking him up. "Why don't you go back to bed?" she said. "You look so miserable lying out here alone. Wouldn't you be a lot more comfortable in bed?"

He rubbed his face, cleared his throat and asked if the morning paper had come. "No," she said, "you know the paper doesn't get here on Sunday before nine or so. Now, Henry, come on." She tugged at his arm as if to pull him up. "You really must go back to bed. You look terrible."

Still half asleep, he remembered allowing himself to be coaxed to his feet and led down the hall. Faith insisted that he take his trousers off; she started loosening his belt. "No," he argued, "leave 'em alone." All he remembered was lying down again, the bed luxuriant, white and cool. Sleep hit him like a black brick.

All at once he sat up, bathed in sweat, completely unstrung. He twisted and looked at the clock. Quarter past twelve. That can't be right! Still trembling, he wiped his face on the edge of the sheet and dragged himself through the tangled covers, out of bed. He ran his hand into his pocket and clutched the gold necklace. It was still there, as he had left it.

In his rumpled trousers and a T-shirt, Slater went down the hall and out through the opulent, tented dining room. He saw Faith outside on the veranda, talking on the telephone. He opened one of the French doors and said, "Why didn't you wake me?"

She covered the receiver with her hand. "I thought you needed your sleep."

Slater stared at her in disbelief. "Who's that on the phone? Did someone call?"

"No, Henry, it's Marietta. Are you expecting a call?"

"I guess not," he said, shaking his head, "I must have dreamt it." He scratched at his eyebrow. "Did we ever get the newspaper?"

"Of course. It's on the breakfast table." For a moment, she spoke into the receiver, "Just give me a minute, Marietta," and again she put her hand over the telephone and looked at him, squarely. "All right, Henry," she said, "what is it?"

But he had turned from her, without answering. He went back through the house. The rubber band was still in place around the local Sunday *Gazette;* it had landed in the rain-wet bushes. The outer layer of pages was soaked, matted together. Slater removed the rubber band and unfolded the bulky paper. Its garish front headline leapt at him: CONVICTS MURDER COUPLE. The photographs of the three escapees filled the page above the fold. But as soon as Slater realized the entire front page had no bearing on him, he hardly glanced at it again. Something wasn't right. By picking the pages apart, he was able to scan the rest of the paper but the news he had waited for wasn't there.

Of course, the omission could be easily explained: perhaps the *Gazette* had already gone to press last night, before the murder happened.

Faith disrupted his thoughts. "You must've had a really crazy dream." With a gentle tousling of his hair, she strolled past him toward the sunny kitchen. "Find what you're looking for?"

"No," he said, "not yet."

"Maybe you dreamed about that, too," she called to him. "Anyway, you'll feel better after you've had some coffee." It took him a minute to focus on what she was saying. "Yes," he answered, distractedly, "that's a good idea."

In the master bedroom, he flipped on the giant TV, turned the volume up and went into the adjoining bathroom, leaving the door open. Minutes later, when he stepped out of the shower, a cup of coffee sat steaming between the large double sinks. Faith had come and gone, without him knowing it—he hated it when she did little things like that. He took a few scalding swallows of the coffee and set the cup aside.

At twelve thirty, while he was shaving, a local news program, *Rio Del Palmos Today*, came on and he watched it from the bathroom doorway. No mention was made of the news he was anticipating, no report of the murder of Rachel Buchanan.

Something's happened. Now he had to come to grips with it and decide how to proceed. His hands were steady; as he finished shaving, the razor scraped his chin and upper lip with short, even strokes. What had gone wrong? He was buttoning his sport shirt when he spoke to himself in the mirror. "Let's get it over with," he said. "Let's find out what the hell's happened." He poured the cold coffee down the drain and, taking his cup, went down the hall into the kitchen.

"Umm," Faith said, "you smell so good. Luisa's still at Mass, so I've whipped up some pancakes." She stopped what she was doing and stepped in front of him. "Henry, sit down. You're making me dizzy."

He couldn't bear to stay in the kitchen with his wife, could not sit at the breakfast table listening while she went on talking about the day ahead. Why hadn't someone called? He couldn't reconcile it. A part of him still expected the telephone to ring at any moment—a friend calling to tell them the tragic news. Again and again, while Faith cooked breakfast, he found himself passing close to the phone, ready to calmly take it up, rehearsing what he would say and the voice he would use—"A tragedy. A terrible, terrible loss . . ."—knowing in advance how horrified he would have to be.

But the telephone did not ring.

He ate Faith's perfectly thin pancakes doused in syrup, drank the coffee that tasted brown, and yet, when he told Faith he had to run down to the office, she was hurt that he would leave her on this late Sunday morning—a hurt that verged on indignation. He was getting into his windbreaker when she said, "Put it off just this once."

"Faith, I can't." He lifted his hands in resignation. "You, above all else, know these people. With the city council meeting tomorrow night, you damned well know what's at stake." He crossed the porch.

"How long will you be?"

"I don't know," he replied. "I just don't know."

HIS CONFIDENCE OF the last few days was quickly deserting him. He even had to think about the trail a telephone bill would leave if he used his car phone to call her. In a booth at the side of a gas station, Slater punched in the Buchanan number, drumming his fingers on the metal sill, waiting for it to ring. Not for a moment did he expect Sheila to pick it up. If a man's voice answered, he would assume that it was the police and hang up; if the voice was full of grief it would be reasonable to conclude that it was one of the neighbors, trying to help. In either case he would know the one thing he needed to know.

On Canyon Valley Drive, the telephone rang twelve times. An image rose in his mind of the girl sitting alone in a funeral parlor. That's where Sheila was, most likely; that's why no one answered. He returned the receiver to the hook. Still it seemed odd that none of the neighbors had been there to help. He couldn't think it through.

At the corner of Alvarez and Franklin, he crested up to the traffic light and stopped. Washed in stark sunlight, the stores were closed, the Sunday sidewalks deserted. No one drove up behind him. Through his open window, Slater could hear the mechanism click on the utility pole when the light changed. He started forward, then quickly swung north on Alvarez Avenue.

If anyone knows what's happened, he thought, it's Reeves.

Burris Reeves, the chief of police, lived on Klamath Drive, a quiet backwater of modest two-bedroom bungalows. Except for its cream-colored porch and trim, the small brick house was indentical to those around it. Slater knew he would have to be careful with Reeves. He stopped at the nearest cross street and contemplated the house through the hard glare of his windshield. Ordinarily Reeves parked his black and white cruiser at the end of his drive, barely off the sidewalk, but this afternoon the front portion of the drive was empty. Unless he had pulled the cruiser up alongside of the house, Reeves was gone. On Sunday.

Slater swung across the street toward the brick house. He hadn't driven far when he could see that the drive was empty. He was about to continue on when a young boy ran toward him through the rays of the sun. The kid's freckled face barely cleared the Eldorado's open window. "Hi, Mr. Slater, you lookin' for my dad?"

Slater eased to a stop. "I wanted to talk to him for a minute, Rusty. Is he around? I don't see his car."

Eight or nine years old, Russell Burris Reeves clutched a regulation-size NBA basketball under his arm. "Naw, he's not here right now. Officer Merriweather—you know him, doncha?—well, he came this morning and got my dad. Some accident happened, I guess. I think that's it. Anyway—hey, Mr. Slater, want to see my new T-shirt?" He pinched his shirt and held it away from his chest. "*Lakers!*"

"That's great, Rusty. Do you know—was he going down to the office?"

The boy shrugged mightily. "I guess so," he said. "He said he'd call; he promised we'd go fishin'. You want him to come by your house?"

"No," Slater said, "that's all right. I'll run into him sooner or later. Tell your momma I said hello. I have to go." He took his foot off the brake and touched the gas.

All right, he thought, something's up.

HE PARKED THE Eldorado off to the side of the two-lane blacktop among the scrub cedars, completely hidden from sight. At the overgrown gate, where he'd last seen Sheila, he stood listening for the sound of a Sunday driver, but the road was silent. I've got to know, he thought. I've got to find out what's happened. Crossing the pavement, he climbed from boulder to boulder until he reached the crest of the high wooded ridge.

With his set of binoculars, Slater studied the Buchanan property: the garage and shed, Rachel's fanciful garden, the white house with the red-tiled roof—all of it magnified before his eyes at a range of ten feet. He had anticipated seeing Reeves's cruiser on the premises, but it wasn't there. The red and brown station wagon sat parked in the graveled driveway but Slater saw no movement at all; the house and grounds were perfectly still. Feeling that he was missing something, he lowered the glasses and wiped his eyes. Where were the police? More should be happening.

Again, through the binoculars, Slater examined the house. Upstairs, at the rear, a window was open. The breeze had sucked the curtains out into the air. Inside the room, he could see a bedpost and a dress hanging on the closet door, even the wallpaper patterned with blue flowers, but no one was there. He lowered the angle of the glasses and turned them slowly to the left, into the neighbor's yard.

The Malcolmsons' grill was smoking; Anne Malcolmson stepped into the frame bringing a salad bowl. It didn't make any sense. How could they be having a cookout with their neighbor murdered right next door? What kind of people were they? How could they act as though nothing had happened? It didn't add up, but his mind, jittery with exhaustion, swam with bizarre illusions. Had Sheila stayed out all night after the prom, at some friend's? Was Rachel's dead body still lying there in the house, alone and undiscovered? He looked at his watch. Quarter to two. He thought: something's got to start making sense. I can't stand this.

Once more, he scanned the house through the glasses.

Suddenly, off the screened-in back porch, Sheila was standing on the walk. *Sheila!* At the sight of her, he experienced a surge of pure joy—but, why was she wearing walking shorts and an old tank top. She shouldn't be dressed like that. Slater kept her in his frame, unable to take his eyes off her. She went into the garage and reappeared pushing a bicycle. When she turned her head toward the porch, he glimpsed her face. She was talking to someone.

Behind her, emerging from the house, he saw Rachel Buchanan.

She's still alive! His heart slammed in his chest; he was frozen with shock.

The sonuvabitch didn't do it!

He didn't do it! He didn't do it!

Sweat crawled from his pores; he was tingling all over. *She's still alive!* He let the binoculars swing on the strap around his neck, threw his hand out and grabbed a cedar branch to keep from falling.

God, he thought. God, she's still alive! He took the money! He didn't do it! He didn't do it! What happened?

What *the hell* happened?

When he, again, put the lenses to his eyes, he could hardly lift them, much less hold them still. His field of vision pitched and vacillated badly. He caught a fleeting frame of Rachel getting into the station wagon. In the backyard, Sheila swung herself onto her bike and rode down the drive, lost from sight. His last impression was of the station wagon following down the drive after her.

He felt weak, cold with sweat. *What am I going to do?*

He thought, Rachel will wipe me out. All she has to do is open her mouth. And she'll do it, too. She'll ruin everything.

The danger was so pervasive he couldn't grasp it. Calm down, he told himself, deny everything. And no more damned waiting. Try to find out what happened. And then—. Henry Slater began to pull himself together. It would have to be quick, decisive, extreme.

She had to be dead.

AT POLICE HEADQUARTERS, the off-duty patrolmen hurried around him. Slater could feel the pandemonium in the room. A few of the men were huddled over what appeared to be a city map, and with them was a fastidious, heavyset man in a tan cotton suit, a bow tie hanging untied against his shirt. He stood a little apart from the others. When he saw Slater, he leaned into the group, issued final instructions and then came forward, his hands extended.

In his fifties, the balding police chief was everything Slater thought an officer of the law should be. He moved with an assurance that belied his position and he was keenly intelligent. Known to be much more flamboyant professionally than he was in his private life, the good-natured impression Reeves gave was real, but it was also a deception—one he liked to cultivate. He was also a cunning perfectionist, determined that, when he took on a job, he was going to do it right. Once started, there was no stopping him.

Slater knew what he was capable of—even for minor offenses Reeves was legendary for his use of trickery, sometimes letting suspects go in order to wear them down.

"What's going on, Burris?"

Burris Reeves took him by the forearm. "All hell's breaking loose. Didn't you read the morning papers?" With a handkerchief, Reeves wiped the sweat from his forehead. "Those three convicts, looks like they're headed this way. I've been on the phone since ten this morning, trying to coordinate with the state."

Side by side, the two men went down the hall toward the police chief's office. "These guys," Reeves said, "they're maniacs. There's no rhyme or reason to the things they do. They broke into a farmhouse this morning at dawn, killed some people; Christ, I've got a make on the stolen car, we know what they look like and that's all. We've called in everybody we can locate; I've got men posted on all the main roads but they could still waltz right in here. All they have to do is change cars."

Reeves stopped walking, his eyes fastened on Slater. "By the way, Henry, what're you doing down here on Sunday?"

Slater felt the impulse to make some excuse and get away—to bolt, right then—but before he could say anything, one of the younger patrolmen went past, buttoning himself into his uniform. "Klueger," Reeves said, reaching out and taking the young man's arm, "you'll ride with Robertson for now. Tell Connors, I want him back here tonight for the graveyard shift."

He turned back to Slater. "Then, for a little local color," Reeves laughed and wearily shook his head, "this guy fries his ass to a crisp—right out here on Route 9."

"What do you mean, fried his ass?"

"Power line's down; dumbass gets out of the car. Zap!" He suddenly popped his big hands together. "Presto: fried ass." He was chuckling again. "It was the steel-belted radials that killed him—you know what I mean, the graphite."

Behind them, one of the patrolmen yelled, "Chief, you got a call up here." As he started to go Reeves moved close to Slater, all the mirth gone from his eyes. "Scared me a little," he said, confidentially. "At first, I thought it was one of our escapees. You ought to see the artillery this guy was packing. Go ahead, take a look; it's all in there, on my desk. I'll be right back."

Slater went through the reception area into the police chief's private office. Cluttering his desk was a big, battered gym bag, a stubby shotgun and a shoe box of odds and ends. The box held the shotgun shells, a handgun, and wedged up in its corner by a worn billfold, a pair of thin, wire-rimmed glasses. The sight sent a flash along Slater's nerves. In an instant, he knew what had happened. *My God, he's dead.*

Only when he heard Reeves out in the corridor did he realize how close to the edge he'd been. He had to pull together some outward semblance of composure—he knew everything he'd worked to build depended on it.

"Bogardus and the Wilson woman embezzled that money," Reeves was telling one of his detectives. "They want to get caught. That woman, Margaret, in particular. Remember: give them enough rope to hang themselves and be prepared to bring them in.

If there's no movement by tomorrow night, then I want you and Berger to start calling them at their homes. Don't say anything; just hang on, let it work on them, one against the other, until they crack . . ."

Slater listened half-heartedly as their conversation drew to a close; he was much more keenly aware when the footsteps started toward him, footsteps that hesitated, then entered the office.

"You still with me, Henry?" Reeves said.

How much do you know, Reeves? Slater didn't dare look at him for fear of what his expression might betray. "I'm still here," he told him, "if that's what you mean."

"You want to see something? Look at this sonuva-bitch." Reeves took up the sawed-off shotgun, broke the breech, snapped it shut and shook his head. "If I shot you with this right now, at this distance, with the shells he was packing, it would tear you in half. Worse than a machine gun. But it's the barrels I can't figure out. Why would anybody go to all this trouble and not replace these Damascus barrels? It's crazy."

In only those few seconds, Slater was in control again. "Any idea who the guy was?"

"No, not yet. We've got some things. He left behind some interesting artifacts, some fake IDs, some money. He sure as hell had it in for somebody." He fished in his pocket and held up a stick of gum. "Want some?"

"No, thanks."

Reeves peeled the wrapper off, stuck the gum in his mouth. "We'll find out who he was. One of these days."

"Let me know what you find out, Burris. And good luck. I've got to get upstairs."

"Luck?" Reeves laughed, but in his eyes there remained a cold resolve. "Don't believe in luck, Henry," he said. "Never had any. I just go about my business an inch at a time."

An inch at a time, Slater thought as he walked down the hall. *I'm losing everything an inch at a time.*

There was a quiet resonance, an empty hum, in the city building that Sunday afternoon. Grateful that the elevator was waiting, Slater stepped in and pushed the button marked 6. The doors creaked shut. With a bottomless groan, the metal carriage began its slow ascent. But when the doors opened on the sixth floor, he didn't step out of the car. He had to do something to make the death real in his mind. He pushed the button in the bottom row, lower level 2, the morgue. It was perverse to go down there, he knew, but he had to come to grips with what had happened.

The chill basement rooms were divided by glass partitions. The main door carried the sign: CITY MORGUE. RESTRICTED AREA. In one of the spaces beyond the door, white drapes were pulled. Slater's moccasins whispered on the painted floor. From somewhere, like a sourceless echo, came a muffled voice. Abruptly Slater stopped, eyes carefully searching the glass enclosures. In the next-to-last cubicle, Dr. Alex Koslow, the coroner, sat at a desk, dictating his findings. Seeing his back was turned, Slater crept past without a sound. The door to the drape-enclosed room opened effortlessly.

The harsh, assaulting stench in the room caused him to snap his head back and catch his breath. Slater grabbed for one of the clean hand towels on the tray by the sink, immediately covering his mouth and nose. On an adjustable metal table in the center of the room, the body lay covered with a white plastic sheet. Slater's shadow loomed over it. Through the towel, he sucked in breath and with his fingertips, he drew the thick covering back.

The face he saw was dead. The closed eyelids had crawled back exposing filmy yellow slits that stared torturously, lips drawn in an agonized grin. Without those wire-rimmed glasses, Slater thought, he could have been anybody. But there was no question who it was.

The diamond gave off dazzling sparks of light as the sheet fell back across the gray features. Slater felt as if he had been kicked in the stomach. In the hall, he dropped the hand towel into a laundry bag and retreated, quietly. A muscle was jumping in the calf of his leg; his hands trembled. He stepped into the elevator. There was a sharp, mean smell in the air now, terrifying and thrilling, the lingering scent of really terrible trouble. *She's still alive.* He couldn't stop the tremors. With a sensation of falling, Slater rode the elevator up to his office.

The sixth floor was silent as he walked through the reception area. The air tasted stagnant and grainy. At the wall thermostat, he flipped the air-conditioning switch and the air began to stir. He shut his office door behind him and went directly to his private bathroom. He rolled his cuffs, drew cold water into the basin and splashed handful after handful on his face.

So that's what had happened. *An accident!* The seventy-five hundred dollars he'd paid up front was sitting in Reeves's credenza right now. Slater was sure of it. But he also knew he couldn't think about the money. *An accident!* He dried his face and hands and drained the basin. Now he would have to do

something else—start all over again. The risk and
tension of the past several days had been wasted—all
for nothing. He had the feeling that something in
the world had been violently disrupted, that the beautiful thing dreaming inside him had been smashed.
Today was meant to be the start of a time when all
could be hoped for; instead, an impossible problem
had been thrust back into his hands.

For several minutes, Slater continued to stand in
the dark bathroom, trying to sort things out. It was
not the first time he had been in serious trouble, but
he had never been in trouble like this. Was there any
real evidence that could link him to the dead man?

There was that day in Delaney's—it was unlikely
that anyone would remember him from that. No one
had come to the table; only the dead man had been
close enough to see what he looked like.

All of a sudden, Slater tried to sweep it all from
his mind like so much clutter.

Still grasping the towel, he walked out into his
office. The large open room was suffused with light.
Through the west-facing windows, the afternoon sun
flooded across the carpet in long shafts, and there,
standing still as an apparition, clutching her purse in
both hands, was Rachel Buchanan.

The blood drained from Slater's face, every nerve
in his body alert to her threat. "What're you doing
here?"

"I called your house," Rachel said, walking toward
him through the bars of light. "Your maid told me
you were here."

"So," he said, "what do you want?"

"I thought we had an understanding," she replied.

What's this woman saying? *You're supposed to be
dead.*

"I thought I made myself clear," she said. "But you won't leave my baby alone." Rachel was coming closer. "You're still after her. I've got proof."

"What proof?" he said. "What the hell're you talking about?"

She relaxed one of her hands from her purse strap, held it out in order to let him see and opened her fingers. The jewel encrusted sea horse lay on her palm. Her fist closed again.

He said, "I don't know anything about that, Rachel. I swear to God, some of the things you come up with." He thought, *You've got to be dead.*

She was still talking: snick-snick, her voice went, snick-snick, like thin sharp blades cutting his nerves. He watched her lips move, tried not to listen to her.

"Oh, I'm still going to tell people about this," she said. "Sheila's just a child, you know. So I have to think of her, what's best for her. I don't want to ruin her life when I tell the newspapers the truth about you."

You have no authority over me, he thought.

Rachel took a step toward him, her voice beginning to quiver with emotion. "So, I'm sending her away. The week after school's out. I've already started arranging it."

He stared at her from beneath his thick brows. "Rachel," he said, "you've really gone off the deep end."

"If you somehow really do care about her," the old woman said, "then you'll let her go peacefully. It's over, Henry. If you try anything, first of all I'm going to talk to Faith. I will, Henry, I swear to God I will; I'll bring the roof crashing down, if you force me to. Some people just can't leave trouble alone, can't get enough of what's bad for them."

He heard himself saying, "You're mistaken," and knew immediately he had not meant to say that. "You're making a mistake," he said.

"No," Rachel said. "You're making the mistake. You'll never lay a hand on her."

"You're crazy as hell," he said. "Why don't you leave? I'd like you to leave."

Her old rock eyes did not flinch or waver. "We understand each other, don't we, Henry?" Snick-snick.

He said nothing.

"Don't we?"

The silence deepened and lingered on. Slater just looked at her.

"Don't we?" she said a third time. "Yes," she answered for him, "I think we do." She wheeled past him, marched to the door and let herself out.

In the kitchenette, he opened a cabinet and lifted the crystal decanter, pouring himself a stiff cognac, drinking it down neat. It hit his stomach like acid; he moaned and blinked his swimming eyes. After a moment he walked toward the windows, his image growing more and more distinct on the glass. It was like glimpsing someone else, someone that merged with him from a different plane, transparently.

The real world below was almost unrecognizable—endless roofs and boats reduced to insignificance, pitched crazily in the sun, the sky absurdly blue. He put his hand out against the window to steady himself. His hatred was still alive and burning, but he realized that none of it was doing him any good, that it never had and it never would. Then that's it, he thought, I won't let you do it. You won't destroy me and you won't send her away, either. His shirt was dark with sweat. Was there anything more detestable than that old bitch?

Oh, God, he thought, I can't lose her.

Time was running against him now. *Three days,* he thought, *school'll be out in three days.* He wiped his brow with his shirt sleeve, his hatred rekindling, beginning to mount again.

What could he do? *I've got to get rid of her and I've got to do it myself. But how?*

At first, even thinking of such a thing was unspeakable.

THE AFTERNOON SANK to dusk. In the hills, Slater followed the drive to his house and parked on bricks still wet from the five-thirty sprinkling. Evenings, here, had an undercurrent of watchfulness, quiet but alive, and for a moment he was part of it, looking, listening. Then, with a deep breath, he went inside.

The lamps were lit in the living room; the dinner table was elaborately set for six. There were abundant flowers and polished silver candlesticks, each with a plum-colored candle. The gilt-edged china sat on clean white damask with his eighteenth-century silver, his irreplaceable crystal still showed the occasional bubble or flaw, a mark of the early glassblowers who had created it. In the kitchen he could hear Luisa raking a pot across the stove. A cunning mixture of seasonings and aromas intertwined in the air.

Goddamn it, Slater thought, moving on down the hall. *Six places.*

Faith was seated in the bedroom at her cluttered vanity, the one place where she allowed herself to be less than meticulous. Only partially dressed, in her underwear and a slip, she was applying her makeup. "So, there you are," she said, glancing up at his reflection in the mirror. "I was beginning to wonder what had happened to you."

There were moments when he looked at her and nothing registered, nothing at all. She said, "You'll have to hurry and get dressed. The Brubakers and Mullers will be here any minute . . . for dinner. Did you forget?" She went back to putting on eye shadow.

He watched her with all the feeling of a dead memory. He couldn't remember the last time he had thought lovingly of her or of anything having to do with their life together. He seldom thought of her at all except as part of his public image and certainly not today, when his mind had been possessed with the girl and with what had to be done. As he walked behind the silk vanity bench, Slater felt so numb, so removed, that even pretense was difficult. "Who invited them?"

"Why, Henry, you did. Three weeks ago when we were leaving the party at Marietta's."

"I did not."

"Look, Henry Lee, there's no use in us quarrelling. They're coming and that's all there is to it. They're supposed to be here at six-thirty—we've got just ten minutes. If you're going to take a shower, you must take it now and be quick. I'll entertain them until you get dressed."

The TV was turned on, tuned to one of the stations that played around-the-clock rock and roll. Slater saw the words "Prince's Trust" and a young Brit with shaggy hair was singing, *"Can't go on . . . sayin' the same thing . . . 'cause can't you see . . . we've got ever'thing, baby, even though you know . . . every time you go away . . . you take a piece of me . . . with you . . ."*

"How can you stand to listen to that drivel?"

Faith narrowed her eyes. "Will you lay off me? For

godsake, either tell me what's wrong ... No! On second thought, Henry, don't tell me. I'm through begging you." She swung back to the mirror and held her silence.

"And another thing," Slater said, stripping off his shirt and going toward the bathroom, "I'm not angry."

"... *every time you go away* ... *you take a piece of me* ... *with you* ..."

Faith watched as he vanished through the doorway, admiring in spite of herself the way his muscles laid across his shoulders. But tonight, he had set her teeth on edge. Holding the lipstick motionless in her fingers, she continued to stare in the direction he had gone. After a moment, she heard him start the water for his shower.

Turning back to the mirror, she completed her makeup automatically, her thoughts elsewhere. Something was working on him and it worried her more and more. Faith wanted to ask him what had taken all afternoon—but that would only be the first of her questions. She stood and slipped into her clothes.

In the shower, Slater set the dial as hot as he could stand it. The trouble with music was that it often seemed to be telegraphing a message to him. The refrain he'd heard in the other room drifted through his thoughts again and again. *"Every time you go away ... you take a piece of me ... with you ..."*

The water splashed over him, beat into his shoulders. He took up the soap, building a lather between his hands, spreading it over his chest and legs. A few minutes later, wiping the water from his face, he reached for the towel and saw Faith come to the doorway, putting on her earrings. She wore her hair in what once had been called a Prince Valiant, black and smooth and roundly tucked-in just above her shoulders. Never a hair out of place. Her straight, black dress was beautifully cut; pinned to it, above her breastbone, was a coral cameo.

Slater turned toward the mirror, running his hands through his wet hair. He found himself not knowing what to say to her or how to get through the impending evening at her side. With Faith in the room, he felt trapped, but he knew he had to pacify her. "I'm sorry I growled at you," he said. "I'm on edge. Work's getting to me, I guess."

"Don't take too long," she reminded him. After a moment, he heard her close the bedroom door on her way out. Knotting the towel on his waist, relieved to be alone, he walked into the bedroom to find that Faith had changed the TV channels as she went past. An attractive female reporter was speaking from the news desk. "We hope to have a live Telecam report from the murder scene later in this broadcast." Only half listening to it, Slater rubbed the towel through his hair.

"In the predawn hours this morning state police and their trained search dogs combed the Fox Creek area south of Strathmore where the convicts were last seen. Authorities now believe that the escapees are led by William Buckram Taylor, twenty-three, who has a long history of mental illness."

The camera cut to a black-and-white mug shot of Taylor, shabby, unshaven. This was a duplicate of one of the photographs Slater had skimmed past earlier in the morning newspaper. The convict's strange, staring eyes gave credence to the report.

"In 1982, Taylor was released from Lakewood Hospital for the Criminally Insane after serving sixteen months for deadly assault. Less than a year later, in March 1983, he was convicted of the brutal slaying of James Madison McCall after an alleged argument over five dollars . . ." Throwing a fresh towel around his shoulders, Slater ran a comb through his hair, opened the sliding patio door and stepped out on the back balcony. Night had fallen.

Okay, he thought, just give me a minute to catch my breath. He was trying to work up some enthusiasm for the evening ahead. He could almost feel the men slapping him on the back, the women kissing his cheek with their little bird pecks. Slater would spend the evening disengaging himself from delicate and powerful hands.

The secluded balcony was like a perch in the vast reaches of the sky. He felt himself standing on the brink of an endless black well. There was no escaping it. Far, far below, the town glittered and she was down there somewhere, too, glittering, impossible to reach, impossible to get to.

Tonight, parked in some dark, out-of-the-way place, a boy would touch her with hands already warmed by her flesh; he would look at her with eyes already drunk with the sight of her and how could she always say no? Surely there were times when Sheila couldn't say no. Just the thought of someone else touching her was driving him crazy. Yet everything about her was dangerous to him, out of his hands, out of control. A man would have to be completely crazy . . .

Slowly he lifted his head and looked back through the sliding door he'd left opened on the night—back at the newscast still in progress. What was it the reporter had said?

He took a deep drink of the night air and folded his towel, preparing to go inside, to get dressed. All at once, he was filled with the insane knowledge of exactly how everything could happen. It would have to be morning. Early. Faith would think he had gone jogging at the club. Not tomorrow, he thought, but the next day, or maybe the day after that. Soon though. It would have to be very soon. He would choose the time, the day, the hour.

He would have to look at the newspaper again. It was all unfolding in him now, perfectly clear, detail by detail, as if all along his mind had plotted in secret and the plan was just now breaking to the surface.

On certain mornings, her house was almost completely buried in fog.

A killer was loose.

It would have to look like the work of a madman.

7

ON TUESDAY EVENING, May 27, a blue and white Camaro convertible pulled up to the Buchanan side door. The car was occupied by two teenaged girls, Mary McPhearson, who was driving, and Cindy Perez. When Mary honked the horn, the door flew open and Sheila came out under the porte cochere, saying good-bye to her grandmother. Ordinarily, Rachel waited in the open doorway, speaking casually with the girls, then waving as the car drove away, but this evening she walked with Sheila to the car. While her granddaughter dropped her overnight bag into the backseat, Rachel, once more, went over the particulars with the girls. Tonight they were going to a party at Ellington Beach, and then later several of the junior girls would gather at Mary McPhearson's house for what they called an all-nighter.

Believing that Henry Slater might still try to make some move, Rachel had agreed with real apprehension to let Sheila stay over at Mary's, but it would be the last time the girls would have to spend together before summer vacation. Tomorrow—Wednesday—was traditionally a free day at the high school, a day set aside for the teachers to compile and tabulate final grades. Then Thursday would be a half day of school, when report cards were handed out, and at noon, the school year ended.

Rachel knew all this and yet she stayed outside with the girls longer than she had planned to; when Sheila started to get into the car, Rachel found herself saying, softly and only to her, "Sheila, why don't you just stay home with me tonight?" It was a feeling, nothing else, something she felt compelled to say.

Sheila's eyes were excited even as her smile filled with tenderness. She reached out and took Rachel's hand. "Now, Gramma, don't be a worry wart," she said, still smiling. She put her arms around her grandmother and kissed her delicately lined cheek. "I'll be your good girl. I promise. Please don't worry so much. I'll be home tomorrow—right after we all get up."

The Camaro pulled forward, turned around and went down the drive, and Sheila's hand came up, as always, with a last-minute wave. Standing at the edge of the drive, Rachel waved back. Then she crossed her arms and watched as the Camaro sped toward town. With her fingertips she massaged her forehead and noticed how cold and damp it was. It's my nerves, she thought. My old nerves.

Alone in the driveway, she stood looking at the empty street. If she had turned then and looked back toward the high rim of her property, she might have seen a glint of light at the top of the hill. It flashed in the stand of Atlas cedars. Still, even though her senses were on the alert, Rachel might have dismissed it as a twinkle of sunlight breaking through the dusk black trees. But she did not turn. Her thoughts were on Sheila and the night ahead. The glint of the binoculars' lenses went unseen.

She didn't immediately return to the house. While it was still light outside, she walked back through her garden to the potting shed, looking for something to do with her hands. It was late in the evening, too late to do any real work in the garden, so she settled on sharpening the tools she would use the next morning. Deeply troubled, she stood at the worktable, turning the blades against the old grindstone and thinking about the woman she had become. Kind and considerate? No. More a hard, judgmental old woman who kept her feelings to herself.

Suddenly Rachel Buchanan began to cry. Her pent-up emotions struck her in waves—feelings of fear and failure and the senselessness of it all. Disappearing sparks flew from the wheel. So often now when she and Sheila tried to talk, it was as if their hearts were giving forth only some remnant of a language they had once known and now had forgotten. She knew that Sheila was older now, separating from her, and she was certain, too, that behind the scenery, behind everything, loomed Henry Slater. She wept hard and bitterly, until finally she had to force herself to stop.

I don't want to hurt her, Rachel thought. God, give me the strength to do this.

Had Sheila stayed home that evening, Rachel would have talked to her about Henry Slater. It was something she continually fretted about—debated back and forth with herself. She didn't believe in being secretive with her granddaughter and yet, at the same time, she didn't want to put wicked thoughts in the child's head either. Rachel knew how tempting, how irresistible the forbidden could be. She found herself in an unbreakable dilemma. I'm damned if I do, she thought, and damned if I don't.

The need to end it, to expose him and destroy his fascination with Sheila, pressed down on her as never before. If only she could vent these feelings, yet she had kept them bottled up inside her, waiting until the arrangements had been made to send Sheila away. Now they nearly were: all that remained was to send the tuition for Sheila's summer classes at St. Francis Academy outside Los Angeles and the girl would be effectively removed from any immediate threat. Tonight, she had decided that it was time for Sheila to be told. She wanted to explain to her what she had done and why, to warn and protect her and arm her with the knowledge of what was certainly going to come from Slater's attentions. It would be ugly, she thought, but it had to be done. And yet, until she could sit down and talk with Sheila, all this stewing about things produced nothing but pain. Tomorrow, Rachel thought, when she comes home, I'll tell her everything.

It was a little after eight o'clock that evening when Marjorie Sanders called, wanting to go over the preparations for the garden show at the annual Founders Day picnic. Rachel had known Marjorie Sanders for forty years and they talked for nearly an hour. As the conversation was winding down, Marjorie said, "Rachel, are you sure you're all right?"

"Yes, I'm fine," Rachel told her, but without her usual zest. There was a pause on the line. "Why do you ask?"

"I don't know," Marjorie said. "You don't sound quite up to par. I've noticed it all evening."

"I'm tired," Rachel said, and suddenly her voice sounded crushed with exhaustion, ragged and old and halting.

"My God, Rachel, what's the matter?"

"It's just . . ." There was a long silence. "There's been something going on . . ." Again her voice seemed to trail away as if her mind was pulled elsewhere. "There's something going on that I can't talk about."

"Is someone else there?"

"No . . . no, it's just me."

"Then what is it? Surely you can tell me. Is Sheila in some kind of trouble?"

"No . . ." This was said in a voice so faint Marjorie could hardly hear her. "I'm taking care of it." Rachel was whispering now. "I tried to strike a bargain with the devil himself."

Marjorie insisted that she go on. "Is this—you know—boy-girl trouble?"

"No, Marjorie, not in the way you mean." Rachel knew she had said too much; she regretted having said anything at all. Her resolve had weakened, and for a moment, she had needed to vent the truth. Now it was better to leave the entire matter alone before it got out of hand. "Everything's all right," Rachel assured her at last. "It's just this fear that gets into me sometimes."

"Are you certain you wouldn't like some company? I could come over."

"Don't be silly," Rachel said, recapturing some of her old energy. "It's after nine o'clock. Don't worry, Marjorie. All I need is a good night's sleep."

"All right," her friend replied, "but I'll call you early tomorrow."

THERE WAS A FOG the next morning, a dense fog that blanketed the entire neighborhood. Looking down from the crest of the hill, the fog was like a gray churning sea, broken here and there by the roofs of houses and the bowers of trees. The red tile roof of the Buchanan house seemed to float and bob idly on the white void like a disabled ship. Not a light was burning in any of the houses.

In the east, dawn was breaking over the mountains. Among the Atlas cedars, the air was cool and fresh. Henry Lee Slater looked at his watch. 5:45. The fog below obscured the landmarks but he had walked the hillside and he knew it well. The terrain was wild pasture. Down across the face of the hill, an overgrown gully edged with saplings and rock ran down to a point near Rachel's garage. That was the route he would take this morning.

He pinched the burning red tip from his cigarette and crushed it into the ground with his shoe. Between his fingertips, he twirled the thin paper sleeve until the shreds of tabacco had emptied and were carried away by the wind. Then he put the filter into his pocket. When he rubbed his palms together, they were damp. He cupped his hands and blew into them, then he pulled the hood of his gray sweatshirt up over his head and tied the drawstring.

Clad in the colors of the morning, faded blue and fog gray, Slater began his descent.

OUT ABOVE THE high treetops, a white barn owl dipped its oarlike wings and swooped silently through the dawn. Rachel loved to wake up to these splendid spring mornings. To her, anyone who slept through the early hours of a day like this one was a wastrel and a no-account. Dreaming their lives away, she thought. All around her, even through the fog, she could feel the world budding and turning green—it was like the first day of creation and she couldn't wait to be outside in the pure new air. Among all her

neighbors, she alone stood awake and ready to meet
the day.

Thinking, Sheila, you really must see this fog, she
started across the bedroom. She was still wiping the
sleep from her face before she remembered that her
granddaughter wasn't home. Rachel shook her head
at herself for forgetting. Then, a fragment of a song
ran through her mind; after a moment she remembered its name, "Harbor Lights," and she was humming as she went down the hall toward the bathroom.
The joists of the house moaned softly beneath her
feet.

Rachel shed her nightclothes and hung them on
the hook behind the door. She dashed cold water on
her face and reached for a towel. Blotting the water
away, she caught sight of herself in the bathroom
mirror. Old, she thought, getting too old, going blind
in one eye. Life's little infirmities. As she quickly
combed her hair she worried that she would one day
go completely blind. She had already had one cata-
ract operation. But then the morning awaiting her
was too inviting to spend time grumbling about herself. Quit it, she thought.

She put on her work clothes: a bulky pink sweater,
a faded print dress, and comfortable leather shoes so
old they were cracked at the creases. Rachel headed
toward the stairs. But she wanted to fill the house
with the fresh air, so she detoured into Sheila's bedroom to open another window.

She wasted no time, going through the room and
raising the window at the side of the house. As she
passed the foot of the neatly made bed, she caught
sight of the large pom-poms of red and black crepe
paper and Sheila's cheerleading outfit, fresh from
the cleaners, hanging in its plastic bag on the closet

door. The vanity table was overflowing with lipsticks and nail polish, makeup and cologne. Once this same table had held a little girl's tin kitchen set; a brightly painted miniature sink, a stove, refrigerator, two small chairs and the set of play dishes she had bought for her granddaughter on Christmas—all of it stored away now in the attic, still good as new. Rachel pushed the memory to the back of her mind. There would be time this afternoon to think about everything. She went downstairs.

The sunlight this morning was split in two—above the fog ceiling, it was a magnificent day; beneath and inside the fog, the light was like putty. A white gloom pressed against the downstairs windows and the air was chilly; the slightest sound seemed to ring in it.

In the kitchen she measured four tablespoons of coffee into the tin cylinder and set the old percolator to brewing. She looked at the clock. Almost six. Marjorie had said she would telephone this morning. And, Rachel realized, Sheila might call before coming home. Surely neither would telephone before seven, but once she was outside, she could easily lose track of time. With the house closed, she wouldn't hear the telephone ringing in the kitchen. The window above the sink faced the back garden; Rachel pushed it open and felt the morning dampness on her face.

That's better, she thought. She took down a frayed straw hat that hung on a nail in the broom closet and set it firmly on her head. Letting herself out the back door, Rachel crossed the screened-in porch and stepped into the narrow strip of yard.

The morning glowed; the fog seemed to capture the light and make it opalescent. The garden was

silent. Rachel followed the cobbled pathways, knowing the way by heart; the fog swarmed and parted
before her like smoke in a dream to reveal the edge
of a trellis, a post, her prized cabbage roses ready to
burst into flower. Each took shape and drifted forward as she made her way past them. The door to
the potting shed was wreathed in mist; when Rachel
opened it, the old hinges squealed sharply. She felt
her muscles contract. Suppressing a shiver, she went
inside the small dim box of a room.

A window at the back of the shed let in light. On
the near wall, the many ribbons and medals she had
won for her roses sparkled in the gloom. Placing a
basket on her arm, Rachel began to collect the things
she would use this morning: a pruning knife, with its
small curved blade, a pair of long wedge-shaped
shears for the larger vines and stems, a trowel to
transplant strawberry runners, a ball of rag strings,
which she had cut and rolled herself. She pulled on
dun-colored cotton gloves and carried the basket out
of the shed.

The brick walks ran foursquare and in an X to a
central circle around the rose arbor. Every morning
she invariably found herself standing before her cherished cabbage roses. They always came first. In 1940,
when she had come to Rio Del Palmos to marry
Charles Buchanan, she had brought five suitcases
packed with everything she owned and a fruit jar of
water-soaked cuttings from her mother's rose garden in Connecticut. Only the climbing cabbage roses
had survived and she cherished them.

Heavy with buds, they towered over her. Some of
the oldest branches were nearly as thick as her arm.
Charlie had helped her build an arbor for them, and
the shoots and runners had interwoven with the

wood lattice until they were inseparable. Always in
need of repair, shored up year after year, the trellis
walls now teetered dangerously to the side, but in a
few weeks, at the height of the season, as if to defy
gravity, a grotto would rise from the earth, a grotto
made of rich green leaves, black thorns and roses the
size of saucers—Rachel Buchanan's famous bloodred
Connecticut roses.

Under the withered thatch, the ground was still
damp from the recent spring showers. Weeds sprout-
ing up at the bases of her rose bushes came loose
easily, roots and all. Rachel hardly noticed the passing of time.

She had cleared the undergrowth from three of
the thorny beds and was tying up some of the trailing climbers when she remembered she had left the
percolater on. "My coffee!" she gasped. Stripping off
her gloves and dropping them into her basket, she
ran through the fog for the house.

Rachel crossed the screened-in porch, threw open
the door and burst into the house. Grabbing a pot
holder, she snatched the percolator off the burner,
swung it toward the sink and put it down. She laid
her straw hat aside and blew out a long-held breath.

From the cabinet, she took down a cup and saucer
and heard a small but distinct noise at the opened
window behind her. She looked over her shoulder
but saw nothing unseemly. It must've been a branch,
she thought, brushing against the windowpane.
Through the fog outside the window, she could just
barely make out the tiny white privet flowers that
lined the side of the house.

Shame on you, she thought, shame on you for
being such a scaredy-cat. She poured herself a cup of
coffee. In the corners of the room the shadows wa-

vered like disturbed water. A twig snapped and she couldn't stop herself: again her eyes searched the open window. No, nothing. Only the fog. And the luminous morning light. Nothing at all. It's this fear that gets into me, she thought. She rubbed at the prickling of her arms.

Holding the full cup in both her hands to warm them, she walked back outside. The sun had begun to burn through the fog; it stood in a layer now, waist high above the ground. The heavy perfume of honeysuckle drifted from a neighbor's yard. Across the driveway, she noticed that the Malcolmsons' kitchen windows were still dark. It was such a rare morning that if she had seen their lights on, she might have gone over, tapped on their door and said, "Have you ever seen the like?" I ought to wake them up, she thought mischievously. It'd be good for them. She smiled to herself as she imagined them in their pajamas and robes, just waking up, sleepy-eyed over breakfast. Rachel drank the last of her coffee, set the cup on a porch step to take inside with her later and turned back across the yard.

Every blade of grass was slick with dew: here and there the precise symmetry of the moisture was broken and ruffled like fur brushed the wrong way. Something had passed through here. The trampled patches formed a disjointed trail, leading from the side of the porch to the garden. She thought, That's what I heard through the kitchen window.

But what came through here? A small animal—a cat or a groundhog—would have left a more discernible trail with smaller prints. She was trying to sort it out, following along beside the rumpled places when she reached the edge of the brick path.

There was a quality of quiet about these past few

minutes that she did not like. In every detail, the garden appeared to be as lifeless as a photograph. She found herself straining to hear even the smallest sound, but if God had struck her deaf, the silence couldn't have been deeper. How can this be? she thought. Always there was something: dry leaves rustling, old bark falling, insects moving, tiny wings whirring. Where were the starlings that came every morning?

The depressions of the grass joined and crossed the brick walkway and mingled with the slick smudges her own shoes had left behind. It was impossible to separate them. An animal of some kind did this, she thought, maybe a big dog. Walking along, still trying to reason it out, she nearly tripped over her basket. It was lying in her path beside the clematis trellis.

It seemed very strange. Rachel couldn't remember leaving her basket there—when she remembered her burning percolater, she had been tying up her roses. Her thoughts swept back, trying to recreate exactly what she had done. She had stripped off her gloves—she remembered that. "I'm getting so forgetful," she grumbled to herself. "I must be losing my mind."

Had she started forward carrying the basket and then carelessly set it down as she rushed toward the house? "I wouldn't put it past me," she said.

Stooping to one knee, she gripped the basket's wooden handle and in the clear gap of air beneath the fog, very close, the thatch splintered and burst—a streaking shape shot before her eyes—a blur right in front of her that scared her silly.

The blood rushed to her head; she was shaking all over. Down the brick path, she glimpsed its white tail as it leapt into her rows of spring peas: and she knew what it was, a rabbit. *A rabbit!*

So that's what it had been all along, making that noise, leaving those tracks. *A stupid rabbit!* Ten feet away, sitting among her rows of peas, nibbling at a leaf, its large glassy eyes seemed to mock her. Keeping him firmly in her line of sight, Rachel lowered her hand, reaching for a rock to throw, but her fingers brushed over something round and grooved and rubbery instead. She looked down.

The toe of an athletic shoe protruded through the weeds. Her first thought was, Who'd throw an old shoe into my garden? Then among the green stalks, she noticed the faded bottom seam of blue jeans, the pant leg rising through the foliage. Inches from her face, half-hidden in the vines and fog, a man was standing over her.

Rachel could not stop staring; she wanted to but she couldn't. She had a terrifying impression of how big he was. Suddenly she stood straight up, her arms locked at her sides, all of her locked.

At once, the entire fabric of vines and fragile blossoms exploded in front of her and Rachel was gazing at a face among the clematis—at his emerging eyes, driven and dark, burning like coals.

"You," she gasped.

She meant to say, What're *you* doing here?, but only the *you* came out. It was all happening too quickly, moving far too fast for her. He said nothing; he was smiling, oddly. The thought ran through her mind that he was trying to show her something—he was wearing her glove and in her glove, he clutched her pruning knife.

"What d'y—"

The words were never finished. The blade edge, gleaming and sharp, flashed through the air; there was a sudden hiss of movement and a burning slash opened across her throat. She couldn't scream. Her plangent cry was air. She was stumbling backward, away from him.

I can't breathe, Rachel thought. Her hands plucked at the wound as if to snatch it away and then her hands were slick with her own dark blood. All at once she tasted it, like salt; blood, hot and coppery, spilled from her mouth.

Her throat was on fire; she almost fainted from the pain. The garden went black then flooded back into focus. Again, she tried to scream—heard the cry she couldn't make burst through her mind. For an instant she saw his face, rigid with hatred and fear, lunging at her.

Twice the pruning knife came at her and twice it missed her altogether, but the hand she threw out, trying to defend herself, could not feud it off. The third time it severed her windpipe. And then everywhere Rachel turned, everywhere she looked, her blood speckled the bright green leaves.

My God! God, help me!

The green morning revolved around her. She could see her hands grasping for a post, something to hold on to—the edge of the trellis broke under her weight like matchsticks—but she couldn't feel anything. It was as if she were floating.

Then something struck her hard in the face. A bone cracked. The stench of rotting leaves filled her senses, and yet precious seconds passed before she realized she had fallen facedown beside the brick walkway. A gush of red warmth soaked the front of her dress. She felt her blood spilling out on the ground and she knew that she was dying.

Lifting herself on her hands and knees, she tried to crawl, but she couldn't see where she was going.

Her mouth sprang apart as if to cry out but no cry was there. Suddenly her spine tensed and her body jerked in uncontrollable spasms. Then her movements slowed. She was lying on her side, her head tilted skyward. Somewhere hovering near, she heard the sound of his hoarse, hollow breathing, but along with everything else, even that was receding. With her last flicker of recognition in this world, Rachel saw them—the starlings that came every morning, thousands of small black wings rising in a wave, then a spiral ascending through the fine, wet mist.

Her last thoughts were of the starlings and these splendid spring mornings, of her roses and of Sheila, all the things she loved, as if suddenly her memory had run backward through the fading circuits of her mind. Silence again prevailed. Rachel Buchanan was dead.

8

SLATER STOOD OVER the body, still clutching the pruning knife, shock running through him. He was shuddering, breathing rapidly through his mouth. He felt that if he moved, some delicate, finely tuned part of him would shatter.

In a moment of wild clarity, the urge struck him to gather the old woman up in his arms, wipe the blood away and tell her it was all a crazy mistake. Just as quickly the feelings left him. He felt paralyzed. The blade clattered against the bricks and the sound echoed on and on. He thought it would never end.

The remaining ceiling of fog stood at a level over his head, leaving a muzziness in the air. He looked frantically about, searching for anything that might later betray him. Fingerprints, he thought. *Jesus!* He grabbed the handle of Rachel's garden basket and wiped it on his sleeve. Then his eyes darted in a frenzied reconnaissance of the neighboring windows. Hadn't anyone heard them struggling, the crash as the trellis broke? In the house across the driveway, he noticed for the first time that the lights were on, and all at once, he expected the entire neighborhood to come running.

A voice in his brain kept shouting, *Get away! Get away! Run! Run!* But as Slater backed away, he forced himself to look at the inert body one last time.

She was dead, no mistake. With a quick last glance at the surrounding windows, he turned to make his escape. He ran across the graveled driveway and down past the side of the old garage, his tall shadow rippling over the vines and the peeling paint. He crossed the rear of the shed to the corner. With his sleeve, he wiped the sweat from his forehead.

All right, it's all right, Slater thought, still feeling sick with panic. Surely someone'd heard the commotion, but no . . . *it's too early. Nobody saw me. It's over. It's over.* No noise came from the garden, the air seemed empty and timeless.

He broke from the corner, legs tearing through the high grass, his head twisting to look back, eyes afraid. He tried to listen for some cry of recognition and heard nothing but the crashing of his own footsteps. He reached the gully and plunged into it, small stones tumbling in after him.

Gasping for breath, Slater raised his head above ground and peered across the field the way he had come, into the weedy gap beside the shed. Again he expected to find the garden crowded with neighbors, but nothing had changed. Through the fuzzy remnants of the fog, the morning appeared undisturbed.

Then the noises came to him, distant noises that seemed to waft through the damp air and fade away: the prattling of birds, the keen whir of the wind, voices. He heard a woman cry out: *"Rachel!* Call an ambulance!" Someone in a bathrobe was yelling, then still another, "Over here! Give me a hand here!" Their shouts sent his heart pounding up into his throat. He dropped from sight below the rim of the gully. I knew they heard us, he thought.

Slater climbed quickly upward along the old floor

of the gully, through the underbrush and saplings and the outcroppings of rock when, suddenly it hit him: all the fear and horror at what he had done surged in his gut. He stood gripping his knees, heaving with nausea. His stomach was empty, but when he tried to go on, he felt drained, without strength.

Pushing harder and harder, he reached the flinty summit where he fell headlong onto the mat of dry needles, out of breath, his lungs wheezing with the exertion of his flight. As soon as he was able, he stood up among the wind-bent trees, desperate to see the Buchanan house through the drifting tent of haze. But he could see nothing. Only one thing was certain: no one was chasing up the ravine after him.

Relieved, he dragged the gray hood off his head. Already his terror was beginning to dissipate, as if a long, bad dream had suddenly burst inside him, stunning him momentarily. Drinking in the high clear air, Slater felt giddy with triumph, almost light-headed. But it was short-lived. From deep in the distance came the whine of a siren. Immediately he turned and moved through the patch of cedars. Taking a zigzag course between boulders, he went down the backside of the ridge to the Old Sawmill Road.

He had harbored the perverse fear that the Jeep would be overrun with police. It wasn't. The Jeep was sitting exactly as he had left it—off the road, among the grove of trees. It was when he slid into the seat that he remembered to take off the blood-stained work glove that still covered his right hand. Panicked, he groped inside the pouch of his sweatshirt for the other glove. It was still there. With shaking fingers he turned the key; the engine started and he pulled out through the overgrown gateposts onto the pavement, heading farther inland where he would take secondary country roads back to the farmhouse.

Christ, it had been awful: how could he have lost his head so completely? The stroke of his arm had been like a mindless thing, the knife like something with nerves of its own. Now, when he tried to reconstruct exactly what had happened, he discovered that he couldn't. How many times had he struck her? How long did it take?

He couldn't remember.

His grave, white face stared back at him in the windshield glass.

And the blood. *Christ, the blood!*

When had the lights come on in that window? Had someone actually watched him do it? Again Slater felt his stomach contract with nausea. He swallowed air. The window had been a good distance away—he remembered that—so far away that he couldn't see anything except the blank surface of its glass panels. He had to believe that it would have been impossible for a witness to have seen him clearly, if at all. If there was a witness.

"Well, it's over now," he muttered to himself. "So what does it matter?" He couldn't go back and change things. Nothing could be undone or done over. But it mattered. It mattered.

Off to his left, the windows of a farmhouse slipped by, catching for an instant the reflection of the speeding Jeep. Farther on, a pickup truck clattered past, headed toward town. The sun was striking the Jeep's windshield—it would be impossible for the other driver to see him clearly through the glare.

The fog had all but dispersed. Slater drove four and a half miles and turned onto a dirt road known as McCovey's Lane, cutting across the narrow width of fifty acres of pastureland. He followed the old cow trail through a stream, then a long grove of cypress and came to a junction with the road he wanted. Within five minutes he pulled into his converted stable and turned the motor off. The Eldorado sat in the next stall.

Leaning against the steering wheel, he pressed the heels of his hands to his eyes, inhaling slowly until the nausea began to pass away. He looked at his watch. 6:55. So far he was close to keeping the schedule he had set for himself. He would have twenty minutes to take care of things here and get dressed, then another fifteen minutes for the drive back to Rio Del Palmos. At seven-thirty, he wanted to be sitting in the Beachcomber Cafe having his breakfast, as he did every weekday morning.

He got out of the Jeep and walked to the wide doorway, to the edge of the intruding sunlight. Slater listened intently for any unusual sound and heard the creaking of the plankings overhead, the thousand small scattered sounds of the wind in the trees and bushes. At the same time, his gaze swept over the silent yard, along the repaired porch, across the shut windows and doors to the gate that was closed as he had left it. Now, at last, he breathed a little easier. No one had been here. No trap had been set. Again, irrationally, he couldn't dislodge the feeling that he had made some obvious and disastrous error.

He stripped off his clothes. Dark flecks of Rachel Buchanan's blood had splattered his sleeves, the lower legs of his jeans and his running shoes. All his clothing would have to be destroyed. Moving quickly, he dropped the clothes piece by piece into a wire basket, then carried it outside, doused the clothes with kerosene and set them ablaze.

He remembered the gloves, went to the Jeep, retrieved them and tossed them into the burning basket. The rubber soles of his shoes would take the longest to burn. In the end, all that would remain would be the rivets from his blue jeans and the chrome-plated eyeholes of his running shoes, both easily disposed of. Inside the stable, in the small bathroom, Slater picked up a clean towel and a bar of soap and went out to the yard. He shed his shorts, dropped them into the fire and holding the soap in his hand, dove naked into the clear, deep water of the rock pool.

AT 7:27, SLATER pulled the Eldorado into the municipal parking garage. From beginning to end, the killing had taken him an hour and a half to complete.

With his hand sliding on the smooth metal rail, he walked down the concrete stairs: second landing, ground level, the concrete cubicle deserted as usual. The thick walls muffled the noise from outside. He realized he was just standing there, lost, exhausted, terrified of going out. As he gripped the handle and pulled the door open, the latch clapped, sending a cascade of echoes up the stairwell. He looked back in sudden fright. Only particles of dust rising through the gloom met his gaze. Shaking off the fear, he stepped outside.

The throb of the awakening city was like an assault. From everywhere, the sunlight struck—from chrome, glass, even flecks of mica in the sidewalk sparkled, burning barbs of light into his eyes. He had sunglasses in his pocket but he left them there. Nothing could look suspicious.

Today of all days, he would behave exactly as he did on any other morning. He went to the corner of two streets and stood waiting for the light to change, looking around him. Across the wider boulevard, a few people strolled by, singly or in pairs. Always before they had been just another part of the background but now, suddenly, he was acutely aware of them and of his place among them. He was the mayor, dressed for business, on his way to get a cup of coffee before going to the office and everyone was his friend.

"Hello, Henry," they said as they passed on the sidewalk. "Hi, Henry . . . Hello, Mayor . . . Beautiful day, isn't it, Mr. Slater?"

Charlie Ulrich leaned out of his open car window and said, "How's it going, Mayor?"

"Fine," Slater answered him, "never better." And, finally, he meant it.

On his face, the air felt bright and fresh, tinged with salt. A sweet, new sensation welled up in him, the promise of unimaginable pleasure. There was nothing to stop him now, no one to hold him back. Sheila, he thought. Now there would be time, endless time, for everything . . . *everything* he wanted. The realization made him feel giddy.

This must be, Slater thought, what a man feels like when he's let out of prison. I did it. I really did it. It's over. All across the city, bells in church steeples struck the half hour. 7:30. And he was Mayor Henry Lee Slater, walking along the sidewalk at seven-thirty on a bright May morning, feeling ecstatically happy.

Keeping a steady pace, his necktie flapping gently against his shirt, his hands thrust carelessly into his trouser pockets, he walked the last half block to the Beachcomber Cafe. At the locked newspaper dispenser near the front door, he dropped two quarters into the slot and bought the morning edition of the *L.A. Times*.

He went inside and took a table beside the large

front window. The tablecloth was white and starched.
The restaurant seemed oddly uncrowded—only a
few men sat at the counter drinking coffee. Somewhere above him, a paddle fan made a tiny, repetitious shriek in its rotation. He unfolded the newspaper
before him and let his eyes wander to the mirror
behind the counter, then along the wide Mojave
mural to the waitress, in her red-checked uniform,
who was coming toward him.

She ought to look at me with horror. Setting the glass
of ice water on the table and taking the pencil from
her hair, she simply said, "You just missed your
buddy, Mayor."

He could feel himself looking up at her blankly.
"Who's that, Gina?"

"Oh, you know who I mean," she said. "Chief
Reeves. One of the patrolmen came in and got him
and they left. Something must've happened."

"No telling," Slater said with a little shrug. "Where's
the crowd this morning?"

"Oh, a lot of 'em left already for the weekend. You
know, Memorial Day."

"That's right," he said, "probably so."

"Cinnamon roll and coffee, like always?" she asked
him.

With the same controlled ease, he nodded, then
changed his mind. "No . . ." he said. "This morning
I want your country breakfast, eggs sunny-side, pan
sausage, a biscuit and black coffee."

After the waitress left, Slater sat feeling pleased, as
if he had just negotiated a difficult and trying arbi-
tration. Before it hadn't meant anything—one breakfast roll had been like the next. But now he wanted
to savor everything, to add any and all pleasures to
this new sensation of freedom.

7:48. Almost an hour had passed since he had left the garden. Shouldn't there be sirens by now? Why were the streets so quiet? Surely they've moved the body by now.

What if she wasn't really dead?

No, he decided. No. I know that's not possible. Otherwise Reeves would be here by now—looking for me. Slater took a drink of the ice water, noticing the coldness of the glass on his fingers—the fingers that had held the knife. And while his mind leapt from detail to detail, it seemed now that any one of them could blow everything sky high.

People came into the restaurant; others went out. Empty coffee cups were left on the counter, then whisked away. His breakfast came and Slater ate it with good appetite. Lifting the buttered biscuit to his mouth, sipping the hot coffee, he was aware of the customers around him, coming and going. A few of the men spoke, one patted his shoulder; most did not even look at him. He sat alone, enjoying his breakfast, feeling thoroughly strange and marvelous.

The waitress cleared the plates from his table. With a second cup of coffee, Slater smoked a cigarette and wondered what was happening in the garden. Outside on the sidewalk, a girl walked by, a plain girl with a firm, lilting glide in her walk. A thin banner of light, threading through the gap between buildings, wrapped over her dark hair, catching its reddish highlights. All morning long, he had kept the thought of Sheila Bonner buried deep and now it came. How much had Rachel told Sheila? The hard little barriers of happiness he had been enjoying began to dissolve. Through his shoulders now and in the back of his legs, he felt a dull, ominous pain. Of course, he had known all along that this would be a horrible blow to Sheila.

I'm terrified, he thought. I sit here and terror comes in spurts.

Trying to appear nonchalant, he looked around to see if anyone was watching him. No one was, that he could tell. It made sense that the old woman would go to any length to poison the girl against him.

All the feelings he had been holding back began to pour forth: feelings of conscience and an awful fear, guilt, remorse. He'd have to go to her. He would talk to her, comfort her, spend time with her—he would do anything to see that Sheila did not suffer. But not now. He would have to wait. Slater crushed the cigarette in the ashtray.

I'll just have to get through this, he thought, one thing at a time. As he collected his things he looked at his hands again, clean, innocent-looking hands that now snapped the newspaper back into shape. Hardly instruments of death.

With his left hand, he reached for the check; the gold ring on his middle finger shone dully. Then the white tablecloth framing his hand began to shift and swim under his eyes. The noise in the room hummed like static in an old radio. His power for thought seemed to disintegrate in the air, leaving only a quivering fright in his nerves. He continued to stare at his ring.

The gold setting was empty.

His diamond was gone.

PART
TWO

9

AT TEN-FIFTEEN that morning, Faith Slater left the house and drove down the long brick driveway overarched with oaks. Since Luisa was coming in late today, she stopped at the end of the drive to pick up the mail.

It was a rare spring morning, the air fresh and warm. Birds fluttered in and out of trees, building their nests. All around her, buds were giving forth new young leaves. As she pulled open the metal flap and took out the thick wedge of mail, a second car appeared, swinging up over the knob of the hill and braking on the pavement behind her. Aware of who it was by the bright red streak of the car, Faith waved to her neighbor and extracted the last remaining envelopes from the box. With her left arm full of mail, she started toward the Corvette. "Good morning, Sarah," she called out, smiling. "Where're you rushing off to?"

Sarah Murtaugh beckoned for her to come faster. "Haven't you heard what's happened?"

"No, I guess I haven't." Faith crossed the pavement's double yellow line to the side of the car. "I've been making my morning calls. What's up?"

"Rachel Buchanan's been killed. She was murdered."

"Rachel?" she uttered, in disbelief.

"Yes, you know who I mean," Sarah was saying, "don't you, Faith? She's one of those older Garden Club women."

"Of course I know her." Faith stood stiffly, leaning over the open convertible, clutching the ream of mail against her stomach. "My God, Sarah, we lived across the street from her . . . when we first moved here. Are you sure about this?"

"I couldn't believe it either, nobody can, but I—"

"Killed?"

"Yes. Murdered. They've been announcing it all morning on the radio."

Faith looked straight into Sarah Murtaugh's face, trying to study out the fallacy in what she was saying. "I can't absorb this," Faith said. She drew a deep breath to try to calm her nerves. "Where? Did it happen in town?"

"It was at her house. They're saying those convicts did it."

"Oh, no—But what about the girl? Rachel's granddaughter?"

"They haven't mentioned anyone else."

Trying to clear her head, Faith straightened, and as she did, she saw a dark brown station wagon climbing in their direction. "Here comes Nancy Herbert," she told Sarah. "I wonder if she knows about it."

"Hey, sweetie, I gotta go," Sarah Murtaugh said with a mechanical grin. "Nannie and me—we don't get along. Besides, I'm running late. Give my best to Henry." She wiggled all four fingernails in a wave good-bye and sped away. But, by then, Nancy Herbert's car was rolling up beside Faith in the opposite lane, Nancy's familiar face tilted out the window. "Did you hear about Rachel?"

"*Yes,* my God. Do you know how it happened?"

"All I know is Sue Bruckner called somebody she knows over there and he said Rachel was cut to ribbons."

"No!"

"It's a nightmare. A real one. I've gotta go." And a little wave left Faith alone in the street.

The image of Rachel Buchanan loomed vividly in her mind—ragged straw hat, always wearing an apron, hands on her hips as she surveyed her garden, her crabby voice and her smile that seemed to say it was all a joke anyway. "Who could do that to her?" Faith whispered to herself. How can it be true? Good Lord, there're far too few Rachels in this world as it is.

She couldn't stop imagining Rachel's face. My God, she thought as she slid into the driver's seat and dropped the mail beside her, Rachel was our neighbor for almost four years! She rolled down the side windows for the fresh air, released the handbrake and turned down the hill. Faith switched on the car radio, whipping the dial to one of the local stations.

"Details remain sketchy at this time. Investigators from the Rio Del Palmos police department and the California State Police have confirmed a homicide this morning at 522 Canyon Valley Drive. The victim has been identified as Rachel Buchanan, sixty-eight . . ."

Faith could feel the icy certainty of it spreading through her body. Her hands were cold; she was cold all over.

"Police are asking that friends of the victim remain calm and vacate the scene. We repeat. Please avoid the scene of the crime."

When the national news came on, Faith turned the radio off. It was true, then, after all, no matter how impossible it seemed—her old neighbor, her friend had been murdered. All of a sudden, Faith's eyes filled with tears.

Speeding through the outlying neighborhoods, on her way downtown, she noticed how vacant the city seemed. Even the traffic seemed lighter and slower than usual. The houses looked closed and locked, their porches empty. Parks and sidewalks were deserted; no one walked by. But school was out. Maybe that was the reason. This was one of the first days of summer vacation. So where were all the children? Her stomach felt hard, like a clenched fist. Faith tried to keep a grip on herself, tried to control her unreasoning sense of panic.

But the closer she came to the downtown business district, the tighter the fist grew inside her. The traffic thickened, surging around her on Concepción Avenue, forcing her to slow down. Faith noticed shopkeepers standing in doorways, talking excitedly with passersby. Along the sidewalks, in clumps of two or three, other people scurried past, talking and gesturing to each other.

Faith felt the sun beating down on her through the open car window, but more than that, she was aware of a mounting disorder in the atmosphere—a sense of people verging on frenzy, rushing through the streets. She stopped behind two cars, waiting for the light to change, when a figure ran up to her passenger window—Millie Dougherty, a woman she recognized from church but hardly knew. "Mrs. Slater, didn't you hear about Rachel Buchanan?"

"Oh, Millie, yes," Faith said, leaning over the passenger seat, "I can't believe—"

"Then what're you doing *here?*" the woman broke in, her eyes anxious with fear. "*They're* here. Those convicts are here. Shouldn't you be home? That's where I'm going."

Before Faith could reply, the woman darted back to the sidewalk and away.

Then she was driving again, the sick knot twisting tighter and tighter in her stomach. Those convicts, she thought, here? . . . loose? Someone in a Mercedes pulled out directly in front of her. Slamming her brakes, heaving up against the wheel, Faith squeezed her eyes shut, certain they would crash, but with a whoosh, the Mercedes sped off. Unstrung by the near collision, the muscles in her arms and legs vibrated. My God. Convicts *here,* in Rio Del Palmos? She could feel gooseflesh up and down the backs of her arms.

The next intersection—where Mercantile Street crossed Concepción—was the one Faith wanted. It led to City Hall half a block away, but she found herself mired at the end of a line of traffic so stationary that she sat through the light, twice. Unwilling to wait any longer, Faith pulled to the right around the car in front of her, rolling slowly forward, threading into the gap between the line of traffic and the cars parked at the curb.

Through the open car windows beside her, Faith heard their radios—one after another, discordant voices but all part of the same fragmented stream:

". . . neighbors discovered the body . . ."

". . . for years a teacher at Uriah Elementary . . ."

". . . a brutal attack of such savagery . . ."

". . . Sheila Bonner, seventeen, lone surviving member . . ."

". . . president emeritus of the Garden Club . . ."

". . . still at large . . . urged to stay at home and lock their doors . . ."

Oh, Rachel, she thought. Rachel, Rachel.

She reached the corner and saw immediately what had caused the backup. The street was cordoned off. A patrolman, directing traffic, motioned for her to stop. "Lady," he said, "where d'you think you're going? You can't go in there."

"But I've got to," Faith told him. "I'm Mrs. Henry Slater, the mayor's wife. It's extremely important that I see him."

The patrolman eyed her, quickly. "I thought you looked familiar," he said. "Mrs. Slater, you won't find a place to park in the lot. You could park there on the corner, but you'll have to walk it."

"That's all right," she told him. "I have to."

The patrolman waved her past. Faith parked where he had indicated, on the corner near a yellow line. She turned the engine off and saw the tumult spread out before her. Halfway down Mercantile, in front of City Hall, television vans and crews clogged the street. Up and down the sidewalks, crowds collected and split apart in roaming, murmuring pockets. She could almost feel their fear.

Wasting no time, Faith rolled up her windows, got out of the car and locked the driver's door. Throwing her purse onto her shoulder, she hurried down the sidewalk, dodging through the crowds, skirting the larger gatherings of people, moving out into the street and around parked cars.

Outside the True Value store, a young housewife clutched a tray of potted geraniums and spoke into a reporter's microphone. "It scares everybody," Faith heard her say. "She was a very highly thought of person . . ."

In front of Delray's department store, a large throng spilled across the sidewalk into the street, completely surrounding the window display of television sets, watching and listening to a news update by way of the outdoor loudspeaker: "Mrs. Buchanan is survived by a granddaughter, Sheila Bonner, seventeen. Although Miss Bonner is in seclusion and could not be reached for comment, others in this exclusive community of fifty-nine thousand are less restrained . . ."

From the loudspeaker, Faith heard a noise that sounded like a Teletype, and the crowd quieted. A newsman was saying, "We go now live to . . ." and instantaneously, Henry's face appeared duplicated many times over on the stacked display of monitors. But after the first glimpse, Faith couldn't see him. The crowd had closed ranks in front of her. She stepped off the curb.

Patrolmen manned the yellow barricades around City Hall. The first policeman she approached recognized her right away. "Of course, Mrs. Slater," he said, drawing the barrier aside, letting her through. Faith ran up the shallow flight of steps and crossed the open civic plaza, where cables and power lines crisscrossed the inlaid tile like tentacles. Television crews moved in and out of the emergency doors. "What's going on?" she asked one of the electricians.

"Press conference," said the man. "We've been live now for about five minutes."

"Where's it being held?" she asked, but he had gone toward the remote van. Faith pushed through the revolving glass doors, into the milling crowd that occupied the lobby. Following the heavy cables, she made her way toward the main floor conference room. When she reached the entryway, she caught the attention of the security guard, Radley.

"Is that where Mr. Slater is?" she shouted above the bedlam.

He nodded.

"Which way will he be coming out?"

Radley pointed toward the end of the corridor, where a few of the city council members stood at the back door.

"Please let me in," she said, going around those men who knew her. "Excuse me," she whispered. "Hello, Emery. I'm sorry, excuse me," weaving past their sweat-streaked shirts, hardly aware of their greetings, so focused was she on getting to Henry.

Resounding through the public-address system, she heard her husband's deep, forceful voice. "These convicts must be caught. These brutal murders must be stopped before more innocent blood is spilled."

Flashbulbs went off; the air itself seemed to quake. The theaterlike room was brilliant with klieg lights. Faith felt as if she had rushed into a white-hot sun. The ranks of cameramen and reporters were impassable, but she could see over their shoulders if she rose on tiptoe.

Standing side by side at a podium, accompanied by an older uniformed state policeman, she saw Henry and Burris Reeves. Unflinchingly, Henry faced the barrage of light. "Only minutes ago," he continued, "the Rio Del Palmos city council met in executive session. By a unanimous vote, we are offering a ten-thousand-dollar reward for information leading to the arrest and conviction of each of these deranged killers of Rachel Buchanan."

Again the chatter of cameras and flashbulbs. Burris Reeves stood jotting in his small notebook, sometimes staring at a point on the floor. In all this chaos, he was its still, grim center.

Slater waited for the noise to die down.

"We invite and we will accept any private funding that increases this reward. But let it be known"—he shook his fist angrily and still again the room exploded with flashing bulbs—"I say, let it be known that this city government will not rest until these three murderers are captured and rightfully brought to trial—according to the sacred laws of this state."

The iron-hard forcefulness of his voice sent a shudder of relief through Faith. He was her ballast when the world was trembling beneath her. Questions rang through the air, shouts merged into confusion, but he didn't respond. After a moment, Slater motioned for quiet.

"Ladies and gentlemen, that concludes my remarks this morning. Rio Del Palmos Police Chief Burris Reeves, the officer in charge of this morning's investigation, has prepared a brief statement regarding Rachel Buchanan's murder. With your kind indulgence, he will entertain your questions at the conclusion of his remarks. Thank you. Chief Reeves."

From the alcove at the side of the room, Faith watched Henry relinquish the microphone and step back toward the long conference table—while Burris Reeves unfolded his reading glasses and took the podium. Henry's back was turned toward her when he quickly drank half a glass of water, his legs slightly apart, his left hand plunged into his trouser pocket. Even in the midst of turmoil, he looked powerful, entirely in charge of the proceedings. Faith felt a tremendous peace of mind now that she was here, able to see him and to know firsthand what was actually being done to find Rachel's killers.

Reeves said: "At approximately seven A.M. this morning, we were called to the residence of one Rachel S.

Buchanan, age sixty-eight, at 522 Canyon Valley Drive. An ambulance from St. Mary's Hospital preceded our arrival by a few minutes and Mrs. Buchanan was pronounced dead at the scene. The body had been discovered by neighbors. She was the victim of a violent attack, apparently during the commission of a thwarted burglary. She had been struck repeatedly with a single knife, which we have recovered, although the exact cause of death has yet to be officially determined. We are assisted in this investigation by the California Highway Patrol, namely Lieutenant Detective Nolan Ellis, who you see now standing to my right, and by the crime lab facilities and personnel in neighboring Santa Barbara."

He removed his glasses to wipe the sweat from his brow and put them back on. "There are a number of things I could point to," he continued, "but our first overriding opinion is that this unfortunate woman happened to be in the wrong place at the worst possible time. Further, it is our immediate impression that Mrs. Buchanan was apparently the latest homicide victim of escaped killers William Buckram Taylor and his companions, the brothers Ned and Bobby Rice."

A reporter yelled, "Does that mean you think these killers are still here—in Rio Del Palmos?"

"It's a possibility," Reeves said.

"Possibility? Or probability?" came a shout from another area of the room.

"It's possible—if they follow their usual pattern. We're advising people who call our headquarters to stay at home and take the usual precautions."

Faith listened as Reeves summarily described Rachel as a highly independent woman, who lived quietly with her granddaughter, Sheila Bonner, seventeen. He emphasized that the girl was emerging from a "state of shock" brought on by the killing and that Bonner, while never an actual suspect, had been completely cleared of any suspicion. He pointed out that Buchanan and her granddaughter were known to be "very, very close."

Then, he called Ellis to the microphones, introducing him as a twenty-eight-year police veteran. Ellis said, "As you know, these three escaped killers are convicted felons, with criminal and institutional records. They are considered extremely dangerous, now with nine alleged murders credited to this current crime spree."

Someone shouted, "What progress have you made in their capture?"

Ellis scowled into the audience. "Let's just say," he said, "we're not optimistic. We're dealing with a highly volatile, unpredictable element here."

Reeves clasped Ellis's shoulder, conferred with him a moment, and bent to the microphones. "That's all we have at this time. Thank you." The questions continued but the briefing was over. As Reeves and Ellis exited through the alcove, Slater shook their hands and then Faith was beside him. "I'm glad you came down," he said, taking her arm while they headed down the corridor. The security guard removed the rope; two patrolmen escorted them through the crowd, toward the elevators.

Someone thrust a microphone at Faith. "Give us your comments, Mrs. Slater."

"It's a tragedy," she said, feeling herself jostled forward. "Rachel Buchanan was the last of her kind; someone fine and rare is gone . . ." Moments later, as they entered the elevator, she wondered if she had even partially communicated her own sense of loss.

The pneumatic doors closed, sealing them in an unquiet hush. No one spoke. Maybe it was because she was next to him, but for the first time, Faith noticed how electric with tension Henry was. He let go of her arm and began to pace back and forth in the small confines of the compartment. She said to him, "Darling, calm down. The worst is over now."

He seemed to look beyond her when he said, "I hope you're right."

The elevator slowly rose. Only one of the patrolmen remained with them; in silence, with Henry pacing restlessly, they rode to the sixth floor. Again they were besieged by reporters.

"Don't you guys ever get enough?" Slater asked them, waving them aside. "I've got nothing else to say." Then turning to Faith, he said, "Go on in. I'll be right there."

His office reflected the morning's confusion—leather chairs sat in disarray; dirty ashtrays and coffee cups, some half full, had been left on the occasional tables.

Running the back of her hand across her damp forehead, Faith thought about tidying it up, but there wasn't time. The door to the outer office stood open, and she saw Abigail dashing about. All seven buttons on Henry's telephone were lit and blinking. Faith went into the private washroom and blotted the perspiration from her face, still trying to steady her nerves. She ran a comb through her hair, quickly touched up her makeup and went back out.

Henry was sitting behind his desk, talking quietly with Abigail, who had handed him a stack of messages. Faith went to one of the two chairs that faced his desk and sat down. While he listened to Abigail, Henry turned, picked up a note from his desk and inspected it, but there was little doubt where his attention was. "Who's screening my calls?" he asked, irritably.

"I've been screening most of them," Abigail told him.

"Good. That's good; that's what I want you to do. What about the press release?"

She said, "It's copied and on my desk."

"Then you know what to do. Let me get this straight: none of these calls are reporters, is that right?"

"Yes," she said, going quickly across the room. "That's right." She smiled a quick, businesslike hello at Faith before leaving the two of them alone.

Stripping off his suit jacket and throwing it across a chair, Henry moved behind his desk and sat down. Sweat beaded his eyebrows and he wiped it away impatiently. "Jesus! Jesus! Jesus!" he kept whispering over and over in disbelief. Faith watched him lean forward with his elbows on his knees, taking a moment to collect himself. He said, "You surprised me—when I saw you down there."

"It's unbelievable," she said. "I was so shocked; I just had to see you for a minute—to touch base. I can't get over this, Henry, I can't."

He sank back in his chair, but then immediately got up and started to pace behind his desk. "I can't talk about this right now," he said. "I've got to get these calls. I've got a thousand things I have to do."

"How can I help?" she asked in an even quieter voice. "What can I do? Isn't there something I can do?"

"I don't know, Faith; I can't think of anything."

He returned to his chair, took up the telephone with his left hand and pressed the first blinking button. "This is Henry Slater," he said.

He clamped the receiver under his chin, unbuttoned and rolled his sleeves. "Yes," he said, flipping the page of his calendar. That was when Faith noticed that he wasn't wearing his ring. His hand looked robbed of its character without it. "Yes, I'll be there," he said. "One o'clock, Thursday." He hung up, scratching the appointment in his book.

"Henry, where's your ring?"

His hand stopped. Still studying the page, he said, "Oh, I'm giving it a rest." He raised his head and looked at her. "You know how it irritates me in the summer—it gives me a rash."

"I just wondered," she said.

Again, he reached for the telephone. "Faith, can't you see that I'm very busy?"

"Give me one minute more," she said, "then I'll leave." She cleared her throat. "What do you want to do about the funeral?"

"We'll have to go."

She sat forward on her chair, her fingers laced tightly around her knees. "No, darling, of course, but I meant, what about flowers and . . . ?"

His hand was still hovering over the telephone; now he drew it back in frustration. "Why don't I leave that to you? Actually, Faith, I thought—why don't you arrange an anonymous donation, maybe through Father Vasquez. We should do everything we can."

She nodded. "I think so, too." As she got up from the corner of her chair, she said, "Henry, I think I'll go out there. To Rachel's."

He glanced at the ceiling and tapped his pencil on

the desk. A slow heaviness settled through him. "My God, Faith, why would you want to?"

"Maybe I can do something to help that young girl."

"That's not such a good idea. From what I hear, it's a madhouse out there. I'm sure she's inundated with well-meaning neighbors and—Faith, who knows, she may not even be there, by now." He walked around the desk, came and put his arm around her. "Why don't you leave well enough alone?"

"But I'd think you'd want me to. If this had happened to you, God forbid, Rachel would come to me." Faith waited for him to object. "I don't want to, but, Henry, I feel I have to."

She collected her purse. "I'm going now," she said softly. For a moment, she regarded him, waiting to see if he had anything more to say, but he wouldn't meet her eyes. His hand clasped the telephone. "Then I'll see you later," he said as she drew away toward the door.

IT WAS SHORTLY after one that Wednesday afternoon, when Faith drove out to Canyon Valley Drive. In either direction, cars were strung out along both sides of the road, parked haphazardly on the grass. Searching for a parking space among them, she felt her apprehensions mount.

As she drew nearer Faith began to see the police cars clustered at the edge of the Buchanan property— never had she seen so many at one time in Rio Del Palmos. There must have been thirty or more, some from bordering counties. Rachel's front yard had been cordoned off, but the neighbors' yards on either side and the yard across the street where she and Henry once had lived, were full of milling people.

Rachel's iron fence and her empty driveway were surrounded by slick yellow police tape. At the foot of the drive, an officer sat in a folding chair. Faith parked half a block away, on the grassy shoulder, locked and left her car. Instead of following the pavement back to the house, she went around to the Shultzes' backyard, where she had seen Beth Shultz and two or three other women. "Beth, isn't this awful?" she said.

"Faith, you can't imagine. We haven't seen you for so long."

The women were watching the slow, weblike movement of the police across the face of the long ridge behind Rachel's house.

"What're they looking for?" Faith asked.

"One of the Lorentzen kids said they saw a man run back that way," Candy Hutchens explained. "But who knows? God, it was foggy this morning."

"What's happened to Rachel's granddaughter?" Faith asked. "Is she there in the house?"

"No," Beth told her, "they've got her next door, at the Malcolmsons'. She's taking it very hard; they had to call a doctor."

"We could hear her screaming clear across the street," said Candy.

Faith shivered. She couldn't imagine how the child must have felt.

"It was crazy—the way it happened," one of the other women said. "She was with her boyfriend and another couple and they pulled into the driveway maybe a minute before the ambulance got here. So she saw—well, almost everything."

"I want to see her," Faith said, "if they'll let me." She said good-bye to the women and walked across the backyard, again with that sensation of the ground beginning to float and spin away beneath her.

When she went up to the Malcolmsons' back door, she could not stop herself from looking across the driveway at Rachel's flower garden, trying to search out where the murder took place. But from what she could see, the garden looked serene and untouched.

Annie Malcolmson pushed open the screen door for her to come in. "Faith, it's nice of you to come."

"Annie, how is she?" Faith asked softly, stepping into the kitchen.

"Oh," the heavyset woman said, averting her eyes, "she's a little better now. It's been a living hell. We had to actually pick her up and bring her here by force."

"Did the doctor see her?"

The woman nodded. "Yes, but Sheila wouldn't have anything to do with him. I thought we might have to hold her down, but he finally said to just give her some time. He left some sedatives but she won't take them; I was thinking I should try again."

"Let me try," Faith said. "Where is she?"

Annie handed her the vial of tablets and a fresh glass of water. "This way," she said. She led Faith down the hall to the den, where an older woman and a boy in dungarees stood near the doorway, talking in hushed voices. Once he was introduced, Denny Rivera said, "I'm here with Sheila," and the woman said, "I don't believe we've met. I'm Marjorie Sanders. Some time ago, Rachel asked me to be Sheila's guardian. What a horrible shock this has been. I never really thought I'd be starting a family at my age."

Feeling the gravity of the moment, Faith stepped into the small, booklined room. The drapes were pulled on the bow window. Sheila was curled up on the window seat, her arms wrapped round her knees, her head buried in her arms. She was rocking, slightly; now and then she gave an exhausted sob. When Faith sat next to her, Sheila looked up with a start. "Oh, Mrs. Slater," she said, "what're you doing here?" Her eyes were swollen almost shut; her face looked raw from tears. "Didn't Mr. Slater come with you?"

"No," Faith said, "he couldn't." She felt the girl's pain—not just her grief, but her overwhelming anguish.

"I want my Gramma back."

Tears stood in Faith's eyes. She was profoundly moved by a mother's impulse—a poorly controlled, incomprehending but undeniable reaching out to a young girl so in need. "I know," she said. "I know, Sheila. I want her back, too."

"I don't know why . . . I don't know . . . why can't they . . ."

"You're so tired," Faith said, "Sheila . . . don't be afraid. We all want to help you."

"No, help," Sheila whispered, "no help, now," and the tears ran from her eyes.

Faith set down the glass of water, opened the vial and shook out one of the tablets. "The doctor left this for you. Would you take this for me, please? It'll help you sleep."

"I don't want to sleep. I want . . . What if . . . I've got to go home."

"It's all right. Don't worry. I won't let anything happen."

"But they said . . . They won't let me get back home."

"You're too tired to talk. I know you don't want to,

but you have to rest. Just do this for me. Please take
it. You'll feel better, Sheila, I promise you."

Through tear-strained eyes, Sheila stared at her,
dazedly. She held out her hand and Faith placed the
tablets in it and gave her the glass of water. Without
further hesitation, Sheila took the medication.

"Let me put my arms around you," Faith said, and
together they moved to the couch, the young girl
and the woman who was once her neighbor long
ago, Sheila struggling against the inexorable tide of
sleep, giving now and then a soft moan and Faith
holding her, speaking as gently as she knew how.
"Don't be afraid," she said, "don't be afraid anymore."

When they were certain Sheila was asleep, the two
women in the hallway came forward to help lay her
down.

FAITH RETURNED HOME in the middle of the afternoon. She didn't put the car in the garage; she
turned off the ignition and sat behind the wheel with
her eyes closed. Then taking her keys, she opened
the driver's door, twisted back and picked up the
armful of mail from the passenger seat. Faith got out
of the car and started toward the house, but she
didn't want to go in. Not yet. A part of her was still
propelled by the day's events; she was too wrung
out, and the afternoon was too beautiful to shut
herself away inside.

Faith walked out across the lawn to the stone bench.
From there, she could look out through a crevice in
the trees and see the small white city, glistening in
the sun. She closed her eyes and let the spring air
saturate her senses. Minutes passed before she began
to idly sift through the mail.

A church announcement, the gas and telephone

bills, an estimate from the caterer, a notice from the
dry cleaners, sale circulars and a mail order catalog:
Faith had nearly gone through them, when she came
to a square-shaped envelope addressed to her. It
looked like a formal invitation of some sort; the
heavy paper was old, faintly yellowed at the edges.
What's this? she thought as she tore open the back
flap.

The envelope contained a single sheet of writing
paper. Old note paper, Faith realized, unfolding it.
She didn't recognize the handwriting, so she glanced
down at the signature, full of surprise.

It was signed: Rachel Buchanan.

She held a letter from Rachel Buchanan in her hand.

Faith stared helplessly at the signature for a moment, disbelieving. *My God!* Her eyes flew to the top
of the page:

Dear Faith,
    I tried to reach you this afternoon but you
weren't home. I was afraid to leave word with
your maid because I didn't want Henry to know
I called. I must talk to you. Some serious trouble has been brewing a long time that you should
know about. This has to do with Henry. Would
you please come by yourself and visit me in my
home in the next few days? If not, I'll be forced
to do something I don't want to do.
    I'm sorry to bring you into this now since I
believe you are a woman of good character.
But I have to.
    If I don't hear from you, I'll know he has
stepped in. I wish you no harm.
                              Yours truly,
                              Rachel Buchanan

Faith was covered with sweat now, a fine warm suffocating sweat that she could feel breaking out all over her body. This was incredible. It was like being in the throes of a bad dream—if only she could open her eyes and the letter, the murder, this panic, would all go away.

But she's dead. Rachel's dead.

She sat staring at the note. With a floating, disembodied sensation, she read it through again—". . . *Some serious trouble has been brewing . . . This has to do with Henry.*"

What has to do with Henry? When did Rachel send this? Faith still had the impression she had read it too quickly and missed its most salient point. The letter was undated. She snatched up the envelope, flipped it over. The postmark showed today's date.

How could that be right? When did Rachel write this? When did she try to call? But Faith's thoughts were too muddled to riddle it out. How was it that God in heaven had given her a last glimpse of the very person she had been thinking of and then have it come in the shape of an awful letter like this?

Terrified, too lost within herself to move, Faith was completely unaware that Luisa was walking toward her across the lawn. "Telephone, Mrs. Slater," the maid called as she approached.

Faith quickly glanced up. "All right," she said. Her throat felt thick and choked. "All right, Luisa, tell them I'll be right there."

"Mrs. Slater, you okay?"

Faith stuffed Rachel's letter back inside its envelope. "Yes," she told her. Put it away, she thought. "Yes, I'm fine." Until she could decide what to do, she laid the letter along with a few bills she'd sorted and shoved them all into her purse. "You can go now, Luisa. I'm coming." The maid trotted back inside the house.

Faith found a Kleenex in the bottom of her bag, blew her nose and again took out the square-shaped envelope addressed only to her. But she couldn't bring herself to look at it again right now. Quickly she put it back. There was nothing in it anyway, nothing that would relieve her tension and set the world right again.

Rachel was cranky, Faith thought, but what would cause her to write a letter like this? What had happened?

She raised her head and looked at her beautiful house. A soft breeze made the surrounding branches sway; leaves were trembling. The air sparkled with instability. In the play of shadows across the old brick and the freshly painted trim, the house rippled cheerfully with life, but in the shade of the veranda, the windows were dark, as if the rooms inside held, not happiness, not the joy of a family she once had dreamed of, but a ripe and brooding plague.

Oh, my darling, what did you do? What have you done this time?

10

"MAN THAT IS born of woman hath but a short time to live, and is full of misery . . ."

In the dancing white heat, the cortege sat parked on the winding lanes of Mount Calvary Methodist Cemetery. The crowd was still gathering, large and somber, around the canopy of the small graveside tent. "In the midst of life," the minister's voice intoned, "we are in death. Of whom may we seek for succor, but of Thee, O Lord?"

It was 3:20 on Saturday afternoon, the last day of May. Draped in orchids and lilies and blood-red cabbage roses, Rachel Buchanan's coffin waited atop its metal bier, suspended over the grave. The minister raised his hands.

"Let us pray."

Ignoring the friends that tried to hold her down, Sheila Bonner rose unsteadily from the folding chair, her eyes closed, weeping. The girls attending her had put her hair up; it swooped back over her ears into an elaborate bun. Her black dress was plain and unadorned and perfect and her hands, crossed in front of her, grasped a tissue, which she wound again and again through her fingers.

"Forgive us our trespasses as we forgive those who have trespassed against us . . ."

Henry Slater watched the pale blond strands escape the French knot and catch the sun like golden filaments; the tiny hairs on the back of her neck glistened like fine gold dust.

"And lead us not into temptation . . ."

Sheila wiped her eyes.

Although she moved her lips, trying to recite the familiar prayer, she felt the pressure of someone's eyes watching her, and Sheila slowly turned her head. Her sight cleared. In the crowd at the foot of the grave she saw Henry Lee Slater etched against the columns of trees and the white sky, standing with his wife. He was looking at her as if there was no one else in the world.

For a moment, their eyes locked and they stood as though alone, timelessly and in silence. She felt his strength reaching for her. Sheila's lips parted; a sob broke the secret language of their eyes and she was lost again, gone from him in the hard weaving rhythm of her grief.

"Thou knowest O Lord the secrets of our hearts. Shut not Thou merciful ears to our prayers . . ."

The two of them stood in the glare, the clear, merciless glare. They were so close—so close to freedom now: even the tips of his fingers were heavy with the desire for her. She feels it, Slater thought.

Faith stood at his side, her arm through his. The fragrance of flowers and the sharp scent of newly mown grass were overwhelming, but these were nothing compared to the sensations flooding him. In the shade of the canopy, Sheila's grim-faced boyfriend stood like an usher, uncomfortable in his suit, still very much a boy. Sheila seemed wasted on him, too rich for him, too sumptuous, and Slater hated that he was forced to watch them: the girl who had al-

ways wrung his heart and the boy who took what
Slater knew should be his. It was elemental, what he
felt for her.

But he was also aware of Burris Reeves, nondescript in his seersucker suit. Be careful, he thought,
be particularly careful right now. Because Reeves
sees everything. Out of the corner of his eye, Slater
watched as the chief of police stalked back and forth
at the edge of the crowd, near the black limousine.
He knew he could never let Reeves see the effect
Sheila was having on him today. He tucked his head
slightly and didn't move, but beneath his heavy brows,
he tracked Reeves's movements. He waited until he
saw the assistant funeral director strike up a conversation with the police chief; then, he raised his hungry eyes. Never had Sheila been so untouchable, so
forbidden and removed from him.

"O Lord God most holy, O Lord most mighty, O
holy and most merciful Savior. In sure and certain
hope of resurrection to eternal life through our Lord
Jesus Christ, we commend to Almighty God our
sister Rachel as we commit her body to the ground."

The blanket of flowers was drawn away and on
wheezing hawsers, the big oblong casket slipped massively into the ground. Sheila's hands fled from her
face, her stare wide with anguish. Watching her,
Slater could feel his own face tighten painfully, a
sympathetic ache that glowed deep behind his eyes.
"Dust thou art and unto dust shalt thou return . . ."

Not for a second did Slater's eyes stray from her
now. The minister crumbled dirt into the grave, and
a wail wrung from Sheila's throat like a sound at
the end of sound. "Gramma!" she screamed—the
incandescence of grief. Only then did Slater avert his
face, cringing, feeling her cry rip through his body,

unable to go to her, unable to move, his fist clenched and white, hanging helplessly at his side. "She's going to faint!" some of the women whispered, and a contingent of Sheila's high school friends closed around her, drawing her down into her chair.

The minister closed the Bible, his eyes cast beseechingly toward the brilliant sky. "Lord have mercy upon us."

The litany spread throughout the mourners. An older Catholic lady clutched a crucifix to her breast, moving her lips silently. Faith leaned like a dead weight on his arm. "The Lord bless us and keep us . . ."

The crowd began to shift and disassemble at the fringes; several of the mourners drifted away on the hedge-lined paths toward their cars. Many lingered behind, murmuring, shaking their heads. Greetings were brief and solemn. As the service drew to a close Reeves abruptly retreated to his cruiser and drove away. Feeling waves of relief, Slater moved to speak to those around him, full of solicitation.

The well-mannered whispers began.

"Rachel didn't stay in touch with them," one woman said. "A few distant cousins, that's all. In Connecticut."

"The poor child . . ."

". . . so young and left alone. What'll she do? What'll happen to her?"

"They said it was sudden," said still another, lips pale and hardly moving. "Rachel never knew what hit her."

"This is the worst thing that could've happened," Slater told Gil Burnett, shaking his hand, "a very sad, terrible day." Standing a step behind him, touching his sleeve, Faith said, "Henry, I'd like you to meet someone. This is Marjorie Sanders. She's going to be Sheila's guardian." She directed him to the elderly white-haired woman at her side. "Mrs. Sanders, this is my husband, Henry Slater."

"Oh, Mr. Slater," the woman said. "I always hear so many good things about you."

And the minutes wore ceaselessly on under his watchful and calculating eye.

The minister bent to Sheila, speaking softly, offering her the benediction of his warm brown eyes. She heard only scant fragments of what he said. Then began what seemed to her an endless multitude of hands, touching her shoulders, faces swimming before her, whispering condolences, faces she had never seen and would never see again. Suddenly she felt as though she were suffocating. Her head darted from side to side and she said, "I'm sorry. I've got to stand up." Hands, anonymous hands, helped her to her feet.

Denny Rivera and her other friends from high school, many of whom had accompanied her to the cemetery, stood several paces back to let the slow receiving line pass. From the corner of her eye, Sheila caught sight of him, but only for a moment.

"I have forty wonderful years of memories of her," said an older pink-haired woman, squeezing her hand. "Whether you think so or not, you're a lot like her." It went on and on—a woman with plucked eyebrows pushed a five-dollar bill into her hand; a middle-aged couple offered her a job as an au pair girl—and then at last, the line was beginning to diminish.

On the lane, doors were slamming, cars were whisking away. Sunlight snapped on their polished roofs. In the distance, someone yelled, "Come on! We'll meet you there." The hearse had gone; the black limousine glinted at the curb.

Faith Slater gently touched Sheila's shoulder. Bracelets of silver and bone clicked on her wrist. "I'm so sorry," she said. "We're with you in this, Sheila. We're with you. Let us know," but Sheila had closed her eyes. "Okay," the girl muttered and Faith withdrew in silence and went toward Meg Winters and three other women, who had motioned for her.

Someone else was whispering then, and when Sheila finally felt the voice's shadow depart, just when she thought she would lose her mind, she opened her eyes and all she could see before her was Henry Slater.

He was leaning toward her slightly and when he gazed at her with those great brooding gray eyes, she could feel her heart throbbing in the hollow of her throat. She felt embarrassed being so close to him, here, but when he spoke, she looked up, her eyelids heavy and swollen. "Sheila," he whispered, "baby, don't you cry any more. I'll take care of you."

Her lips were moving and Slater had to strain to hear. "Oh, Mr. Slater," she told him, her voice small. "I'm so scared."

"It's okay," he reassured her. "I promise it'll—"

Her voice overlapped his. "I don't want to die," she pleaded, utterly sincere and irrational. She kept searching his face to make sure he didn't miss a word she said. "If I'd been there, they'd've killed me, too," she muttered. Her hands, cold and wet, took his hands. Sheila had always believed that Henry Slater was a tough man, severe and decisive, perhaps the only adult man she knew who loved her—in a way. It had given her a feeling of the same constant, reassuring, occasionally uncomfortable protection that her grandmother had provided through the years.

And now she desperately needed him. "Mr. Slater," she whispered, "won't you help me?"

Slater could almost taste the feel of her. For him, it was like the smell, the crackle of rain and electricity before a storm arrives. "Sh-h-h," he said, rubbing her icy hands. He looked out among the elaborate winged monuments at his wife, still talking with her friends. "Tell me quick. Where're you staying?" Little by little, he was letting her go.

"At Mary McPhearson's."

"When will you go back home?"

Sheila shrugged listlessly. "Maybe Monday sometime . . . afternoon."

Again he leaned toward her and for an instant she thought he was going to kiss her cheek. But he didn't. "All right," Slater said, his voice smooth and quiet. "Don't worry about things. I'm taking care of it. I'll find you." His hands were in his pockets when he casually walked away. It was as if he had taken something from her, something that she willingly gave, while they spoke.

Denny Rivera watched the mayor talking to her, and when Sheila's eyes lifted, he saw a devotion in them that hadn't been there for him in a long time. As Slater went to join his wife, Denny watched the way Sheila's gaze followed him.

"So," he said, making an appearance at her side, "what was he trying to sell you?" Denny meant it to be light and diverting, but Sheila gave him a scathing look and didn't answer. "Never mind," he said, feeling as though he had committed some sacrilege. "I was just wondering—what you two were talking about?"

She gave no indication that she heard him. She felt steadier, now, a little firmer on her feet. So when the sexton released the canvas straps and pulled

them out of the open ground, Sheila did not look
into the grave a last time. She had observed more
than her mind could hold. Her grandmother was
down there now, at the bottom of the world, and
nothing would ever bring her back. Nothing would
ever be the same again. But knowing it and trying to
resign herself to it still seemed impossible to Sheila.

A temporary marker had been placed at the head
of the grave, a two-inch paper nameplate in a tin
frame on which was engraved: RACHEL SIMMONS BU-
CHANAN. REST IN PEACE. Sheila leaned down and
touched it.

"Bye, bye," she whispered, "bye, bye."

Folding her damp tissue into smaller and smaller
squares, she turned toward her friends. Denny put
his arm around her waist, the same way he had done
many times before. "Tell me what I can do to make
you feel better," he said, quietly.

For the first time since the murder, she tried to
smile, her face, her eyes in particular, still puffed
and traumatized, her teeth dazzling white against
her pale lips. "It doesn't feel like it's over," Sheila
whispered. Then, she was quiet again.

"Babes—" he began.

"It's all right," she said. "Really, Denny, I'll be all
right. Just stay with me. I'm sorry I'm such a mess."

He tried not to think about anything else, concentrating entirely on her. She still wasn't herself and
she was worrying the hell out of him. At eighteen, he
was not quite as young as he had been a week ago;
now he was part of something that was more important than himself.

"You're no trouble," he said. He hadn't kissed her
for a long time, nearly four days. "You know I love
you, Sheila," he said, devotedly. "You know I'll do

anything for you." He bent his face toward her, but Sheila whispered, "No," and turned her head away, slipping out of his arms toward their friends. "Not here."

Neither of them looked back at the winding cemetery lane, neither saw Henry Slater as he opened the door of the Cadillac for his wife, and then watched them over the blue sunstruck roof of the car.

THEY WERE SILENT on the way home, both preoccupied with their thoughts, Slater at the wheel and Faith watching the afternoon drift past her window. The Eldorado ran smoothly through the sunlit city streets, full of Saturday traffic. I have to ask him, she thought.

Some serious trouble has been brewing a long time . . . I must talk to you . . . This has to do with Henry. Rachel's letter kept repeating itself in her mind, a thousand times, ten thousand times, till now it lay open like an unhealed wound. There had been times over the past days when she wanted to thrust the letter at him and scream, *What is it, Henry? What did you do?* But at the same time, there was a small, secret, afraid place in her heart that insisted: you don't really want to know. You don't. You don't.

But she did.

They were headed through the northside neighborhoods before she laid her head back against the seat and rubbed her eyes. Whether from dread of what she might uncover or fear of the thing she was about to attempt—she hardly knew which it was— Faith's heart was beating heavily.

"Wasn't it awful?" she said, lifting a hand and brushing back a limp lock of hair with her wrist. "I can't imagine it getting much worse than that."

Henry glanced at her, then turned back to the road. She noticed how his attention wandered disconcertingly from object to object, from noise to noise. "It was bad," he said.

Faith laced her slim fingers together and stared at them in her lap, afraid that if she looked at him for even an instant, her eyes would betray her true purpose. "I've been trying to remember the last time I saw her," she said.

"Rachel, you mean?"

"Yes."

"I saw her only last week," he said, straightaway. As he spoke, Faith shifted around on the seat and faced him. He smiled—and his smile was melancholy. "She came to the office; I don't recall which day it was. Anyway, she showed up." He shook a cigarette from the pack in his shirt pocket, punched in the car's lighter. "She was the same as always, still irascible. You know how she was."

He loosened his tie and unbuttoned his collar button. The lighter popped; Henry lit his cigarette, but his face showed nothing other than the sad hangover of their friend's death.

"What did she want you to do?"

"It's the same thing every year. She had some questions about her quarterly taxes." He expelled a stream of smoke. "She was complaining when she got there and she was complaining when she left."

He's lying, she thought. I don't know why, but he is. Faith ran her fingers along the pleats in the upholstery. "I thought you turned that tax work over to Bryan while you were still acting mayor—before the election."

"That's right," he said. He chuckled—still sadly, but disarmingly, Faith thought. More his old self.

She noticed that his throat had grown slightly flushed above his opened collar. "But that didn't stop her from coming around whenever she damned well felt like it," he was saying. "Rachel questioned every dime; I'm sure she thought we were all cheating her."

Faith thought, What was Rachel trying to tell me? What did she have that Henry could conceivably want? Nothing. There was nothing. "When did you have time to help her with her taxes?"

"What is this?" he asked, making a face, squinting at her. "What's with you and all these questions? I had time whenever Rachel wanted it. Christ, you knew her." He smoked, put out the cigarette and turned up Condor Pass. "Faith, I told you about this."

He hadn't told her, but he was explaining the circumstances with such begrudged sincerity that there was little reason to doubt him. Faith almost believed he was telling the truth. So that must be it, she thought. Taxes. Is that really what that letter was all about?

"No," she said. "No, you never did."

"Well, anyway, that's the way it was." Again he looked over at her, then back at the road, swinging into a familiar curve. "But, I really don't like all these questions. What's past is past." A line of sweat ran down his forehead and soaked his eyebrow. She knew she was brushing too close to a nerve.

Let the dead bury the dead, she thought. But it was no longer that simple. The dead had risen up and handed her a letter. "Darling," she said, "if you're too warm, why don't you turn up the air conditioner?"

"Very funny," he said, mocking her. He rubbed the sweat from his brow.

She waited, thinking her silence might draw a little

more out of him, but he pulled into their driveway without further comment. Some inclination tugged at her to open her purse, show him Rachel's letter and have it over with, but she had learned long ago never to ambush him; she knew how far she could push things and when to back off. He was her husband and Faith loved him; she wouldn't risk damaging the one thing she guarded above all else—her marriage—certainly not for the sake of a letter, no matter how threatening it was. She knew she had come to the point where she had to accuse him directly or let it go, and the questions she wanted most to ask withered on her lips. She would have to think of something else. In the end, Faith changed the subject and in a more amenable voice said, "I don't think the poor girl recognized me at all. God, it was hard. She seemed to remember you though."

"Who knows?" he replied. Henry pressed the garage door opener. "You can't imagine what she said to me. She said, 'If I'd been there, they'd've killed me, too.' "

"Oh, I know. She's so young." Full of compassion, Faith put her hand lightly on Henry's arm. "She must be frightened out of her mind; I would be. Henry, shouldn't we try to do something more for her? What can we do? Do you think she's going to stay here in town?"

"I have no idea."

The Eldorado sank into the garage and he pushed the button to shut the door. They got out of the car with Faith still talking to him. "I suppose she'll have to stay until the estate's settled—with Mrs. Sanders. And she still has a year of school left. But won't she need money to live on—to pay expenses? Henry, couldn't we give her some money? Help her that way?"

"How much have we given already?"

"Thirty-five hundred, which pretty well covered the funeral, minus some incidentals."

"Through Father Vasquez?"

"Yes, like you told me to do."

Slater pinched the bridge of his nose, idly, then studied the floor. "If you wanted to drop a few hundred into an account for her, periodically, I'd have no objections as long as it's kept confidential. You'll have to check; Rachel's account may be frozen in probate."

"I hadn't thought of that."

"That's right," he said. "There're a lot of things to keep in mind. Faith, if you do this, leave me out of it. I don't want people camped on the doorstep, thinking I'm the goddamned public dole." They were going in, now, through the door to the laundry room. "More than anything," Slater continued, "what she'll probably need is a summer job."

"When she gets over this," Faith said.

"That's right."

"But you can help with that, can't you?"

"We'll see. For you, we'll move mountains." As they went through the arched kitchen doorway, his arm came up around her shoulders momentarily, but when she turned to him, he let his arm drop. "What?" Faith asked.

"Nothing," he answered, on his way to check the afternoon's messages. "Where's Luisa?"

His back was half-turned but Faith was sure he was smiling. "In her room, I suppose. Why?"

"Just wondering."

Faith waited and when he didn't go on, she asked, "Were you going to say something else?"

He shook his head and, after a moment, she went down the hall to the bedroom to change clothes. She was thinking, My God, he's in a happy mood. And it wasn't the damned taxes. Rachel wouldn't write a letter like that because of some tax irregularity. Would she? No, something had happened. Something else had happened. *But what the hell is it?*

NO CIGARETTE HAD ever tasted so rich. Slater leaned against the refrigerator, smoking, leafing through the half dozen or so messages; he felt he could sleep for a month, so great was his relief. He was conscious of how totally isolated he was now, but things had always gone better when he was completely on his own. All his plans were proceeding beautifully.

None of the messages required an immediate reply. He slipped them into his jacket pocket and entered the living room. With the mounting pressure of these last few weeks, he had forgotten how much he liked this vast quiet room. Now it was too quiet: it needed music, lusty and convivial, no matter how inappropriate—but there would be plenty of time for that.

Slater ran his fingers over the old mahogany pieces, breathed in the orderly scents of furniture wax and polish, lemon and almond. Clean as a whisker, he thought. It's over, thank God. Done. The days of numbing urgency were behind him. At the bookcase that framed the fireplace, he pushed the spine of *David Copperfield.* Hydraulics whirred, the shelves parted and the bar rose to his fingertips.

Whistling through his teeth, he took down two plump tumblers, filled them with ice from the ice

maker and, although he would have preferred straight
whiskey himself, he mixed two faultless manhattans.
He could still see the strands of her tawny hair
catching the sun; he remembered the black begging
centers of her eyes. Slater stood there, in a moment
beyond life and death, giving himself up to the all-
consuming wish to be with her. It's over, he thought,
and it's working. But he had other things to attend
to now.

Taking up the two drinks, he went down the hall,
mulling over what it was Faith had been trying to get
at in the car—but it couldn't be anything. Why should
she doubt him? It hardly mattered any more. There
were other places he wanted to be, a girl he longed to
see, but he was married and he knew he had to stay
married for his own reasons and ambitions. Why
look for trouble where there wasn't any? Faith was
always disagreeable when he had been inattentive to
her. All she required was some preventative mainte-
nance, a little fence mending.

Going into the bedroom, he swung the door shut
with his elbow. He found Faith where he knew she
would be, in her dressing room, in her black slip.
"This is for you," he said, handing her one of the
manhattans, "for always sticking with me." He smiled
at her.

"But that's"—she was caught off guard—"darling,
that's what I'm here for." Faith took the squat glass,
and a fretful, knowing look came into her eyes. "Are
you sure you're all right?"

Yes, he was all right now. He belonged, at last, to a
world he had created.

With his fingers, he took down the thin, black
strap of her slip and kissed her bare shoulder, moving in toward the side of her throat until his cheek

had tenderly lifted her hair. When he whispered against her skin, telling her what he wanted her to do, the dimness of the dressing room filled her eyes and the world seemed faraway. There was only the touch of her husband and she reached up for him.

HER BODY STILL strummed with long, deep waves—turning slow as honey. Her mouth hung open in a slack and perfect oval, drawing in the heavy summer air that surrounded their bed like a tent. Faith loved the feel of him, his weight crushed upon her. The closeness. The enduring, the abiding. Her hands were limp but she wanted to hold him and she ran her fingers over his back, feeling the hard articulation of his muscles, gently stroking the short, clipped hair at the nape of his neck. She clung to him. My darling.

Over his shoulder, Faith saw the stars off the back balcony, soft and infinite, and a moon like a tiny horn had risen. So lovely. Why did I have to get that letter? If only I hadn't gotten that letter. Oh, if only I could give it back, unopened.

11

ON SUNDAY MORNING, Burris Reeves stood leaning against his cruiser outside the Holy Redeemer Presbyterian Church, waiting to take his son home from Sunday school. A few people that he knew greeted him and went inside to await the nine o'clock service. Lagging behind them was an elderly woman, smartly dressed, who climbed the stone steps, but halfway up, he watched her stop, slowly turn and come back down the steps toward him. "Excuse me," she said. "You're the chief of police, aren't you?"

"Yes, I'm Burris Reeves," he said.

"My name's Marjorie Sanders," the woman said, clearly uncomfortable in his company. She looked at the sidewalk for a moment, either with great uncertainty or as a means of collecting herself; then she raised her head. "I'd like to talk to you for a few minutes, if I could."

Marjorie Sanders was slightly stoop-shouldered, and her face was patterned with wrinkles, but her alert brown eyes were like a doe's, honest and skittish. "I was afraid to say anything at first, I'll admit it," she said, "but something has been on my mind day and night. I know this isn't the right place to do this but—there's something I have to speak to you about, Mr. Reeves."

He smiled to himself. It was oddly moving all the same, this respect she attached to speaking to an officer of the law. "Mrs. Sanders, we can talk here, if you want to," he answered. "Or you can come down to the station tomorrow."

"No, I'd better do it now," she said. "This is a private matter. I don't want anyone else to hear me." Stepping up closer to his side, her voice hardly rising above a whisper, she began. She had talked to Rachel Buchanan the night before she was murdered, and Rachel had been terribly upset. "I've never heard her so upset. I asked her if I could come out but she said not to." Mrs. Sanders recalled wondering at the time if it had something to do with Sheila and she had pointedly asked Rachel if that was the case, but her friend had answered that it wasn't.

With his head bent toward her while she spoke, the police chief nodded now and then as if to say that he knew what it was like to lose a dear friend. He noticed that a faint nervous twitch, like a tiny buried heartbeat, was emerging in the wrinkled flesh above her left eye.

"Then she said something I'll never forget." Mrs. Sanders leaned toward him confidentially. "Mr. Reeves, she said, 'I've made a bargain with the devil!' It was such an odd thing for her to say. What can you make of that?"

"You tell me, Mrs. Sanders," Reeves replied. "What do you make of it?"

"Oh, but, sir, you didn't know Rachel, did you?" she said. "She never shared personal matters. Never. I never once heard her talk, you know, the way most women talk about their ups and downs—not in forty years. That's the thing that struck me right away. For her to say that, something awful must have been happening to her. Mr. Reeves, there was some kind of trouble going on, you could hear it in her voice."

"Are you sure you might not've imagined—"

"Yes, I'm absolutely certain. I'm telling you exactly what she said." Marjorie Sanders looked him square in the eye for the first time. "I want to help," she announced. Reeves could see that she was beginning to choke up. "Do you think my coming forward will help at all?"

"Of course. Everything helps," Reeves told her. "Mrs. Sanders, Rachel was your friend. Do you have any idea what this might've been about?"

"No. I've racked my brain but I don't know." She started to back away. "I really should go now," she said, "if you'll excuse me. We're about to get started. I'm in the choir, you see."

Reeves nodded and thanked her.

A pair of older women about her age came hurriedly across the street and she went to join them. Reeves stood looking after her. The church bells started to chime the hour and he went around the cruiser to his door, hardly conscious of the expensive cars lining the street, the sleek Alfa Romeos, the Bentleys. That's right, Reeves thought, feeling his jaw muscles tighten. That makes sense. That's the kind of thing I've been waiting for. Wasn't it all just too damned slick, too damned pat! He watched Mrs. Sanders as she went up the stone steps. *A bargain with the devil.* That's just the kind of thing.

What Marjorie Sanders had told him had its own logic; it seemed right and, to Reeves, it had the reverberation of truth. Now it's up to me, he kept thinking. I'm going to find out who killed that Buchanan woman or know the reason why. You can damned well bank on that.

Coming out through the gold-tipped iron gates, the children swarmed over the sidewalks. "Rusty!" he called, "over here!" while the bells rang to a shuddering silence. Like a murmur through the open church windows, the choir had taken up the first stanza of "Old Rugged Cross." Reeves tousled his son's hair and started the cruiser. It was time to go on about his business—an inch at a time.

BEHIND CITY HALL, the parking lot was all but deserted. Seeing that Reeves's cruiser wasn't there, Slater drove out to the house on Klamath Drive; he caught the police chief as he was backing out of his drive. "Burris," he said, "let's get a cup of coffee. I need to know what you're doing about these convicts."

"I'm on my way out to the Buchanan house now. Why don't you ride along?"

Rachel's house! "You mean to the murder scene?"

"Yeah, something's been on my mind. I've got to go back out there again."

Slater was staring at the police chief as if spellbound. Come on, he thought, get a grip on yourself. "How long will you be?"

"Fifteen, twenty minutes. You can leave your car here; nobody'll bother it."

Slater hadn't counted on being drawn back to the scene of the crime so soon or so directly, but now that he had confronted Reeves, he couldn't think of a graceful way to bow out of it. Completely aware of the risk he was taking, Slater left his car parked at the curb and got into the cruiser. Once they were moving, Reeves said, "So you want to know where we are with this Buchanan thing?"

"I can't ad lib it with the press much longer. I've got to give them some straight answers."

Reeves chuckled. "Christ, Henry, if I had answers, I'd've called you." He fished a toothpick from his shirt pocket and started to chew it. "All I've got is questions."

Immediately, Slater was conscious of a needling uneasiness, an anxious feeling of trouble. His throat was dry. He swallowed and coughed into his fist, but he couldn't shake the way he felt.

"You knew Rachel Buchanan fairly well, didn't you, Henry?"

"I suppose. Probably as well as most people. Why?"

Reeves shrugged. He maneuvered the toothpick into the corner of his mouth and chewed it, the end twitching. "The picture I get of her is of a reserved woman, tight with her money, conservative, not given to sharing intimacies. Would you say that's an accurate depiction?"

"Some people might say that," Slater told him, feeling a trickle of sweat break under his arm. "It's one side of the coin. On the other side, she was more generous."

"Yeah," Reeves said. "We're all like that, I guess. What I meant was: I don't see her as a gossipy woman. Do you remember her talking much about herself—you know, about her ups and downs?"

"No, not really. Rachel wasn't like that."

"That's what I thought. That's what I wanted to hear you say."

It hummed on the air like a pronouncement of death. *But I didn't say anything. My God, it was nothing at all.* So why did Slater feel as though he had just made the most irretrievable blunder?

The traffic that morning was thin and scattered and they drove through it smoothly. In short order, Reeves swung onto the on ramp and they were headed south on the interstate. "I wanted to have this thing neat," the big policeman was saying, "with no loose ends. I wanted it bad. Maybe you think that laying this murder off on those convicts was the obvious thing to do—but, Henry, it wasn't. It was easy."

All the time that Reeves was talking, his hands were moving: he kept taking the toothpick out of his mouth and putting it back, he flipped on the turn signal, he adjusted the rearview mirror. And Slater thought, What's the matter, Burris? Nervous about something? But he, also, cautioned himself not to read too much into it.

"It seemed right, at first," Reeves said. "I bought it—the whole nine yards. So did you. We even got up in front of people and told them how much we believed it."

Don't let on, Slater thought. Say whatever he expects you to say, act the way he wants you to act. Slater raised his eyes and wondered if there was any color left in his face. He said, "So what're you telling me?"

"You're no dummy. You know what I'm saying."

"No, I don't think so."

They swooped down the Canyon Valley exit and turned left through the underpass, following the meandering country lane. We're going too fast, Slater kept thinking—we're getting there too fast. He could feel himself rushing headlong toward the one place he ought not go.

Reeves said, "Henry, goddamnit, it wasn't the convicts."

You can't know what really happened, Burris. You *can't! You just can't.* Slater stared at him. There's no way. "Now, wait a minute. Hold on for just one damned minute, Burris. Four days ago, you told me this thing was cut and dried."

"Four days ago, I thought it was."

"You've got to be kidding. What changed your mind?"

Reeves bit the toothpick and just looked at him.

"You've found something."

Reeves returned his attention to the curving road. "Not a thing," he said. "I don't have a damned thing." He was slowing down, putting on his brakes; he pulled up sideways at the end of the Buchanan driveway and cut the engine.

We're here. God help me, we're here.

"Then how can you say—"

"Henry, this is the slickest murder I've ever seen, I have to say. Before I came here, I worked homicides all up and down this coast, and I've never seen a slicker one. We combed this place, I mean *we combed it* and I swear to you, there's not a shred of concrete evidence out here—not a single fingerprint, not a hair. I'll take that back—we did find half a shoe print, man's size eleven, which we made a cast of. But that's it; that's how slick it is."

"Jesus," Slater muttered. He sat looking at the band of yellow, plastic police tape that marked off the entire area around Rachel's house. He was thinking about the graveled driveway and his diamond—the countless thousands of rocks. "So where are we, then, Burris? Up the creek, without a paddle?"

"Not quite."

It was twenty past nine, and the surrounding houses lay in a deep, slumbering silence. The sky was overcast. An occasional squirrel or bird darted among the trees, but no one ventured forth on the silent lawns. Reeves opened his door. "I want to clear this barrier before that girl comes home tomorrow." He took the toothpick from his mouth; its end was frayed and splintered like a tiny broom—he flipped it out the window. "How about giving me a hand, before these neighbors get back from church."

Slater felt a stony reluctance to do anything but stay in the car, but at the same time, he knew he couldn't refuse such a simple request. Unable to shake the feeling that something more was going on with Reeves, he said, "Sure, all right," and the two men got out of the cruiser, slamming their doors.

He followed the police chief across the shallow, grassy right-of-way toward the far corner of Rachel's iron fence. "We'll be getting organized here in a minute," Reeves said.

What does that mean?

Reeves unclasped the larger blade of his penknife and handed the knife to Slater. "You can cut it down," he said, "and I'll roll it."

Why did you give me the knife, Reeves? What're you trying to do?

They started at the corner, Slater cutting the bindings and Reeves collecting the yellow tape in a loose roll. Working quickly along the front of the fence and across the driveway entrance, they turned up the near side of the perimeter lilacs. "Burris, are you sure about this?"

"Henry," Reeves said, as they arrived adjacent to the porte cochere, "did you ever have something caught in your craw? Know what I mean? It always sits right about here." He clamped the rolled tape under his arm and massaged the hollow at the base of his throat. "You can't get it up and you can't get it down and it never goes away. I drink a glass of water and it's there; I have a sandwich and it's there; I go to sleep and I wake up and it's there. Do you know what that's like? Well, I've got this murder stuck in my craw like a goddamned rock."

"So what're you getting at?" I can't stop sweating, Slater realized. He could feel it, wet, under his arms like hot slippery paste.

A second cruiser pulled up behind Reeves's and two younger patrolmen got out. "Henry, let me have that," Reeves said and Slater handed over the knife. Now there were two additional cops coming toward him. What the hell's going on?

"You guys get your beauty sleep?" Reeves chided, walking down the drive to meet them. "Looks like you could use some more. Here, take down this line, pick the place up a little." So it was nothing to worry about; Slater felt a momentary respite. "Then you can go on to your regular assignments," Reeves concluded, starting back. "Come on, Henry, let's walk this through. I want you to look at this with me."

Wait a minute. I can't go through it again, Slater thought. I can't. But with every step, he could feel himself drawing closer and closer to *that* place. A big drop of sweat trickled slowly through his hair, down his back. I shouldn't be here. Why did I ever come here? Now it was too late: he couldn't get away.

"A lot of little things just keep nagging at me," Reeves was saying, but Slater was only partially aware of him. Everything was now filtered through his fear. "Nothing about this case makes sense. I have to believe there's something I'm not seeing."

"Which is?" Slater said.

"I don't know. I don't know what the hell I'm looking for. There's something out here though— there's something; I know it—but I can't find it."

They had come to the wide gap in the hedge between Rachel's driveway and the Malcolmsons' backyard. Slater felt as though he were entering a zone of inescapable danger. "In case you're interested," Reeves said, tugging at an earlobe, "that's where we found her—over there beside that graveled walk."

It's a trap. A breeze shook the bushes and Slater thought he could hear life surging from the house. It was a sound like a waterfall. *What should I do?* Time seemed to be speeding by him and he knew whatever he did, Reeves would not fail to notice. *Can I bear to look? Or not?*

"See? Where that trellis's broken down."

I have to, Slater realized. *No time to deliberate.* He lifted his head and looked roughly in the direction Reeves had indicated, toward the place where he knew Rachel had fallen. He reached his hand up but couldn't stop it: he felt the phantom knife slash his throat.

"Christ, Burris," he panted, "I don't need this. Don't forget: I knew Rachel. She was my friend. We used to live right over there, in that house across the street."

"Sorry, Henry. I forgot about that," the police chief said and a moment later he changed the subject. "Look at those starlings. Filthy, damned things." When he stooped to gather a few stones, Slater noticed half a dozen or more of the brownish-black birds, sitting perfectly still on the trellises and arbor. Two were on the ground, pecking at the gravel among the broken-down clematis vines.

The birds fastened his eyes to the spot. *Blood! The blood! It's all over the place!* Slater closed his eyes but the blood was still there. For an instant, once again, he could feel Rachel struggling at the ends of his hands. *God help me! I've done it! I've done it!*

"Hey, Henry, what's the matter?"

Slater gasped with relief as reality flooded back—the graveled drive, the late morning sunbeams where all was sane and orderly. Reeves clasped his shoulder. "Say, buddy—are you all right?"

"I can't help it," Slater said, gulping a breath. "It's this place. I was thinking—Rachel. I think—it's getting under my skin."

Reeves gave him a look of absolute sympathy. "Know what you mean," he said. "Just try to take it easy. I never get used to it either." Choosing a piece of gravel from his hand, he fired it at the birds. "She must've fed these starlings. I've always hated them; you couldn't drive 'em away with a bazooka."

One at a time, he sailed the handful of stones into the garden, the birds fluttering up when the gravel struck too close to them, and then resettling. "See what I mean? There must've been a hundred out here that morning, but they're impossible to get rid of." He slapped his hands together, knocking off the dust, and slid the garage door open on its creaking pulleys. Old and rusty, the red and brown station wagon sat before Slater like an unwanted dream. It brought to mind the last time he had seen Rachel driving it—the same evening that Sheila had flashed her fingers for him to meet her.

"What I'm going to tell you, Henry, has got to be strictly off the record."

"Fine." He was still having trouble controlling his voice.

"Between you and me, right?"

"That's right. The way it's always been."

From inside the dark garage, Reeves said, "I'm out on a limb with this thing. The way I see this case is not the way anybody else sees it. Okay, the murder itself; that could be—that's the kind of shit these convicts would do. But I keep going over it in my head, coming out here, trying to reconstruct what actually happened. Her car, for example. Why didn't they take her fucking car?"

The sun had come out. Slater gripped the edge of the door frame, trying to stop his fingers from trembling. Reeves opened the doors of the station wagon and then he opened the hood. "They didn't take *anything*," he said. "Nothing was stolen. I'm not saying they're logical; that's not possible. But, Henry, they always steal things. One of 'em killed a guy for a fountain pen, but as far as I can tell, they didn't even go inside the house. Buchanan's purse was lying there, money in it; nobody touched it. Car keys. Car in the garage. That's one of their favorite things—they get their rocks off stealing cars." He was poking around under the hood. "So tell me, Henry, does what I'm saying make any sense to you?"

Slater stepped into the dim garage to escape the sun. "Don't ask me," he said. "Maybe something scared them off."

"That's what Ellis says. That's the official line." Reeves had opened an old newspaper on the floor and was down on his back, examining the undercarriage.

"Burris, what the hell're you looking for?"

"Just checking things out," he said from the caverns of the engine. But Slater knew he was searching for something; anything. Reeves stood up, shaking his head over yet another small defeat. He wiped his hands on an old rag. He couldn't have seen the shadow came to the open garage door—his back was turned. "Chief," said the younger patrolman, "we're outta here."

"Go ahead," Reeves said, going to retrieve his knife. He shut the station wagon doors, shut the hood.

"Then, all of a sudden, this morning, it hits me. These convicts—they're messy; they're not slick. It's the things they didn't do that're remarkable." He walked past Slater, outside. "I swear, Henry, I can feel it. There's just no way those convicts killed this old lady."

Slater said, "So we stood in front of those cameras and told a lie."

"No, not a lie, exactly. We gave them the official line."

Staying behind Reeves, he stepped into the sunlight and had to block the white hot glare with his palm.

"There're other things," Reeves said. "The hour that it happened, for instance. Very unusual. I'll bet you could count the number of murders that take place at seven A.M. in this entire country on one hand." Waiting for his eyes to adjust, Slater lowered his hand to the garage door and slid it shut. The sky was so blue it seemed almost purple. He saw that Reeves was also shielding his eyes, staring at the ridge that ran behind the property. "No, sir. It will be a frosty day in hell before I'll believe that those convicts did this thing."

"So, who's your suspect?"

"Jesus! I have to figure out what I'm looking for, first. Then I'll worry about who." He was still studying the landscape behind the garden.

He knows the killer ran back that way, Slater thought.

"I don't mind telling you, though, I had a feeling about the girl's boyfriend. But he's in the clear." Reeves turned, his hands on his hips. "Christ Almighty! Would you look at that!"

The yellow police tape had been left in loose untidy piles. "These guys wear me out! But what can you do?" He shook his head in disgust. "There's an empty trash barrel back by the garage. Henry, if you'll get this, I'll go around front for the rest."

"Okay, Burris, but then I've got to be getting back."

He watched the police chief make a little detour around the corner of the house before he gathered up the piles of tape and started across the backyard garden toward the trash barrel. The cabbage roses had opened their colossal red blossoms and a delirious sweetness tinged the air. It brought back memories of their suffocating sweetness from years past. He thought he had forgotten the scent of love and death, but it came to him now, much sharper and richer than ever before. It was the smell of a place long shut away and uninhabited, strange, almost magical: it was the stench of an old woman's dying perfume.

The smell of the roses only intensified as he crossed the garden. When he passed too close, several of the starlings flew into the air, scattering into the trees—at the periphery of his sight, he saw a spark streak through the sky. Quickly, he turned his head but it was gone. It had fallen like a shooting star. I'm still seeing things, he thought while one by one, the birds returned to their roosts.

He had trod this same ground Wednesday morning, in his getaway, and now it placed him close to the place where Rachel had died, within a few feet of the brick walkway where the crevices were filled with pea gravel. He looked over his shoulder, but Reeves was still out of sight behind the corner of the house. Slater felt the muscles in his jaws contract. He couldn't stop wondering if Reeves had maneuvered him here deliberately.

He knows part of it, Slater thought. But it could be worse, a lot worse. Still, he knows something . . . he hasn't told me everything.

As Slater dumped the tape into the barrel, one of the starlings pitched forward from the rose arbor. It swooped over his head and landed on the graveled path no more than a few feet away from him. "Get out!" Slater said, stamping his foot.

The bird hopped into the air, its wings flapping, and drifted back to the ground in much the same place it had occupied before. Eyes, black as onyx, stared fiercely at him, then in a quick tilt of its head, the starling scrutinized the path. The bird strutted over the gravel with its quirky gait, comically awkward on sticklike legs, tilted forward and pecked among the stones. The thought passed through Slater's mind, What's it after in those rocks? A spider? Again he looked toward the corner of the house and saw Reeves sauntering into view.

Come on, Burris, he thought, let's get this over with and get away from here. But he knew he couldn't appear too impatient. He shoved his hands into his pockets and the waiting went on. He looked around at the starling. Now it had something in its beak. He thought about motioning for Reeves to come on, but he didn't even begin the gesture. The starling was dragging whatever it was along the rough surface of rocks. Again, Slater started to stamp at it, to frighten the bird away. Instead he carefully put his foot down and froze. A hideous moment passed when everything was caught in silence and immobility. The object in the starling's beak gave off steely points of light.

Suddenly, there it was. *It's my diamond!*

The hair stood on the back of Slater's neck. For a

split second, he remained motionless, flooded with joy and terror, his heart hammering so fast he could hardly breathe. He threw a wild, light-headed glance at the figure now approaching from across the garden. Slater thought, *I've got to get it! He's coming!* He also thought, *You can lose your life this way.*

He leapt for the diamond, kicking at the starling.

"Get out!" he gasped. "Get out of here!" and the bird clattered to a hovering height in the air, unafraid.

He glimpsed the fading spark of facets in the bird's beak. It was all he could do not to yell, It's mine! Wings pumped downward. Slater swung at the starling and nearly hit it; he felt the turbulent air rush off its wing. Dislodged, the diamond fell, tumbling into the grass and he was on his knees, running his hands over the green blades.

Then he had it, in his fingers, in his closed fist. My God, I've got it, I got it, I got it!

Where's Reeves?

His head shot up. It felt as though a steel wire snapped shut on his throat.

Standing on the grass, across the path two feet away, Reeves said, "What're you doing? Henry, what've you got?"

The sun streamed down on his back. His eyes began to water with the glare and he squeezed them shut. Did you see it, Reeves? How long have you been there? What did you see? Slater knew he had to get himself under control. He dug his fingernails into his palms, trying to pull out of his fright, but the wire on his throat was choking the life out of him. He opened his eyes.

It's nothing, he almost said, all the time thinking, Don't risk it; you cannot risk it. He wanted desperately to throw his hands behind his back, like a child, and hide it. But he couldn't.

Reeves chuckled good-naturedly. "Come on, Henry. Let's see it. What'd you find?"

He'll know for certain if you try anything, anything at all. There was nothing Slater could think to do, still he delayed the inevitable as long as he dared. My God! My God! My God! Trembling badly inside, he cleared his throat and pushed himself upright. "You won't believe it," he said, and it was tearing him up, "see for yourself." Struck by his own grave mortality, fighting to hold himself still, he extended his hand and unfolded his fingers. He had grasped the diamond so tightly that it left a red indentation in his palm. "That damned bird had it."

Reeves made a rush for the brilliant stone. "Jesus!" he shouted, his voice cracking with triumph and excitement, "look at that!" He took the diamond from Slater's palm and held it to the light. "By God! Look at this thing, Henry!" Reeves laughed out loud. "We're damned lucky you saw it. Wonder whose it is—who the hell it belongs to." He continued to examine the diamond, then he tossed it in the air and caught it. "Don't think about it, Henry," he went on. "Maybe it was Rachel's. I know you don't think so and I don't think so either, but we won't know until I look into it."

Slater's only conscious thought was of Reeves jamming his hand into his pocket, with the diamond.

Reeves stuffed his armful of the plastic police banner into the barrel. With splashes of gasoline from a gas can in the garage, he set it ablaze.

Time no longer flowed around Slater but coiled upon him like a rope. The only real disaster that might have happened, already had. Seconds passed before he came to himself, standing alone in the driveway. He could still feel the diamond pressed into the palm of his hand. He hated Reeves with a strength he would never have believed possible.

Slowly, he backed toward the car, still waiting for Reeves but aware of every step as if he were walking underwater. It was then that he noticed the tiny sticks littering the gravel—the toothpicks chewed into little brooms lying all around him. Reeves had been here many times before. *What does he know? How much does he know?*

The police chief checked to see that all the doors of the house were locked and secure. Then, leaving the fire to burn itself out, the two men returned to the cruiser. Cars were passing now, the neighbors coming home from church.

They were on the interstate, headed back toward Rio Del Palmos, when Reeves said, "If I showed you the statistics on crimes like this, Henry, they would say that, nine times out of ten, the victim knew her assailant and that the murder grew out of some domestic dispute. So if I listen to that reasoning, then I have to believe that Mrs. Buchanan's granddaughter knows . . . well, something. When I tried to talk to her that morning, she was incoherent. But now I've got to have a long talk with that young lady."

Slater rubbed his eyes. *God knows what she's going to say.*

"Christ, Burris, don't bother her. You saw what she was like at the funeral. I can't believe she had anything to do with this."

"No, I don't think she did either and I'm not unsympathetic. But my ass's on the line with this thing. So's yours. I'll give her time—a few more days. Of course, there's always the possibility that I'm wrong. But, Henry, if I'm wrong, we won't have long to wait. These fuckers are like buzzards. If they did this, they're camped in the hills somewhere and they'll be back. Then, God help us. But I don't know—I don't think that'll happen."

"Scares the hell out of me," Slater said.

"It should."

"So what're you going to do?"

"I'm going to find the sonuvabitch that did this. That's all there is to it. I'm going to try to find him fast." Reeves touched his brakes and swung onto the off ramp. "It's still a slick piece of work, almost perfect—and we've played right into his hands. The bastard just didn't dig deep enough—didn't do his homework. He didn't find out what these boys are really like."

Slater turned to gaze through the windshield and it was like looking down the shiny muzzle of a gun, where at the bottom, death waited, compact and hypnotic.

"Jesus," he said, "what a mess."

12

BACK IN HIS own car, Slater's nerves finally cracked and he let go of all his suppressed terror. If it wasn't for you, he thought, I'd have my diamond back. I'd be in the clear. If it wasn't for you, Reeves. Even after he had turned the corner and the black and white cruiser vanished from his rearview mirror, it took a long time to escape the firm persistence of Reeves's voice.

As the Eldorado sped recklessly down the quiet streets, it seemed to him that the small pastel houses and vine-covered courtyards, the sunlit walks and token palmettos—all the mundane and recognizable images of his world—were suddenly whirling away from him. He saw them and forgot them in the same instant. The realization came over him that somewhere, stealing out of this bleak late morning still again, was the same frenzy that had taken him over less than a week ago. If Reeves figures it out, then I'll have to kill him. I'll have to. Through his open window, Slater breathed the air with its ocean smell. He felt the pounding weight in his chest. No, that's crazy. That's *crazy!* That would bring the roof down.

In vain, he tried again and again to convince himself that he had gotten through the incident unscathed. But no, he could never be sure with Reeves.

His first impulse was to get in touch with Sheila; if only she could meet him somewhere. But he knew that was the one thing he must not do. If Reeves were actually on to him, he would be waiting for just such a move. Slater debated with himself about going out to the farmstead, where he could hide for a few hours until he could think straight. But in the end he decided to surround himself with the familiar—with men he trusted and understood. With friends. He had always experienced the greatest sense of safety in a crowd.

At the house, he got on the telephone and repeated the same invitation to each of the men he called. "Let's play poker." He left a note for Faith to meet him later for dinner and drove to the Rod and Gun Club.

In the first hour and a half, he won close to two thousand dollars; then his game turned sour. He ordered a fifth of Old Grand-dad and started to drink it down. *He'll track that diamond to me. I don't know how, but he will.* He had three jacks and knew Ben Lapham was bluffing, bet his hand to the hilt and lost to a nine-high straight—a goddamned impossible hand to fill in five-card straight poker.

He laughed when the men ribbed him. And he drank. He had tens over aces and lost to a straight flush. The whiskey wasn't working. Through it all, he kept seeing those little brooms. Perspiration coated his face; when he least expected it his hands shook— once or twice he nearly dropped his cards. "We've got you this time," Bill Franz said, cheerfully needling him. "You don't know how long I've waited to see you sweat."

"Yeah, well, Bill, that's how it goes. That's poker. I guess it had to catch up with me sometime." By three-thirty, he had lost his winnings and was down a thousand dollars. Men left the table, went home; others sat in. He hit; he won four hands in quick succession, which nearly brought him even. Then it spiraled and snowballed, downward. He didn't care about the money, but he couldn't afford to lose so much that it would be talked about at length. When he tore the deck in two at quarter to six, barely an inch of whiskey remained in the bottle, but Slater had never been more sober.

What am I going to do? In the locker room, he plunged his face into a basin of cold water, holding his breath as long as he could. He studied his face intently in the mirror while he combed his hair. *Didn't do my homework.* He was down not quite twenty-five hundred when he went out to have dinner with his wife.

He couldn't eat. Faith remarked about it but he shrugged it off. He was thinking about the convicts, aware that they might be caught at any time. Then it would be too late to do anything. Something else was going to have to happen fast. It would have to be something that would cause great confusion, big enough to distract Reeves and send him right back after the convicts. And it would have to be under his control, something he could arrange secretly beforehand.

Reeves has too much time, he thought, too damned much time and I have none.

At ten, they got ready for bed. He waited until Faith went to sleep, then, in his robe, he went through the house to the garage and turned on the single overhead light. Against the wall, near the door to the laundry room, lay a stack of old newspapers that Faith had saved for the church's paper drive.

From the top of the pile, he began to go through them, one by one, taking them up, unfolding them, searching for any reference to the convicts. The papers were full of them—always the same story, it seemed, told in different words, again and again. *Homework,* Slater thought. In order not to miss what he was looking for, he was condemned to read the stories practically word for word. With every page, he hated Reeves more. Didn't dig deep enough, he thought. Goddamn you, Burris.

He had gone through perhaps thirty newspapers when the laundry room door opened and he nearly jumped out of his skin. Faith stuck her head out. "Henry, are you all right?" she asked. "Is something the—"

"I'm all right. What do you want?"

"What are you doing?" she said sleepily.

"What the hell does it look like? I'm looking for something. Christ, Faith, can't I have a few minutes to myself?"

"But—"

"Go back to bed."

"Well, Henry, excuse me for intruding." She slammed the door.

Intruding, he thought. That's right. Intruding. Tongue like a damned whip. He let loose a deep breath. "She'll get over it," he muttered. "She always does."

Close to midnight, when he was near the bottom of the stack, he came to an issue of the *San Francisco Chronicle* dated Sunday, March 30. That's when he found what he had been searching for.

BOMBING DEVICES FOUND
IN KILLER'S CAR

A stolen car driven by escaped killer William Buckram Taylor was found to contain timers altered to detonate explosives, this according to search warrant affidavits opened today by agents of the Alcohol, Tobacco and Firearms (ATF) Division of the Department of the Treasury and the FBI.

Also found in the trunk were several pounds of gunpowder, boxes of .445 caliber lead shot and other materials required in the construction of small-scale bombing devices.

Escaped mental patient Taylor is the subject of a statewide search for the recent double murder of Jack and Betty Sewell, in rural Pinewood. He is still considered a prime suspect in the series of explosions that rocked Sausalito in 1984, which claimed five lives.

Explosives, Slater thought.

That's what Reeves had been getting at—*Christ,* that's what he had been looking for under Rachel's car! A bomb!

Slater read the article through again, then a third time. He restacked the newspapers in a tall loose pile, placing the March 30 edition close to the top so he would immediately know where to find it. The article was almost as interesting for what had been left out of it as for what it contained. Anyone with any knowledge of even basic chemistry would recognize that necessary materials were missing. To build a bomb, Taylor would also have to have batteries, probably six volt, or some other power source, blasting caps, and either timers or a radio.

Slater's hands were smudged black with printer's ink. He washed them in the sink beside the workbench. So many years had passed. He would have to dig out the old textbooks he kept in his father's trunk at the farmhouse. And any large construction site would have an explosives shack. Or he'd have to mix his own compound.

Too preoccupied to go to sleep, Slater turned off the lights, opened the garage door and walked out into the starry night.

Explosives.

ON MONDAY MORNING, he went down to the office an hour early. He knew what he had to do, but not yet how to go about it. I've got to get on with it right away, he thought. I've got to get Reeves off the track.

Before Abigail and the girls started to arrive in the outer offices, Slater went to his private bathroom and closed the door. And I've got to see Sheila. The funeral was behind her; this was the time to see her. Without delay. And yet his mind kept straying back to the more immediate problem of the police chief. Slater washed and dried his hands, but what he wanted, he realized, was one last breath of fresh air. Cool, clean air that would help him think.

In the wall facing north there was a small window of opaque glass, two feet square. He turned the crank and the window rotated wide enough on its axis for a hand to clean it. A gust of wind hit him in the face. The art of distraction, he kept thinking. I've got to distract Reeves. The hand is quicker than the eye.

Even at this altitude, he could smell the salt from the ocean, but this morning it was like the scent of blood, and washing in with it, riding on the back of these turbulent airs came the shape of another crime, or perhaps more than one, that he was now forced to commit.

Placing his hand against the window frame, Slater stood, looking out, soaking up the damp, morning air. He saw the weblike city streets, the vivid, silver bows of bridges spanning rivers and inlets. He saw the railroad tracks, shining like ethereal knife strokes, all gossamer, and quaint, and doomed to rust. On the Rialto River Bridge in the distance he watched a black and white car drive toward him over the pavement's long middle hump. A hard red spark revolved on its roof. That's a cruiser, he thought. I'll bet that's Reeves.

Slater's foot began to slowly tap on the green marble floor. He watched the cruiser drift to the end of the bridge, turn right, and park in the lot across from a donut shop he and Reeves had once frequented. The Hole in One. Old habits die hard.

So Reeves still stops there in the morning, Slater realized. He even knew what the chief of police would have: two glazed donuts and two cups of coffee, black. He glanced at his watch. 7:15. Some things never change. He would have to check to make sure, but he was convinced that that was Reeves's cruiser.

Gradually, Slater straightened up and smoothed back his hair. The plan rose in him, fully formed and in possession of him, as if the handmaidens of sleep and nothing else had delivered it to him like a garment. Now his mind could not let go of it.

The art of distraction, he thought.

Suddenly he was drained by all his plotting, weary of the spiral of lies he had had to weave. But he had come too far: he couldn't turn back. God, what've I gotten myself into? Sheila's so young. Whenever Slater closed his eyes, he always thought, Now I will be with you. He knew he had to see her again. Once more and forever. God damn, now I have to do this thing, he kept telling himself. But, Sheila, I'm doing it all for you.

He remembered her standing before him at the funeral, looking small and defenseless and badly hurt. She'll be home this evening; I'll go see her, to pay my respects.

Across the far-flung countryside, he saw only the black and white cruiser in a parking lot, waiting for him. For Henry Slater, it was a day unlike any other. It was Monday morning, Monday, and there was no end to it.

13

"IT'S NICE THAT you stopped by," she said.

"You've become a stranger. I thought I might see you in town."

"I hoped I'd see you." Sheila stood at the kitchen sink, looking over at him. Her voice was soft, fading on every few words. "I've not been very brave at all." She turned her head, gazing into the gathering dusk. "I can't tell you what this is like . . . to come back home with her gone."

"Don't try to be brave," Slater said. A week had passed since he had last seen her at the funeral, and now a sense of unreality cloaked everything. To him, even their most insignificant gestures seemed false and formal.

Sheila had curled and brushed her hair, but she hadn't put on makeup or lipstick. Her eyes were an abstracted blue, her mouth pale, her face bereft of color. She was wearing blue jeans, Weejuns and an oversized, starched white shirt. "Isn't it risky for you to be here?" she asked, turning to him slowly and leaning back against the countertop.

He looked at her uncertainly, not sure what she meant. It was, of course, capricious for him to be here without Faith, even dangerous, but Slater knew of no other way to see Sheila alone. "I spoke with the neighbors on my way in," he explained. "They know I'm here to pay my respects." The house was empty and strange, but its emptiness seemed right.

Sheila smiled unhappily and nodded. "I saw you out there talking with Mr. Malcolmson."

"How are you feeling?"

"I don't know. I know my Gramma's gone, but I can't get it through my head."

Slater felt oddly in sympathy with Rachel and the care she had given the neat kitchen. The counters gleamed, the embroidered tablecloth, anchored with a bowl of roses, still showed its creases; the two chairs at the table faced each other, snugly tucked in as if at any moment the room would undergo a minute inspection. In its plain familiarity, it defied his intrusion.

"Did the police treat you all right?"

"Yes, I guess so. Considering what happened. Mr. Reeves—he was especially good to me."

"I suppose they asked you a lot of questions?"

"The usual thing," Sheila replied, as if none of it mattered. "It was like a movie." She was clearly not interested in talking any further about it.

"Let me put on the light," he said.

"No, please don't. I look awful. I don't want you to see me too much."

In the bowl, some of the big cabbage roses had curled for the night, but others had dropped their petals like red sparks on the tablecloth. Seeing that he'd noticed them, Sheila said, "Mrs. Hagerty brought those here from the funeral. Don't ask me why. I guess she thought she was being nice." Her voice was robbed of all vitality. The tilt of her head, the curve of her shoulders, spoke eloquently of her loneliness.

Her friends had returned to their lives yet she remained, standing at the window of Rachel Buchanan's empty house.

"Would you like to go in and sit down?" she asked
him, as if only then thinking to ask. "I've put on
some coffee. It's almost ready."

"Sheila, I don't think so." Slater looked at his watch.
"I shouldn't stay." He shifted uneasily in the doorway, as if preparing to go, but he wasn't ready to
leave her. "I was on my way somewhere else but I
wanted to see you for a few minutes."

She gave no indication that she heard him. Night
was falling. The darkness entered the kitchen in
eddies; already the corners of the room were dark.
But Sheila didn't move to turn on the lights; she
hadn't moved at all for several minutes. "We have
many things to discuss," he said. "You're going to
need some help."

"Oh, I know," she readily agreed. "I know. I meant
to tell you—it was nice of Mrs. Slater to come see me
the day that it happened."

He hadn't come to talk about Faith; he let it go
without comment. "Where're you going to live?"

Sheila shook her head. "It looks like I'll have to
stay with Mrs. Sanders . . . for now. They explained
it to me. I guess next year when I turn eighteen . . .
then I can do whatever I want."

"Yes," he said in affirmation, wanting to say
more but letting it pass. "Are you still with the
McPhearsons?"

"Yes, but only for the rest of this week." She fingered the top button of her shirt. "I'm supposed to
get settled in at Mrs. Sanders's this weekend. I don't
know why they won't let me stay here. There's so

much to do—so much stuff to go through. I don't know how I'm going to get it done all by myself."

While she spoke Slater moved into the kitchen, adjacent to her, to the row of windows overlooking the driveway. Sheila's hair billowed richly about her shoulders; it seemed to attract the waning light, turning dark copper. He remembered how it felt, touching his face; it was the most vibrant thing in the room. Parting the curtains, he looked out.

She said, "What is it?"

He noted the fear in her voice. "It's nothing," he told her. Trying to appear nonchalant, Slater let the curtain fall. "I thought I heard something."

"It might be Denny. He's supposed to pick me up at seven-thirty. He sometimes shows up early."

"No," Slater said, "it's no one." He stood an arm's length from her, but the distance between them was incalculable. The slow filtering evening lay between them in a deep gray gulf. "I've brought you a couple of things, Sheila." He withdrew an unmarked business envelope from his inside breast pocket. "A couple of things for you to think about."

With her close now, he was afraid of making some small but irreversible mistake. Slater yearned for her. He wanted desperately to soothe and reassure her, but he thought he knew what would happen. She was so susceptible to him now that even the slightest touch might easily flare and reduce them to ashes. I'm doing all of this for you, he thought. If only he could hold her and wipe out the horrible thing that was going to happen. I'm going to do something unimaginable. For you. Do you love me? Do you?

Eyes somewhere were watching these gray windows; he was sure of it. Many things hung in the

balance—he still wondered what Sheila had told
Reeves. But until he could speak with his heart,
everything he said, everything he tried to do seemed
stilted and incomplete, as if his only lifeline to the
world was badly frayed, awaiting and depending on
her acceptance of him to mend it and set things right
again.

"I believe Rachel had a little insurance, didn't she?"

"Yes, she did."

"You'll have to file for that, but you should get
that money in about thirty days. In the meantime,
I've put a little cash in here—that you don't have to
tell anybody about—to tide you over."

"Mr. Slater, you didn't have—"

"Just take it, Sheila, and don't argue with me about
it. Just take it." Through the twilight, Slater handed
her the envelope. He watched her bend forward, the
strong, young line of her bare forearm as she took
the money.

"Thank you," she said, grateful for any kindness,
and she smiled, still very unsure of herself. To him,
her helplessness was enormously appealing.

"Sheila, can I trust you?"

A frown gathered around her eyes. "Oh, but . . .
you know you can. What about?"

"I don't know. I want to trust you. You won't ever
repeat the things I tell you?"

"No, I *never* . . ."

"It's important," he said. "Don't tell anyone anything unless you've talked to me first. Do you know
what I mean?"

"Of course. I won't; don't worry."

"All right, the other thing," Slater said, "is something you'll have to keep between you and me. Do
you understand?"

Sheila nodded but he continued to study her for several seconds. "If a time comes, when you'd like to get away from all this, I have a place—a place that no one knows about. It's hidden, it's quite safe and comfortable; there's even a small pool. You can go there and stay as long as you like. No one'll ever know. No one'll bother you. All you have to do is say so and I'll give you directions. Or I'll go with you, if you like."

"Okay," she said, but behind her voice he heard misgivings. "I might want to sometime."

He was watching her carefully. "I know how hard this has been for you. I was thinking: I'm driving up to Pacific Grove on Monday next week for a meeting. I'll be tied up most of the afternoon. Why don't you come along? Nobody needs to know. You could soak up the sun and if there's time afterward, I'll take you to dinner." He waited, his eyes full on her face. Sheila hesitated for what seemed a long time before answering.

She knew what her Gramma would have said about this and she remembered Mrs. Slater's kindness to her on the day of the murder, but she couldn't deny how she was feeling now. The need to escape from her grief overcame her grandmother's persistent lessons. When she finally spoke, it was to ask, "What day did you say?"

Patiently, he repeated it. "I'd like you to, Sheila. I'd like—couldn't you arrange it? It would mean a lot to me if you'd let me do this. Won't you come? You need to get away."

The indecision had left her face. "Yes, I think I would like to. Where should I meet you?"

"I have a stop to make first in Vandalia. Do you know where that is?"

"Yes. About what time?"

"Ten sharp. The football field on the north end of town."

"Okay, if I can work it out, I'll be there by eleven. You're sure . . . Mr. Slater, are you sure you want me to?" Her hair had fallen forward. Sheila lifted strands of it back, first behind one ear, then the other, all the while looking at the envelope in her hand. "I don't know why—"

"Sh-h-h," he said. "One thing at a time. Of course, I'm sure. I told you I'd look out for you and I am, but I should go now."

He waited for some word from her that would release him and send him away. Sheila folded the envelope in her fingers. She straightened, pushing away from the counter. The room was almost completely dark now. He thought he could follow her anywhere by the perfumed scent of her hair.

Turning toward him, she said, "Won't you let me give you a cup of coffee? I'm sure it's ready. I remember when I was little you used to come and have coffee."

The bare simplicity of her request—that it had been years since he sat in this kitchen, drinking coffee, and she remembered it; that she had made the coffee purposefully in anticipation of him—moved him nearly to tears. It evoked a forgotten memory as full and bittersweet as anything in his life: Sheila had been ten or eleven, a tomboy, the warrior princess, he'd called her. But as quickly as it came the image deserted him and he realized she probably was asking him to stay because she couldn't bear to be in this house alone. There was nothing he had to do that couldn't wait, nowhere else he wanted to be, but here, in this old kitchen, with this enchanting, grief-stricken girl.

"Okay," he said, "but on one condition. If you'll turn on a light."

"There's a switch," Sheila told him, "there by the toaster. You know where it is."

He flipped on the switch. Above the sink, recessed behind the valance, the fluorescent bulb hummed with light, spreading blue-white illumination into half the room. As Sheila prepared to serve the coffee, she moved from the cupboard to the cabinet to the counter. Watching her, he had no sense of time. When she placed the teacup on the saucer, it was Rachel's hand putting it there just so; when she grasped the handle of the old percolator, pouring the coffee, it was with Rachel's good generous heft.

Ice ran down his spine. He would never know how long he stood there before he realized Sheila was shaking with sobs. In her hand, the cup full of coffee chattered on its saucer.

"Sheila, don't . . ." he said, starting toward her. He lost his head. The coffee spilled and she was in his arms, weeping on his shoulder. He could feel the length of her pressed fiercely against him, the soft shuddering collapse of her body as she gave in to wave upon wave of tears.

"Oh, Mr. Slater, what'm I going to do?"

The folly of it, the insane spontaneity of her need filled him with such lust that he covered her hair with kisses, feeling its silky turbulence slide and un-coil across his face. He started to gather her up, but at the edge of his sight, he saw headlights illuminate the front rooms of the house and flash through them—a moment's pale brilliance struck the kitchen's half-light. As the motor rumbled past outside on the driveway, Sheila drew quickly away. "I'll be all right," she whispered, wiping her eyes with her hands. "Really. I've been doing this off and on for days."

They heard the door slam. "That's Denny," Sheila said.

"Then I'll go."

But when Slater started out, the screen door under the porte cochere clicked open. Sheila slipped the envelope he'd given her inside her purse, threw Slater a glance and said, "Denny, we're in here."

They heard his steps in the hall; then he appeared in the doorway, the same boy Slater had noticed at the funeral, a strapping kid, dark, his black hair rumpled. Slater guessed him to be about Sheila's age, maybe a year or two older, athletic and well built, honest brown eyes—but a face with a history of misdemeanors, the thin white groove of a scar near one corner of his mouth. Without hesitation, Sheila said, "Mr. Slater, I'd like you to meet my boyfriend, Denny Rivera."

Slater smiled and offered his hand. "Hello," he said, "I'm Henry Slater. I've been hearing a lot about you."

Surprised and at the same time resentful of his being there, Denny muttered, "Hi," and abruptly shook Slater's extended hand.

In the awkward silence that followed, Slater finally said, "I really have to be going." When he stepped past the boy, he said, "You take good care of her, Denny." The boy regarded him sullenly.

Sheila hastened to say, "I'll walk out with you." Then to Denny, "I'll be right back."

On the driveway, in the dark, Slater reached out his hand and took hers in a pantomime of a hand-

shake. It was the most reassuring thing she had ever
felt in her life. His hands were hard and strong: she
remembered how they had always swallowed her
fingers. "Be good," he said. "If I could hug you, I
would." He was looking at her with eyes that were
pure and loving and kind. Slowly he let go. "You
know what to do?" he asked, under his breath.

"Yes." Her hands floated up nervously but didn't
touch him. She started to speak but instead looked at
the kitchen's curtained windows and changed her
mind.

He said, "Good night, then."

When he was halfway down the driveway, Sheila
followed after him a few steps, but already the distance between them was too great. "Good night!" she
called. "Good night! Thank you!"

She watched the darkness absorb him until all that
was left of him was the faint tread of his footsteps in
the night. She stood perfectly still in the driveway,
afraid of the house, dreading the hours still ahead.
A moment came when she thought the echo of his
footsteps returned to her—that he was coming back.
But it was only a trick of the night air humming
around her; his footsteps had faded completely although she believed she could hear them long after
they were gone.

ONLY A STREETLIGHT here and there illuminated the
darkness. Canyon Valley Drive lay mostly in shadow.
The night air was soft, as subtly perfumed as her hair.
Slater was savoring an extraordinary happiness. He
had what he had come for: she would keep quiet
and she would see him again.

A car sat half-hidden in the darkness between the

streetlights. The moment Slater saw it, the queasiness he had experienced only the day before surged through him again. *Reeves, you bastard.*

He stopped, trapped, at the edge of the street. I should've known you'd be around here, somewhere. Watching. Slater considered going on, acting as though he hadn't seen the car, but he knew he couldn't. He had stopped cold in his tracks. Reeves would've had to be blind not to have noticed his reaction. Turning, Slater walked directly to the police chief's open window.

"Evening, Henry. How's our girl?"

Slater wondered if Reeves could detect anything peculiar about him, wondered suddenly what he could say to make his being here appear more legitimate. "She's still—rocky," he said. "She can't take too much more. I thought you said you wouldn't push it."

"Sometimes things don't work to plan."

"Goddamnit, Burris." The curse escaped him. "I've been thinking about what you said and I don't know. I think you might be on a wild goose chase with this thing. Why don't you just round up those convicts and leave the girl alone?"

The police chief chuckled. "Henry, you can't put heat on me. I *am* the heat. Don't concern yourself with this: I'm handling it. I'm gonna give her another day or two. I saw your car and thought I'd see how things are. That's all."

You wait, Slater thought, after tomorrow you'll give her a lot longer than that. "Well, maybe you do have a heart, after all, Burris. She'll snap out of it, but she's going through hell right now. Listen, I've got to go."

"So do I," Reeves said. The cruiser started up and

rolled forward. With a wave, Reeves drove past him as Slater walked to his car.

You wait, Slater thought. Just you wait.

SHEILA WENT INSIDE, shut and latched the door. She imagined she could still see him, standing in the kitchen doorway, tall, vigilant, a man of influence who had said he would always take care of her. What a relief it would be not to have to figure everything out on her own. She liked being looked after, she liked the tender expression that came into his eyes, she liked the feel of his hands. When she turned into the kitchen, her fingers ran over Denny's shoulder in a quick, flirtatious pass. "You're in a good mood," he said.

"I'll just be a minute." Moving swiftly, she cleared the counter, rinsed the cups and emptied the old percolator. She knew she couldn't mention that she was planning to meet a married man and it made her feel guilty.

"Sheila, are you okay?" Denny came up behind her. "What was he doing here anyway?"

"You know," she said. "I've told you. I had other visitors, too. The minister came by for a while."

"So . . . what do you think of hizzoner?"

Sheila didn't answer.

"What did you think of him? Come on, Sheila, I want to know."

"What do you mean? He's just a friend, just a longtime family friend. I think he seems nice . . . sincere."

"How old is he?"

She took a deep breath and let it out. "How should I know?"

"Jesus Christ! Don't you think it's weird, Sheila? Why's he always hanging around? What is it with you two, anyway? I come in and here you are—standing around in your kitchen with this big, rich, powerful, *married* guy!—with one goddamned light on!—in the whole damned house! Don't you think that seems kind of odd?"

All at once, Sheila leaned forward and gave him a kiss. "Oh, shut up, Denny," she whispered. "You know there's no one but you."

14

THE PACIFIC LAPPED at the old waterfront of Rio Del Palmos, the ripples all but motionless, the water black, reflecting every star. It was as if there were no sky, no ocean, only a vast twinkling void. A woman, bending down to kiss her children goodnight, whispered, "Don't the stars seem close tonight? Don't they look like little pieces of heaven?" Life was peaceful in Rio Del Palmos, lying beside the glittering night.

The light gleamed from the houses, tarnishing the grass in long copper shafts. In the rooms, seen through windows, the lamps glowed prettily in their shades—sometimes a breeze played at the curtains only to disappear like breath taken away. At eleven-thirty, after *The Tonight Show*, the last lights began to go down. Here and there. An upstairs light continued to burn all night at the Schullenburgs'; they had a new baby girl, four days old. The other houses were dark, all was silent, all secure.

No one heard the muffled engine prowling up and down the streets. In the sleeping houses, no one had any reason to notice that a nondescript Jeep was weaving through the city, crisscrossing back and forth, stopping at the old boatworks—where a figure left the Jeep and placed two ten-inch packages low beneath the derelict hydrangea bushes, one at each side of the large frame structure—then looping around, doubling back and going on. Twice that night, patroling police cars appeared on the street in front of him and Slater veered off into the surrounding neighborhoods, hid the Jeep among other shadowy parked cars, killed the lights and engine, and waited. But he wasn't being followed.

On Klamath Drive, the black and white police cruiser sat at the end of Reeves's drive. No one living nearby would remember the sound of the engine that softly died or the metal door closing. In his gloved hands, Slater carried electrician's tape and a thin coil of soft wire; his dark windbreaker concealed a parcel already wrapped in tape. In the neighbors' slumber, the whisper of his footsteps crept over starlit lawns and vanished through a hole in their dreams.

Faith had been sound asleep at two-thirty when Slater left the house; at four-fifteen, when he got back into bed beside her, he could see that she had hardly moved.

In the hour before dawn, the milk trucks turned slowly into their fog-bound routes, yellow beams smoking before them. Half an hour later, the whir of bicycle tires spun down the dream-thick streets; newspapers hit bushes, sidewalks, porches. Slowly, in the foothills and across the basin of the city, sixty thousand lights were coming on in bedrooms.

In the East, the first clear rays of dawn streaked over the Sierra Madres. Layer by slow layer, the fog dispersed and sunlight dappled the sidewalks like white drifts of pollen. It was morning in Rio Del Palmos, June 8; peaceful and serene.

A breath of wind stirred the palms at 6:55 when Slater crossed the plaza to City Hall. He stopped momentarily outside the revolving glass doors to let it bathe his face. The day's perfect, he thought. A smile touched the corners of his mouth. In the lobby, the large granite reception desk was unoccupied as he went past. Stepping into the elevator, he pushed the button for the sixth floor.

The cubicles were deserted when he walked down the narrow aisle and unlocked his office. He checked his watch. 7:06. He left the door conspicuously ajar. Abigail would not arrive for another half hour, the rest of the staff closer to eight.

Without haste, he took up his briefcase, went into the private bathroom and pushed the lock in the knob. He turned on the cold water tap to mask any incidental noise and, also, to alert anyone that he was there and not to be disturbed. Sliding the thumb latches, Slater opened the briefcase and took out the small set of binoculars and a transmitter roughly the size and shape of a garage door opener.

With a twist of the handle, the opaque window swung open. He drew back and glanced at the locked door, listened, then he looked at his watch. 7:14. Opening the window to its full pivot and taking up the binoculars, he looked two blocks north, drawing into sharp focus the Rialto River Bridge, which rose above the surrounding trees. The morning rush hour wasn't fully underway. The seconds ticked within him. He watched and waited until he saw the roof of Reeves's black and white cruiser rise over the hump of the bridge, its number—5022—painted in block letters on the curved brow above the windshield. Okay, he thought. Come on.

Slater checked his watch. 7:16. Right on time. The tremendous panic he had experienced a few days ago with Reeves was gone now, completely. Again he calculated the distance and it was right. The time couldn't be better. In another twenty minutes, the traffic coursing the bridge would be dense, headed toward the interstate. Slater took up the transmitter and threw the switch to turn it on, activating its batteries.

Reeves's cruiser came off the end of the bridge, turned right and swung into the lot. Come on, Burris! What're you doing! Slater's nerves were taut as wires. The car door swung open and the police chief got out, ambled across the street and entered the donut shop.

The binoculars swerved from the glass door to the parking lot. Another car arrived—there were eight now altogether counting the cruiser—and Slater waited for the driver and his companion to go inside. Quickly he examined the lot. No one else had driven in.

Do it, he thought. His thumb pressed the black button.

There was a thudding blast, a flash of light. The floor of the building shuddered under Slater's feet. He was certain he saw the cruiser bounce into the air, but a huge cloud of smoke and dirt billowed over the wreckage that was taking place before his eyes. As the dust drifted away, he saw the crazy angles of the badly battered cars. The cruiser had actually rocked backward a few feet, its hood torn off, its entire front end blackened. The cars parked on either side of it were wrecked.

In those first few seconds as he surveyed the damage, there came a second blast—the cruiser's gas tank exploded and then the rear of the car next to it heaved up. Its tank exploded. Flames leapt into the sky. It was happening so fast that Slater couldn't

take it all in. "Goddamn," he whispered to himself.
"God—damn!"

He waited until he saw the men run out of the
donut shop and into the street, where they stopped
and stared, Burris Reeves among them. Okay, Reeves,
he thought, now what are you going to do?

Slater stepped back, cranked the window shut, returned the transmitter and the binoculars to his briefcase and snapped it shut. The other bombs were
rigged with timing devices—there was nothing he
could do about them now. It was out of his hands—
irreversible. He had chosen the places and times as
carefully as he could. A vision came to him then, just
as if he stood on the sidewalk in the crowd: the riot
of blue police lights, red ambulance flashers, sirens,
fire equipment, TV crews—all gathered at the car-
cass of the black and white cruiser.

Now you see the diamond, now you don't.

The art of distraction.

SLATER HAD PLANNED four bombings in all, three the
first day, two within the first hour, in rapid succession.

The second explosion came at 8:19—flames shot
fifty feet into the air. The unoccupied new addition
of the St. Pius Grade School, which Slater had dedicated only a couple of weeks earlier, collapsed in
fiery ruin.

Through the heavy plate-glass windows of his office, he watched the fireball lick the air but he could
hardly hear it. Bulletins were coming from the radio
behind his desk: "We interrupt this broadcast . . . an
explosion has occurred at Three Points Avenue near
the entrance to the Rialto River Bridge. Police are
asking that commuters please avoid the area. We
repeat—"

No mention was made of the convicts. It's too soon, he thought, too much confusion. He kept changing the stations. "KRIO has just been informed that the city of Rio Del Palmos has been shattered this morning by two explosions. We will be keeping you up-to-date with those locations as soon as they are verified. Police officials are advising that residents stay inside their homes unless it's absolutely necessary to go out—"

Slater paced beside his office windows, watching the devastation and waiting. Running through his fingers and in his mind was Sheila's gold necklace, a single gold thread, pliant as her hair. I'm closing this city down, he thought. It'll all grind to a halt, all for you. It occurred to him that this was one of the few times in his life when he knew exactly what had to be done. Never had he been so careful; he had to think of everything.

Two gray pillars of smoke curled into the early morning light. It was awesome to watch the world blow apart with forces only he controlled. Never in his life had Slater felt more in command, more omniscient. He heard the dim wail of sirens but the noise rose to him as if from the depths of the ocean. Only the two columns of smoke made it real. And the ringing telephone. He put the necklace into his pocket, reached across and picked up the receiver. "This is Henry Slater."

But it wasn't Reeves.

Frightened herself, Abigail came in and tried to elaborate on what the bulletins were saying on the radio. Faith called, obviously upset, wanting to know if he was all right and Slater assured her that he was. She wanted to come down, to be with him, but he told her not to—to stay home.

The intercom beeped on his desk as Abigail screened and announced his incoming calls. It was ten o'clock, it was eleven. With the receiver tucked between his cheek and shoulder, he shuffled through the blue slips she periodically brought in. Still nothing from Reeves.

When Slater wasn't on the telephone, he paced in front of the windows, his hands in his pockets, his right-hand fingers wrapped in gold. Then Abigail said Burris Reeves was on line three. This is it, he thought. *Finally.* But Reeves was only giving him an early assessment of damages, reporting that he had requested additional manpower from neighboring communities. "You do that, Burris," he said. "I want some answers."

"I'll get back to you," Reeves told him.

Slater hung up. I'm still waiting, Burris.

The morning was spent on the telephone, the afternoon in emergency meetings. Rumors flew; men raced in and out of his office; implausible theories took on the ring of truth. At one o'clock, Slater stepped before the microphones and cameras and expressed his shock and outrage, calling the bombings "fiendish" and "insane," and assuring the public at large that immediate action was being taken.

Through it all, he waited for Reeves to call him back. And again, the only call that mattered didn't come. The afternoon and evening newspapers began to arrive. The local *Gazette* carried a small header above the double banner headline.

Police stymied, no leads, no critical injuries
2 EXPLOSIONS SHOCK RIO DEL PALMOS
BOMB DESTROYS POLICE CHIEF'S CAR

The *Santa Barbara News Press* devoted the entire front page to the bombings and the *L.A. Times* carried the story below the fold:

TERROR ERUPTS IN RIO DEL PALMOS, FEAR STALKS THE STREETS

Two bombs in less than an hour sent waves of panic through affluent Rio Del Palmos at dawn this morning. The powerful explosions jarred homes as far as a mile away, although miraculously no one was injured.

He saw his own words—*fiendish* and *insane*—quoted in headlines. The police chief was quoted again and again, but nowhere were the convicts mentioned.

Slater shoved his hands into his pockets. Again, he paced. The intercom beeped but he ignored it. A minute elapsed, then two more—minutes when he imagined Reeves thinking that the worst was over. At 4:26, there came a noise like an immense thunderclap. His pictures shook against the office walls. In an instant, the old abandoned boatworks collapsed in a heap of dust and rubble. That's three, he thought. Talk to me, Reeves, or I'll bring you to your goddamned knees.

Abigail stood at the doorway. "Oh, Mr. Slater!" she exclaimed. "My God, did you hear that?"

Her face was more frightened than his own. It fed him with strength.

Night fell. Barricades and emergency torches sealed off entire neighborhoods. Slater took a roundabout way home, talking with the patrolmen stationed at intersections, passing through the roadblocks surrounding the city.

And again the next morning, a bomb blew at 6:48 while Slater looked at his watch and got into the shower. He walked through police headquarters on his way to the office, but Reeves wasn't there.

Noon came and still no call, no word. Slater was hanging up the telephone when he realized that the door to his office was open and that Reeves was looking at him. In the way the police chief stood, Slater could see the man's exhaustion.

"Well, Henry," Reeves said. "I guess everyone's entitled to a mistake once in a while. I was wrong. It's been those goddamned convicts all along—Christ, have we ever got a situation on our hands."

Okay, Slater thought, now it can stop. It's over. It worked.

"Close the door, Burris," he said, measuring his tone, getting up and going around the desk to meet him.

It worked. It worked.

And yet there was still that lingering doubt.

You're too damned smart, Reeves.

15

AN ILLUSION OF smoke haunted the air over Rio Del Palmos, although the mornings were clear and unclouded. A smaller, low-intensity bomb had been set off in an open field, which investigators now considered the work of a prankster, and there had been an undisclosed number of bomb threats. But people knew about them. Both a nursery school and a restaurant had been evacuated and thoroughly searched. The fear of a sudden cataclysm did not stop. In a plea for reason, the harassed police chief issued a statement telling the city the rage was not over. Until the convicts were captured, nothing, it seemed, could stop the bomb threats. But for years to come Denny Rivera would mark those few days of terror as the time when his life fell apart at the seams.

That first week after the murder had been a tender time for Denny and Sheila. Mornings when she let him into the house after the McPhearsons had left for work lingered in Denny's mind long after they were over. Even if he was running late, he always stopped at the bakery and got half a dozen pastries—Sheila liked eclairs—and she made coffee. Nothing much ever happened and yet, the hour or so they spent together seemed full and quiet and rich.

Mary would leave them alone in the kitchen to drink their coffee and talk. It was as though Sheila were giving him a glimpse of how it would be—the two of them married and living together. Seldom had Denny felt more privileged. She was funny and sweet in those first moments after waking up, her face soft and clean, still puffy with sleep.

He was careful not to mention the murder or anything having to do with it, unless she did. Many times during the week that had passed, he knew Sheila was longing for her grandmother. The undercurrent of her grief was ever present. With that in mind, most of their conversations were subdued and about the immediate future.

"I don't know," Denny told her one morning soon after he had arrived, "I don't think I should leave you right now. To tell you the truth, I almost called Burgess last night and canceled, so he could get somebody else."

Licking a smear of chocolate from her lip, Sheila smiled and said, "Oh, Denny, what's wrong with you? It's only for six weeks. You've talked about working at that sports camp all winter."

"Well, it's not really a camp; it's a clinic."

Mary agreed with Sheila. "But it's got to be easy money, Denny. Where else're you gonna do that well?"

And he backed down. "All right," he said. "It's probably too late to get out of it now, anyway." He watched the two girls move idly around him in their sleep-wrinkled gowns and loose robes. Then Mary was gone and Sheila was smiling at him. He was crazy in love with her.

Then, two days after the explosions, Sheila met him at the back door but she stayed inside the screen.

"Maybe you forgot," she said. "I've got to go to Mrs. Sanders's tomorrow and—Denny, I've got a thousand things to do."

"I guess I did forget," he said, "but I can give you a hand."

She was still in her robe, but he noticed that she had already taken her shower and that her hair was brushed and silky clean. "Denny, not now, okay? Not this morning. I've got a lot of things I need to do by myself. Why don't you wait and come by tomorrow afternoon? You can ride with me when I go over there."

"Okay—but wait a minute," he persisted. "If this is your last day here, then let's take off somewhere. I can get away and I'll help you with your stuff tomorrow. Come on, let's go some place . . . to the beach—"

"I can't," she said. "I really can't. You have no idea what this moving from place to place is like." Her eyes slid away. "I'm going to be tied up all day and half the night. Don't make me feel so pressured."

Denny stood, clutching the bag of pastries in his hand. It was true. He had no idea what it felt like to be so unsettled. "I know a way to change your mind," he said. "Here, you and Mary have these. They're for you anyway." He pushed the screen door open, handed her the bakery bag, kissed her on the cheek and headed down the side of the driveway toward the street.

Sheila dropped the eclairs on the kitchen counter and ran upstairs.

"Is he gone?" Mary asked.

"He's gone. But I've got a feeling he'll be back."

Mary rolled over and sprawled across the bed, her chin propped in her hands, watching Sheila strip off the robe and run to the closet in her bra and panties.

"If he's coming back," Mary said, "I'm not staying here, either. If he gets mad . . . Sheila, I don't want Denny mad at *me*."

"He won't do anything," Sheila countered, clearly preoccupied with what she was going to wear. "He's always mad at somebody and he's never done anything before."

"So?"

"I can't help it," Sheila said through a dark red Thai silk dress she was pulling on. Lifting her hair from the yoke, she stepped quickly to the mirror, turned twice and shrugged the dress off again. "I need to get away," she said, as if to explain. "I just have to get away for a while." This time Sheila stepped into a chamois minidress, fawn colored, and pulled it up over her shoulders. "So, I'm talking to Annie Gilbert and she asks me to come spend the day. What am I supposed to do? Say I can't? Mary, you've got to cover for me, just this once."

"Once! Did I hear you say, *'Once'*? How many times have I covered for you?"

"Okay, okay." Sheila laughed. "But you will, won't you?" She cinched a wide red belt at her waist and pushed on red cowboy boots. "What do you think—do I need stockings? I look awful, don't I?"

"With that tan? Don't make me sick!"

"No, seriously."

"You look fabulous."

At a raffish angle, Sheila put on a big, red, straw hat so that it shadowed half her face. "Is this all right?"

"Absolute depravity."

"Thank you," Sheila said. "You will take care of things, won't you, Mary?"

"Have I ever let you down?"

*   *   *

THE FLORIST SHOP was called The Artesian and it was just opening its doors. Denny counted out thirty-eight dollars from his pocket. He had to keep five for something to drink, five or six for gas, leaving him with twenty-seven, twenty-eight dollars. The roses were a buck fifty apiece; he did a quick calculation—he could afford eighteen of the white bud roses.

"How much for that pink tiger?" He motioned toward the four-foot-high stuffed tiger sitting behind the counter.

"Twenty-two, fifty."

"What d'you think is better for a girl: the tiger or roses?"

The florist laughed and shrugged. "I'd take the roses," said the woman arranging flowers at a table.

Denny had roses in mind, but he had wanted a roomful. At the same time, he worried that they might remind Sheila of the funeral. "Okay," he said, "but could you wrap 'em up nice in that white paper? It's a surprise."

With the eighteen roses in a cone of white paper lying on the seat beside him, he swung by the garage and asked Gonzales if he could keep the pickup for the day. "When you gonna pay me back these favors?" the mechanic called after him, but Denny was away, winding through Woodrow Estates and coming out on Belvedere Avenue, two blocks from the McPhearson house.

He let up on the gas, shifted back a gear, traveled the two blocks and cut the engine at the curb. The Dutch Colonial sat across the intersection, on the opposite corner. Afraid of breaking the wrapped roses, Denny cradled them protectively in his arm and got out of the pickup, moving around to the sidewalk.

He was about to cross the street when he saw the door at the side of the house fly open. Sheila came out. Quickly he hid the flowers behind his back but Sheila didn't turn around. Why was she all dressed up? She wasn't in mourning; she looked fabulous. What's going on here? Denny watched as she ran for the alley. Where's she going in such a big hurry? He started after her, but directly ahead of him, down the next block, he saw the old red and brown station wagon whip from the alley and sink from sight in a patch of gray exhaust.

Denny stood rooted where he was, peering into the thinning fumes. What is this!

He ran to the pickup, tossed the roses onto the seat and jumped in beside them. He tried to tell himself that she must be running out to her grandmother's house, but his instinct got in the way. Why would she dress like that—to go out there? Denny tore after her through the intersection, pushing the truck faster and faster. He thought, Let's find out where the hell she's going.

He let her trail ahead of him. As long as he could keep her in sight, that was all he cared about. She was headed east, into the country. You goddamned little sneak, he thought. You *lied* to me.

SHE WASN'T THERE.

Slater parked the Jaguar facing the closed stadium, snapped the engine off and slid lower in the cockpit to wait. He told himself he was behaving like a schoolboy. Through an open portal, he could see a patch of the Vandalia Tigers playing field—silent, artificially green. 10:06. Six minutes late. Christ. His eyes were riveted on the rearview mirror, waiting to see the station wagon among the approaching cars behind him. But it was still another five minutes before the wagon appeared. He watched as it turned and parked a short distance away in the shade of old mangroves. *She's here.*

STOPPED AT THE corner traffic light, hemmed in by other cars, Denny sat frozen in the pickup, watching with amazement as Sheila darted toward the low-slung car. There wasn't a thing he could do. He saw the passenger door swing open and then Sheila was getting into the bucket seat.

The traffic light flashed green; the cars ahead of him in the turn lane started to move. Denny slid his foot from the brake to the gas and let out the clutch, still thinking he might catch them. *Come on! Come on, let's go!*

"I ALMOST DIDN'T see you," Sheila said. "Is this your car?"

The moment the door shut behind her, Slater backed out of the parking lot, but his eyes were lit up with amusement. "Of course it's my car." Sheila was breathless, her face flushed.

SLOWED BY THE movement of the cars in front of him, Denny turned left through the intersection just as the Jaguar shot straight at him, going the other direction. As it sped by, Denny looked down from the high cab of the pickup and there was no mistaking who the driver was. *Slater.* That was all Denny could see but the sight burned him. *I knew it!* "What're you doin', Sheila!" He struck the wheel with the bottom of his fist. "What the hell're you doin'!"

The wheels of his pickup squealed into the stadium parking lot, skidded into a U-turn and bounced back onto the street. "You won't get away with this," he said in the hollow cab. "I'll show you! You don't know who you're messin' with!"

But at the intersection, where he was forced to stop, Denny could see that the Jaguar was gone. He threw his cap onto the seat and ran his hands through his hair. Then he remembered the roses. He grabbed up the flowers and slapped them again and again against the window until a riot of bruised buds covered the dashboard. "All right!" he said to himself. "All right! I'm never gonna forget this, Sheila. Never!"

SHEILA WORE SCULPTURAL gold orbs, like scarabs, on her earlobes. "I didn't see your big car," she said. "I didn't know what to look for. What happened to the Jeep?"

"I only use the Jeep when I'm not on the job," he said, shifting into third gear.

If she noticed that he was taking back roads out of town, Sheila didn't mention it. "What kind of car is this?" she asked, her expression bright with curiosity.

As he drove, Slater sketched the Jaguar's history for her, what make it was, where it was manufactured, all the time picking up speed. "One of these days," he said, "I'm going to have it restored."

Always afraid that they might be seen, he felt tremendous relief when the town of Vandalia fell away behind them. His hands relaxed on the wheel; his anxiety dissolved, only to be replaced by an extraordinary awareness of how close they were in the outmoded cockpit.

"How are you feeling?"

"I'm better today," she said. "How fast will this go?"

"Fast enough."

Sheila leaned toward him. "Wasn't that something? Those explosions!"

"Sheila, you have no idea," he told her.

She thought for a minute, then she smiled. "Can we have one ground rule?"

"You know I don't believe in rules."

"Just this once. I don't want to talk about anything awful that's happened. Okay, Mr. Slater? I don't even want to think about it."

He saw how suddenly serious she was. "Of course," he said. "And there's another thing. When you're with me, I'd like you to call me Henry. We've been through this before."

"Maybe I will this time," she said.

He luxuriated in her presence. The floppy wide brim of her hat was loosely woven, sending splinters of light across the shaded side of her face. "Could we put the top down?" she asked. Her tanned arms were flawless, without mark or blemish and her eyes were heavily lashed, beautifully shaped—great, lustrous blue eyes.

"You might lose your hat," he said, grinning.

"I'll take it off."

"Let's put some miles behind us first," he said. "I was beginning to think you weren't coming."

"I told you I would."

On the open road, the wind and engine noise made it difficult to talk. He wondered what she was thinking. He rejoiced at being confined with her in so intimate a space. The explosions had worked even more beautifully than he'd expected. With Reeves buried in investigations and paperwork, Slater could devote himself to her, and he wanted to be with her as often as it could be arranged. When he wasn't looking at her, he felt her presence surround him. It was like a radiance that filled the car.

Twenty miles down the highway, they slowed to go through Glen Terrace. "You've changed," he said. "You seem full of yourself—more grown up."

"No," she said, "I haven't changed." When she laughed, he felt young again himself. She said, "I'll bet you do this kind of thing all the time?" He saw the gleam in her eyes—her delight in being able to tease him. "Don't you?"

"What's that?" he asked.

"Take girls riding in your car?"

"Not for a long time."

"But you're so good at it," she said. She smiled playfully. "Haven't you done this before?"

"Only with you," Slater said. "I'm fairly new at this."

"Really?" she replied. "I'm not."

After they were out of town, he stopped by the side of the highway to put the top down. He wanted the ride to be glorious for her. He drove leisurely through the hamlets and towns, streaked over the foothills and between the long fields of artichokes, rich and verdant. "I love the speed," she shouted.

All the way there, again and again, she was aware that he was smiling. "What's the matter?" she asked more than once, "why are you smiling?" but he only shook his head.

At a few minutes past noon, they rolled to a stop at the corner of Twelfth and Navarro in the renovated older section of Pacific Grove. Slater pointed out the shops and restaurants, arranging to meet her at six.

"I'm sorry I have to leave you like this," he said. "I thought we might have time for lunch, but I can't stay. Why don't you buy some new clothes? I'd like to see what you would do. Change yourself completely."

"What's wrong with the way I look?" she said. "God, you must think I'm made out of money."

Slater shook his head indifferently. The thought of transforming her filled him with recklessness. He got out of the car, opened the trunk and put on his suit jacket. From his wallet, he took out several bills and folded them into her hand. "Don't look at this now," he said, "and don't bring any of it back. Don't save a penny. Have a good time; I won't take no for an answer." He told her the name of a boutique, to ask for a woman named Harriet Holt. "Tell her you know ex-senator Tripplet's wife. She'll take it from there."

I shouldn't do this, Sheila thought. Gramma wouldn't let me—but she's not here any more. Oh, forget it; why spoil the fun? Just forget it and take the money because he wants you to. Slater wasn't smiling exactly, although it seemed he might smile at any moment and she wished he had. What she saw, instead, was so naked it embarrassed her—Sheila had never seen a more defenseless look than the one he gave her, never before.

Sheila nodded to herself then, and in that single movement, she seemed to him to be very young and very lost. "Mr. Slater, why d'you always do this?" she said in a low voice. "Do you want me to come to you for everything?"

And Slater thought, If I destroy everything around you, then you'll have to come to me. He grinned at

her. "Sheila, if you'd let me, I'd take care of everything for you from now on."

She still couldn't meet his eyes. "What kind of
changes do you want me to make?"

"You decide. Something expensive and extrava-
gant and sexy. Maybe you don't know it yet, but,
Sheila, you are a really expensive girl. Tell Mrs. Holt
you're going to a fancy dinner. She'll know what to
do."

"Am I going to a fancy dinner?"

"You'll see." He opened the door for her.

It was as if a secret drum had sounded: the men
having lunch at the sidewalk café casually raised
their heads when Sheila got out of the car. Slater saw
their eyes drift from their conversations and sandwiches and slowly attach to her. One man nudged
another when she bent into the open car for her
straw hat and purse. She would always be noticed; it
unnerved him at times, knowing that her beauty,
alone, could be their undoing.

Sheila said, "See you at six," and walked away and
the men followed her as if she existed only for their
eyes and for the sweet switching rhythm of her hips.

HE HAD ONLY a passing interest in the conference he
was to attend, but he knew he had to be there and he
had to do more than merely go through the motions.
A certain attitude, a questioning cast of mind had
become expected of him. In the lobby of the First
Pacific Mercantile Bank and Trust, Slater stood at
the mirror in the public rest room, setting his tie,
running a comb through his hair, rearranging his
jacket on his shoulders, trying to collect himself for
the monotony of the hours ahead. He was thinking
that he had wasted so many years of his life—the

only life he would ever have—on meetings and con-
ferences much like this one. The world would never
be new again. Only Sheila was new—hers was still
the life of old dreams.

He threw off the lightheartedness he'd felt with
her in the car and his face became serious and hard.
He took the elevator to the twenty-first floor, got out,
stepped past the placard that read: ENVIRONMENTAL
IMPACT REVIEW FOR CITIES AND TOWNS. QUARTERLY
MEETING.

Identifying himself to the guard, he entered a
second elevator, ascending to the penthouse suite.
He was greeted by Vern Tripplet's private secretary,
a pleasant woman he had seen here many times
before, who showed him into the conference suite
with its towering Palladian windows and vast views.
"We'll be getting started in about ten minutes," she
said. "Mr. Tripplet had a small luncheon brought in.
You're familiar with how we do things—you're welcome to help yourself. There's coffee and iced tea."

"Yes, thank you, Marie. I would like something."
He scanned the long room, the small coteries and
clusters of men.

"Would there be anything else, Mr. Slater?"

"No, thank you." He smiled and thanked her again.

At the elaborate rosewood buffet, he selected among
the finger sandwiches and miniature vegetables. Taking up his plate, he went toward the windows, aware
that several of the other men, singly and in pairs,
would eventually join him. There would be twenty of
them in attendance, mayors of municipalities with a
population of less than a hundred thousand. He
knew he would be asked about the explosions; Slater
braced himself with noncommittal answers.

"Hello, Whitey, you old rascal," Slater said, extend-

ing his hand to the mayor of Villa Grove. "Good to
see you, McGuiness."

"You've had your hands full down there, haven't
you, Henry?"

"Yes, you'd better believe it. It's been one hell of a
mess." He talked with the men and ate the sandwiches and drank coffee. He looked through the
windows at the city. Sheila was out there now, away
from home and waiting for him, three miles away, in
the gray-green maze of streets.

16

"COUPLE OF SIX-PACKS, cold," Denny said, leaning his weight against the counter. In the old jukebox, the needle slid off the record and the turntable whirred to a stop. He flicked the ash from his cigarette on the floor.

Florence, the big black woman who owned the place, eyed him. "Sweets, you're not legal. I can't sell you no beer."

It was one-thirty in the afternoon. Except for a hobbled old black man who was rearranging the chairs and cleaning the ashtrays, the place was empty. Denny kept his voice low. "Come on, Florence, you've done it before. Don't you recognize me?"

"Everybody's always in a hurry," the black woman commented. She smiled, exposing incredible white teeth and purple gums. "When you take up smokin'?" She was dancing a little samba behind the counter on her way through swinging doors to the kitchen. "Put some music on my jukebox," she said. "I dance when I work."

He fed two quarters into the jukebox, punched in Aretha twice and a Billy Ocean.

"Give me three dollars," the black woman said, putting the brown bag on the counter. "Six Miller in here, that's all."

"I'll leave you a tip," Denny said and held up a five. She leaned over the counter and stretched out her fleshy arm to take it. Then she was moving again, feet shifting, massive hips shuddering, doing the samba to the cash register.

Outside, in the Firebird, his friend Tommy Ames said, "Where to next?"

"Just go." Denny popped two cans and passed one over. Finally, he said, "I don't know what I stay here for. I wish to hell I had enough money to get away for good."

"Sheila giving you a hard time again?"

"Nothing I can't handle. Got any weed?"

"Yeah. You want to get really fucked up, try some of this."

They slammed out through the country on back roads, pushing the Firebird up to a hundred, once, just to see the needle jiggle on the two zeros. They drank the cold beer, three apiece, threw the cans at road signs, and couldn't think of any place that would sell them more in the middle of the afternoon. After a while Denny drove and Ames rolled a couple of joints of what he claimed was weird Panamanian. It messed them up, but nothing did Denny any good. It had eaten into him by then—the horrible, numb feeling of his loss.

"So . . . ," Ames said. "Where d'you want to go?"

"Just drop me off downtown."

They drifted back into Rio Del Palmos.

"What're you gonna do?"

"I don't know," Denny said. "Something. I'm gonna do something."

"Why don't you just kick her ass?"

"I might. That's what my old man used to do."

It was three-thirty when he got out and the Firebird rumbled off. The sidewalks were busy and he turned again to look at the flow of afternoon shoppers, thinking he might see someone—some girl—he knew. For several seconds he watched a huge man leading a fox terrier. Then a woman in a dark blue suit caught his eye. He thought she looked familiar, but at first she was obscured in the crowd. Something self-assured in her manner stirred his memory. A name slowly detached itself and rose in his mind: that's Mrs. Slater. He struggled to clear his head. He thought, That's the bastard's wife. I met her. So what was her first name?

Denny was trying to remember the rest of her name when it occurred to him what he should do. Suddenly he stood up, straight as a stick, resting his hands on his hips and turning over in his mind the possibility of actually talking to her. Faith. Yeah, that's it. Faith Slater. Wonder what she knows about this. He made his way across the street through traffic.

He watched as she waited in line at the cash register of an outdoor market. Her straight black hair was cropped at the shoulders, pushed behind her ears—a slender, dark woman, tan, polished. She had been nice to Sheila the day of the murder, Denny thought. He wondered if she was always so kind. Maybe she knew something he didn't know.

He watched Faith Slater pay at the checkout counter and move along through the crowd; she paused for a moment and looked around. He worried that she wouldn't recognize him. He felt nervous about talking to her, he had to admit that. Apathy fell upon him and Denny gave himself to it. What the hell good would talking to her do anyway?

Suddenly he was struck with an image of Sheila in

that short little dress that hardly covered her and
those high-heeled cowboy boots. Two months ago,
they had been talking about getting married; he had
been making a real effort to save some money so
they could be together and there came to his mind
that picture of Slater, in that sports car, with *his* girl.
Denny was seized with jealousy. "I'm gonna do it,"
he muttered, girding himself. "I'm gonna ask her.
I'm gonna goddamn do it."

Immediately he set off through the milling crowd
with their shopping bags and newspapers and vin-
tage wines.

"Mrs. Slater?"

Faith raised her eyes with a start and saw a
young man coming toward her. "Yes?"

With every step, Denny felt more and more uncertain. Struggling to appear levelheaded, he stopped a
short distance from her. "Hi," he said, "maybe you
don't remember me, Mrs. Slater. I'm Denny Rivera.
I met you that day at the Malcolmsons'. I was with
Sheila."

"Oh, yes," Faith replied. "I do remember you now."
Denny noticed that she held herself very straight,
like a lady poised on a horse.

She seemed too carefully made up, her black hair
perfectly in place. She was holding a small leather-
bound notebook and a pen. Denny looked at her
cool, languid hands, her bracelets and rings. Doubt
settled over him like a fog; he had trouble meeting
her eyes.

"Nice to see you again," Faith said. She looked at
her watch and started to walk away.

"I thought . . ." he began. "I wanted to talk to you
for a minute."

She stopped. A look of concern came into her face. "How is Sheila?"

She *is* nice, Denny thought, and somehow that made it worse. "Don't you know?" he said. "I thought maybe you'd tell me." She heard the bitterness in his voice, the note of desperation.

What's this all about? Faith thought. "I'm sorry but you've got me at a loss. What do you mean by that?" She slipped the pen into the notebook and returned it to her purse. "Has something happened to Sheila?"

"Yeah. Kind of. It kind of has. Mrs. Slater, does Mr. Slater drive around in an old sports car sometimes?"

Her eyes widened in bewilderment. She thought, What's wrong with you? There was something definitely wrong with him. Without knowing why, she was beginning to feel uncomfortable. Still, she smiled. "Well, yes, once in a while," Faith said, "but I don't see what that has to do with anything."

"Is it black and dark red? Is that his car?"

Suddenly, she ran out of patience. "Oh, come on, what is it? Has there been some kind of accident? What're you talking about?"

"Then it is his," Denny said in triumph, as if he'd known all along. "So, Mrs. Slater, what I want to know is this . . ." He started to walk toward her, opening his hands out before him in supplication. "Why did Sheila drive to Vandalia this morning and go off with him in that sports car?"

Faith stared at him, then she stared down at the palms of his hands.

"Know what I mean, Mrs. Slater?" He moved to take her arm but Faith sidestepped back, away from him.

She looked around at the passersby to see if anyone she knew might have heard what he said. Then she laughed, lightly and naturally. "I'm sorry. I really don't know what you mean." There was, now, a dry patch at the back of her throat. "Of course, we are both very fond of Sheila, as we were of her grandmother." The boy was staring straight at her and it was then, exactly then, Faith realized what was wrong with him: he was drunk.

"I think you've had too much to drink," she said. She tried to be firm, but her voice sounded weak to her. All at once, she felt weak all over. Faith wondered if he noticed it, too. "You'll have to excuse me," she said. "I really have a great many things to do. I don't think you know what you're saying."

"No, I'm not drunk, Mrs. Slater. Let me tell you something—"

But she was leaving—it happened so fast. Before he could even reach for her, Denny heard her high heels striking the tile mosaic as she rushed away. Jesus, he thought. She's running away from me.

Faith was across the street, headed into the parking plaza by the time he caught up with her. "Get away from me," she snapped, glaring at him.

He said, "Don't you know what's been going on? Don't you know what they're doing?"

She was walking so fast he could hardly keep up with her. A passerby parted them temporarily. Denny grew even more intent. "Sheila'd say anything to pump things up and make them more exciting. Okay, look, I love her, okay, but she doesn't know what she gets herself into sometimes. You don't know her, Mrs. Slater." But he found himself rushing along beside an impenetrable silence. "Maybe you could talk to her—"

Faith would not look him in the face. "You're drunk," she said.

"Mrs. Slater, maybe if you'd talk to her ..." he implored. "She seemed to like you ... trust you. Maybe you could straighten her out."

Abruptly Faith turned on him. She was far beyond charity now. "You force me to say things, you force me to be unkind. I don't know what's happened between you and Sheila. Whatever it is, I don't care." Faith lowered her voice to emphasize the importance of what she was saying. "But—*but* if you think I'll stand by and let you make these ridiculous accusations, you're badly mistaken. How dare you say these things! There are laws against this—against harassment and against libel. I don't think you understand the seriousness of what you're saying or realize who you're going up against. If my husband gets wind of this, he'll file charges against you ..."

Red-faced, Denny looked away; Faith stared straight through him. "I know, for a fact, that my husband's old car is home right now in our garage. So forget about what you think you saw and leave me alone. We'll always help Sheila as much as we can. But I won't allow you to spread this madness. Do you understand? Don't repeat it. Not one word, or I'll go to my husband myself. I'm doing you a favor, believe me."

He put his hands into his pockets and quickly took them out; he shifted his weight, but in the end, Denny stood with his hands on his hips, staring at the sidewalk. "Christ," he said, "I thought you were nice." His voice was ragged and he cleared his throat. "Okay, so I won't say anything. But, Mrs. Slater, if you don't believe me, why don't you follow them sometime? You'll see I'm not lyin'."

"Not another word," she said. She was white with anger and fear; she was trembling, but her eyes didn't move. She could see that he was just as upset and afraid as she was.

Slowly he lifted his hands in a hopeless gesture, crossed in front of her and walked away. She realized her teeth were clenched so hard they hurt. What gets into people; my God, what got into me!

I don't believe this, Faith thought. I swear to God I just simply don't believe it. The last several minutes had been like a bloodletting. She had done what she had to do, what any wife would do, she told herself. Only now could Faith allow herself to feel sorry for the boy. His pain had been obvious and honest. They've had a big falling out, she thought, and the damned thing lands on me. When her eyes brought him back into focus, Denny Rivera was receding with every stride. Faith looked at her watch again. Time to get home. *I know it's not anything*, she thought, *it can't be. Only I don't see how* ... She shook her head.

The traffic she drove through that late afternoon seemed as distant and removed from her as the background traffic in a movie. Don't be silly, she kept thinking, Henry and Sheila Bonner; it's impossible.

But the Jaguar was not in the garage, as she had believed it would be. She closed the overhead door and went swiftly toward the house. Now, all at once, everything felt disrupted, uprooted. Luisa was just beginning to start dinner and Faith dismissed her. "Take yourself to a movie," she said, "and have a good time." On the nightstand in the bedroom, she found a note from Henry.

Picked up the old bucket—motor needs a tune up. Meeting in Pacific Grove, maybe poker after. Home late. H.

Faith looked at the clock. Ten after four. She took up the telephone and dialed Henry's office. "Abigail, this is Faith. I know Henry's in that meeting in Pacific Grove, but I've misplaced the number he left me. Do you have it? I never know when I'll need to get in touch with him."

Abigail Giddings gave her the number.

She told herself she would put it out of her mind. But some great doubt refused to be still. He's just involved with his work, she thought. At this stage in a marriage, you have to expect this sort of thing.

Maybe he was giving Sheila a ride somewhere. That would be like him. A harmless ride. But then why didn't he mention it in his note? And what was Henry doing in Vandalia—why meet her there?

For a second, she thought of going out again and doing something, anything. She could go to the club. At least there would be someone there to play tennis with. But it was only a moment's attempt at escape. Faith knew perfectly well that she would stay right where she was. This was her place—the one place where she belonged and she would stay.

But how quiet it was. How lonely.

The desolation of the house was complete without him, like a deserted fortress: the emptiness of the bedroom, the useless opulence of the dining room, the vast silent efficiency of the kitchen. Her life was one of tranquility and service. So why did it now seem filled with portent?

At ten till five, she called Pacific Grove and asked for him. A secretary took her number. Faith put the receiver down and kept waiting for it to ring. Standing right beside the telephone, she took off her earrings. She tried to think of something to say to him when he called her back. What would she say? She was so consumed by her thoughts that when the telephone did ring, it startled her; Faith jumped and snatched it up. "Oh, Vern," she said, "is Henry still there?"

No, the ex-senator told her. Henry had been gone for about half an hour.

"Did he say by chance where he could be reached?"

"Sorry, Faith," Tripplet said, "but I assumed he was headed back home."

"I think Henry mentioned something about a poker game."

Tripplet chuckled. "If there's a game, he damned well better have invited me along—but he didn't. I'm sure he's on his way home."

As soon as Faith had hung up, she flushed with embarrassment. What would he think of her calling about her husband? Would he mention it to Henry? How stupid she had been to invite such humiliation—and Henry's volcanic temper.

Toward evening, trade winds blew through the rooms, cooling them, but afterward when the winds died down, the house felt hotter than ever. Twilight was well advanced; the sky was growing darker. She thought, If he was only giving her a ride, Sheila's probably back home by now. In the bedroom, she dialed the McPhearsons' number, and on the third ring, a woman answered.

"I don't believe we've met," Faith told her and then without hesitation, in a move to protect herself, she did something she had never intended to do. She lied.

"I'm Mrs. Marilyn Hughes," she explained, "and I knew Rachel Buchanan years ago, when she was teaching school. I understand that her granddaughter is staying with you."

"Yes, that's right," the woman said. "Sheila's practically a member of our family. She's always welcome here. We're grateful that our daughter, Mary, has such a good friend."

"Mrs. McPhearson, would it be possible for me to speak to Sheila?"

"I'm sorry, Mrs. Hughes, but she's not here right now. Sheila spent the day with a friend and I'm not quite sure when she's getting back. Should I have her call you?"

Faith wound the telephone cord on her finger. "No, it's really not at all important. Please don't bother her. Won't she be moving soon, to live with Mrs. Sanders?" She listened as the woman explained the arrangement. "Then I'll call her there in a few days, once she's settled." As quickly and tactfully as she could, Faith hung up.

She's not there.

On the nightstand was last month's copy of *Art & Antiques*. She turned on the lamp, took up the magazine, opened it in the middle and forced herself to focus on the text. But her heart was beating so hard, she could hardly get her breath. The article had to do with Gauguin; still, Faith's thoughts were so muddled, she didn't know what she read. No matter how much she tried to concentrate on the words, she couldn't. Finally she realized she was waiting for the sound of Henry's car outside on the drive, convinced that he would appear at any moment. But on Condor Pass, nothing moved.

Faith lay back on the bed, on top of the covers.

Her wild imagination kept growing, feeding on her adversity. As each minute passed and he still had not come, she grew increasingly distracted, and she was aching. Faith burned for him. The violence of her feelings surprised even her.

In her hands, she held the stiff sheet of notepaper that once had been white but was now creamy with age and cross-sectioned from its many unfoldings. *Some serious trouble has been brewing a long time that you should know about. This has to do with Henry.*

17

AT SIX, SLATER found her waiting in the deserted lobby of the Casa Del Mar Hotel, where he had arranged for them to meet. No one else was about except for a solitary businessman at the desk. Sheila was sitting in a canvas chair under one of the huge, beige, market umbrellas. When she saw him, she smiled, but just as quickly a cloud of doubt crossed her face, as if she was uncertain she'd done what he wanted. She rose from the chair, gathering her things, and he had what he'd asked for.

She was transcendant. She wore a pale blue-gray evening gown, devoid of ornamentation except for its thin braided straps. The gown clung to her body, eased softly over her waist and hips and fell tapered to the floor with a little excess flare of cloth off her ankles. A slit ran to mid thigh on her left side; it parted as she came toward him. He watched as her long leg slid in and out with each step. Her lips and nails were coral, her beautiful eyes sea colored and her hair more abundant than he'd ever seen it.

She smiled, anxious for approval. "How do I look?" she asked.

He was filled with incredulous pleasure. "You're spectacular," he said, taking her hands. "But we can't stay here on the street. Let's go." A subtle perfume hung over her. All he wanted to do was take her in his arms. Instead, he gathered the three boxes of clothes she had worn earlier and they went around the corner.

"Mr. Slater, don't you like what Mrs. Holt picked out for me?"

He laughed. "Of course; I told you—"

"Yes," she said, "but don't you think I'm pretty?" She stepped out in front of him and did a pirouette.

"Oh, you're prettier than pretty. You're exquisite."

Sheila lit up at his praise. "I'll settle for pretty," she said.

His eyes had a look of mischief Sheila had completely forgotten, one that reminded her of the first time she had seen him when she was ten. Seeing it again this evening erased all the years.

"Where's your car?"

"Here." He was smiling, his face was glowing. "Come, look," he said, directing her toward a polished white Karmann Ghia convertible.

Sheila looked at him. "No," she said, her eyes sweeping the lanes of parked cars for the Jaguar that wasn't there. "Stop teasing me. Where is it?"

"Come and look," he repeated, smiling at her over his shoulder. "Get in." He opened the door for her and started to laugh. "Actually, it's not my car. It's your car." He held the keys out before her.

"No," she said. "No, Mr. Slater, it isn't either. This is going too far."

"All right," he said, "calm down. I'm having some work done on the Jaguar, so I rented this for the evening. And right now we've got to go." Leaving the passenger door open for her, he stashed her boxes of clothes in the trunk and then got into the driver's seat, beside her. "The truth is, you ought to think about it, Sheila. This is a good little car. If you like it, I could help get it for you." She could see that devilment still in his eyes. "Or maybe you'd rather have a new one?"

"Mr. Slater, you know I like it," she told him. "But I can't afford this. You can't seem to get that through your head. I have to face facts and get by on my own and I'm broke."

"Yes, but all that's changing." Then he turned her words around and gave them back to her. "You don't seem to get the point. I said I'd take care of you. I'll buy you this car if you want it. You can test it out on the way home."

He assisted her into the Karmann Ghia, got behind the wheel and they moved into traffic. "You need a good little car," he was saying, "something that suits you. You can't run around forever in that old station wagon. The damned thing's falling apart."

Sheila looked at him, full of uncertainty. "But what would I tell people?"

"You could say you bought it with the insurance money," he told her. "But that's lesson number one. You should never tell anyone what you're doing." His voice had hardened. "It's none of their goddamned business."

"Okay," she said and she smiled. "What's lesson number two?" And they both laughed.

THE COASTAL TOWN of Clementine was in deep shadow when they arrived; they could feel the melancholy of dusk in the air. To the west, the sunset still etched the tops of clouds, leaving the streetlights with the spent, empty glow of imitation pearls. They rode down avenues of palms, headlight beams flickering over gray trunks wrapped in ragged gauze.

"Where are we?" she asked.

He lit a cigarette and let the wind snatch the smoke from his mouth. "Far from home," he told her.

They turned into a street that seemed hardly more than an alley. A mugginess hung in the air, a sticky heat that saturated their clothes. It was even worse when Slater stopped the car and the wind flowing around them suddenly ceased. In the stillness that rushed in, they could hear telephones ringing in houses half a block away.

The restaurant was called simply C'est Bien, its name written with small white lights across its tall brick front. "I think you'll like this," Slater told her, opening her door. He extended his hand, and Sheila's grip tightened in his fleetingly as she swung her legs out of the car, oblivious to the flashing of a nylon-darkened thigh, so taut, so secret and quick it swiped his eyes.

They entered through a small courtyard, with a trickling stone fountain—a narrow walled garden where fig trees and roses and tiny-blossomed star jasmine grew. Vines grew up the walls and over the entryway; tendrils hugged the white awnings. It was quiet and discreet, with an oriental air of privacy. With his hand grazing the small of her back, he led her up the steps between topiary elephants to a black louvered door set in a large archway fitted with black shutters. As if on signal, a gaunt majordomo, his black twill uniform trimmed in gold, opened the door and stepped aside.

Sheila walked by him and felt a cocoon of breath-taking opulence wrap around her. The air was scented and cool; she felt the chill of the marble floor even through her satin slippers. From the corner of her eye, Sheila saw Henry Slater step inside and heard the shuttered door gently close behind them.

The majordomo went behind his large carved desk, hardly looking up as Slater spoke to him. He nodded, checked his reservation book and pressed a button. "Thank you, Matthews," Slater said, watching her now to see her reaction as he came to her side.

"You're making me feel very grown up," she whispered, delightedly. "Is everything all right?"

"Of course. What makes you think it wouldn't be?"

But Sheila hardly heard him, she was in such an excited state. "I don't know." The aroma of hot baguettes, fresh and crusty from the oven, drifted toward her from the kitchen. "Is this a private club?"

"No," he said, warmed by her enthusiasm. "If it were private I couldn't bring you here. I've got a little stake in it, that's all."

"Are you serious?" Her face collapsed behind her hands in soft laughter. "You mean you own it?"

"No. I have an investment."

"I don't believe you."

He winked. "No one knows about my part in this, Sheila, except for the few people I do business with. And now you." Odd the effect she had on him, as if, in all the world, there was not enough air. He felt tight inside, ready to burst out and say things he knew he shouldn't. He could see the enchantment waiting in her eyes.

"I love it here," she said.

Whatever happens, he thought, it will be irrevocable. He knew he was coming to the end of something.

The lobby ran the full depth of the building to another archway, which was glass-enclosed. Three stories up, a long skylight let in illumination that died somewhere above their heads. The walls were lined with mirrored panels; huge crystal chandeliers hung suspended in the air.

A waiter led them down the long corridor past period furniture, plump sofas, soft lamps receding at intervals before them, and Sheila thought there must have been a thousand candle flames flickering—all multiplied a hundred times over in the cross fire of mirrors. And flowers: old fish carts laden with them, huge tubs and pots overflowing with ferns and gardenias, orchids, flowering fuchsia, hibiscus, delphinium and more.

Doorways stood open to large dimly lit rooms. Through the openings came the pleasant murmur of dinner being served, of subdued conversation and the tinkling of silver, glasses, ice. Huge tapestries covered the walls. Slater remained a step behind Sheila, watching for the unexpected familiar face, aware of the huge risk he was taking just by bringing her here tonight.

A waiter led them outside, across a terrace, down a small flight of steps and out a wide white gangway toward a maze of thatched huts some twenty yards offshore. Other waiters jockeyed past them, bearing trays of steaming bowls and chafing dishes. The floorboards creaked, sagged unnervingly under their steps now and then while below, against the pilings, the water lapped steadily. In the huts, behind layers of mosquito netting, figures drifted slowly and in secret, like ghosts.

Drawing the gauzy netting aside, the waiter showed them into one of the huts. It contained a single room, with a round table and a pair of fanciful bamboo chairs. The floor appeared to be covered in cream-colored marble; there was crystal and silver and unlit candles. Like a sacrificial offering, a great sheaf of flowers lay across an antique sideboard. The ceiling was open at the peak, a paddle fan circulated the ocean air. Helping Sheila seat herself comfortably, the waiter then tied back a panel of netting where it faced the Pacific and departed.

Slater moved his chair next to hers. With great propriety, they sat side by side. "I'm sorry about the heat," he said. "We could still go inside if you'd rather."

"But we just got here," she said. "It'll be cooler when the sun goes down."

In the middle distance, the silhouette of a fishing boat went by, its outboard sputtering, a myriad of silver splinters, like minnows, following in its wake. Long after it had passed from sight, its waves splashed against the pilings beneath them.

"It makes me want to dive right in. How about you?"

"Speak for yourself," Slater said, clearly enjoying himself. "What would you like to have to drink?"

Sheila looked at him uneasily. "Can I . . . here?"

"No one's watching."

"What are you going to have?"

"Maybe a martini."

"Okay," she said. "Then, that's fine with me."

"They're fairly potent. Maybe you'd rather . . ."

"No, I want what you're having."

When the waiter returned, Slater ordered champagne. Sheila laughed and waited until the two of them were alone again.

"What's the matter?" she asked. "Don't you trust me? Didn't you think I could handle one little martini?"

"It's not that. I thought champagne seemed more appropriate."

"Oh, I don't care what we have," she said, "except sometimes you treat me like I'm still ten years old. I can take care of myself."

The sleeve of his jacket, that brushed her wrist, seemed to have the texture of some rich and delicate cashmere. It was immensely flattering to be here with him, to feel the attention he lavished on her. After all, he knew so much more about the world than she did. Sheila thought he couldn't really be so pleased with her as he appeared, or so interested in every word she uttered, but it made him wonderfully attractive. When she saw him again after sometimes weeks had passed, it always took her by surprise to discover that he remembered everything she had said the last time they had talked during some brief chance meeting. It was easy to understand why shop clerks and bankers and housewives voted for him, why sixty thousand people, who might have met him once and shaken his hand, called him by name as if they had known him all their lives.

Occasionally, she would see him downtown, the mayor on his way to lunch with other men—an influential man, distinguished and powerful. He seemed entirely different to her then, like a man she had never known and could never know; almost like her own father, whom she had no real memory of and could only imagine. Sheila liked the fleeting sensation of completeness and definition it gave her to think of Henry Slater that way. But tonight, she was happy to be with the other Mr. Slater—the one she had known over the years, who gave her things and didn't mind coddling her, a man whose gray eyes continually smiled upon her with approval.

Presently, a second waiter wheeled in a cart filled with small oval dishes containing hors d'oeuvres and served them, one by one, onto their plates. Sheila nibbled a fantail shrimp dipped in mustard so hot it took her breath and made her eyes water.

"Whooo," she said, "now I've embarrassed myself." She wiggled back in her chair. "I can't sit still. Do you mind if I get up and look around?"

He said he didn't mind. He asked if she still needed to call the McPhearsons, and Sheila told him she already had, while she had been waiting for him in Pacific Grove. It was almost enough then for Slater to unwind in his chair and let his mind become saturated with her—her fingers that ran along the old sideboard and then went to her throat as she bent to breathe the indolent flowers, her leg that peeped from beneath her skirt in a wild, reappearing surprise.

"What about your boyfriend? Won't he wonder where you are?"

"Don't worry about that," she said. "I don't want to talk about him."

"But you're in love with him."

The light changed in her eyes; she was looking at a place in the air between them that he couldn't see. "Something's happened to me since my Gramma's gone and I really don't know if it's me or if it's him, but Mr. Slater," she said gravely, "I don't think I love anybody anymore."

"You're too young to be so cynical. Maybe you do and just don't know it."

He saw her shrug. "I always thought when I really fell in love, I'd do it in a big way. I've known Denny since the seventh grade, almost as long as I've known you, and he's my friend, but we don't get along anymore. We fight all the time and it's—"

The champagne came, interrupting them. Curiosity lured her back to her chair; her manicured fingers lifted her glass in a toast. As they drank she smiled, watching him over the glass's transparent rim. Hers was a look that came with the speed of dreams, a look almost shy—but aware—that no experienced woman could ever duplicate.

They talked and drank, meandering through six courses. They watched the night overtake the Pacific, saw white sails turn gray-purple as the sundown collapsed. In the candlelight that followed, his thoughts revolved only on her. If only I could touch her, he thought. Slater reached out for her hand, and Sheila laced her fingers through his, spontaneously, like a child. At the same time, a photograph of Sheila as a child shown him once by a proud grandmother rose up in Slater's memory and, in an instant, faded. It rocked him. The touch of her, the fact that he always had to seek her out in secret, was a communion with the darkest tyranny in his life. Slater pulled his hand away.

He said, "Sheila, what would you do, if I said: let's go away somewhere? Come live with me and we'll leave all this behind?"

Sheila laughed and slumped back in her chair. "I don't think I could right now, tonight; I think I probably have to wash my hair. Where would you want to take me?"

"Where do you want to go?"

Her eyes were flashing with playfulness. He could see that she was carried away with the charm of make-believe. "I don't know. What would I be—your kept woman?"

"I wouldn't care what you were."

"God," she said, "it would be, wouldn't it—just like being married. Would you ever marry me, Mr. Slater? Would you divorce Mrs. Slater, throw everything away, just to go off somewhere and live with me?"

"What if I would? What if I did that and more?"

Her face, much like his own, was all aglow, a delicate pink in her cheeks. "But you're so much older than me," she said. Then all at once, Sheila couldn't maintain the pretense any longer; slowly her beautiful head turned away. "This is making me really nervous, Mr. Slater. You've always been so nice to me. But I don't always know when you're kidding and when you're not. I think I know and the next minute I'm not sure. You shouldn't say these things unless you mean it, because I start to get carried away—I start wanting to believe it."

"Never mind," he said. "I sometimes start to believe it, too."

After he'd had his coffee and Sheila the chocolate soufflé, while the waiter was clearing their table for the last time, Slater asked not to be disturbed again. Over the years he had stopped believing in simple happiness, only taking real enjoyment in hard-won successes. But with the night outside surrounding them and no one stirring in the dark hut next door, he felt safe for the first time all evening and relaxed completely.

Sheila insisted he undo his tie; she slipped out of her shoes, folding her feet up under her. He saw her toes sheathed in thinnest nylon, watched a wave of gray silk drape over a drawn-up knee. Slater thought he had never seen a girl so dangerous.

"Thank you for this," she said tenderly, her splendid shoulders turned toward him.

Taking the champagne from the ice, she leaned close to refill their glasses, her face passing within inches of his, the tip of her tongue curled on her upper lip. "This is my last one," she announced. "I don't want to get plowed."

"I don't want you to, either."

"Are you sure?" she said recklessly.

"You're really a nice girl," he told her. "I thought you might grow up to be only gorgeous." When he lifted his glass and drank, she watched his fingers, the clean, trimmed nails, the strength of their grasp. "I'm not always so nice," she said.

All evening she had laughed at any trifle, and when she was not laughing she was smiling. Her eyes sparkled. Young and unsophisticated, she had been charming even to the waiters, probably because, Slater thought, without ever being aware of it, she had been trained in trust and decency. Rachel's strict domination had, at least, given her that. "You know what they say about you?"

"No." Her eyes widened suspiciously. "What?"

"That no one stands a chance with you."

"Who told you that?" She tried to laugh it off. "Gramma told me that's what you men talk about. I'm beginning to believe a lot of the things she used to say." Sheila waited for him to reply. Some part of her, schooled in Rachel's caution, was now wary. She shrugged with exaggerated carelessness and smiled uncertainly, not knowing what or how much to reveal about herself. "I . . ." She looked down at the billions of stars reflected in the water. "Do you think I seem like that? I don't give myself as easily as a lot of the girls, if that's what they mean."

Again he waited, still watching her.

"Well, now I've told you almost everything," she

said, tossing it off as unimportant. "But let's talk about something else."

His eyes seemed to her to be softly lit with understanding. "Sheila, don't be afraid to show me how you feel."

She nodded and fell silent. She fingered one of her earrings. Her frivolity wavered. He could see that she tried to laugh again and couldn't.

"Mr. Slater," she said, "you shouldn't take me so seriously. I'm just a girl who looks good in a room. That's all."

Except that he loved her. He knew that now. No one else mattered. At the slightest sign of her discontent, he moved to correct it. In a quiet, humorous voice, he said, "Come on now. Who're you trying to kid? Modesty doesn't suit you."

Sipping the champagne, she looked at him and lowered her eyes, her long lashes nearly touching her cheek. Then, as if she could read his thoughts and knew his mind, she lifted her eyes and said, "Mr. Slater, tell me the truth: why are you doing this? I mean, what do you want with me? I'm a nobody and you're married."

And she saw it come fully into his eyes—the sudden taut leap of fire.

She thought, My God, this can't be happening. She said, "Why do I feel like you planned all this and we'll never be like this again?"

"What time do you have to be getting back?"

"I didn't give a time," she answered. "I said I might be late."

Slater said, "I don't want to go back yet, do you? What if I said I didn't want to ever go back? What would you do then?"

His eyes were fastened on hers like magnets.

"Couldn't we just go for a walk?" she asked. "Some-where . . . maybe out to that point? Unless you'd rather get started driving."

Most of the huts were dark when they returned along the gangways and across the flagstone terrace. They didn't speak. Sheila glided beside him, her body now and then brushing against his sleeve, but she didn't take his arm. A band was playing in the cocktail lounge; while Slater paid the check, she stood near the doorway, listening.

She was only partly aware of the people around her, except once, when she spied a group of young men wearing fraternity jackets. Denny could look like that, she thought. If he wanted to, he could be one of them.

She was completely unprepared when one of the fraternity men asked her to dance and before she could decline, she was whisked onto the dance floor. The musicians let loose, the congas' rhythm releas-ing her to the spirit of the moment, and Sheila surrendered herself to it with the same exuberance she had shown all evening. Unnoticed behind the crowd, Slater went to the end of the bar and ordered a double brandy.

"Who are these college kids?" he asked the bartender.

"UCLA," was the answer. "Guests of Cal Dawkins."

Slater had never heard of Cal Dawkins—that's good, he thought as his eyes slowly canvassed the crowd. He saw no one he knew.

Sheila danced with an abandon that was mesmeriz-ing, so total was her enjoyment in the music and in the evocative shapes she made of it. As she whirled among the other dancers, Slater saw flashes of the clinging evening gown and he felt his throat tighten.

He saw her now in her world, her young world,

lost and immersed in it, irrepressible and resilient and full of life. Once, like a bright ribbon thrown above the music, he heard her ecstatic laughter and it thrilled him. It all seemed so right; Sheila looked completely at home, as if to be dancing among young people was her proper place. And Slater felt drawn to them, wanted to become one of them. Was that what she really meant to him—had she become his last frail link with a world he could never be a part of again?

My God, what am I doing?

I'm in love with that young girl, he thought. Slowly it dawned on him that his plans for the night ahead shouldn't happen. This is wrong, it's all wrong. God, just look at her. How could he hope to hide her away and deprive her of this—this hungry young life? If you really do love her, Henry, you won't draw her into this. You'll let her go. Let her go.

I can't, he thought. I can't. I can't do this.

She danced through two numbers with a succession of admiring partners, and when the set was finally over, she sank onto the stool next to him, her eyes bright, her color high. Sheila leaned against his shoulder, plucking her dress away from her skin. "Oh, that was fun," she gasped, "just what I needed." He put his arm around her and she accepted it without a word.

"Could I have a taste of that?" she asked and he gave her the brandy. With a sip and a shudder, she handed it back.

The band started up again. "Let me have one more," Slater told the bartender, "and we'll call it a night."

No one saw them go out through the black shuttered door. With her arm wrapped in his, her head resting lightly against his shoulder, they stepped into a night that was warm and damp and luminous. Following the path under the coconut palms, they passed behind a row of bathing huts, which were standing like lonely sentinels, canvas walls swelling and collapsing in the breeze. Gradually the path narrowed to nothing. Sheila perched on the low sea-wall, crossing her legs to remove her slippers.

"Let me do that for you," he said and he cupped the backs of her calves, first one then the other, to slide off her shoes. He could feel a shivery ripple run deep into her thighs.

For her, it was one of those inconsequential moments that linger in the mind and take on a kind of immortality. The firm delicacy of his hands seemed to stay there longer than was conceivably possible. Even after he was through and her slippers were removed, she could still feel him holding her legs. A voice inside her said, You'll remember this the rest of your life. Still, he had hardly touched her. This man she had known half her life, and the other man, the stranger, she was sure she could never know.

Telling him to turn his back, Sheila drew aside the slit in her skirt, unhooked her stockings, and took them off, stashing them in her purse. She reached for her slippers. "I know where to put them," he said, and watched as she walked out on the beach, the sand giving way beneath her feet.

Slater took off his own shoes and put them with hers under the base of a spindly lifeguard's station. He rolled the cuffs of his trousers. With his jacket over his shoulder, Slater went across the sand after her, still watching her go before him, with that slow, sliding kick in her stride. He knew that they would never reach the point.

They were quiet, walking side by side. She was trying to recapture the feelings she'd had only a month ago, before her grandmother's murder, but she couldn't. There came into her heart a painful yearning for the world she had lost, irretrievably. The night, the empty beach, the abandoned promenades of palms, only reinforced the emptiness welling up inside her. In front of her, out through the starry dark, stretched the enormous panorama of her loneliness. When she looked around, Henry Slater wasn't looking at the ocean. He was looking at her, and she thought how much she wanted to be with him. She even thought she might do something quite unlike herself, something rash and quite immodest.

She looked down at herself. Here I am, she thought, in this beautiful dress. Gramma would have never let me have a dress like this. Look at my nails; look at my hair. Only he sees me like this. Look what he bought for me. He's made me feel good for the first time since she died.

She waded into the shallow depths, startled by the water's coldness, kicking at it, splashing. Despair washed over her. Now even Denny was leaving her. She walked slowly along, remembering with a strange delectable pain how much she had once liked him too, and how even that was receding from her.

They went along behind an old beachfront hotel, only a few curtained windows burning with lights. Why was he married?

Sheila wondered if maybe it was a mistake to be doing this. She knew what she was supposed to do and think and feel and say—she remembered Rachel saying, "Don't get confused and think you're in love when you're not." But I'm in love with him, she thought, I've always been in love with him.

The moon sailed high, and the strip of sand, broken here and there by upright boulders, curved before them like a long, white tusk, stretching to dark
infinity. Far in the distance, across a gulf of water, a
bonfire burned like a tiny collapsing coal and the
minuscule sounds of laughter and music wafted to
them through the darkness. "It's like walking on the
moon," Sheila said, tilting her head to look at him.

"Yes," he said, "and listening back to earth," while
his eyes explored the terrain. He listened to see if
anyone was about, but around them the air had
condensed to stillness. Only his heavy heartbeat
sounded in it.

He felt the sand sliding and sinking under his feet,
enveloping him. Offshore, he could make out an
abandoned rig of some kind, lightless, rusting—once
in a long while metal clanged with an empty sound.
It seemed, then, that his life was like that rig, stark
and cut off, floating through a gray universe. Waiting. Decades passing.

The scent of the ocean drifted over them. With a
repetitious hiss, the water broke in gentle, ever-
running waves, leaving behind traces of froth. Above
them, the moon shone so brightly that nothing escaped its pale glow and the infinite roof of the night,
shot through with innumerable stars, was like a great
and splendid jewel—it was as if they had stepped
into the dark, blue, sparkling heart of a sapphire.

"I want to tell you something about myself," Slater
said. "There are so many things you don't understand, Sheila; so much I can't tell you and you'll
never know. You have no idea what you mean to
me." Once he had started, his feelings came pouring
out, but his words seemed trivial, like bubbles that
effervesced as soon as they were spoken. Yet he

persisted. "The few times I'm able to see you, it always seems unreal to me. Every morning I wake up and I think about you, I remember dreams about you . . . I never stop thinking about you. Maybe you can't see it, but for a long time, a very long time, something's been going on between us. I think you must know . . . you have to know. If I'm wrong about this, tell me to stop."

Half-turned, she raised her head, and for a long moment she looked at him but with an expression he couldn't clearly see in the dark. Then she looked down again at the sand.

"Tell me I'm wrong about this, Sheila."

"No," she said. She tried to sound firm, but fear and excitement undermined her. "You're scaring me a little."

"I don't mean to scare you." Surrounding the beach was a snarly mass of cypress and maritime pines and one towering weeping beech tree. "I'd never let anything hurt you. Sheila, don't you know me at all? I would never. I'd die first. No one will ever love you the way I do. No one could. You don't know."

He had meant to wrap and bind her with all the things a young girl would want to hear; now, he would tell her the truth. It was as if he had known the words all his life, holding them in, waiting for this moment to spend them, but even as he spoke, Slater wondered what she would do. He half-expected her to try to end it swiftly, to demand he take her home at once, but instead there she stood only an arm's length away, listening.

"What I felt for you years ago just never stopped. I don't know what you think of me or even if you think of me at all, but don't hide from me anymore.

I don't even care if you can't love me, but I want to know."

Slater opened his jacket and set it around her. His hands began to caress her shoulders through the jacket with light, slow, hypnotic strokes. "I love your beautiful face. In my dreams, I hear you laugh. I love the way you move: I love your body. Just the fact that you exist fills me with—it fills my life. You could have any man you want, you know that and I know it, but you won't ever find again what I feel for you. I'd give you anything I have and I have nothing you need. You're the only one I've really cared about—for years and years. Sheila, don't you know what I mean? Haven't you felt it?"

"Yes," she whispered, "I know what you mean."

But he knew she couldn't know the depths he had gone to and there was no way to tell her. He let go of her shoulders. And he knew he couldn't do it; he couldn't end it. "I brought you something," he said. In her hand, he placed the gold necklace she'd left dangling for him in the night.

"Oh," she said. "I had decided you didn't see it." Sheila opened the tiny clasp and slipped the chain around her neck. But still she wouldn't look at him.

He said, "Don't you know I'd do anything for one of your kisses?"

It was then, when all his words ran out, that he saw how sad she seemed, sad and skeptical, both. She raised her head and took a long breath. "You wouldn't lie to me . . . ," she said, "would you?"

"No, I never would."

"Then you mean it . . . what you said?"

"By my sacred oath."

"Oh . . . ," she said, and something that had been knotted up inside her suddenly came undone. Her nervous fingers touched his arm and slipped into his hand, trailing flames along his wrist. She smiled at him, and it was right this time. It made his heart feel impossibly heavy and yet her smile grew until there was nothing in the night but her upturned lips, and he thought, This is wrong but God help me, I can't stop it. I can't. I can't. The stars, the dimness around her faded to nothing; in the world there was only her face and her smile and her tender, trusting eyes.

Her hand went out. His jacket fell from her shoulders and she let it fall. Ever so lightly she put her hands up along the sides of Slater's face as if trying to recognize who he was through touch and then, she closed her eyes and kissed him. With her lips softly on his, she did not murmur or whisper; she opened her mouth and put her life into one kiss—he could feel it vibrate through him.

Never with anyone had she opened and laid herself so candidly bare. She knew that for her there could be no turning back. She put her pain into her kiss, and the awful grief poured out of her, all the lonely hours of her suffering. And when it was emptied from her, all that remained was herself, alone, and her inviolable sad, sweet trust in him. In those brief seconds, she died in his arms; her past died and now she would start again.

Slater didn't speak when she drew away; he knew that his hands were empty. Sheila continued to look at him for several seconds as if coming to a decision all her own. With her back turned to him, she suddenly started to walk away. He was at a loss; all confidence abandoned him. She stopped after a few steps, poised in midstride, muscles tense, as if debating what to do next, and without looking around, she lowered the dress straps from her shoulders.

"Sheila," he said, taking a step toward her, but she took a corresponding step away.

Reaching awkwardly behind her back, Sheila pulled the zipper down and her dress parted like a peel, swooping open to the lowest curvature of her hips. The sight of her came at him with such speed and it struck with such force that Slater felt a moment's foolish disorientation, as if he had never believed that this could actually happen.

With a shrug, the dress bunched at her waist, catching on her hips. She pushed it down, wiggled it over her hips, and then stepped out of it and into the shadow of a boulder.

Her reemergence from the gloom was like an illusion, as if she were cast of moon rays. She was wearing a white lace merry widow. A trifle of lace ran just above the band of her very brief panties. "You bought this, too," she said. "Do you like it?"

"I like everything you do."

"You'll never get rid of me now," she said, in a soft, insatiable voice. "I've always loved you."

"I'll never want to," he said. He took her in his arms and kissed her with burning slowness, until every inch of her smoldered. His hands were still moving over her when she tried to undo his shirt; she unbuttoned one button, then gave up. "You'll have to do it," she said, "I can't get my fingers to work." He could smell the clean scent of her hair, the faint perfume.

"Sheila, this isn't the place for this. Let me take you somewhere else."

She laughed edgily and caught her lower lip between her teeth. "Please let it be here. No one'll come. It's the middle of the night." Lifting her hair from the nape of her neck, she twisted, presenting her back to him. Her bare shoulders were blue with moonlight, blue as dawn. "Undo me," she said. "I can't reach it."

He experienced a sensation like dreaming as he felt the skin he had so long and so often imagined. He unfastened the small hooks down the back of her merry widow. Without hesitation, his hand slid over the taut band of her panties and down across her swollen mound.

"Let me take them off."

"No, Sheila, hold still and let me."

But quickly she had done it. She was trembling. She was naked. A gust blew and she turned her face toward it, lapping it in. He saw the wind harden her nipples, saw her turn dark lavender with moonlight. She still wore her necklace and earrings, nothing else, her hips firm and very round.

"Is this how you've wanted me?"

"Yes," he said. He reached for her but Sheila twisted playfully away. Her eyes never left him. He said, "I believe you're the most beautiful girl in the world." Where the sun had not touched her, her skin was like ivory, a smudge like pale smoke between her legs.

"Then why don't you kiss me again?"

Joyously, he lifted her up in his arms and she threw her legs around him, letting his hands run all over her. When he let her down, she remained close, standing on tiptoe.

"Can I take your jacket?" She stooped and picked up the jacket where she had dropped it. "I'll wait for you," she said. She brushed it off with her hand and hiding nothing from him, walked naked toward the weeping beech tree. Pulling apart the branches, she disappeared among them.

Slater saw himself poised at the brink of a chasm, and all his work, his life as mayor, everything he valued, plummeting into it. I'm risking it all, he thought and dropped his unbuttoned shirt. Pushing off his trousers and shorts, Slater entered the tent of branches. Immediately, she was there; he felt her hair against his cheek, her body pressed to his. "I don't want it to be fast."

He started to answer but her mouth rose to him, still murmuring. "Touch me. Please. Hurry up, before I change my mind."

It was a small space; the two of them nearly filled it. Going to his knees, he kissed the warm hollow at the small of her back, between the dimples from which her buttocks swelled. He was rubbing his hands over them and his hands were like torches. He was quivering, even his voice was quivering. "Lie down," he said.

She knelt facing him and slid down on his jacket. He moved his body slowly, full of reverence, then his hands moved over her again, feeling her, caressing her belly, his fingers searching between her legs and then going on around her until she was completely surrounded by him. With every breath, she shuddered. He pulled her to him, his mouth hard, his body hard. "Kiss me," she said, "keep kissing me."

And he kissed her. In his embraces, she gave him back long kisses, and when she shifted under him, she was wonderfully inexpert, but in full possession of her place. Slater proceeded to kiss her all over, nibbling, biting her gently, scores and scores of kisses, insistent, soft, then fierce, as if she were succulent and he were famished. "Oh," she sighed, "Oh." He sucked her nipples and licked her throat, her body rippling now to every swift stroke of his mouth, and then all at once, he folded his arms under her thighs and sank deeply between her legs.

"You're too big . . . you're too big . . . ," she whimpered, but she was aligning herself, searching for him. Then, "Please, Mr. Slater, don't . . ." and then with the last of her breath, Sheila gasped, "Oh, goddamn . . ."

Suddenly, massively, she felt him entering her.

Everything seemed to stop: he was sliding into her and she felt full of him and it hurt. She could hardly move. For seconds at a time she forgot where she was. Even the ground where they lay seemed to recede. Sheila moaned and clung to him. She leaned forward, pressing her mouth to his shoulder, muffling her cries, feeling him begin to push in and out.

Everything was stopping and going on and on at the same time. Her eyes were shut; she reached down to feel herself with him inside her. And then, for her, it began, and Sheila gave herself up to the long winglike beats of her passion. Her hair was all over her face; panting, she snatched it away.

"A little longer," she pleaded, "a little longer," and she could feel herself enter another dimension of movement, one in which her body claimed its own fluidity and pleasure and speed. And the sweet pressure grew, layer upon layer, wave upon wave, to an intense trembling peak that wouldn't fall. She was like a sleek powerful cat running effortlessly at top speed, muscles gathering and exploding and gathering again. She couldn't slow down, and not wanting to, not even knowing how to, she began to come as he plunged into her; she could feel herself erupt from every sweet nerve, from her fingertips and toes, as she cried out.

For long minutes afterward, he hardly moved. He

wanted nothing more than to stay as he was, completely steeped in her. He sought and found her mouth and his kiss was now lingering and devout. When he began again, he was infinitely slow and tender, his circumference gradually ebbing out of her and just as slowly sinking back in, sensing her with it, tasting and savoring her.

Having her was far beyond anything he had ever experienced before, or dreamed of, or imagined. It was beyond anything that he could have expected or foreseen. Not the act itself, but the enormous purity that surrounded and attended it. For the first time in his life, he felt himself immersed in and bathed by a girl's young body, a girl whose goodness he believed to be unconditional. He had plunged to the very heart of something excellent and divine. A feeling of gratitude welled up in him, that she had given herself so completely. To him. It was as though, in the blind blackness where they lay, her body had slowly shaped and accepted that part of him that had no shape and that no hand could touch. Everything that had troubled him had been left behind without any thought or memory, like a life shed and disposed of after long sleep. The doors of heaven had been torn away and the cold breath of fear that had haunted his heart vanished—only this girl, who opened herself beneath him, this girl who was invested with a wild, improbable splendor that rang over all his life.

There was no need to utter a word, but he whispered into her ear, "Forgive me."

And her answer came back to him. "Oh, yes, Henry. It's all right. I wanted you to."

*   *   *

SHEILA REMEMBERED HOLDING him tightly, not wanting to stop or ever let go, afraid it would never be the same again. When it was over, when, flung out beneath his exhausted weight, Sheila opened her eyes, she saw only the moon-streaked leaves above them. A breeze blew, shaking the air into black and silver bits. Everything was new. Even the darkness itself was transformed.

Slippery with sweat, she lay utterly spent, unwilling to move, reverberations still quivering in her belly and legs. Her body ached all over, oh, not ached, stung, so delicately, as if she had been burned—as if she had passed through fire that had scorched every part of her. Even minutes later, after he had slipped to her side, Sheila was still aware of the fluttering between her legs.

For a moment, she sat up in dazed delirium, her hair a soft cascade in her face. The night slowly resolved into focus although particles of moonlight still stirred above her.

"I never dreamed," she murmured.

"I've always known," he answered.

And that was how it began.

18

THE SOUND ACCUMULATED until it rose above the noise of leaves and the lowing wind—a motor that amplified and then abruptly died against the dew-wet bricks.

Almost three in the morning. Faith raised her unsteady fingers to her face and then forced them to stop shaking over her eyes. All right, she thought, he's here; he's home. What should I do? She heard the car door close and the muffled clatter of the garage door shutting down. She sat on the bed and listened for him until her ears rang with listening. Somewhere in the house a light came on—a thread of dim illumination outlined the bedroom door.

He's got to be exhausted, she thought. He'll come straight to bed. Still, her mind was rampant with questions and doubts. A minute or two later, the light disappeared. What's he doing?

Faith, don't let him see that you've been waiting. Act as though you're asleep. Quickly, she stretched out on her side between the smooth sheets, leaving one leg straight and drawing the other up akimbo, her dark head burrowed into the pillowcase. She draped her arm gracelessly back over her head, arranging the arm in such a way that the crook created a ledge over her eyes, hiding them but also allowing her to watch him, undetected. She could hear him distinctly now: Henry was coming toward the bed-room door. He was whistling, low, between his teeth. Why is he so happy? It's five to three in the morning.

When the doorknob to the bedroom clicked open, her eyes were like an animal's eyes peering out from a cave. Pretending to be asleep, Faith drew slow, regular breaths, feeling the sheet ride lightly on her nightgown. She tried to force her muscles to relax, but her nerves were as tense as wire. His whistling stopped; the door swung open and his big, blurred shape advanced over the threshold.

He was close. She thought he stood perhaps ten or twelve feet away. The closed curtains let in a thin light, dark and coarse as pumice; through it, Faith saw the pale sheen of his white shirt. Why are you standing there? What're you doing? she thought.

Ice clicked against a glass. He was having a drink.

He walked straight to the foot of the bed, where he remained for another minute, looking at her, almost studying her, it seemed. This is ridiculous, Faith thought. I'll just turn over and pretend to wake up. Already words of welcome had formed in her mind; she could hear herself saying, "Oh, I'm so glad you're home." But she didn't move.

Henry took another drink. Again Faith heard the soft clatter of ice against the glass, then the slow release of his breath, as if some pressure had given way within him. He was making a small noise that came from deep within him; Faith had to strain to hear it. He was humming to himself, but after a few seconds it stopped. *Why are you so happy? Did you win at poker?*

He came up the side of the bed. Here, away from the windows, the room was even darker. He slid past her angle of vision. Faith heard him put his glass on the nightstand. She could sense his body near her, big, supple. Henry was taking off his shirt. She saw the blur his arm made in the corner of her eye as he peeled it off, heard it drop with a faint rustle in the chair. Then she smelled him, the scent coming to her of his bare skin and of his clothes, of sweat and cologne, the smell of stale smoke, tobacco and whiskey, all the things she had always smelled on him and loved. She closed her eyes and listened while he emptied the contents of his pockets onto the nightstand.

Her left foot was growing numb and Faith shifted, as in sleep. Instantly, she felt his warm whiskey breath gliding over her arm and shoulder. After a time, he stretched out his hand—some part of him grazed her naked knee. Faith started, but concealed it by turning deeper on her side. He was lifting the sheet over her, and yet seconds had passed before she realized: he doesn't want to wake me up.

She felt the cool, thin material collapse over her and all the time Faith was breathing his familiar smell, still damp with the night's moisture. Now there was something else, too, raw-smelling, fresh, but faint—an odor she recognized. It was old and fertile, as primordial as black mud. Henry had undone his trousers.

She had always found his animal scent arousing. She could almost feel herself falling back, her body opening to him. Faith watched him recede across the room, carrying his clothes and his shoes and she was struck with a violent longing.

She heard a soft click. The louvers in the door to his dressing room were suddenly shot through with light. Putting away his clothes. It's the usual thing, Faith thought, the same as always.

The ladder of light went out, the door opened; she was aware of him going to the bathroom, the door closing, the light that cast a thin white shaft around the door. She heard him start a shower and lowered her arm, looking at the clock. Now it was five *after* three. What should I do? she deliberated. Faith glanced behind her at the felt-lined tray on the nightstand where he had emptied his pockets and saw only a few bills, not the great wad of money he would bring home on a winning night.

I don't think I can sleep. Should I confront him? From the bathroom came the sound of running water. She didn't know what to do. She was lying in bed, in much the same place, head in the pillow, eyes closed, when he came out. Faith heard him sigh. It seemed a sigh of deep pleasure. He started humming, deep in his throat, again. Faith anticipated him lifting the sheet and sliding beneath it, the familiar sag of the mattress. Now come to bed, she thought.

The latch in the door opened. When she could tell by the nature of the silence that he was no longer in the room, Faith opened her eyes. The bedroom door stood ajar, leaving only the stillness behind. The relentless seconds wore on. Her anger mounted, and at the same time, she felt disconnected, outside everything. What're you doing? Why won't you come to bed?

Through the open door, she heard music. Very low and faint. At first, she thought she was imagining it and looked querulously at the clock. 3:12. Faith sat up in bed and listened again, but now the sounds had faded and she was alone in the emptiness. She was about to lie back down, when it started up again. Music. Is he playing music?

That's it, she thought, I've had it. I'm going to find out what's going on. An icy draft of contempt blew through her. She left her slippers by the bed and silently, on bare feet, made her way out the opened bedroom door and down the dark hall. The voice met her as she went forward, floating through the darkness—a melancholy, haunting voice, soaked in violins.

"You ain't been blue . . . till you've had that mood indigo . . . that feelin' . . . goes stealin' down . . . to my shoes . . ."

The music was coming through the closed study door. Faith stopped dead still and listened, her eyes blazing. That's what Henry had been humming only moments ago.

"Always get that mood indigo . . . since my baby said good-bye. In the evenin' when the lights are low . . . I'm so lonely I could cry . . ."

Her face took on an expression of pained surprise. Frank Sinatra?

"When I get that mood indigo I could lay down and die."

It was after three in the morning and he was playing an old Sinatra recording—the same song that he had played for her, again and again, when they were first married. She had been waiting for him all night and the sentimentality of hearing this music again, now, at this insane hour, was overwhelming. Uncontrollably, her eyes filled with tears. On the album, she remembered, there were two tracks that Henry had particularly loved, and this was one of them.

This was one of the songs he had always played for her, years ago, while they were making love.

But he wasn't in bed now and he wasn't making love to her. He was playing the other cut.

"When you're alone . . . who cares for starlit skies . . ."

In the hall, outside his door, Faith began to pace without direction.

"When you're alone . . . the magic moonlight dies. At break of dawn . . . there is no surprise . . . when you're lover has gone."

She wrapped her arms around herself. A sob rose in Faith's throat and she swallowed it. Still she paced the hall, back and forth outside his door—and the pain began to come. He *did* it. He *did* it. She heard Henry's voice weaving through Sinatra's, like a trailing echo, heard one mingle with the other when Henry sang, "There is no sunrise."

His deceit washed over her—Faith felt her entire body break out in gooseflesh. Again and again, her hands doubled into fists and grasped only air. She stalked back and forth in front of his door as Sinatra's ache knifed through her. Would he, she stopped to ask herself, feel her tortured presence outside his door? No. He was oblivious to her.

He was singing. Drinking and singing.

"What lonely hours . . . the evening shadows bring . . . what lonely hours . . . with memories lingering . . . like faded flowers . . . life can't mean anything . . ." Sinatra's voice was the loneliest voice she had ever heard. Her body shuddered; the slow, steady drag of his pain answered her own. She couldn't get away from it. It came and it hurt and her hatred spilled like venom.

You did it, didn't you, Henry?

You did it.

You were with her all night.

All night.

While I sat here.

Waiting.

Waiting and waiting.

You fucked her.

All night.

It's been going on for a long time.

The burning inside her was not simply pain. It was pain beyond pain, a fire all through her body, all through her life.

Trembling with the effort to control herself, Faith stood at his door. *That kid was right.* She took the doorknob in her hand, silently, savagely, and then—

She put her head in her hands and continued to pace. Henry, if only you knew, she thought. If you knew what I know.

This has to do with Henry.

My God, Henry, you're not really doing this? Surely to God.

And she began to crack. She felt a cry surge in her throat and her hands flew to cover her mouth. A terrible premonition, sharp as grief, filled her. You couldn't. She's just a kid—she's still in high school. I know you couldn't. I don't believe it. I won't believe it. No. There's got to be something else, something I don't know. But if not—then why this awful music? Sobs filled her throat, too many, too fast; Faith could no longer contain them.

Sinatra's voice smothered her now with its crushing sadness. Oh, my darling, I don't want to know. I swear to God, I don't want to know.

And then, in her two hands, finally, the tears.

19

LUISA GENTLY SHOOK her for the second time at eight fifty-five the next morning. "Mrs. Slater will want breakfast?" she asked.

"No, Luisa," Faith answered, pushing herself up on the bed. "No, just coffee. You can go do your shopping. I'll help myself." She tried to wipe the sleep from her face and heard the sandals flap softly across the room. "It waits for you," the maid said, closing the door behind her.

Faith sat quietly for two or three minutes, struggling to stay awake. "God," she moaned. *What's wrong with me?* She felt drained, thoroughly wasted. I can't wake up. She rubbed her face again and looked at the clock-radio. Almost nine. Henry would have left for the office over an hour and a half ago.

Her eyes felt scratchy and sore; they ached and her eyelids were tender. I must've been crying, she realized. But in my sleep? She reached around, running her hand over her pillowcase—it was dry. Then it all came flooding back.

She remembered breaking down piece by piece and then fleeing from his study door, not wanting to see him, unable to face him and hear his excuses and lies. She remembered running into the bathroom and swallowing a Nembutal. After the first she gulped down a second in order to be unconscious with sleep before he came to bed. She remembered thinking, Don't let him see you cry like this. At the time, nothing had seemed more important. The last thing that came back to her was trying to suffocate the sound of her sobs in her pillow.

It's the Nembutal, she concluded. That's why I feel so out of it. She had never taken more than one. Her drowsiness came back in waves; Faith let her head fall back into the pillow and looked up at the ceiling, smooth and white and sturdy as a vault. Protected was far from the way she felt this morning.

How could her husband have spent the night with a seventeen-year-old girl?

The threads of deception that wove into something large and ominous and irrefutable the night before, now in the cool wreckage of daylight, seemed insubstantial and full of holes. It didn't make sense. In fact, no matter how it looked on the surface, Faith didn't believe it. Henry wouldn't do something like that. She knew him too well. Of course, he was a gambler; she was convinced, if the stakes were high enough, he would weigh the odds and wager this house and everything they owned for that moment of high tension when the cards were turned. *She knew*. It had happened once before. He loved the risk, the mental maneuvering. It was that fearless, dare-me attitude so many people found attractive in him. Including me, Faith thought. But not this—not Sheila Bonner. For godsake.

"It's absurd," she said aloud to herself. "You went off the deep end and now you're making everything worse by being silly." Faith got out of bed, went to the bathroom and stripped off her gown. She took a long, leisurely shower, letting the hot water pound into her shoulders and then pummel her face. That's what it was. The pressure of waiting for him all those hours had gotten the better of her. I lost it, she thought. Whew, did I ever!

In her robe, Faith padded into the kitchen, poured herself a cup of coffee and brought it back to the bedroom. I must be looking for trouble, she thought while she dried and shaped her hair. And when I do, God puts it there for me to find. All she could do was laugh at herself.

Sitting at her vanity, she made up carefully, putting on mascara and lipstick with the assortment of tiny brushes. What's the matter with me? she thought, blotting her lips on a tissue. Men in power are always viewed with suspicion. It's human nature. They always have enemies. But I can't live like this—suspecting things, doubting every word Henry says. She leaned close to the mirror, studying her eyelids, and saw that the shower had relieved most of their puffiness. I'm in love with him. I've got to stop dwelling on this.

In the dressing room she pulled out an understated, pajamalike blouse and trousers in pink crinkled silk—she knew the color flattered her—and dressed with more speed and ease than usual. Of course nothing had happened. Her earrings were on, and her bracelets. Faith picked up her purse. But before she left the bedroom, she took out Rachel's letter for the last time. She didn't open it; she held it in both her hands. I'm not ever going to look at this again, she thought and tore it in two. The impulse was strong to tear it into pieces—flush it down the toilet. No one would ever know. She couldn't imagine ever having any use for it, and yet, at the same time, she knew that once it was gone it would be gone irretrievably, and in the shadowy depths of her mind a whisper stirred, Don't do it. Keep it. Hide it. So she looked around the room, and instead of tearing it to shreds, Faith slipped the two pieces of the letter under the heavy silver tray on her vanity.

She was grateful for the distracting errands she had to run for the Founders Day barbecue she and Henry held every year. In ten years, their invitation list had grown from less than thirty guests to more than five hundred. For this year's event, Faith had in mind something on the order of a day-long banquet.

Working through the details with the caterer later that morning kept her firmly rooted in the here and now. She was going to make this year's barbecue the most talked-about event of the summer; she would be a credit to Henry. On her way to the marina for a lunch date with Nancy Herbert, Faith felt her world was almost intact again, almost.

After lunch, in the nook under the potted palms at The Wharf, she sat sipping a wine spritzer, listening to Nancy gossip. "Jeannie Whitman! Oh, God, yes. It's madness, of course, but she's left Jack, cleaned out their bank accounts and taken the kids, skidaddled God knows where—with Bernie Piper."

As Faith nodded and smiled at Nancy, she was thinking, What was it that boy said? What had he said exactly?

It was approaching two o'clock when they parted on the sidewalk. Faith liked walking out through the sunlight; ordinarily it gave her a sense of bright, sharp definition. This afternoon, she wondered if it wasn't the residue of the sleeping pills in her system that caused her head to feel so strange and light. Driving to the library for a meeting of the League of Women Voters, she felt an unsettling sense of detachment, as if she had separated from something of great importance to her.

Why don't you follow them sometime?

When she arrived at the Audubon Room, the meeting had already begun. Several of the women already seated turned and greeted her with a smile. Faith recognized every one of them. Tiptoeing to a chair in the back of the room, she was again struck by the same sense of unreality, of separation. It all seemed to her, then, vaguely distorted—that either the women weren't really here or she wasn't. The scene before her—the particular rows of chairs, the guest speaker standing at the lectern addressing the women—was impossibly familiar, yet impossibly foreign.

What's happening to me? She put her purse aside, opened her notebook and took out her pen, trying to give the appearance of being attentive and taking an occasional note. But she couldn't think; she couldn't concentrate.

Mrs. Slater, if you don't believe me, why don't you follow them sometime? You'll see that I'm not lyin'.

She thought for a moment she was going to faint. Was it possible that Henry was actually involved with a very young girl?

If she hadn't arrived late, Faith might have left the meeting right then, but she sat through it, minute by dragging minute, struggling to pay attention to what was being said in order to filter out the dread, to keep at bay the sense that when she stood and went outside, the thing, the failure of her marriage—whatever it was—would still be waiting for her and would devour her.

Finally, she couldn't stand it any longer. Toward the end of the meeting, she had to get up and leave because if she didn't she knew the tears would run down her face. Only one of the older women, a Mrs. Howell, took notice and came to Faith as she was drinking from the water fountain.

"Mrs. Slater," she said, "don't rush off so soon. Don't forget we'll be having cookies and punch after the meeting." And Faith had to explain that she couldn't stay.

She kept telling herself, Nothing's happened. It's just the stress of last night still affecting me. But on her way out, she stopped at the shelf of telephone directories and looked up Marjorie Sanders's address. *1210 Balboa Avenue.*

Starting the car and heading for home, she scolded herself severely, *You said you were going to quit this.* Again she resolved to put it out of her mind, and yet, driving through the old downtown neighborhoods, she began to notice the street signs flashing by. Faith drove slower and slower. There it is, she thought, Balboa Avenue. A sudden surge of anger caused her to press her foot down on the accelerator.

On the deeply shaded street, she watched the house numbers until she saw 1210 on the pilaster of a white stucco house. Taking her foot off the gas pedal, she coasted by the front of Mrs. Sanders's house. A car sat in the driveway, but no one seemed to be home. Balboa Avenue was narrow; the house faced across it, onto a small ornamental park.

Unfamiliar with this part of town, Faith turned and stopped parallel with the house but on the opposite side of the park. She found a gap in the hedges and evergreens where she had an unimpeded view of the stucco house. She checked her watch. It was three-forty-five; she had decided she could wait no more than a half hour. *Why don't you follow them sometime?* What Faith really wanted to do was to follow Henry, but she knew it would be too risky. He would recognize her car.

Twenty minutes later, a white Karmann Ghia convertible swung into the drive at the side of the white stucco house and the figure of a girl ran for the front door carrying a bundle of what appeared to be clothes. Faith was too far away to be certain who it was, even after the girl put the bundle down and fumbled for a key. But she *knew* who it was.

A blonde like that—there was little room for doubt.

THEY HAD DINNER guests that Friday evening, and in light of the bombings, Faith wondered at Henry's expansive mood. He ate as though famished; he poured and filled glasses and drank wine. When the conversation turned serious, when the only thing anyone wanted to discuss was how to protect themselves from these madmen, Henry cajoled them back into feeling safe again. He razzed; he teased the men's wives. These were their oldest friends, but even so, Faith listened to his reassurances and watched him again become a consummate politician in the face of this crisis.

After dinner, as the men walked out on the veranda with their brandy and cigars, she overheard him offering to loan Jack Sutcliffe ten thousand dollars. She thought, Where did a young girl like that get the money to buy a sports car?

When the last couple sped into the night, Henry turned to her. "Let's get to bed, Faith, what do you say? I'm beat." He was asleep before she had changed into her nightgown.

In the middle of the morning on Saturday, he said, "Faith, I'm going to run into town and see if I can talk to Reeves. Then maybe I'll find a game somewhere. You want to meet me at the Rod and Gun around six-thirty?"

Faith gave him a ten-minute lead and drove down to Balboa Avenue. The white Karmann Ghia convertible was gone. She pulled away. She could feel the pressure building inside her, drop by drop, but the car's not being there didn't tell her anything. I can't believe I'm doing this, she thought.

At five-thirty—an hour early and dressed for the Rod and Gun Club—she sat waiting on the other side of the park. The white Karmann Ghia came back at six-fifteen. It seemed an odd, coincidental time for Sheila to be returning—Faith had barely enough time to get to the club.

On Sunday, after a late and leisurely breakfast, she didn't wait to hear his excuse for not staying home. She wanted to see what he would do. "I'm thinking I'd like to drive into San Francisco," she said, "and spend the day browsing through the galleries and antique shops—would you like to come along?" He appeared to consider it for several minutes before he said, "I've got a lot of things I should do around here. Why don't you go without me?"

At the bottom of Condor Pass, where the hillside met the city, she pulled into the back parking lot of the combination gas station-coffee shop. With her car concealed among other cars, she went inside, took a booth near the large front windows and ordered coffee. Then she waited, watching the hill road for Henry's car to appear. Her fingernails tapped on the Formica tabletop. If he was going to go to the girl, Faith had given him a clear field—to do so. She wondered if she had been too obvious about what she was trying to set up. She waited, sipping cup

after cup of coffee, until the waitress became a nui-
sance. Nearly an hour and a half had passed. He
wasn't coming. Convinced that if he was ever going
to, Henry would still make a move, she paid, went
out and drove to the park across from Balboa Avenue. The white Karmann Ghia sat in the sunny drive.

It wasn't until after lunch that Sheila went out.
Faith followed her all that Sunday afternoon. She
was clumsy at it, at first. On Canyon Valley Drive,
she saw the girl going into her grandmother's house
and drove past, thinking, This is stupid. By three
o'clock she was trailing behind the little car more
easily. Patiently, silently. Faith watched Sheila go into
Mary McPhearson's house. Minutes later, the girls
came running out and jumped into the car. She's not
doing anything out of the ordinary. Stupid. Stupid.
But she made herself stay with them.

In his rusty old Bronco, Denny Rivera pulled Sheila
over in the late afternoon and Faith quickly stopped
at the curb only a few cars back, afraid of driving
past and being seen. She saw him grab Sheila by the
arm and yell, "All right! To hell with you then! I'm
going tomorrow. Don't you think I know what you're
doing behind my back?" Sheila pushed him away
then, and Denny pushed her back. Faith could hear
their raised voices but she couldn't make out everything they said. She didn't want to know what they
said. Doors slammed. Tires burned. Denny was gone;
Sheila drove away.

Faith couldn't remember ever spending a more
miserable or humiliating afternoon. I'm never going
to do this again, she thought. This isn't like me. And
besides, it's a complete waste of time. Chasing around
after a high school girl! *For godsake!* I'm just not
going to do this anymore.

On Monday evening, Henry called to say he would be in meetings until late. "Mr. Slater not coming home again tonight?" Luisa asked as Faith sat at the dining room table, looking at his empty place. She could hardly bring herself to answer.

On Tuesday, they had a quiet dinner at home, then he had to leave.

Late Thursday afternoon, when she hung up the telephone after he had called, she said, "Luisa, you can stop making dinner and take the rest of the evening off. I won't be needing you tonight."

Faith was wearing a black velour sweatshirt and black velour sweatpants and she had her car keys in her hand as she went out.

20

DOING SEVENTY ON the interstate, the girl's white Karmann Ghia switched lanes and dropped from sight on the Bay Court exit. A few seconds later, Faith executed the same maneuver, sliding across lanes, cutting dangerously in front of another car and hitting the exit ramp in time to see, at the bottom, the girl's brake lights go dark as the car turned left.

At the bottom of the ramp, Faith hesitated at the stop sign, shifted gears and turned quickly in the direction the girl had gone—to the left, through the underpass. In the distance, perhaps a quarter of a mile away, she saw the rear of the white car sink into a tree-shadowed curve and disappear.

It was twenty past six—clear, deepening dusk. Faith knew she had to remain far enough back not to be seen but close enough to the Karmann Ghia to keep it in sight. I can't stand it anymore, she thought. I'm going to find out what you're doing or know the reason why.

Running beside a stream, the road twisted and curved, crossed a narrow bridge and cut due east through rolling farmland. Now and then, through the frieze of branches, she spotted the white car shooting away before her over a knoll. But the distance between them continued to widen. Faith thought, She's driving too fast for this road. Then it occurred to her: she's got to know this road like the back of her hand. Again, coming up over a rise, Faith caught a glimpse of taillights blazing, dipping from view.

She was trying to keep track of her mileage. She pushed her own speed up to fifty—as fast as she dared to go—and held it there. When she had driven about fourteen miles from town, she came over a hillock and saw the land fall away in a long sweep of fields. In the twilight, the road descended through it like a snail's shiny track. Not a glimmer of taillights met her gaze, not a speck of metallic white paint— the girl and the car had vanished. Only the winding ribbon of pavement lay before her.

What's happened? she thought.

Immediately, she let up on the gas and put her foot on the brakes. Clasping the wheel, she looked around. It's not possible, she said to herself. Nothing moved. Off to her right, at the top of a grassy ridge, she saw a thin veil of dust flying in the wind. *Where did she go?*

Did Sheila pull off the road? Could I have passed her without knowing? Not possible, Faith thought, angrily. No, I couldn't have; I would've seen her.

She tried to calculate how far the girl had been ahead of her—half a mile, a quarter—and couldn't. *She has to be down there somewhere.* Faith continued driving for another mile, then two, then three miles, carefully looking for a place where the girl could have pulled in and stopped. She passed entrances to pastures, long rising fields edged with trees, a graveled place beside a big oak—the Karmann Ghia was nowhere in sight. *She got away from me. But how?*

An intersection appeared before her, a one-lane

dirt road that crossed the pavement at right angles. If Sheila had slowed to take it, Faith would have noticed the boiling up of dust, even at a distance. And yet, as far as she could see down the sandy side road, the air was clear.

Dust, she thought.

All at once she wheeled in the crossroads and went hurtling back. That dust, that damned *dust!* Now she could think of nothing else.

The fence surrounding the old orchard was broken out completely between its posts. She could see what appeared to be parallel indentations in the grass as if, long ago, a lane had been there—a lane that was now completely overgrown with grass. So that's it, she said to herself. That's got to be it. Wherever the girl had gone, it lay over that ridge.

She pulled through the broken fence onto the grass until the car was safely off the paved road. She turned the engine off, set the emergency brake, and taking along her purse and keys, got out of the car. A gust of wind whipped around her.

She discovered two shallow paths beneath the grass, with a slight hump between them—she could feel the topography beneath her shoes as she went up the rise. It left no question in her mind: it was a kind of invisible lane and it led somewhere.

At the top of the ridge, she drew a deep dizzying breath of sweet honeysuckle mingled with wood rot. She had the illusion she could see for miles, like a hawk. In the immediate valley below her, in the hollow between hills, sat an old farmhouse—it was so well concealed among trees that, at first, it appeared not to be there at all. Walking higher along the ridge, Faith could make out a shed or stable adjacent to it. Behind the shed, a stream ran to the ocean through a wide gorge in the hills and there, at the end of all she could see, lay the Pacific. The sun was going down in the west, giving the valley and the farmstead a brilliant patina.

But there was no sign of the Karmann Ghia.

This isn't right, Faith thought. Where could she have gone? If the girl had come this way, the farmhouse was her only possible destination—the creek would have prevented her from going farther. *So where is she?*

Faith wiped her eyes. The top of the ridge was worn, sparsely matted with grass, the earth dry and powdery. She kicked up a little puff of dust. I'm not seeing something. She turned, still wondering, still looking around, and started back toward her car.

Maybe it was the nap of the wind-blown grass or the angle at which she looked or the shadow that had fallen across the back of the hill throwing it into stark relief, but she noticed it, then, clearly: the grass chewed in places, bruised by the tread of tires—the unmistakable twin tracks of tires, one of which ran between her feet. *She is here! She did come this way!* Faith whirled and ran back, up and over the ridge.

At the bottom of the long slope, a broken line of hedge flanked the imaginary lane, setting the house and yard apart from the derelict orchard. The evening was very still. Crickets were chirping all over the hillsides—a noise like slow, incessant sleep.

Its upper story hidden in leaves, the back of it built into a steep bank, the early nineteenth-century farmhouse looked as much a part of the landscape as the massive gray oaks that sheltered it. A spooky desolation hung over the barn lot; a soundless night bird darted through the air. Not a light burned in the house. The grounds were deserted; no one was about. On the other side of the tiny front yard, Faith could barely make out a pond shining up like a mirror in the dusk. *Does someone live here?*

Never had she felt so alone and exposed. The main road over the ridge, where she had left her car, seemed to exist in another world. A voice in her head kept repeating, Don't go in there. Go back. *Go back.* But she knew she had to do it. I won't be able to live like this, she thought. Forever in the dark, never knowing from one minute to the next what's going on. I just can't bear it one more minute.

Her hearing sharpened for the slightest disturbance, Faith looked back to estimate how far she had come and then went on toward the old stable—the only place where Sheila could have hidden her car. The weathered clapboard siding showed dull gray in the twilight. Keeping an eye on the front of the house, half-expecting someone to rush out demanding to know why she was there, she crossed the pebbled barn lot as silently as she could. To Faith, even the soft grit of the gravel under her sounded grotesquely loud.

Suddenly there was a deafening shriek. Her fist clasped to her chest, she twisted, eyes startled, searching the empty lot. Again the wind blew; the weathervane atop the stable roof pivoted, metal scraping metal.

Completely shaken, she reached the only true door among the six closed stalls and tried the handle. The door opened; she stepped inside. She was in a dark vestibule, a sort of wind trap, then in front of her, a second door. She opened it and took the step down into the stable. The deep room was dark, shards of light filtered through chinks in the siding, but even before her eyes completely adjusted, Faith recog-

nized their cars—Sheila's white car and, parked beside it, Henry's dark Jaguar.

She felt sick. It was as though she had never once
expected it. So they're here, she thought. They're
here, together, after all. In admitting it to herself,
she grew weak, her legs melting under her. When
she put her hand out to steady herself, her fingers
brushed across a light switch. Faith hesitated, then
flipped it up.

A single bare light bulb came on above an old
workbench, cluttered with tools. She saw that the
Jaguar XK 140—which he had said could take a few
months to restore—was already done, the new black
and burgundy paint sparkling, the rechromed bump-
ers smooth as bright silver. And the leather, the new
dove gray leather—she could smell it across the room.
Kept here, secret from her. All of her anguish attached itself to that beautiful little car and she nearly
wept. Instead, she let the misery she had felt, all the
hate she had tried to suppress come to a boil.

And then, after that, everything came a little
unstuck.

She thought, They're here . . . someplace . . . hiding from me.

The next minute she was wondering if they actually knew she was there. Surprise would be to her
advantage, not theirs. Faith turned and went out of
the stable, carefully shutting the outside door and
crossing the pebbled drive. Now the crickets seemed
to mock her with their raucous chatter. The flagstone walk leading to the house was so old that dead
moss withered in the crevices. She stepped up on the
shabby porch where the windows were boarded shut.

She had an urge to bang demandingly at the front
door, but she wanted to come upon them together.

Determined, now, to put an end to this thing, Faith wanted blatantly to expose him, whatever the result. Without making a sound, she tried the doorknob. It was locked.

Shading her eyes, she squinted through a knothole, but the room inside was dark. Where are they? In minutes, it would be night. Time was abandoning her. Faith looked over her shoulder for the sun, trying to gauge how much longer she would have its waning light, but the sun had gone down over the Pacific.

What was that? She stiffened and raised her head. Not a breeze sighing on the eaves, no, but a sound like that. Or a bird cooing.

Quietly she went down the porch steps and looked straight at the windows upstairs—open windows. And there it was again. *Music.* She thought, crazily, *it is music*—leaking from the windows. Maybe that was why they hadn't heard her. As though from faraway, a note of laughter passed above her head; it was a sound that almost wasn't a sound, drowning in the music. It lurked. It played on the air, like a whisper, teasing, mocking her through the red-gold gloom.

She thought, They're upstairs.

It's got to be them.

Moving as silently as she could, she went down along the side of the house toward the rear, looking for a means of getting up there, some other entrance. The back of the house was built into the slope of the hill behind it, but she saw no door. Faith started backing up. Maybe on the other side. She noticed a kind of beaten path going up through boulders at the side of the slope—there wasn't enough time to search for anything else. Crossing through weeds, she started to climb among the large rocks.

She climbed until she found herself shielded behind a large protruding boulder and across from a rear window. The window was open.

She heard them before she saw them. Small but unmistakable sounds.

Through the music, a girl was moaning.

Then Faith heard his voice.

And in a gap of silence on the record, there were other sounds. She had no trouble recognizing them; they were all too familiar. Instinct warned her, Don't look. Don't. You really don't want to look.

The window was open and gave in on a small dim bathroom with its door ajar. Through it she could see a portion of a larger room, which was fire colored; even the shadows were molten. The harder she looked, the smaller the room seemed to become. At first, against the vivid glare, Faith hardly realized what she was seeing. She thought she saw only the girl kneeling face down on the bed. Sheila was swaying up and back, gently, rhythmically.

This is evil, she thought. This is an evil place.

Still rocking, Sheila unfolded, rising, pushing herself up on her arms and the radiance streamed in, tracing her bare pink body in gold. From beyond Faith's angle into the room, dark hands came up, rubbing the young full breasts. For an instant Faith felt the insane urge to be touched in just that way.

Sheila wiped her mouth with the back of her hand, arched up, slipped lower on the bed and bent downward, her hair a gold turbulence, and Faith saw what they were doing, where her mouth went, the man she straddled. Then his voice, Henry's voice: "Sheila . . ."

Hearing him say it sent the blood singing through Faith's head, but already her eyelids were shut, while the hard thumping of her heart went on and on as though it would never slow down. She didn't re-member getting down from the hill. Her face burned with blood as if she had been beaten. "Caught you," she whispered, no louder than her breath. Eyes closed, fighting to keep herself quiet, she was standing deathly still, shaking with hatred, wave upon icy wave of it.

"Caught you," she murmured. "Caught you at last . . . you stinking bastard."

So it was over. It was *all* over. She would no longer have to suspect or doubt anything about him. *She knew.* Finally, she knew, after eighteen devoted years of marriage. Faith's rage gathered until it loomed stronger and larger than she was. She hated him. Her body throbbed with it, her chest ached with it, her face was consumed with its fury. *I'm going to kill you.* Taking up her purse, she stalked across the pebbled lot. *I'll set the fucking house on fire.*

She spent swift, urgent seconds digging inside her purse, sifting through its contents for matches, but none were there. Inside the stable, she found a hatchet, the blade the color of gun metal except for its sharpened edge.

Adrenaline blew through her veins. *I'll kill you.*

Grasping the stubby handle in her fist, she whirled to go back to the house—and noticed their cars. No one was escaping this. She was crying by then, sob-bing, tears running from her open, angry eyes.

The hood of the girl's car was still warm; Faith put it up and swung the hatchet, driving it down with a careful, deliberate fury, the blade hacking through hoses and wires. The wires she couldn't cut, she yanked out with her hands, connectors popping from spark plugs.

The noise, she thought suddenly. *They'll hear me.*

She ran to the door and peered across the barn lot

at the house, waiting for Henry to come tearing from it. But no. They had music on and they were too far away to hear. There was nothing to hold her back. Faith rushed back to the Jaguar's hood, folded it up and over. Again she destroyed—new red rubber hoses, new electrical wires, anything she could cut.

When she was sure both cars were immobilized, she felt a welling up of gleeful relief, yet she was still shaking with hatred—trembling so hard she thought the air around her shook with it. "To hell with you," she gasped, barely able to speak. "To hell with you both."

Sweat covered her face, and she could feel it dripping down her sides, under her arms. Tossing the small hatchet aside, Faith grabbed her purse, flipped off the light and ran out, closing the two doors behind her.

The music still leaked from the windows. *They're still at it.* A flurry of stars lit the night sky. *I'm going to be sick.* She reached the split row of evergreen hedges barely in time; she stumbled into the weeds, doubled over and threw up. Grabbing a handful of waxy branches to keep from falling, she vomited a second time and then, feeling weak and light-headed, she straightened to look back at the house. No lights burned.

She started to sob uncontrollably as she scrambled through the darkness up the hill. By the time she got to her car, she was calm. Deathly calm. Caught you, I caught you. She started the motor, shot back across the pavement, ground gears and tore away.

21

NINE-THIRTY.

They dozed, Sheila curled to his side, her arm draped loosely over him. The upstairs room was like a black ship adrift in the slow, spinning currents of starlight. A breeze stirred the air; Sheila's lashes rose and fell and she was awake. She didn't want to be awake. She touched Slater's hair and then held it between the scissors of her fingers, thick and damp and luxurious. "You're so warm," she whispered.

She waited, but he didn't answer. Dreamlike, with a slow, roving hand, she felt the hair on his chest, then his stomach, his genitals. She nestled her cheek against him for a moment, then raised her head and kissed his ribs, looking up at him, smiling.

"It's late," he said, quietly. He shifted, stretching out, and reached to turn on the night-light. From its sconce, the white beam leapt up the wall, spilling its reflection over them. He took up his watch, looked at it and put it on his wrist, but all the while Sheila was sliding on the bed. She kissed his chest, then turned her head toward him again.

"Yes," she said, "yes, I know."

The house was quiet as a stone. "Come here first," Slater told her and drew her into his arms, bringing the sheet up over them. She was damp with his sweat. She liked the intimacy of being here, hidden with him, the world awaiting them outside—so far away, it seemed.

"I love it here," she murmured.

"This place?" he said. "It doesn't exist. It disappears when you're gone." He ran his hand between her legs and Sheila wanted it never to end. This was the feeling of time standing still, waiting for her, that she always wanted, having him inside her and the forgetting. "I want it always to be like this," she whispered. "So you'll never forget me." She tried to grasp his hand with her thighs when he took it away.

"I never forget anything about you," he said. He got out of bed, and she went after him, playfully throwing her arms around him, pulling him back. "Now I've got you," she said, smiling up at him. "Come back."

"I think I'd better not," he said.

Her arms went tightly around him in an impulsive embrace. She was keenly aware of who he was going home to. She covered his shoulders in kisses, took his hand and slid it under the sheet, onto her skin. "For a minute . . . ," she said, "for just one more minute."

"No, Sheila," he said. He disentangled himself from her a second time. "I've got a full day tomorrow, even if you don't."

"Won't you ever stay with me?" She stroked the bed between them.

He started to laugh. "You know I have to go home. Come on, get with it." He pulled the sheets from her and she lay there naked, her breasts curving softly toward her upper arms, her eyes half-closed watching him. He groaned and looked away.

"My God," he said, "you drive me crazy." He took his clothes into the bathroom to get dressed.

Sheila rolled into the middle of the bed. I don't want you to go home to her, she thought. In the other room, she heard him turn the water on. The bed was a cool white field and she luxuriated in lying there, hearing him move about. On the other side of the world, Faith Slater would be waiting for him, Sheila was sure, in an elegant silk negligee. After a moment, she stood and slipped into her brassiere. She knew how dangerous this was for him politically. But I'm taking risks too, she thought.

She was pulling on her khaki shorts when he returned to the room, immaculate and distant now in his thoughts, his neat, dark hair with its silver cast, his shirt dazzling white, the creases sharp in his trousers. It was as if for a while they had forgotten who they were and now had to assume different identities. It always left her feeling a little unstrung.

He watched as she finished getting dressed, as he always did, admiringly, she thought. Sheila buttoned her blouse, stepped into her Weejuns, ran a comb through her hair.

When she was nearly ready, he went around the room closing and bolting the windows. He turned off the night-light and flicked on the flashlight in his hand. In the few minutes that remained they would say very little to each other. As she turned to leave with him and he took her arm, Sheila felt unaccountably vulnerable, as if she didn't quite know where she was. He must have sensed it for he took her in his arms and kissed her, saying he was sorry that they had to go. All the things she needed to hear.

They went down the old stairway, where she waited for him to lock the steel door on the landing, and on out across the gutted parlor to the front door, which he also locked. A full moon had risen in the east; the night was bronze and black. A step or two ahead of him as they crossed the barn lot, Sheila turned, stepped quickly up to him and kissed him. "Tomorrow, then," she whispered.

"Yes," he said.

"Where? Could we go for a moonlight swim?"

"Is that what you want to do?"

"I'd love it."

She was still ahead of him when they entered the stable and she opened the second inside door, reaching through the beam of his flashlight and hitting the light switch. A pungent chemical odor assailed her and she turned her head, questioningly, but already Slater had pushed past her.

"My God," she said, swallowing her voice.

They stood a few steps apart, surveying the wreckage: the hoods of their cars gaped open, bits of wire and hose were strewn about, dark liquid stains soaked the floor. "What the—" Slater said. "Who the hell did this?" For the barest instant, he stared at Sheila, jaw muscles clenched, eyes cold. "Who did this," he kept muttering, "who did this?" There was a sudden hardness about him that made her want to back away, but just as quickly, his eyes shifted back to the room.

Someone knows.

All at once, Slater flew past her outside. In seconds, he was back, still studying the darker corners of the stable. "They're gone," he told her, his voice choked with tension. "Whoever it was—they're gone."

Sheila wanted to touch him for her own reassurance, but he trailed into the room, crouched and picked up a few of the severed strands of wire. He examined the ends as he stood, then slapped them against his pant leg like a cat-o'-nine-tails. "Look at that," he said, motioning toward their cars. "Would you look at that? Christ, look at it! Son of a bitch!"

"You're scaring me," Sheila said. "Do you think someone did this because of me?" She could see how hard he was trying to overcome his rage. "But who?" she said. "Who would do such a thing?"

"I think you know," he said.

"Me? Are you kidding? No, Henry, I swear . . . I don't . . ."

"That goddamned spaced-out boyfriend of yours."

"No . . . *Denny?* No. He's not even around this summer. He's seventy miles away from here."

"We'll see," Slater said. "If it's not him, I don't know." She could feel the anger in his voice. "But you'd better damn well believe I'm going to find out."

"Well, it's not Denny. I can prove it; I can call him—"

"Don't you dare. Don't you even goddamned think about calling him. That's all the hell we need—"

"Why are you so mad at me?" Sheila said, aghast.

This seemed to bring him to his senses. "Christ," he said, now angry with himself. "Christ, I'm sorry. Sheila, I'm sorry." But even as he was comforting her, he realized the immediate danger they were in. *Someone knows!* The thought of it wouldn't let him alone. *Someone knows. Someone knows.* He was covered with sweat, a burning cold sweat. With the back of his hand he wiped his eyes clear. He had loved her too much and far too long, now, ever to give her up. "We've just got to be a thousand times more careful from now on."

"I've wondered all along," she said, softly, "if we

could really pull this off. I've dreaded that something's going to happen every minute. Now I can't even get home."

"We'll find a car," he said. "I'll go find a car."

"And leave me here? No way. I'm sorry, but Henry, there's absolutely no way I'm going to stay here by myself tonight."

"All right," he said, "then we'll have to walk it. It's going to take us all damned night."

"I don't care," Sheila said, heading out as he reached to take her arm. His fingers were hard as they pressed into the soft flesh of her underarm. "Ouch," she protested. "That hurts. Don't do it so hard."

Slater immediately let go of her and went about shutting up the stable and locking the outside door. Even then, as they followed the white beam of his flashlight into the darkness, he could feel it all along his spine, like ice, terrified of looking back as if a dark shape stood watching them. Not since that morning in the garden with Reeves had he felt so close to the edge.

Slater couldn't think straight. None of it was making any sense. Who would do a thing like this? If it wasn't that kid. No matter how ridiculous it seemed, only one name continued to surface, again and again, in his thoughts. *Reeves.*

But Reeves wouldn't stoop to this. Would he?

My God. Was he here? Trying to force my hand? *Does Reeves know?*

22

FAITH WAS HOME, in her dark bedroom.

Leaving the light off, she sat on the side of the bed, hands folded in her lap, wretchedly and convulsively crying. She had cried before but tonight the tears rose from the depths of her body, hard wracking sobs.

"Oh stop it . . . ," she gasped. "Oh, God, stop it . . . please make it stop!" Her face, her neck, her collar were all soaked with tears. Now her monstrous rage had compressed to a white burning core.

I knew it was coming, she thought. I could smell it.

Oh, grow up, she told herself, and live in the modern world. *"But I'm not modern,"* she said, weeping, *"I'm not modern."*

It hurt. Oh, God, it hurt so bad. It hurt like a son of a bitch.

He loves her.

She simply couldn't make it stick in her mind.

Wearily, Faith sat there, shuddering, staring out at the night. With every convulsive breath, she could feel him being ripped from her insides. All the time, she was listening for the sound of his car on the drive. Everything was waiting for him, she was waiting for him, the house waited. Condor Pass was quiet and empty; no one drove by. Henry would come home that way. The clock showed a few minutes past eight-thirty. How could it be so early?

It was still some minutes before she realized he would be late coming home tonight. Very late. If at all.

"He loves her," she said aloud. She seemed to speak by rote, as if she had rehearsed saying those three easy words so many times that they were now stripped of all importance, devoid of all feeling.

Well, Faith, what're we going to do now?

Presently she stood and went into the bathroom. She flipped on the light. Who was that woman in the mirror with the wrecked stare? Her face was streaked with grime, her eyes so red they seemed bloody. That was when she noticed it for the first time—the cold hardness in her eyes. It made her uncomfortable; she pushed the image from her mind.

What can I do?

Faith sat on the edge of the bathtub and looked at her hands. Her palms were red, nails broken. There was a thin, brown scratch of dried blood on her left thumb. I must have done it on those wires, she thought, distractedly, but she couldn't remember. It was frightening how little she could actually remember.

Turning on the tap, she splashed handfuls of cold water on her face. "I mustn't let him see me like this," she muttered as she undressed, dropping her clothes where she stood, stepping into the shower. The ice-cold water took her breath. Afterward, she felt refreshed but drained. With her hair in a towel, she put on a nightgown but quickly changed her mind. I can't stay here, she thought. In the dressing room, while she slipped on clean clothes, she began to actually think it through. I don't want to see him.

She would give anything never to lay eyes on him again. She dried her hair, brushed it into place. *He doesn't know it was me that was out there; he still may not know anyone was there at all. If he'd seen me, he would've come down. On some pretext.*

She could almost hear him fabricating his lie. *That's what he would do.* She trimmed her broken nails and rubbed lotion onto her hands. *Henry wouldn't hide. Sheila would hide, yes, but not Henry.*

Going back through the bedroom, Faith turned on her bedside lamp and sat at her vanity, quickly applying the rudiments of fresh makeup. "I wish to God I'd never gone out there . . ." Deep in her memory, she heard her father's big, mocking voice, "If wishes were pennies, Faith, we'd all be rich."

With an ease and control she did not feel, she painted her fingernails. *Henry won't know who trashed his car. He can't. The farmhouse was dark; he was still in bed—with* her. *When could this have started?* Faith remembered him looking at his watch. *We were at dinner. And the stinking son of a bitch was fucking his brains out all along. No telling how long.*

Too late, the web of his lies seemed utterly transparent. Looks Henry had given her, offhand remarks, even his impenetrable silences took on significance where none had been before. In her mind, Faith could still hear his excuses for working late or for playing poker into the night—poker games from which he had begun to return empty-handed. *I should've known. I should've.* "I've got to stop doing this," she muttered to herself, "before I lose my head completely."

Fanning her wet fingernails before her until they dried, she paced the room. *If Henry thought about it, logically, he could probably figure it out—that it* could only have been her. Yet she knew he seldom gave her a second thought now. Would he believe that she could do that? Not Faith! Not stylish Faith. Oh, Faith has much too much style ever to do such a thing. She drew a grim satisfaction from that.

But if he sees me now, he'll know. I can't stay here.

All at once, desperate with the thought of his coming home, Faith started throwing clothes into an overnight bag. She wondered if Henry might have somehow patched up one of the cars, if in fact he wasn't already speeding for home; she wondered if they were screwing again. She hated him for this. She ached for him.

She ran back into the bathroom, retrieved her dirty clothes, and stuffed them into a plastic bag. She'd take them along and dispose of them—wherever it was she was going. She tossed the plastic bag into her suitcase, shut the lid and snapped the latches. Then she stood in the room, unable to think, numb all the way through. She nearly wept again, because in those few seconds she realized she'd reached the end. She had nowhere to go. She had made a solid life with him here; he obviously hadn't with her.

This is *my* home, Faith thought, although she knew now she would never have the rocklike comforts of home she'd always wanted.

"Of course, I'll leave him," she said, talking to herself. "I'll get a lawyer. I'll leave him penniless." All at once, she spun around, staring at the windows that faced the driveway and the garage. Every little sound from outside, now, startled her. The publicity alone would destroy him. His political life, all his ambitions would be over. She knew people—lawyers—

men of enormous power and finesse. "All right," she muttered, "that's what I'll do. First thing tomorrow."

Faith took a pencil and pad from the drawer of the nightstand and wrote, *Henry, I'm leaving you,* but just as quickly she tore it off and put it in her purse. No, it had to come without warning; he couldn't have the slightest clue as to what she was up to. See how you like it. She scratched a second note, saying matter-of-factly that she'd tried to reach him at the club and missed him, that she was driving into Santa Barbara to see Meg Winters, who was in the hospital, and if it got too late, she would find a hotel and stay over. "I'll call you in the morning," she wrote, "one way or the other."

You bastard.

She hesitated, then as if nothing had happened, she signed it quickly "Love, Faith," folded it into a crisp peak and left it on his pillow.

She tidied up the side of the bed where she had been sitting. She grabbed up her bag and left the light burning on the nightstand so that it shone on the note. The hall was dim and silent. The Chinese runner sank beneath her hurrying steps, the walls shifted backward, but she felt as if she were hardly moving. It was impossible, but the air in the house seemed to tug back at her, as if it knew the depth, the limitless dimension of all she was leaving behind.

PART
THREE

23

_____

YEARS HAD GONE by since the trouble the last time—so
much time that the past sometimes seemed like a
long bad dream to Faith Slater.

They hadn't been married a year when Henry lost
their money, a great deal of money, including the
inheritance she had received only a few months earlier from her father's Winnetka estate. "I was set
up!" Henry ranted. "The bastards set me up!" But
no one had set him up. "You got in too deep," she
tried to tell him again and again. But he couldn't
accept it. "They're vultures, Faith. Vultures! Christ,
they'd take the damned shirt off my back, they'd
pick my bones if I'd let them!"

She remembered how frightened they had been,
the wild paranoia of those last days in Chicago when
they stayed up nights, trying to decide what to do,
afraid for the phone to ring—the talk about filing
for bankruptcy, the evening they returned to find
their furniture and paintings gone, the foreclosure
notices. Sleepless nights when it was finally decided
that they would have to get away, as far away as
possible, to begin again. They would go to California, he decided, and build a new life there. She
remembered how Henry had pleaded with her to go
when she didn't want to—"Oh, my darling, please,

this is home to me. This is my home, don't you see?"
she had begged him. "We can make it here. We can
get by." But he wouldn't be swayed. "I'll make it up
to you, Faith—I promise. I started out with nothing
when we met and I'll make it all back again. Just
remember: it's you and me Faith, no matter what
happens. It's you and me."

"Always," she vowed, "always, always."

IT'S YOU AND me, Faith, no matter what happens.

It's you and me. You and me.

Always. Always.

And then to awaken this morning and know she
was alone.

Alone.

Faith opened her eyes to the piping of sea gulls.
Where am I? she thought. How did I get here? What
in the name of God has happened to me? She was
stiff and sore. When she pushed herself up in the
car seat, she remembered driving the night before,
driving and driving until she couldn't go any farther.
The parking lot where she'd pulled in and fallen
asleep overlooked an empty white beach. Now, the
air was crystalline and blinding bright. Faith ran her
hands through her hair, put on lipstick and sunglasses, trying to get her bearings. Sliding over behind the wheel, she started the Mazda.

It was the kind of day that the middle of June was
supposed to bring, warm, fresh-scented, with an occasional chase of clouds across the blue sky. Half an
hour later, she turned toward the old coastal highway, a road she hadn't taken from this direction
since the days when she had first arrived in California. She passed the Palomino Beach sign and turned
to the right, still heading south. For the next few

miles, the ocean and the long, bone-colored beaches skimmed by as slowly the elevation began to rise.

The pavement narrowed to a two-lane blacktop that climbed steadily higher and higher through rugged terrain. This strip of road was among the most hazardous in the state, and for the next forty-five miles, she drove through its deep, twisting curves. Eventually she passed the entrance to the settlement for refugees coming in from Central America, and the church hospital where she did volunteer work every Friday and Monday morning.

Five miles farther on, she reached the gas station-restaurant called Mama Emilia's, the last outpost before Rio Del Palmos. Mama Emilia's was a small cluster of buildings with corrugated tin roofs and beer signs blinking in the windows, but the place was always crowded with tourists this time of year. Mama's empanadas were famous.

Making a U-turn, Faith pulled her car across the road onto the shoulder, where there was barely enough room for one small car to park. It was rare that anyone else used this space because it was so narrow. Off the passenger's side of the car, the drop was so precipitous that to look down at the waves crashing below made her stomach crawl. And yet, she loved this view of Rio Del Palmos more than any of the others: the miniature city in the swollen green lap of hills, the ocean sparkling in the bay, the mission-style domes and spires all but unrecognizable at this distance. I don't want to live anywhere else, she thought. This is what I want.

Taking her purse and keys, Faith got out of the car, crossed the old highway on foot and went through the crowded parking lot to the restaurant, inside.

"Ah, Mrs. Slater, how're you today?" said Miguel

from his usual place behind the counter. "You're running a little late. Same as always, yes?"

"Yes," she said, nearly shouting above the noise in the crowded room, "but please put them in a bag today. I'll have them while I'm driving. I'm afraid I can't stay."

"*Sí*, Mrs. Slater."

LEAVING HER CAR on the brick driveway, Faith went toward the house. Immediately, she could sense it: Henry wasn't there. Her beautiful, white morning glories were thriving, choking the porch posts of the veranda, but the desolation she felt extended beyond the familiar eloquence of the flowers. This was the life she had elected to live—a mild, protected life, removed from the chaos she knew life could throw her way. *I wanted a home and a husband and this is how I end up,* she thought.

It was 9:35 when she stepped into the hollow sanctuary of her own home. She had tried to keep the world at arm's length, and by and large she had succeeded. Her marriage, her life with Henry, was not something to be tampered with. And yet, today, the house had an unfamiliarity about it, the same as it sometimes did when she returned from vacations. The living room looked as if everything in it had been slightly upset by some thorough but urgent cleaning. Absurd as it was, Faith kept wanting to blink her eyes and set things right.

I can't help it if he loves her, she thought. *I'm his and he's mine; he belongs to me.*

"Luisa," she said, shuffling through her telephone messages and finding nothing from him, "did Mr. Slater have a good breakfast this morning?"

"No," the maid told her, "Mr. Slater, he say, 'Only coffee. Black.' "

The first thing she did was to call his office, simply and directly, as she would have done if nothing had happened. Faith had to find out what he knew about last night. This would be the first time she had talked to him since discovering him with Sheila and she dreaded it. Stay calm, Faith told herself as she dialed the telephone. Act normally.

"Abigail," she said, "this is Faith. Could I please speak to my husband?" She waited until she heard his voice on the line.

"Good morning, Henry," Faith said, as cheerfully as she could. "I just got home and thought I'd check in. How's everything?"

If Henry noticed her strangeness, he didn't let on. His voice flowed into her ear, full of its old music; she could feel it in the pulse behind her knees much as she had felt it, last night, when it came through the farmhouse window. She couldn't stop seeing that young girl on top of him. The flood of images was driving her wild. Why do I ask for this? she thought. Why don't I just go?

Suddenly, she tasted the salt of tears on her upper lip and licked them away.

"Did you sleep well?" she asked. Her entire body trembled with the effort not to sob. Removing herself from Luisa's hearing, she carried the phone, trailing the cord, out onto the balcony. The tears ran. Burying the receiver against her shoulder for a moment, Faith fought for self-control.

" . . . but it was fine," she heard him saying. "I turned in early."

She wondered how he could miss the emotion flooding her voice. "Don't forget," she reminded him, struggling to sound calm, "about dinner . . . tonight at the Parkinsons'."

The line was dead with silence. "Christ, what time?" he asked.

Below, as far as she could see, sun struck the cresting waves in an ocean of sparkling light. "They're serving cocktails"—Faith put her head in her left hand and then wiped her eyes—"at six-thirty."

Henry said, "Sounds like you've picked up a cold."

Tempted to spit out the truth, she hesitated a moment, then held it back. "Oh, I'm . . . okay," she answered.

Alone.

When she hung up, her hands were shaking so badly that Faith couldn't make them stop; she went quickly down the hall to the bathroom to straighten and repair her face. God, that was close, she thought. Too close. I mustn't do that again. He can't ever know that my life is torn apart. I'd rather die than give him the satisfaction.

He's still lying to me, she thought, returning to the bedroom. He must be going out of his mind with worry. Suddenly she realized: *He doesn't know who it was.* He had no idea who it was out there last night. If he knew it was me, why would he lie? He'd know that I had seen him. With her. Faith felt like laughing out loud. He probably just thought I wasn't feeling well. Faith's got the sniffles. Whatever his imagination had conjured up, she thought it could hardly measure against the reality she had already seen and suffered.

So, what now? It occurred to her that she could talk to Father Vasquez, but she immediately dismissed it. She knew there was no one. And yet,

thinking about the priest brought to mind her com-
mitments, the people who were counting on her.

Opening the appointment book on her lap, Faith
dialed the chancery's number. When the housekeeper
answered, she asked to speak to Father Vasquez, and
when he came on, she said, "Father, this is Faith
Slater. I'm running behind this morning. I'll be there
as soon as I can."

THE MORNING AND the evening were hardly connected.
At her vanity, Faith studied her reflection in the
mirror. With a fingertip, she wiped away a faint red
smudge of lipstick at the corner of her mouth. Opening the bedroom door, Faith straightened her back,
drew herself up to full height, and gracefully moved
down the hall toward the living room where her
husband waited.

This was the hardest part—to meet his eyes and
not flinch—to face the fact that a malignancy, buried
deep within them, had been secretly growing for so
long. Faith, approaching through the dining room,
paled at the sight of him. Tonight, he smiled with
what seemed to her a terrifying cheerfulness. "Ready?"
he asked.

"Yes," she answered. "I think so." It amazed her to
see him performing like this, to show no sign of
nervous fatigue or whatever it was he must be feeling. A defiant hardness rose in her eyes. Well, if he
can do it, so can I. Faith had learned long ago to
discipline herself and she did it now. Composed, she
left the house at her husband's side.

In spite of how she had braced herself against
him, Faith realized Henry hadn't said a word about
how she looked. *And why should his opinion still matter*

to me now? He rarely complimented her anymore. It would be demeaning to ask. A bone to a dog.

"So how do I look tonight?"

"Fine. You look fine, Faith."

She sat next to the window while he drove and watched the lights of the city melt into the darkness. After what seemed only a few minutes, she felt the Cadillac losing speed, pulling to the curb. The night air smelled of jasmine and almond. Haunting and lovely.

The Parkinsons' dinner party was held in the garden. She asked for wine.

"Oh, Faith," Anna Parkinson said, "why don't you let loose? We're having old-fashioneds."

"No, I'll stick with wine." *Don't you know?* she thought. *Faith doesn't let loose. Faith never loses control.*

She was constantly aware of the other guests around her, touching and withdrawing, voices on the air, laughter, muted guitars. In her mind, Faith sat, calm and strangely removed, just listening and waiting to see what would happen next. As she heard the others talking around her, she felt that they spoke of things from another world, to another race blind to the realities of life. *I don't care what they think or how they live or how many husbands they've had or who they sleep with. I couldn't live like that; I've never wanted to live like that.*

Faith watched as Henry talked with Anna Parkinson, who was sitting at the head of the table. She saw how the light of the lanterns overhead played over his hands—they were like beautiful carvings, masculine and hard and strong.

Now she felt an icy shiver of desire. *His hands.* Desire had overtaken her in an instant. There had been a time—long ago—when the more they fought, the more they wanted each other afterward. I'd explode, she remembered, and even now, she could almost feel her body keening towards him. God damn, she thought, oh god damn. I'm still in love with him.

After dinner, home, in the garage, came a moment that might have changed everything for her. When Henry pushed the door open to the laundry room and Faith stepped into the house, she passed within an eyelash of his face. Again, she felt the passion. The instant they were inside the house, she wanted him. But he shrank from her, pretending to give her room in the narrow entrance.

The moment for her was gone.

"I'll get the lights," he said as she walked silently down the hall. Looking back, her hand on the bedroom doorknob, she saw his eyes watching her, his face, like an actor's mask, sculpted with light and his tall shadow flung back across the ceiling and wall. How many times had his hand reached beneath the shade to turn off that same lamp before coming to bed? Night after night after night. Suddenly, she felt sick—sick to death of loving him.

I might as well be dead, she thought. But I'm not. I'm here; I married him, and he's mine. I won't let her take him away from me. For a minute Faith tried to put this hellishness out of her mind, but it wouldn't let her alone. Slowly and decisively, she called up the possibilities: she was going to keep him. She could easily imagine destroying Henry and the girl and herself in the bargain.

I'll make this affair impossible for them both. I'll keep my mouth shut. I'll behave like an angel. Sweetness and light. I've got to get close to this girl. I'll get to know her very well. She'll be my best friend.

For as long as it takes.

It would be a war and Faith would have to fight. *And win.*

Oh, I want, I want—

Unable to go to sleep, she waited until she was sure Henry had drifted off, then she got out of bed and began to roam the room. She would have to learn how to move as a shadow moves. Secrecy was necessary to her. Outside, a breeze ran through the trees, shaking their branches, and the smooth surface of moonlight exploded into a thousand flashing pieces.

But Faith hardly saw it. Almost protectively, she listened while her husband slept, his every breath deep now and softly measured, while in the night, her eyes burned, feeding on the darkness with the fiercest black glow.

24

SHEILA WAS INVITED to all the parties that early summer, but she didn't go to them. The word circulated that she was still depressed about her grandmother's murder, which was true, but the excuse also suited everyone concerned—in particular, she thought, Henry Slater. She often talked on the phone with the girls she knew, although she relied mainly on one or two of her closest friends, like Mary McPhearson, if she wanted to go downtown.

In the mornings, two or three times a week, she put on shorts and a T-shirt and drove out to the house on Canyon Valley Drive to spend the day sorting through Rachel's old things. Sheila poured over old photograph albums and forgotten letters tied in bundles—some were from her own mother, who she remembered vividly. She wondered why Rachel had failed to show her the letters: after her mother had died she had missed her desperately, and now, reading these things written in her own words was like stumbling upon a secret room.

Every day shortly before noon, she'd slip on a bikini and unfold a lawn chair in the backyard. The neighborhood seemed deserted at that hour. Lying in the sun, she dozed or thumbed through magazines or tried to read a book, but after a while—after a shorter while every day, it seemed—boredom set in and Henry Slater occupied her thoughts. They were drowsy, disconnected thoughts: the stirring sound of his deep laugh, things she remembered him saying. He had said he wanted her more than anything else in the world, and she held on to that.

Sheila was driving the Karmann Ghia again—Henry had replaced the wires and belts and hoses. His Jaguar was back in the shop waiting to have the upholstery redone a second time. He had given her a key to a new place, an isolated beach house north of the city. "When you go there," he'd told her, "you've got to be careful, more careful than you've ever been before." His office had changed to summer hours, and as often as he could he left at three and she met him there in the late afternoons.

A staircase led up to the loft, where the only bedroom was. Sheila liked to arrive early, shut the blinds and drapes and be waiting for him in bed. Eventually she'd hear him come in; she'd watch him getting undressed in the semidarkness and hold the sheet up as he slipped in beside her. They always made love, only to part streaming with sweat, spent but never surfeited.

With the edge of the sheet, he always rubbed her down while she lay limp, eyes closed, heart thudding wildly under his hand. He was always the one who said, "It's time to go," and none of her prowess ever stopped him. She didn't ask him where he was going. She knew. To Faith. To his other life. It sometimes made her feel incomplete, as if she wasn't quite all that she should be. He was older and sophisticated and she had so much to learn. When she stayed behind, Sheila waited for ten minutes, as he had asked her to do. Then she was dressed and driving back to Mrs. Sanders's, telling herself it would never end.

IT MUST HAVE been about ten-thirty that Monday morning, because her mouth was dry from the dust on the closet shelves. Sheila was upstairs, going through old hatboxes that Rachel had ferreted away, when she heard tires on the gravel outside. Looking down through the bedroom's side windows, she saw Henry's dark blue Cadillac, pulling up the drive.

What's he doing here? she thought.

The car vanished under the porte cochere. She heard the door slam. Why would he take the risk of being so obvious? Why hadn't he called?

Sheila ran downstairs and out through the dining room, jogging around the half-packed boxes just as the doorbell at the side of the house began to chime. She caught her breath, her stomach jittery with nervous excitement. Stopping before the mirror to check her hair, she went down the short hall between the kitchen and the dining room and threw the door open.

Under the porte cochere, where great bursts of honeysuckle spiralled up the columns, a woman stood with her back turned. Her hair was black, tucked in smoothly at the shoulders. Slowly she turned, crisp in navy and white linen, bracelets of bone and silver clicking on her wrists, and she was smiling.

For a moment she stared at the woman's face as though unable to believe her eyes. "Mrs. Slater," she gasped.

Faith extended her hand. "Sheila," she said, "I'm ashamed of myself. I've meant to come by to see you a thousand times. How've you been? I swear I think about you every day."

Sheila hardly heard a word. She backed against
the wall, aware that the doorknob was still clutched
in her fist but unable to let go of it. All she could
think was—She knows! She knows!—and then wonder in horror, What do you want? Why're you here?
"Wh . . . what is it?" she asked.

"Are you all right?" Faith asked. "Is something
the—"

"I'm all right." *It's his wife. It's Henry's wife. What
should I do?* "You really surprised me, that's all."
Sheila thought she might faint. She forced herself to
let go of the doorknob and clasped her hands behind her back. "You scared me," Sheila said, still
feeling a desperate need to explain. "I was going
through things and the doorbell scared me."

Faith despised her. She had to fight down the
urge to slap the girl, hard, across the face. Instead,
she breathed compassion into her voice. "Oh, then I
am sorry. Forgive me for bothering you. Are you
sure there's nothing else the matter?"

"No. No, it's nothing." Sheila couldn't think of
anything to do, but to say, "Would you like to come
in?"

"Oh, I can't stay," Faith said. "But . . . well, maybe
for just a minute. There's something I've been meaning to talk to you about."

As Faith stepped past her into the house Sheila
couldn't help but notice how she walked, her head
erect, her shoulders square. Shutting the door, Sheila
followed her up the three steps when she heard the
telephone ringing. "Excuse me," she said, walking
rapidly into the kitchen.

While Faith waited in the hallway, she thought
how familiar the house seemed, exactly as it had
years ago when she and Henry lived across the street—

the patterned linoleum, the white-curtained windows. She heard Sheila say, "Oh, Mary, I can't talk long. Someone's here."

Faith scrutinized Sheila now, as she had never studied any other female before in her life. That perfect skin. How could she not have noticed it before? The champagne-colored hair caught at the nape of her neck with a rubber band. Even from this distance her eyes were a drowning blue. She was wearing the briefest of khaki shorts and a white zebra-patterned T-shirt, which left nothing, absolutely nothing, to the imagination. But she knew that body; she had seen it through the window, etched by a fiery sundown. Never had Faith felt such molten jealousy.

"Mrs. Slater, go on in," Sheila said, covering the phone. "You remember where everything is. It's just my friend Mary. I'll only be a minute."

Entering the dining room, Faith looked back, once more, over her shoulder. With one knee bent, her bare foot braced against the cabinet, Sheila stood gazing into the backyard garden, talking into the receiver. Youth, beauty and that body. I wonder what Henry gives you for that body. I'll bet he gives you lots of things.

Moving around the half-packed cartons and boxes, she crossed through the sunlit dining room into the empty hall. Every room in the house appeared to be in a state of upheaval. Faith made her way into the living room, past a massive walnut secretary, its slant-top door left open. She saw Rachel's fountain pen, the one she had always used, the one she had doubtless used to write the note to Faith. She let her fingers run along the back of a chair. My God, she must've sat right here.

But Faith didn't have time to dwell on it. She could hear Sheila coming toward her through the dining room. "I'm sorry everything's in such a mess," Sheila said.

"You shouldn't ever apologize," Faith told her, "at least, not to me. Why, when we lived across the street, we were almost family."

They sat at opposite ends of the sofa. How poised she is, Sheila thought. How polished. She was a woman who would always know what to say. Not like me. Sheila cleared her throat, then said, "Things go to pieces so quick around here."

"What are you going to do? Will you be moving?"

"I don't know. I keep getting bills. They're supposed to come turn off the electricity. I thought that might be who it was, when you came."

The two of them sat in silence.

Tight little body in shorts and a T-shirt.

"I don't know why you'd want to come here," Sheila said. "It's all so horrible."

"But I came to see you. Maybe you don't know it, Sheila, but Henry and . . . well, we've been trying to look out for you. We both know how careful Rachel had to be with her money . . ."

How are you feeling, now, without her? Faith found herself suddenly thinking. Losing your mother at such a young age and now with Rachel gone—but pity was an emotion Faith could ill afford. She reached into her purse and pulled out an envelope. "I've put a little something in here for you out of my own mad money. You can use it for anything you like; it's perfectly all right with me."

It's not about Henry and me, Sheila thought. *She doesn't know!*

Faith handed her the envelope of money.

She doesn't know!

Sheila stared at her, incredulously. She wanted to laugh. Intense, hysterical relief flooded her. But what should I do? Now she's giving me money, too.

"Thanks," she said.

Faith glanced at her watch. "My goodness," she said with great solicitude, "I'm sorry, Sheila, but I really must be going."

At the door, on her way out, Faith turned, as if waylaid by a thought. "I'm driving up to Monterey day after tomorrow. If you're not doing anything, maybe you'd like to come along. I know how awful it must be to be alone, without anyone . . ."

Faith knew she had struck a chord. In spite of herself, Sheila was looking at her as something other than a threat, and Faith marked well the subtle change. She went on, "It's hard without a woman to talk to, Sheila, honestly I know it is. I'll tell you what—I'll buy us lunch somewhere."

"Monterey?"

Faith laughed. "I guess the whole thing does sound kind of . . . spur of the moment."

She doesn't know!

It was madness, but Sheila was tempted to accept. What would Henry say? It would certainly be taking the craziest kind of risk. How do I say no? She's Henry's wife, but how do I get out of it? "What're you going to do there?"

"Just some shopping."

"I don't know, Mrs. Slater. I don't think so. Thank you just the same, but I've got lots to do here."

"It'll still be here when you get back," Faith said indulgently. "Come on, you'll have a good time; I promise you."

A blush appeared on Sheila's cheeks.

"Well," Faith said finally, as if amused by the silence, "you can't blame me for asking."

Sheila suddenly grinned. Her doubts hadn't really lifted, Faith thought, the grin didn't quite ring true, not yet. But one day soon it would. I'll make sure of that.

"Actually," Sheila said, "I don't think I am doing anything on Wednesday."

Faith walked out into the shade of the porte cochere. "Wednesday it is, then," she said and turned toward the Cadillac to conceal her smile.

25

"I MAY NOT always like the law," Reeves had said many times at political rallies. "I might not agree with it, but it's the only thing that stands between you and me and anarchy. And I've sworn to uphold it."

Privately he said to Slater, "Fuck 'em, Henry. I won't break the law to get 'em, but I'll sure as hell bend it. I'll do whatever it takes. I'll squeeze their balls until it comes out their ears."

When at last the calls began to come in that first one and then another of the escaped convicts had been captured southeast of Rio Del Palmos, Reeves was the one who got into his car and drove miles out of his own jurisdiction to question them. Then he had to sit for hours on end pouring over transcripts, which were nothing more than the deranged ramblings of madmen.

He was out of the house at dawn on those pale, shimmering mornings, and if he didn't stay over, invariably it was dark when he returned. The paperwork piled up on his desk. Every day driving and getting nowhere. His shirt stuck to the vinyl seat with sweat. A hundred miles on Monday, a hundred back. A hundred thirty the next day, a hundred thirty back.

"Waste of time!" he snorted as he walked back

alone to his car each evening. The small of his back hurt. Either they didn't do it or they have no recollection of what they did. They're warped, that's all. Crazy.

Thursday in a meeting with the district attorney and Mayor Slater, he gave an inconclusive report— all he could pull together. "I've turned it every way I can think of," he told them, "and it still doesn't make any sense."

Day after discouraging day with nothing accomplished and nothing good to say for himself, Reeves would open his eyes from a shallow, uneasy sleep to a sense of his own failure.

His determination grew.

They didn't do it, Reeves concluded time after time while driving home. They just damned didn't do it.

But all he succeeded in doing was to rule them out—in his own mind—as suspects. He still believed that the devil Rachel Buchanan had bargained with was in all probability her killer. Which meant that it was someone who knew her and that she knew, someone she'd had dealings with, most likely someone living in the area. Maybe someone with a square-cut diamond. That was where his speculations turned to empty air. It could be anyone.

After-hours the next afternoon, he made his way through headquarters and down the corridor to his office. Seating himself in the gray swivel chair, he snapped on the fluorescent desk light. On top of the papers on his desk lay the two lists he'd asked his secretary to prepare earlier that day. He began to go through them, and what he read came as no surprise: the convicts had left behind fingerprints, traces of saliva, skin fragments, blood samples. The list of the items they had stolen was so eccentric as to be almost humorous; but a large square diamond wasn't among them.

He was rummaging in his drawer for toothpicks, when the small manila envelope caught his attention. That's where I put it, he thought, to keep it safe. There it is. He opened the metal clasp. The square diamond, its facets winking in the violet dusk, rolled into his palm. He knew this was the only real evidence he had in a murder case that just wouldn't let go of him. This was the most horrendous thing that had ever happened in Rio Del Palmos. Everything concerning it deserved, now, to be reconsidered from the beginning.

This one's mine, he thought. Nobody's gonna mess this one up. I'll do the work myself. It's my ass that's on the line; I'll get the bastard who killed Rachel Buchanan.

"NO, IT DIDN'T come from here," the jeweler on Bank Street told him the next day. "But this is a fine diamond. It's old, the color's very good, clarity's excellent. It measures almost two karats; there's a small chip in the back, but it's still worth close to eight thousand. What else would you like to know?"

"Who'd wear a diamond like this?" Reeves asked. "An older woman?"

The jeweler handed the stone back to him. "If I had to guess, I'd say it's a man's, probably from a man's ring. The square cut's not that common. Of course, it could've come from anything, but it would be ideal for a man's ring."

In store after store, he was given much the same information. It wasn't until he went into Muller's

Estate & Antique Jewelry to see Andy Muller that he
got lucky.

"You know who used to have a diamond like this?"
Muller asked him. "Mayor Slater."

"Henry Slater?"

"Yeah. I remember his wife bringing in a ring to
be cleaned and reset. I'm sure she did." *That's right!
Henry does wear a diamond ring.* "It's because of this
chip on the back that I remember it," Mullen continued. "If it wasn't for that chip, it—"

"Do you have a record of that?" Reeves asked. *Why
didn't he just tell me it was his diamond?*

"Maybe—but that was two or three years ago. Let
me check my files."

Muller went to his offices in back and, minutes
later, returned with a yellowed piece of paper, which
he handed over to Reeves. It was the carbon copy of
a sales receipt showing an August date from nearly
three years ago, an amount of sixty-seven dollars
marked Paid In Full. Then Muller showed him the
signed claim check with the same series of numbers.
Scrawled across the bottom was the signature: *Faith
Slater.*

"That's all we would have," the jeweler said. "I'm
afraid it doesn't tell you much."

"Let me hang on to these," Reeves said to him.

"What's this all about, Chief?"

"It's probably nothing," Reeves said, half believing
it himself, as he went out.

26

ON THE OUTSIDE, Faith was cool discipline; inside, she was churning rage. She drove Sheila to Monterey that Wednesday morning, her body aching with hate. Again, she was graciousness itself, but the distrust still lingered in the girl's blue eyes.

Through the afternoon they wandered in and out of the galleries, the gourmet cooking shops, the wine bars, the exclusive boutiques. Faith watched as the girl went among the racks of expensive clothing; she saw Sheila's thin, tapered fingers glide over the linens and cashmeres, the hesitations, the pouts, the frowns of indecision, the desire. Faith couldn't help but notice the stylish jacket Sheila was wearing, the gold bracelet and earrings, the designer sunglasses. *You little tramp. I'll bet Henry sees to all of this. He's taking care of you now.*

Oh, Rachel, didn't you know what was growing up under your roof?

The girl was gorgeous; she drew mens' eyes everywhere she went. Faith was sick with envy. *How can I ever compete with her? I'm forty-two years old. No matter what I do, I can't compete. I hate what you've done with all my soul,* she thought. *I could kill you for this.* The realization was staggering. And frightful. *My God, what's happening to me?* Only days had passed and life with her husband was at a standstill. Faith found herself making plans that didn't include him. They ate their meals in silence—when he was home at all—and she took sleeping pills to avoid his touch at night.

This is ruining my life. This affair has got to end.

Dusk had settled in by the time they got back to Rachel's house.

"Thank you for everything, Mrs. Slater," Sheila said.

Faith realized she had to be careful. She was sure that Henry was seeing the girl almost every day now. "I think maybe we should pretend this little outing never happened." She raised a warning finger. "I'm not sure Henry would approve if he knew. He's against my showing any favoritism, and he might get angry with me."

They looked at each other with perfect understanding.

"Sheila . . . I just wanted you to know that he'll never find out about this from me."

Faith searched the girl's face for a clue to her feelings, but she saw only a mask of politeness. "Call me if there's anything you need," she said with a smile. "Anything at all. I'll come by in a day or so to see how you're getting along."

DAY AFTER DAY the thought of her husband making love to Sheila Bonner consumed her, and at night visions of them together tormented her dreams. Who are you? Faith constantly found herself thinking. You're like a neglected child; you belong to no one; you have no home. Why did you have to bring your chaos into my life?

Now the everyday pleasures of living eluded her.

She seldom laughed anymore; she had lost her appetite, and there was something almost violent in the way she tore through her daily chores. Driven by bitterness and pain, she completely immersed herself in the rhythm of Sheila Bonner's world: how the girl dressed, her friends, where she shopped, how she spent her time away from Henry. *I'll know you in ways he never will and then . . .*

Two days later, Faith followed the two girls in the white Karmann Ghia downtown to Concepción Avenue. Keeping a safe distance behind them, she made her way through the afternoon shoppers to Marcella's, her favorite boutique. How could the little bitch afford to shop here? But, of course. She knew. *Henry.*

Grabbing a dress in her size from the rack, Faith headed for the dressing room. She had seen Sheila and the McPhearson girl disappear behind the curtains just as she came in. But she wasn't prepared. She couldn't have been.

Sheila was standing there, the door to her cubicle wide open. She was wearing her pantyhose, nothing more, and the sight of her body was overpowering. Faith tried to keep up a false smile to hide her shock. "Why Sheila—what a surprise!"

Don't look at her! Keep your eyes on her eyes.

"Faith! What're you doing here?" The girl snatched up her T-shirt and covered herself.

"The same sinful thing as you are, I imagine," Faith said, concealing a jealousy so monstrous that she couldn't bear to look at her any longer. "Is this your friend?"

"Oh, you know Mary McPhearson, don't you, Mrs. Slater? I stayed with her for a while after the funeral."

"Yes, of course, I remember," Faith said. "It's nice to see you again under more pleasant circumstances."

"Hi," said Mary. "Excuse me, though, Mrs. Slater, I was just going to try on some shoes."

When Faith turned again to Sheila, the girl had slipped on a dress of rough amber silk and was struggling with the zipper. "Here," Faith said, dropping her things on a chair, "let me." Wrestling with the unbidden images of her husband's hands on this body, she set the hook and eye. Faith could still see them through the farmhouse window, his hands all over her, as she adjusted the material squarely on Sheila's shoulders. *Stop it! Oh, stop it!* With a light touch under the chin, she tipped the golden head toward the mirror. "There. Take a look at yourself."

The girl's eyes sought her own reflection; Faith watched as a tiny knowing smile of approval played at the corners of Sheila's mouth.

Forgive me Rachel, but you see what I must do. I can't let this go on. Some things were never meant to happen.

"I only wish your grandmother was here to see how lovely you look."

Pain, like a blow, flew into the girl's face.

"But I'm here now," Faith said. "Let this dress be my gift to you. I know Rachel would want you to have it."

FAITH GAUGED HER visits to the Buchanan house with care. Every two days or so she would appear to help Sheila pack, bring little gifts, offer encouraging advice or simple conversation, reassurance that this difficult time in the girl's life would pass. How she loathed the perfect body, the unblemished skin, the astonishing blond hair. Her resolve burned: she would turn Sheila Bonner to *her.*

*   *   *

IT WAS TUESDAY morning when the call came from Burris Reeves's office. Faith was again at the house, tagging boxes for Sheila in the dining room.

"Mr. Reeves wants to see me again," Sheila told her. "Right away; this afternoon."

The girl's face was white with dread.

"But whatever for?"

"I don't know. I don't know. They just said a few more questions."

Faith could see the fear, the shrinking uncertainty in her eyes. She said, "Of course I'll drive you there, darling. You can't go alone!"

But it was alone that Sheila walked through the glass-paneled door next to the police chief's office. In the reception area Faith bought a cup of coffee at the coffee machine. She couldn't sit still. Pacing in the hall outside the glass door, wondering what more the police could want with Sheila, she lifted the paper cup and sipped the coffee, feeling it burn the inside of her mouth and her throat when she swallowed.

Through the glass, she could see Sheila sitting through the interrogation. There were three officers in the room with her; Faith caught a glimpse of Reeves, sitting on the edge of the table, his heavy body leaning toward Sheila, his face filled with sympathy. Henry had told her about Reeves. A snake, he had said, slithery as hell.

But not so slithery as you, my darling, she thought bitterly.

The sound of the door opening forced Faith to return to the moment at hand. Now Sheila was at her side, the girl's face filled with horror and grief. Instinctively, Faith put her arm around her and just as naturally Sheila allowed her body to sag against her. *At last.*

Faith led her gently up the stairs through the vestibule, into the sunlight. "Are you all right?"

Finally Sheila said, "They had to show me some pictures. They said maybe something was moved between the time I came ... I came home that morning and when the photographers came." She seemed stunned. "And it brought everything back."

On the way to the house, they were quiet. Sheila sat staring out the window, biting her lips, fighting, Faith saw, to keep control of her emotions. They were on Canyon Valley Drive before Faith said, "Sheila, is there anything I can do? Was it so terrible? Can't I help you?"

"You've been so nice to me; you're always there. But you don't know me. You don't!" Sheila shook her head. "I've done a lot of things I'm ashamed of, Mrs. Slater. I keep thinking about my Gramma. I've been selfish. Believe me, if you only knew, you wouldn't stick around."

"But you're wrong!" Faith protested. *My God! Is she going to tell me?*

Suddenly, Sheila reached out and grasped Faith's hand, and for a moment the strong young fingers clung to her gratefully. "No, I'm not," she whispered.

She got out of the car abruptly. "I've just got to be alone for now," she said, and fled up the walk into the house. Faith watched as the door closed behind her. *All right,* Faith thought, *all right now; let it be.*

SHE'S ABOUT TO fold in spite of herself, Faith thought while driving home. When she walked through her living room minutes later, her back was straighter than it had been in weeks. She hadn't expected Henry

to be home, and he wasn't. She could never forget
that he ran to meet the girl every chance he had.
The truth was still scalding. *For all I know they
could be together right now.* Well, Henry would find
it rough going with her on this day.

Her charade with Sheila had worn her out. Faith
took off her suit and blouse, stepped out of her navy
crocodile pumps, whisked off her underclothes.
Wrapped in a thick, white, terry cloth robe, she
threw a few scented beads into the tub and started a
hot bath. The room immediately filled with a cleans-
ing fragrance.

At her vanity, while taking off her makeup, Faith
began to formulate her plan. Tomorrow at eleven
she had a brunch, and then at one-thirty, Nancy had
reserved a court at the club. *Back here by midafternoon.* She slid the silver tray to the side and there it
was: the two ripped pieces of Rachel's letter. She
could feel Rachel's words fueling her rage, the fine
mean taste of her wrath between her teeth. Faith
stood and stalked up and down the room, striving to
work off her tension. *Stop by to see Sheila again the
day after, maybe for morning coffee. Good,* she
thought.

When the tub was more than half full, Faith lay
back in her bath, the steaming ripples lapping her
body. *The girl would never be able to bear this
burden for long; today was proof of that. One day
soon she would need someone—someone she could
trust absolutely. Someone older. Who would she want
to run to? Henry? No, there were some things even
he couldn't fix. The girl needed a mother.* Suddenly
Faith felt elated, icily certain that when the moment
was right, Sheila Bonner would finally come to her.

27

"WHEN DO YOU expect her?" Reeves asked the maid.

"Mrs. Slater tells me if anybody calls, she be home very soon."

"Then, if you don't mind, I'll wait on the veranda."

That had been twenty-five minutes ago. Why hadn't Henry said it was his diamond? Listening to the late-afternoon silence, Reeves wondered what Faith Slater knew. Well, it's time I found out. Before long, he heard a car coming and the red Mazda swooped down the driveway; it stopped beside his cruiser, and Faith's long legs swung out on the driver's side.

Reeves watched her close the car door and come up the walk, her eyes riveted on the police cruiser. With every step, she moved slower until, within a few yards of the entryway, she stopped, clasping her purse in her arms. She looked right and left, then, through a gap in the bougainvillaea, the police chief's eyes met hers.

A smile of recognition blazed over her face, although it only highlighted the anxiety that quickly overtook her. "What is it?" she asked. "Has something happened?" She stepped up on the veranda toward him.

"No, nothing like that, nothing disastrous," Reeves said, keeping the file folder in his left hand. "Mrs.

Slater, I don't believe we've ever actually gotten to know one another—I'm Burris Reeves."

"Yes," she said. "My husband's told me of your exploits over the years." She smiled courteously for a moment, waiting for him to state his business.

"We're still investigating the Rachel Buchanan murder," Reeves told her, "and I've been meaning to talk to you. You might be able to help us, if you would. I promise not to keep you too long."

"But—I thought those convicts—"

"That's what the murderer wanted us to think," Reeves said. He watched her eyes, but they told him nothing. "Mrs. Slater," he said, directly, "did you see or talk to Mrs. Buchanan in the few days preceding her death?"

All at once he saw something flash across her face. But what? What was she thinking? "Oh, but you must forgive me, Mr. Reeves," she exclaimed. "You've taken me so completely by surprise that I've forgotten my manners." She went to the door and held it open on the lofty, white living room. "Wouldn't you like to come in?"

"If it's all the same to you," Reeves said, "I wouldn't mind staying here on the porch. In the fresh air."

"Then, please . . . make yourself comfortable. May I get you something to drink?" She continued to look at him with grave curiosity. "Iced tea, perhaps?"

"Yes, something cold would be good, but I don't want to take up too much of your time."

"Surely you'll stay long enough for a drink," she said graciously, stepping inside the door and asking Luisa to bring two glasses of iced tea. "Now where were we?" she asked, coming back and taking a place on the wicker settee across from him. She laced her fingers around her crossed knee.

"The last time you talked to Mrs. Buchanan," he repeated. He settled back into the wicker chair, the file folder on his lap.

Faith paused, staring before her into space. Slowly she shook her head. "I really can't remember. It's been—what?—over a month now since she ... I used to see Rachel every so often in town, but ... I'm sorry, but I honestly can't recall."

Some people had trouble looking at him squarely during questioning even if they had nothing to hide; Faith Slater, he thought, was the sort of woman who would look him straight in the eye no matter how innocent or guilty she might be.

"I'm working my way through a list of people who were Rachel's friends," he explained.

But before anything else could be said, the front door opened and the maid came out, carrying a tray with a pitcher of iced tea and glasses of sparkling ice. She put it down on the wicker table at Faith's side and left. Faith said, "Thank you, Luisa," then to Reeves, "there's lemon and sugar, if you'd like." Bracelets clicked on her wrist as she filled the two glasses. Reeves noticed that the hand offering him the glass was not quite steady. She said, "What are you doing to catch the killers? All we ever get in the newspapers is the same old song and dance. Are you on to anything yet?"

"We know quite a lot," Reeves said. "But it's never enough. For one thing, I'm convinced that Mrs. Buchanan knew her killer. And there was only one assailant—not two or three. A lot of things indicate this. For instance, we've been told that Mrs. Buchanan was upset and despondent—very deeply troubled on the evening before she died. I've been led to believe that such depression was unlike her. Would you agree with that, Mrs. Slater?"

"Yes. Rachel was almost always in good spirits."

"We looked everywhere—did you know?—for one solid piece of evidence. We searched that property inch by inch."

"Evidence?" Faith said blankly. "What kind of evidence?"

"Anything—a fingerprint, an article of clothing. Whoever killed Mrs. Buchanan was wearing gloves and they had to have been . . . well, bloody." Reeves noted that she didn't change expression. Her control was remarkable. "We believe the gloves were probably hidden or thrown away right after the murder. By the way, did Henry tell you about driving out to the Buchanan house with me?"

"No, I don't think so," Faith Slater said. She glanced up at him and then away again. "I'm sure he didn't."

"Well, it's not important," Reeves told her, lowering his eyes. *He didn't tell you about the diamond?* Although he didn't move, he could feel her cool scrutiny on him. "Then after we were absolutely sure nothing would be found, not a trace—we got lucky."

He leaned forward, reaching for his glass of iced tea, when the file folder on his knees fell to the floor and a number of black-and-white eight-by-ten glossies spilled across the flagstones of the veranda. "Oh, I'm sorry," Faith said automatically, reaching for them. "I hope they're not . . ." Then she blanched, her eyes immersed in the photograph she held in her hand. It was of Rachel—taken, no doubt, moments after the police had arrived at the scene that ghastly morning. Rachel's old eyes were still staring, her bloody hand clutched at her throat.

Faith shivered, now, looking at Reeves. "My God!"

she gasped, "My God! Why didn't you tell me what those were? Here! Take them!"

"She died a horrible death, Mrs. Slater. Unbelievable. That's what I think about; it's what I dream about at night. A vicious murder."

"My God." She was still visibly shaken. "How could somebody get away with this?"

"It was luck. A run of pure luck." Reeves took the lump of tissue from the small manila envelope in his pocket, unwrapped it and placed the diamond in Faith's hand, his eyes fixed upon her face.

She blinked and—he was sure—almost shuddered.

Both waited for the other to speak. Faith looked up and saw his cold, steadfast eyes.

Faith turned the diamond over and over in her palm. *It's Henry's,* she thought. She could feel the tiny nick on its back. *I'd know it anywhere.*

"Have you ever seen a diamond like this one before, Mrs. Slater?" He asked, and again waited. "You knew her fairly well. Did you ever see Rachel Buchanan wearing a diamond like this, maybe in a piece of jewelry?"

What does he know? Faith found her voice, or thought she had, and said, "No." But she hadn't: her response was choked, hardly more than a whisper. "No," she repeated.

"That's what I thought. A jeweler told me it was most likely a man's diamond."

She was aware by the nature of his silence that although she had told him nothing at all, she had been understood only too well. In spite of the scare he'd given her, she was determined not to let things deteriorate any further. It's Henry's diamond, she thought, it's from his ring. The police chief had been holding it back all along, waiting to spring it on her

after unnerving her with Rachel's photographs. Too
late, Faith realized exactly what he had done. *He
knows something.*

"Where . . . did you find it?"

"Do I need to tell you where we found it, Mrs.
Slater?"

By the way he phrased it, Faith no longer needed
to be told.

"We found it near the place where Rachel was
killed."

Still aware that her face was flushed, she looked
hard at the diamond, trying to compose herself.

"Is there anything else you want to say to me, Mrs.
Slater?"

"No," she said, "nothing." *He's my husband,* she
thought, wanting to clutch the diamond even tighter.
But she handed it back.

Until these last few minutes, she had appeared to
be utterly sure of herself, but as Reeves collected his
things, he saw that she could hardly sit still.

"I'll see you out," Faith said.

He rose from his chair and stood at the railing, a
balding, imposing figure. His iced tea sat untouched
on the wicker table as they went down the walk.
"Sometimes it takes a long time," Reeves told her.
"But sooner or later something breaks and we start
getting close to the answer." He left her by saying,
"Take care of yourself, Mrs. Slater. Thanks for making me feel at home."

Faith smiled bleakly.

Could it be? She went inside, closed the door and
stood in the middle of the room, surrounded by the
echo of every word that the chief of police had said.
Her teeth and her fists were clenched; she had to
keep swallowing to hold back the tears or nausea,

she hardly knew which. The thought that Henry was involved in this in any way was unbelievable. And yet.

That was Henry's diamond, she thought, *I know it was.* She took several deep breaths, waiting for the sound of the motor outside to recede.

But he couldn't have. No, my God. It can't be true.

Faith glanced at the clock: four-thirty. When would he be coming home? *I gave him that diamond!*

She tore through the house.

I've got to find it. I've got to know for certain.

In his study, she quickly went through his desk starting with the large central drawer and working her way down through the drawers in its stout legs. She sifted through stacks of paper and copies of old correspondence, ran her fingers under things and into the corners, but Henry's ring wasn't there.

She stepped into the middle of the room, looking, searching for a place where he might have put it. But what if he didn't want her to find it, she thought, what if he had hidden it deliberately?

Faith left the study and went through the bedroom, into the bath. It would take forever to search this house and even then there was no guarantee that it was here. She opened the medicine cabinet and examined the shelves. Nothing. She ran her hands through the linen closet, again nothing, and stepped back into the bedroom. She felt the hanging clothes and examined the storage bins in his dressing room. The ring wasn't anywhere.

That diamond was his; I know it was.

Where could it be?

Faith ran back toward the living room through the kitchen, where Luisa was preparing dinner, and went through the laundry room, opening the door to the garage. She stepped down on the one concrete step, flipped on the light, and the drab gray walls leapt away from her. Through the gloom she saw the rows of tools arranged and gleaming on the pegboard, but if he had hidden the ring out here she knew she would never find it.

Where? Where?

Then somehow it occurred to her. She thought, What's the first thing he does when he comes home in the evening? Where's the first place he goes? Faith walked back into the living room. With the tips of her fingers, she pushed the red leather spine of *David Copperfield* and the hidden bar rose on whirring gears before her. It's here somewhere, she thought. She looked in the obvious places, behind the rows of liquor bottles and in the area around the bucket for the ice maker; then she remembered the small, secret cash drawer, triggered by a sliding panel on the side of the cabinet. With her fingertips, Faith slipped the panel backward, and the shallow drawer, released, sprang forward an inch. Faith pulled it open and looked down through the square, empty hole in the gold setting of his ring.

BY THE TIME Slater parked in front of the house, it was nearly six in the evening. He was headed for the front door when his eye caught something familiar on the ground. He leaned over and picked up a toothpick that lay among the bricks of the drive. The end of it had been chewed into a tiny broom. *Reeves.* No doubt about it: Reeves had been here.

But when? And why?

The toothpick wasn't weathered. As far as he could tell, it was new. That meant Reeves had been here sometime today. Or yesterday, at the latest. Then he saw more of them, six or eight toothpicks scattered here and there. How long had Reeves been here? How many times?

What the hell's going on?

Faith met him inside with a cold gin and tonic. But in his left hand, Slater still held the toothpick. He twirled it between his fingers. "Was someone here?" he asked.

"You tell me," she answered. "You seem to know already."

"What'd he want?" Slater was watching her carefully, trying to read her expression. But Faith kept her face averted. "It didn't have anything to do with you, Henry. He was making inquiries about Rachel."

Look at me, Faith. "What kind of inquiries?"

"He mainly wanted to know if I had seen her a day or two before she was killed, which I hadn't." When Faith lifted her eyes, she looked him square in the face. "I don't like being cross-examined, Henry. Once is quite enough for one day."

She waited through dinner that evening for Henry to announce that he had to go out. She had a plan in mind for a way she could go about it—the only thing she could conceive of that might reveal to her what she had to know. It would be melodramatic, she knew, but given Rachel's final letter to her, it seemed oddly fitting. At seven-thirty, Henry made his excuses. This time he claimed he had to see the highway commissioner to prepare for tomorrow's budget meeting. Faith walked with him to the edge of the brick drive. She stood alone in the near darkness, watching his taillights disappear.

Back inside the house, she went into the bedroom, picked up the receiver and called the after-hours number at the post office. "If I mailed a card to a local address this evening," Faith asked the supervisor who answered, "when would it be delivered?" Tomorrow, he replied. She thanked him and hung up.

She found a pad of plain white bond paper in a kitchen drawer and a matching small white business envelope, both of them cheap and nondescript. Using her left hand—she was naturally right-handed—and having to restrain and control the erratic impulses of her untrained fingers, Faith wrote:

YOU MURDERED RACHEL BUCHANAN

She drew back and appraised her work. To her eye, the printing wasn't noticeably feminine, only childlike. In the same crabbed handwriting, she addressed the envelope to Mayor Henry Slater at his home address. It would be a test, she thought. It would be like receiving a letter from a dead woman. He would pass. Or he would fail. Then, without giving herself time to change her mind, Faith drove into town and mailed it.

28

THE MAIL ARRIVED between nine-thirty and ten every morning but, knowing that the white envelope she had sent was about to be delivered, Faith didn't want to be there when it came. Ordinarily, Luisa went out to the mailbox and brought the day's mail into the house; Faith discarded the junk pieces and sorted through whatever correspondence remained. Only those items requiring Henry's attention were left on the small walnut table inside the front door. If she was gone for the day, the mail waited on the table until either she or Henry had a chance to look through it.

Faith was impatient for evening to come, anxious to have it over with. This time it was crucial that he receive the letter without it ever having passed through her hands. She needed an excuse to be without a car so she could be with him when he came home. So soon after Henry left for work that morning, Faith called and asked Nancy Herbert for a ride to the Historical Society brunch.

She waited till midafternoon to call him at the office and explain that she was stranded in town and wondering if she could ride home with him after work. "If you're going to be in meetings," she said, "maybe I could wait."

He hedged, then he said, "Don't be silly. We'll go to dinner."

"That would be perfect. I'll call Luisa."

It was after eight-thirty and dark outside when they pulled up in front of the garage. "I'll let you out," Henry said, "before I put the car away." So she got out of the Cadillac, but waited for him on the drive. She didn't want to enter the house first, nor did she want to go in without him.

When they went inside, she walked into the kitchen to the counter beside the telephone and began to shuffle through the messages. He walked into the living room. Two lamps were burning on tables at either end of one of the sofas, and Luisa had left the light on in the kitchen. Faith flipped it off.

Concealed inside the kitchen doorway, she turned toward the long pier glass inside the front door that reflected much of the living room, including the small gateleg table where Luisa always left the mail. She saw Henry enter the frame of the glass. He was smoking a cigarette, the day's mail clasped in his hand.

Faith watched his reflection as he continued to go through the envelopes. Slowly his hands grew motionless. She saw it, then, clearly: he had taken up a small white envelope. It had to be the one she'd sent.

He was tearing it open and even though she had positioned herself some twenty feet from him, Faith was convinced of it now. Impatiently Henry stubbed out his cigarette, a long stream of smoke momentarily clouding the glass. When he opened the sheet of paper, everything stopped. He didn't move a muscle. No movement at all, nothing. Faith could only wait.

Then, all at once, his right hand, clutching the note, fell to his side and his fingers crumpled the sheet of paper into a ball. Without hesitation, he slipped it into his jacket pocket. When he lifted his head, she could see his profile in the mirror. She saw the heave of his chest. His face was drained of all life, all color. He took a step out of the frame of the mirror and she lost sight of him. Time stretched on and on. Only the ticking of the mantel clock interrupted the silence. Finally she heard the tread of his steps—slow, uncertain steps that crossed the living room. Faith had to see what he was doing; she stepped up to the dark kitchen doorway.

Oblivious to her, Henry had smoothed out the crumpled note and was holding it down in the lamplight by the sofa. It was horrible. She could see his nerves were shot. The sheet of paper was lightly shaking as if his hand were palsied. Faith had never seen him more wounded. *Oh, God!* It was all suddenly too much for her and she fled back into the kitchen's comforting darkness.

A few seconds passed before he called to her, "Faith, I forgot something. I've got to go out for a little while. I won't be long." She could hear the tension in his voice.

Although it was nearly nine o'clock, Faith didn't ask him where he was going or why. "All right, darling," came her reply.

Let him run, she thought. Where can he run to? To Sheila? What possible comfort could *she* be?

Faith heard the front door open and close, then the noise of the garage door rising. She waited, listening until he drove away, her heart beating much too fast. Putting her hands over her eyes, she felt the tears held just below the surface, the hysteria beginning to mount. But the worst thought—the one that twisted her heart—was the realization that for no reason on heaven or earth, she still loved him.

Faith rushed to their bedroom and sat down on the foot of the bed. She could feel the panic like waves through her body. Her eyes flew to the vanity. She stood and pushed aside the silver tray and the two torn halves of Rachel's letter were in her hands, aligned again into a whole.

I tried to reach you this afternoon but you weren't home. I was afraid to leave word with your maid because I didn't want Henry to know I called. I must talk to you. Some serious trouble has been brewing a long time that you should know about. This has to do with Henry.

Then the last lines:

If I don't hear from you, I'll know he has stepped in. I wish you no harm.

This time, the letter told her everything.
He killed Rachel.
He killed Rachel to get to Sheila.
My God, my God. He committed murder to get at a seventeen-year-old girl. Why? *Why!* It was beyond her comprehension. This was—*crazy.* And only *I* know. Burris Reeves must know too, but what did he really have? Without the empty setting for the diamond, how would he ever make a case?

"And I suppose you expect to get away with it?" she said aloud. "As usual?" Without being aware of what she was doing, Faith sat clutching one of the bed pillows, her long nails digging into the percale cotton.

For better or worse, she thought. She had taken a vow; she was bound to him forever and ever. But he was a murderer, who would go unpunished—and he deserved to be punished. Oh, yes.

All right, Faith told herself.

All right, God help me, you won't have her.

Now it's your turn to pay.

HE WAS RACING through the city streets now, speeding, hurtling through the night, his foot set solidly on the accelerator, daring the law to stop him. In the older sections of Rio Del Palmos, the pavements were dark with summer, dark as caves; at the intersections even the wide beams of streetlights were all but smothered in the green-black foliage. I'm going to see her: I don't care, Slater kept thinking. I'm going to see her. But how? Call her? And if she's not there—

The danger was bottomless and it was all around him. If only there wasn't this awful fear gnawing at him every time he stopped thinking about her, about the last time they had been together. She was so beautiful, so willing to do anything he asked her to do. "Got to see her," he muttered, "got to see her." Run the risk. Drive by her place, see if she's there. And tell her to watch out—watch out for Reeves. And what if she's not there? Maybe try the McPhearsons'. Or her grandmother's.

Maybe Reeves has already talked to her? Maybe that's why . . . What did you say, Sheila? What did you tell him . . .

Try it. Try it.

Slater ran his hand over his face to wipe away the sweat. You sent that goddamn note, Reeves. To scare me. And you succeeded, you stinking, stinking bastard. Trying to force me to do something. Something crazy. *Reeves!* Watching me. To see what I'll do.

Always watching me!

Watching me right now!

All at once Slater's eyes attached themselves to the rearview mirror, afraid of what was there, expecting to see—but no. The nearest headlights were a block or more behind him. And yet, his instinct continued to whisper that Reeves was there . . . back there . . . following him . . . and he felt frenzy run through his blood as the thought gripped him.

He realized that he was slowing down. Not this street, but the next would be Balboa Avenue, the street where Sheila lived with Mrs. Sanders. Drive by and see if she's there.

Every few seconds Slater glanced in the mirror. "Where are you, you sonuvabitch?" Stoplight coming up. *Reeves, I'll get you for this.*

Don't let him rattle you, he had to keep telling himself. You can't go see Sheila. Don't be crazy. Reeves could be there. Waiting.

The light changed. Slater drove through the intersection. Again, his eyes lifted to the mirror. And waited. And watched. And then, cruising through the patchy light half a block behind him, he saw glimmers of chrome and new paint. Reeves traveling without his headlights on.

I knew it!

Slater was bone cold. I knew it, he thought, I knew it, I knew it, I knew it. He sped past Balboa Avenue, headed in the direction of City Hall and beyond that the interstate. He had to think.

ALL RIGHT, YOU saw me, Burris Reeves thought. You made my car. He slowed, letting the distance between them lengthen. The night had served its purpose.

Where're you going, Henry, driving like a maniac? Nowhere. Nowhere, at all. You know you can't get away from me. I won't let you.

You're the man nobody knows, Henry, nobody but me.

I know. I know what you did.

All I have to do now is keep the pressure on.

And prove it.

29

"I CAN'T TALK long," Slater said the next morning. "I'm at a phone booth."

Sheila picked up the telephone from the dining room table and carried it into the kitchen. "Why're you calling me?" she whispered.

"Are you all right?"

"Yes, I guess so."

"I've been worried about you. Has anyone tried to talk to you?"

"Not really. I don't know what you mean."

"I can't explain right now—it's too complicated. Listen, something's come up. I'm not going to be able to get away this evening. And maybe not for a while."

"But why?"

"I can't go into it over the phone."

She walked toward the deepest set of windows in the kitchen, the ones farthest away from the dining room. "What're you saying? Is this your way of trying to get rid of me?"

"No, Sheila, God, no."

"But you promised—"

"I know what I said. Come on, that hasn't changed. I can hardly hear you. Is someone there?"

"I know I may not be much good to you, but I'm

361

in love with you. Do you mean we shouldn't see each other at all?"

"I can't do it now, baby. I just can't do it now."

There was a strain in his voice, an urgency, a fear, like the night at the farmhouse. He had frightened her that time, too.

Sheila said, "I hardly ever get to see you as it is. Don't you miss me?"

"All the time," he said. "I miss you all the time. But, baby, you've got to understand."

"Okay. For how long?"

"I don't know. A week or two. Maybe longer."

"Why're you doing this?"

"Because I have to. Can't you get it through your head? Because I goddamned have to."

All of a sudden Sheila felt dizzy. "So then . . . what about Founders Day?"

"No," he said bluntly. "No. Absolutely not. I don't think so."

She found herself pleading, "Couldn't you get away? Couldn't you please?"

"No, I told you I can't. Why won't you listen?"

She was trying to control herself and she was losing. "Jesus, you're scaring me." Tears stood in her eyes. One more minute and she wouldn't be able to hold them back.

"All I can say is—oh, Christ, Sheila, you've got to trust me. You just have to, that's all."

She was defenseless. She couldn't get her mind to focus on anything. "Don't you love me?" she whispered pitifully. "Don't you want to be with me?" She was crying now, and when he didn't answer her, she began to sob, the tears rolling down her face. She wiped them on the bottom hem of her work shirt.

"Come on," he said, impatiently. "Come on, Sheila,

I'm sorry but I really can't talk now. You don't know what's been happening. I just can't be doing this. We've got to stop—for a little while."

"No." She was crying. "Wait a minute. Just tell me why. Why?"

"I've got to get off," Slater said. "I can't. I can't stay on the phone. I'm crazy about you; that's all you should think about." And the line went dead.

"Hello . . . ," she muttered, through terrible rasping sobs. "Hello . . ."

From behind her, a shadow ebbed into the room. "Bye," Sheila said quickly and hung up. Putting the telephone on the counter, she wiped her eyes as Faith materialized at the other end of the kitchen. "What's the matter, darling?" she asked. "Boy trouble?"

"Yeah, kind of."

Faith couldn't help it; she saw the blue eyes quivering with big liquid tears and felt a wrench of compassion.

Sheila wiped her eyes a second time with her bare hands. "I loved someone," she confessed, as if needing to explain, "and now it's over." Then she was sobbing again uncontrollably, but before Faith could respond, Sheila darted out the back door.

It's happening, Faith thought, it's happening faster than I'd imagined. Yet, surprisingly, she took little joy in it. *I loved someone and now it's over.* For a second she couldn't help but feel Sheila's pain. I was young once. And in love. I'm sorry for you, she thought. In love with a murderer. Just like me.

Reluctant to intrude, Faith listened with her hands clenched to the girl crying. She waited another minute or so and then walked out to the back porch, thinking, Sheila, if only you knew, then what would you feel?

She was sitting outside on the step. Hearing Faith's footsteps, she let her head fall back to rest against the doorframe, but it didn't last. Quickly she again covered her face in her hands, weeping.

There was nothing Faith could do but wait, fighting back the pity until Sheila's crying subsided. "I can't think of anything to say that won't make this worse, but—" she stopped. She wanted to say, This will all be over soon. Instead, Faith asked her, "Are you going to be all right?"

"I guess so. I guess I've got to be."

I knew it'd all come crashing down.

"Try not to let it get to you," Faith said. "Why don't we drop off these things, have lunch and I'll take you shopping. You'll feel better, I'm sure of it."

He's beginning to panic, to lose his grip.

He'll do something terrifying.

That was the same morning that Faith had slipped Rachel's old dress into her purse. When she first saw it among the other clothes, a new idea began to take shape in her mind. It was completely unlike her, but now she was feeling she could do anything now. Henry's deceit, his compulsion, freed her worst fantasies.

The dress was pale blue, worth next to nothing and over the left breast pocket, in large elaborate letters, was the embroidered white monogram *RB*. Faith took it from a box of old clothes going to charity while Sheila was outside. Afterward, when they had dropped the boxes off at St. Vincent DePaul, she took Sheila to a very expensive lunch.

She bought the chicken livers early the next day, along with several other small items at the grocery; then she stopped at a gas station. In the ladies room, Faith disposed of the livers by flushing them down a toilet. All that remained was the red-black blood. There's no mercy, she thought, in prolonging this. She took out Rachel's dress, poured the blood over it and slipped the bloody dress into a Ziploc bag. This one's for you, Rachel, she thought. I'm doing this for you. But Faith knew she was in the grip of something far larger and more vicious than simple justice. She knew she could hardly contain what was happening; even she sensed that she had entered a new realm entirely.

Then it was a few minutes past twelve, and from the open plaza across Concepción Avenue, Faith watched Henry leave City Hall in the company of three other men. She rose from the stone bench and started toward his office, carrying her package.

30

COMING BACK FROM lunch a few minutes early, Slater noticed that the receptionist's desk was deserted. He went through the secretarial lair and passed only one of the clerk-typists, who happened to be painting her fingernails. Even Abigail was away from her desk. Everybody gets lazy in the summer, Slater thought, walking into his office. When he pushed the door shut, he found himself staring straight into Burris Reeves's face.

"Christ, Henry, look at that view," the big man said. "Always knocks me out. Maybe you don't know how lucky you are. If you ever miss·the common touch, come camp down in the basement with me, then you'll appreciate all this."

All Slater's instincts were ringing with danger.

"Oh, I think I appreciate it, Burris. What're you doing here?"

"I'm in the Traffic meeting you called for one-fifteen. That's where your secretary is right now—getting coffee. Your coffee maker's on the blink."

"Then make yourself at home."

Reeves's face broke into a smile. "Already have."

The other city officials were beginning to come in, shaking hands, drifting toward the conference table: Massey, the city clerk, Neil Hardwick, the commissioner of streets and highways. Bill Corbin, from the committee for urban development, came in with the representative from the research firm, who began putting up an easel and flip charts. Abigail followed soon after with the coffee urn.

Slater had gone behind his desk, some fifteen feet or so from the others. He dropped his suit jacket across the back of his chair and rolled his shirt sleeves. Taking the last cigarette from his shirt pocket, he lit it and tossed the crumpled pack into the wastebasket. When Abigail came by to ask if there was anything else, he said, under his breath, "This isn't the time or place, but we've got to find a better system for manning these offices at lunchtime."

"I'm sorry," she said. "I really don't know what happened. The girls must've gotten their wires crossed. Anyway—it won't happen again."

He couldn't say that it was already too late, couldn't say that he never wanted Reeves in his office, alone. Slater stubbed out his cigarette. "All right," he told her.

While the men began taking their places, Slater sat down at his desk to collect his notes for the meeting. Suddenly, he caught a whiff of a faint, rancid odor. But in an instant, it was gone. What was that? he thought, but couldn't place it. The midday sun beat viciously into the room. He ran his hand over his shirt pocket and realized he was out of cigarettes. When he opened the center desk drawer to get another pack, the smell flew in his face.

All he saw at first was blood—red-black blood—and he swallowed hard at the surge of nausea in his throat.

It took a moment to realize exactly what it was he was looking at. Beneath the vivid, dark splashes of

GARY DEVON

blood, he saw the old woman's dress with the monogram *RB*. Slater shuddered involuntarily. *Rachel's dress.*

Who did this?

He nearly panicked. Quickly, he pushed the drawer shut. *Oh, God . . . oh, God . . .*

He lifted his eyes to see who, if anyone, had noticed his shock, but no one was looking at him, no one except Reeves. Who was smiling.

God help me.

Still feeling sick, a fine, damp sweat turning cool on his forehead, Slater sat forward on the edge of his chair, clasping his trembling hands below the surface of the desk. Against the background of quiet conversation, he tried to gather his wits, but he couldn't focus on anything for more than a few seconds. *What am I going to do?* He was afraid to leave his desk, afraid that someone—Abigail perhaps—might come and open the drawer in front of his staff. Stop it, he told himself. Get a grip. Don't let Reeves see what he's done. Slater didn't have time to reason things out; he was aware of the men, one by one, turning to him, waiting for him to start the meeting.

His mouth felt dry and sour. He got up, and as he did, he felt the room swerve gently around him. He clutched at the edge of his desk for support. Divert them, he thought. Get them to focus on somebody else.

"All right," he said. His voice was hoarse. He coughed, cleared his throat and began again, "Let's get down to business . . . we're here to consider"—he paused and went on—"the expansion of Willow Creek Lane to a four-lane thoroughfare."

He didn't immediately take his place at the table but stepped in front of his desk, placing himself protectively between the men and the bloody drawer. Slater looked at each face in turn. "Let's get started with the traffic impact studies conducted recently by TSE Research. Mr. Eades, if you'd like to begin."

The men's faces turned from him. Everywhere he looked now, Slater seemed to see affirmation that things had gone wrong, dreadfully wrong. He couldn't see how he was going to get free. For the last seven weeks now, he had tried to brace himself, knowing that something was coming, sensing Reeves drawing nearer and nearer the truth. But he had expected a warning—or some veiled threat. This was worse. Much worse. Slater felt sick to his stomach as he listened, in a kind of a trance, to Eades's droning voice: " . . . resulting in an increased traffic load of thirty percent or roughly eight hundred fifty passenger vehicles per day."

All he could conjure up was the smooth, tan-pink tautness of Sheila's body, her lovely shadowed eyes. Sheila, Sheila, he kept thinking. What if Reeves knows all about you, too—my God, he's got to know about you. It'd started that night at the farmhouse. And been going on ever since. But how? Reeves, how did you get on to me?

The diamond. What did you find out about the diamond? Reeves, if you know, then I'm done for.

Suddenly he was filled with bravado, knowing that this life he was leading could be over in seconds. Make your move, Reeves, he kept thinking defiantly, if you're going to. All you have to do is open the drawer and it's all over.

The meeting was ending. It was four in the afternoon. Slater concealed his impatience as well as he could; he was constantly aware of Reeves watching him. Slater knew that the police chief could not be deterred in his pursuit of the truth in any way. How long have you been watching me, Reeves? How long have you been waiting for me to incriminate myself?

Then the men were gone and the room filled with the long emptiness of the sinking afternoon, all the minutes he would sit alone. Somewhere out by the elevators he could hear Reeves whistling a light, happy tune. Getting up and going to the door, Slater asked Abigail, "Was anyone here when you left at noon?"

"No."

"But—how did Burris know you had gone for coffee?"

Abigail smiled. "He was getting on the elevator when I was getting off on the second floor."

He nodded. "See that I'm not interrupted until quitting time."

Returning to his desk, Slater pulled the drawer open, and again the stench of old blood filled his senses. Again there was that twisting pain, dull this time, under his ribs. He closed the drawer as tightly as it would close; he sat down in his chair; he got up, but he couldn't avoid the stench—it was all around him. He breathed it in, deeper and deeper until he felt his lungs were contaminated with it.

My God. *Her blood.* I can't get away from it. It keeps coming back. He'd have to get a container—a plastic bag, he realized. Then he'd have to get it out of the building, without anybody seeing what it was, and destroy it. Burn it.

Sitting there, trying to muddle it through, he felt the cold rush of truth. The diamond! That had to be what it was. His diamond was the only piece of hard evidence Reeves could possibly have. That damned diamond!

I've got to kill him. Nothing else made any sense.

He knows too much. It was terrifying enough never knowing what Reeves was planning for him, but nothing was worse than coming face-to-face with it. Reeves did this—he's been dogging me all along and his timing was perfect—today, even Abigail was gone. He's still setting me up, still testing, waiting to see what I'll do. He's driving me crazy.

Damn you, Reeves, he thought, you know I can't live like this. I should've taken care of you a long time ago.

Downstairs, in police headquarters, was the man Slater was going to kill, the man who had to die. He felt curiously resigned about it now—more than resigned. He was thinking about a gun, a hired killer's sawed-off shotgun lying in a leather bag. An evil bastard of a gun, Reeves had called it.

Sheila could never know what his love for her had led to. But I can't see her. Reeves will be there—watching.

He knew how it would be done and where—the day, the hour. Slowly the anxiety and the dread left him.

When Abigail came into the room to say good night, he was sitting at his desk in the great flare of evening sunlight, apparently going over some of his notes from the meeting. Slater was attentive and pleasant to her but he didn't hear a word she said. His eyes were fixed the whole time at a point above and to the left of her head.

31

FOUNDERS DAY FELL on a Saturday at the end of June. It was the kind of vibrant summer day that drew people out of doors to spruce up lawns, to wash and polish cars, to light the charcoal in their grills. And Sheila felt, as she always had, the thrill of unbridled expectation. Every year, from the moment she woke up, it was the one day that was always charged with excitement—and this year that feeling of anticipation was even more pronounced. Because tonight she would see Henry Slater again; it would be unavoidable. She knew exactly where he would be this evening and she would go to him. He would have to look at her, speak to her. She didn't intend to make it easy for him to resist. To be down on the courthouse commons, tonight, with the orchestra playing and the scent of flowers everywhere—those were the minutes she lived for.

If she had been asked to account for her actions that morning, Sheila couldn't have, and yet there she was, driving slower and slower up Condor Pass, until she had hardly enough speed to carry her up the road's twisting curves. All she was aware of was an overwhelming need to see him. Where the pavement widened, cars were parked on the side of the road. In the opposite lane she saw one of her classmates transporting guests in a golf cart. Farther along, through the foliage, she glimpsed a milling crowd wandering through striped tents, then the Slaters' lawn opened fanlike before her. Across the lawn, she could hear violins.

Suddenly, emerging through the guests, Sheila saw him. She knew who it was by the confident way he moved.

So this's what they do, she thought. This is the party he couldn't invite me to. Or Faith either, for that matter, but Sheila put the blame squarely on Henry. Thinking she was being treated like an outcast, she experienced an intense, prickly jealousy. When she stopped parallel with the long slope of the lawn, she saw a boy she knew from school, a senior, coming toward her. "Hi, Sheila, you invited to this shindig?"

"No," she told him, "wish I was though."

"Hey, what do you hear from Denny? You two still going out?"

"Yeah, kind of. He's gonna be back in a few weeks. What're you doing here?"

"Taking invitations and parking cars," he said. "If you don't have an invitation, I'm supposed to tell you to move along."

"Oh, I'm not staying," she told him. "I just wanted to see what it was like up here." She shifted gears and hit the gas. "See ya," she called. She whipped into the end of the Slaters' driveway, swung back and headed down the hill.

The McPhearsons had invited her over for a cookout but Sheila didn't want to go. She hated having to invent lies in order to explain herself but she chafed under their solicitations. Still, that was where she ended up. It was quarter to three in the afternoon when she left, saying good-bye to Mary and promising to call on Monday. She had an appointment with the real estate agent at three-thirty—papers to be signed before the closing on the house. She dreaded going back out there—maybe, she thought, because she really didn't want to sell it after all, especially now that it was too late to change her mind.

Canyon Valley Drive was quiet. There was seldom any traffic at this time of day, even on weekends. Porches stood empty. A muggy oppressiveness hung on the air, a penetrating heat that seeped through Sheila's clothes. The sidewalks and lawns sweltered. Two old pickup trucks were parked in her driveway, so Sheila pulled off the pavement at the front of the yard and turned off the ignition.

Under the relentless sun, the staff of gardeners the real estate agency had hired made little headway. Three of them were at work now on the front yard, Mexican-Indians, she guessed them to be. One rode a noisy power lawn mower, another clipped the hedge and the third was wielding a machete against weeds that had sprung up among the dwarf trees edging the property.

Sheila was wearing shorts and the skimpiest halter-top she owned but still the humidity saturated her skin. She didn't relish the men looking at her so she got out of the car, ran up the driveway to the house and darted around back. She realized at once that something had changed. The grottolike rose trellis had caved in. It lay collapsed in a widespread ruin across the backyard.

Sheila remembered how much Rachel had loved those red roses. And the honeysuckle next door. It climbed the neighbor's clapboards, sending out long wavy tendrils into the air, their pale yellow blossoms like frilly trumpets giving off the sweetest perfume. Sheila remembered when she was young enough to sneak up on her grandmother while she gardened, catching her around the waist. Rachel's craggy face lit up as Sheila swung her round and round in a dizzying circle, the honeysuckle falling over them as if from the sky. "Sheila, let me go!" she'd cry, "now let me go, honey!" At times these flashes of memory struck Sheila with such blinding force that she would find herself standing as if paralyzed, sudden tears in her eyes. She could almost feel, again, the two of them buried in yellow leaves, with Rachel grinning up at her. "Gramma, d'you give up?" she'd urge, "d'you? d'you?" Then the picture would fade, and when Sheila pressed her eyes shut and tried to bring it back, nothing was there. The starched white curtains on the kitchen windows, the taste of the cookies the two of them once had made—they were only mere suggestions of the woman who had lived and breathed. And they were so few.

The kitchen felt stale, forgotten; the cupboards were empty. Almost all the packing was done. The things that were left had been tagged with sale numbers by the auctioneer. Sheila tried to imagine her grandmother sitting in that chair by the table, but now it was impossible.

She thought, The old trellises fall, we die and go away. Nothing stays the same. What do I have left? What could I bring back if I tried? Was she good to me? Yes. Gramma was good to me and I miss her. And yet, even my closest friends can't take the sadness away. Only being with Henry helped. And now, oddly enough, Faith.

Taking the tablecloth off the table, she went out to the backyard. When she shook it out, the starlings flew up in a dark, frightened cloud. Once the garden had been carefully tended and well kept, but now it lay in weedy ruins. Going inside, Sheila looked at the clematis near the place where Rachel's body had been found that morning. Could it have been only four weeks ago? Again, she felt a moment of frozen fear while the scene of that fog-bound morning replayed vividly in her mind. She almost expected still to find something—a trace of blood or some other horrible reminder left behind. But there was nothing. Only the sandy brick walkways. She would never get used to the thought that her grandmother was murdered, never as long as she lived. A mosquito whined in her ear; Sheila slapped at it and blew a wisp of hair from her eyes. I'm afraid of so many things, she thought. Sometimes for no reason at all, she would feel her muscles tightening up and that cold, cold feeling begin.

She was still standing at the edge of the garden when the real estate agent arrived. Sheila signed the contracts quickly. The property was sold. The realtor had scheduled the closing in ten days, asking if that was suitable. Sheila shrugged and said it was, as if the fact that she would no longer own Rachel's home meant nothing to her. After the woman had gone, she sat there at the kitchen table, utterly immobilized by dread.

She wandered upstairs into the big bedroom where Rachel had slept. The bed still stood where it had been for a lifetime. When the door swung shut, Sheila was confronted with a sharp image of herself in the full-length mirror, eyes meeting eyes irresolutely. I'm not like her, she thought. I wish I were.

The dusty room, long unaired, closed around her. Sheila crossed the landing to her own room and was comforted by it. It, too, never changed. She still kept some of her things here, even a few changes of clothes. The mahogany bedstead stood exactly as it always had, with its cracked finish and its vague smell of linseed oil: the result of years of Rachel's polishing. The windows were closed, windows that let in the dawn every single day for the last seven years.

I like it here, she found herself thinking. But was that possible? She had always dreamed of getting away. The times she had actually been away—even if it was for nothing more than staying overnight at one of her friends—she had not missed this place at all. Now as she went about opening the windows and shaking the dust off the curtains, there was a hollow ache in her stomach, an emptiness.

Strange, she thought. How awfully strange.

She went out to the Karmann Ghia and came back carrying her dress in a clear plastic bag. The gardeners had gone, taking the noise with them. As the afternoon wore on, Sheila glanced repeatedly out the window, humming softly to herself, waiting for nightfall and thinking of Henry, hiding her nervousness in the dozens of unnecessary tasks she set for herself.

Sheila turned back the covers on her own bed and smelled the warm damp odor of the unused sheets. She slipped off her clothes and stretched out naked between the sheets, feeling their coolness surround her. She could feel the sadness of dusk in the air. Occasionally, in the stillness, she heard the lonesome barking of a dog. Distances were already beginning to recede.

She listened to the last sounds of the afternoon— sounds she had been hearing, it seemed, since that first evening when, as a ten-year-old, she came to live in this house. The crickets began to signal in the grass and the yelling of children playing down the street dwindled away. This time of day, the advent of night could be frightening to a child coming to a strange place; tonight it only made Sheila feel more and more alone. She heard the abrupt flurry of the starlings in flight, and for an instant she imagined the sky alive and trembling with their wings. Suddenly, she thought, What if I never see him again?

That was something she couldn't imagine.

And besides it was time to get ready. Sheila took a bath, rinsing her hair in vinegar to bring out its golden highlights; she painted her nails. Her anticipation grew; her eyes glowed with expectancy. She couldn't bear to think that she had to waste all this sweet urgency she was feeling on waiting. She wanted to go to him and cling to him and be with him. This is the worst, she realized, because I didn't know what it was like to be really in love with him before, but I do now. And how did it happen? Henry brought me back to life.

I've got to forget about Faith; I can't think about her.

Tonight Sheila would wear the new dress of rough amber silk. Its cut was impeccable; the soft skirt moved when she moved. Spreading it out on the bed, she sat in her underwear and stretched out her splendid long legs, running her fingers over them as she pulled on her nylons. She slipped into the dress and thought, I shouldn't have sold the house. I should've found a way to keep it. But I didn't. Whatever happens, I did it; I did it to be free for him.

She was running a comb through her hair when she remembered Rachel straightening the part for her just so, cupping and lifting her chin ever so gently, looking into her eyes all the while asking, "Now who's the prettiest girl in the world?"

WITH FAITH AT his side, Slater looked very sure of himself, standing at the gateway to the barbecue, greeting late arrivals and saying good-bye to the guests who left early. But inwardly his nerves were about to snap. The pressure had been on him now far too long. Except for the diamond, Reeves had no evidence, no case, nothing; yet the pressure went on and on.

But now he waited; there was nothing he could do but wait. The party was teeming with guests, and he had to subject himself to their flattery and small talk. Soon it would be over. All afternoon and into the evening, he wondered where Reeves was and what he was doing. He hadn't appeared at the barbecue; there had been no sign of him. No matter where you are, it's going to happen tonight. You're going to die, Reeves. Nobody can stop it.

It was a quarter to six and the string quartet had packed its instruments before Slater made his way to the master bedroom. He stripped out of his suit and pulled on a navy blue golf shirt and dark blue poplin trousers. Faith asked him if he knew how long he would be and he told her that his shift at the booth ran until ten-thirty but he might be tied up until after midnight.

He drove the Eldorado into the municipal garage attached to City Hall and parked in the space marked RESERVED, MAYOR. But instead of heading for the commons, he took the elevator up to the second floor of the garage. Around the first turn, the Jeep was parked among other cars, waiting for him exactly as he had left it. Satisfied that everything was in place, he turned, went down the stairs and outside.

People spoke to him as he crossed through the park and he answered. Night had settled in. Clouds raced northward, sweeping over the city. Minutes later, Slater entered the Chamber of Commerce booth at the entrance to the midway. The members of the city council were out in force, selling raffle tickets for a new Ford Taurus, the money to be used to build a new bandshell. Slater shook hands all around; he shook Reeves's hand. "Evening, Burris, how's it going?"

"Fine, Henry, how about yourself?"

Thirty yards away, the crowd at the street dance applauded the end of the first number. No one knows what I'm about to do, Slater thought. He stood next to Burris Reeves and smiled out across the crowd. Through the loudspeakers, the sound of the orchestra was reedy and thin, the vocalist unintelligible. Down the midway, children were knocking over bottles, breaking balloons with darts, shooting ducks. At a glance, Slater saw a merry-go-round, a Ferris wheel, octopus rides and caterpillars, a tunnel of love. Girls were screaming joyously. In the sticky heat, the smell of sex hung in the air like woodsmoke; men and women bumped against one another, brushed shoulders, rubbed hips, until the air was rank with it. Slater thought this was true every year. His eyes missed nothing, every muscle in his body alert, sensitive to the whirl of movement around him.

It surprised him how easy it was to carry on ordinary conversations, even when his throat was dry with nervousness. So he talked on but his mind did not veer from the task that still lay before him, what he knew he had to do. A woman said, "Excuse me, Mr. Slater."

He said, "I'm sorry. But don't I know you?"

"Meredith Pannett," the woman said. "Shame on you, Mayor Slater, I worked as a volunteer for you last fall."

"Of course." Slater's face broadened into a magnanimous smile. He held out his hand. "It's great to see you."

SHEILA GOT BEHIND the steering wheel of the Karmann Ghia and started the engine. She looked at the large, square house flooded with streetlight as if seeing it for the last time, trying to imagine the place belonging to someone else. Never before had she been so acutely aware of time passing and of the changes that inevitably had come and were still to come. A gust of love for her grandmother came into her heart. Where do I fit in? she thought. What will become of me?

She turned into the driveway, backed out and sped down the winding lane. For Sheila, it was always a mysterious, thrilling feeling to be driving through the night. Within minutes, she was in the thick of things. All around her, drivers sat in their expensive cars, waiting for the light to change. Somewhere a bell was ringing, and grade school girls crossed through traffic in shorts and T-shirts, their tanned arms and legs quivering like deer. Sheila parked on a side street a few blocks away from the carnival lights and hurried from the car.

She could feel the danger she was bringing down upon the two of them. She had never defied him before, but tonight she couldn't help herself. She had to be close to him.

Sheila made her way through the crowd until finally she saw him. A week and a half had passed since she had spent any time with him and again she tried to rehearse what she would say and do. Act nonchalant, she told herself. Sheila knew exactly what she wanted, but not quite how to go about it. What should I say? I had the weirdest dream about you. No, too trite. Maybe: I don't know what got into me; I came into town so I thought maybe I would . . . She knew she couldn't very well say, This is a matter of life and death, although, to Sheila, it was.

I had to see you. I couldn't wait any longer.

She arrived at a place ten feet in front of him with the crowd flowing both ways around her when she stopped, afraid to go on. How would Henry react? He would be surprised, naturally, but would he be happy? What exactly did she think she was doing? Sheila couldn't make sense of it, even to herself. Then she realized that she had been holding her breath all that time, and she gasped for air.

It was at that moment he saw her—her hair tumbling over her shoulders, her eyes moist with love and so blue they pierced his heart. His first thought was, How could I do without her for so long? His second, What's gotten into you? Don't you know what you're doing?

Slater watched her walk toward him, zigzagging through the crowd, her skirt shifting softly about her knees. As if oblivious to the attention she generated from the men around her, concentrating entirely on him, she looked shy and scared coming across the midway.

She was there, before him.

My God, Sheila, why're you doing this?

She looked down at the toes of her shoes, then up

at his face. Under his breath, Slater said, "What're you doing here?"

"I had to see you," she answered quietly. "I had to—"

Quickly he glanced to the side and saw the bottom half of Reeves's pant leg six feet away. "Fill out these tickets," he told her out of the police chief's range, then he slid a booklet of raffle tickets across the makeshift counter of plywood.

Reeves saw it unfold: suddenly Slater's attention was no longer on the booth and it was obvious where it had gone. He couldn't see Slater's eyes, but the look the girl was giving back to him was deep and seductive and intimate. Much too intimate. There was no mistaking the willfulness that flowed from her. It was pure voltage and it was concentrated directly at Slater.

Suddenly, for Reeves, it all fell into place—all the loose ends that he had struggled with. He knew.

He knew why it had happened. It was all in the girl's face.

Now Reeves knew everything he needed to know.

"Don't do this," Slater whispered and immediately turned to greet a couple that had come up for tickets. I'll never recover from this now, he thought. When Reeves sees her here, he'll know for sure.

He took her tickets when Sheila had finished filling them out and collected the five dollars she placed in his hand. "What's wrong with you?"

Her smile withered. "Nothing," she said, "nothing's wrong with me."

"You shouldn't be here like this," he whispered, his face grave.

Outwardly Sheila maintained her composure while inside she yearned for him; she wanted to touch him and to be touched. "Don't hold it against me," she said. She didn't like to think that she had caused him trouble, but she was taking risks too and she thought he might appreciate it. She wanted him to do something, say something. She wanted him to tell her he still loved her, still wanted her. She needed to hear him say these things.

"Why don't you just go?" he said and turned away, abandoning her. He was gone—down the counter to talk with someone else.

How could you? she thought, astonished with the swiftness of his departure. Don't leave me standing here. How cruel that he had the power to destroy all her warmth with a few words. Sheila backed away and fled through the crowd to her car. "Well, thank you," she muttered to herself, "thank you very much."

Then it came to her for the first time: Henry had dropped her. Sheila tried to resist believing it, but she couldn't. He wasn't coming back. How could he change so much? In such a short time? I must've been out of my mind to think— Panicked, she wheeled the Karmann Ghia out into traffic.

Biting her lips to keep back the tears, she drove recklessly up the ramp, onto the interstate. She drove but there was no thrill in the speed, no joy in the rush of wind. "Henry—" she sobbed. She continued south, driving aimlessly, speeding, the needle twitching on seventy. The highway had filled with trucks; oncoming lights blinded her. Hopeless. Hopeless. She ached with exhaustion and loneliness and desire, wanting to be in his arms and to go to sleep with his warm body lying crushed upon her.

Why did I do it? Why did I say those things to him? It loomed in her mind larger and larger. Fleeting lights, silhouettes of trees, starlight—she turned into the graveled driveway on Canyon Valley Drive, leaning her head against the side window. Sheila felt as if this day had taken place a long time ago. It seemed like a year had passed with each minute.

She climbed out of the car and ran into the dark, empty house. *Home,* she thought. *I'm home! Gramma, I'm home!* Until this moment, it had seemed that Henry Slater and their time together was the brightest, clearest thing in her mind and that this house and Rachel's memory existed only in a haze. Now everything was reversed. Now only this home was real. But Sheila had sold it. For him. She couldn't get it back.

The hard truth of what she'd done brought back the sorrow of these many weeks, the sweet and exquisite pain ... the loss ... the life she'd had with Rachel and the time when all Henry did was give her things, the beautiful feeling she had lost and couldn't get back again, the place she could never return to, the dream of finding that place again and struggling not to let go, lying in bed clutching the past to her breast and yet feeling it slip away, like breath. That was when it was finally gone, when she could no longer bring back the memory of her own innocence, even in her dreams.

The tears were running down Sheila's face and she threw back her head and screamed.

THE MALCOLMSONS, NEXT door, heard the long, thin, eerie cry through their open windows. Then came a second, like an echo of the first. And a third.

Ted Malcolmson, his hands full of the Saturday evening newspaper, came into the hall from his study. His wife met him from the kitchen, wiping the dishwater from her hands on her apron and reaching behind herself to untie it. "My God," she said, "that has to be Sheila. You'd better go over there. I'll come with you."

It was hardly ten minutes later that the telephone rang at the Slaters' and Faith picked it up.

"Could you come right away?" asked Annie Malcolmson. "It's Sheila. She's awfully upset, Faith. She's asking for you."

32

AT A QUARTER to ten that evening Slater walked across the midway and ordered a dozen barbecue sandwiches at the Lions Club concession. Reeves thought, What's going on, Henry?

Shortly after ten, he slapped the police chief on the shoulder, picked up the bag of sandwiches and set off through the crowd. When he was nearly out of sight, Slater cast a glance back at Reeves silhouetted against the spinning, multicolored lights of the Ferris wheel.

Reeves stepped aside to allow free passage to the people moving around him, but his eyes were on Henry Slater. *Now what've you got up your sleeve?* He couldn't be sure of anything tonight; the man was too much of a wild card. Especially now that the girl had entered the picture. Reeves could see that Slater was really strung out. All his instincts told him to get to the District Attorney right away, but he didn't want to let Slater out of his sight. Tomorrow morning would have to be time enough to swear out a warrant for his arrest.

With the sack of barbecue sandwiches clutched in his left hand, Slater struck off through the park toward City Hall and was soon swallowed up in the crowd. All was in readiness, or nearly all. He walked briskly, keeping to the schedule he had set for himself hours earlier. The timer controlling the lamp in his office would come on at precisely ten-fifteen. He'd have twelve minutes, no more, to get past the policemen on duty and vanish down the lower-level hallway; they would think he was going to his office by way of the back stairs. It was going to be a little tight.

Slater didn't hurry; he was deliberately matter-of-fact in order to give the impression of not hurrying. He could feel the deep pulse of the city. The sound of a produce truck crossing the intersection echoed in the street. The city park and its crowds sank behind him. The street was empty now. He passed dark stores, locked doorways, parked cars.

He entered the municipal parking garage at the Concepción entrance, immediately took the elevator down to Lower Level One and got out. He looked at his watch. 10:12. Perfect. The door to the police department was three steps down. Going inside he always had the sensation of passing into a cavern hung with torches, bathed in half-light. As his eyes focused, a figure appeared—a patrolman faced him behind the front desk. "Evening, Mayor Slater."

"Good evening," he said. He saw two other patrolmen come to their feet in the background. "Thought you guys might like a snack," he said, offering them the bag of sandwiches. "You having a fairly slow night?"

"There's nothing going on," one of them said. "We've got a couple drunk and disorderlies dryin' out. That's all."

After minutes of small talk, Slater winked and said, "I guess I'd better get on upstairs. You guys have a nice evening."

"You, too," they said. There were three of them, altogether, one about to go on patrol.

The hallway was quiet. His shadow loomed up and switched behind him as he went through pools of fluorescent light. Three quarters of the way down the corridor, he looked back over his shoulder: it was exactly as he'd hoped. The officers were too busy eating and laughing to notice his hand on the doorknob to the police chief's outer office. Slater turned it and stepped inside, immediately shutting the door behind him without a sound. The darkness sealed around him—he felt as if he stood in a black pit. For a moment, he leaned against the door frame, listening, listening. Nothing. Holding his hands out before him like a blind man, Slater moved forward until his fingers brushed the side of the secretary's desk.

He shut his eyes to let them adjust to the darkness, still trying to listen for any odd sound at all. Unless Reeves kept the diamond on him, which seemed highly unlikely, it was here somewhere, but Slater didn't have the time to search for it. Taking the penlight from his pocket and directing it at the floor, he turned it on.

A halo surrounded the thin projectile of light on the carpet. He moved behind the secretary's desk and opened the top right-hand drawer. He found what he was looking for in the rubberized compartment tray: the small ring containing the keys to Reeves's office and credenza.

He slid the drawer shut. Keeping the penlight aimed at the floor, Slater moved directly across the room, inserted the key into the office door, and switching off the light in his hand, let himself in. The drapes on the one large window had been left

open and a beam of light from the parking lot outside cut through the office in a wide stripe. Remaining in the shadows, he crossed to Reeves's credenza
and unlocked it.

The rectangular door clicked open. In seconds
Slater found what he had come for—he lifted the
LeFever shotgun from the oversized gym bag, checking to make sure Reeves hadn't dismantled it. The
gun was assembled and in good working order and
the thought of what it could do chilled him. Feeling
through the dark, his hand closed on the cartridges—
three of them, which he put in his pocket.

Taking the shotgun with him, he went around to
the office door, stepped out, locked it and put the
key into his pocket. His eyes had grown so accus-
tomed to the dark that he was now able to navigate
his way without using the penlight. Again, he listened, pressing his ear to the door that opened onto
the hall. These were moments of intense danger; he
could feel himself sweating and wiped his eyes and
his brow with his sleeve. Placing the unloaded shotgun inside his jacket, he turned the knob and eased
the door open two or three inches.

Through the gap, he studied the front desk at the
end of the hall. Now even the smallest mistake would
be disastrous. A lone officer sat at the desk paging
through a magazine when a second policeman drifted
into view and started a conversation. Slater couldn't
decipher what they were saying but he heard them
laughing. The officer at the desk turned a page;
after a few seconds the other one sauntered from
sight. Slater knew he couldn't wait any longer. Biting
down on his lower lip, he stepped into the corridor,
keeping close to the wall. With his free hand, he
pulled the door gently shut.

He went out through the fire door and climbed the fire stairs two at a time to the second floor. From there he took the skywalk across to the parking garage. It was 10:29. There was no one in sight. Everything was so still that his light footsteps resounded from the concrete walls. Slater got behind the wheel of the Jeep and thought about his next move without haste. He started the engine and drove slowly out of the garage.

Slater inhabited a night world full of waiting. Waiting for Reeves. He kept wanting to turn his head, wanting to search the street behind him, but he knew he shouldn't. He strained, listening for the sound of another engine turning over somewhere on one of the nearby streets, but he heard nothing. He was a man alone driving through the streets at night, nothing more.

Reeves must still be at the picnic.

I've got to put myself in his path.

When he drove by the entrance to the carnival, he saw him. There you are, Reeves. Confident, menacing Reeves, leaning against the front fender of his new cruiser. Slater drove past him without appearing to look, but he saw the long, sleek shape of Reeves's new cruiser. Now it was only a matter of time.

Reeves's headlights flashed in his rearview mirror as the cruiser swept round and into the lane nearly a full block behind him.

That's right, Reeves, follow me.

They were driving along Columbia Avenue, bypassing the interstate, coming steadily closer to the old parkway that ran south along the oceanfront then tapered inland through the country. Never had he noticed how deserted this section of Rio Del Palmos was at night. The pavement narrowed, the trees grew thicker and more erratic, garden walls were interspersed with fields. When he looked in the rearview mirror, headlights reflected in his eyes.

I must be crazy, he thought.

Sheila. Will you forgive me for this, Sheila? God, you don't know what I've had to do. Don't you see? Sheila, don't you see I have to do it?

Every fraction of a second he and Reeves were drawing nearer and nearer the place where it would happen and Slater could feel his heart beating, marking off the time. He wanted to get out of the car and run and run, but there was no getting away from this.

He sped through the darkness, heading out of town. Again he glanced in his mirror and saw the headlights. Stay with me, Reeves. The lovely slickness of the night moved with him. He saw Sheila's face staring after him, all great wide eyes, as he sped deeper and deeper into darkness. It's almost over, he thought. He wanted to tell her so many things.

The road he was looking for was unmarked and overgrown with honeysuckle. Finally it was before him. Vines trailed across his windshield; branches full of leaves brushed the bottom of the Jeep. Somewhere to his right, beyond the black rim of trees, was the glimmer of the ocean.

The thicket gave out onto a grassy glade that hissed in the breeze. Across the bay, the red, yellow and blue lights reflected in the water like glittering pendants for a young girl to dangle in the night. Slater stopped the Jeep, let go of the steering wheel and felt how wet his palms were. He flexed his fingers, surprised to find them aching from his grip. Everything he touched was slippery with sweat. He knew it had to happen and yet he felt empty, as if he'd never really believed it could come to this.

It will be here, he thought.

REEVES CAUGHT THE gleam of red taillights and slammed on his brakes. "He's turned off," he said to himself, grinding the accelerator to the floor. The cruiser fishtailed, skidded to the shoulder and spun around. He returned to the mouth of the old trail and pulled up. It didn't make sense. Why would Slater take this old road? Where was he going—to meet that girl? There was nothing down there but an old lovers' lane; not even a lane any more, just an old dead-end trail going down to the ocean. Reeves knew the place well from his nights on patrol before he ran for office. A shelf of grass overlooked the Pacific there, but what could a man alone want down there on a hot June night? Unless he was meeting the girl?

Crouched forward over the steering wheel and peering through the overgrowth in front of him, he turned into the forgotten lane. Ruts in the old road caught the cruiser's tires and made its progress a clumsy zigzag. Reeves couldn't see the taillights of the Jeep now; he couldn't hear its engine. He had all he could do to hold the steering wheel on course toward the faint glimmer of night sky at the end of the green tunnel. Gradually, the trees thinned. No power on earth could have stopped him now. I'm going to find out about you once and for all, Reeves thought, and I'm going to put a stop to you. As he broke into the open, he cut his headlights and slowed even more, hoping to remain undetected until he got his bearings.

The night, the beach: Slater had driven the Jeep

right out to the edge of the grassy shelf above the water. The driver's door hung open like a broken wing. All right, Reeves thought, where'd you go? Down to the beach?

He swung the steering wheel to the left, bringing the cruiser onto the high grass to place it between himself and the Jeep. Quickly, he got out of the car and closed the door. The ocean gleamed through the foliage. And yet, what if it wasn't the girl? What if it was something else? Unbuckling the leather strap on his holster and letting his right thumb rest on the handle of his Magnum, Reeves started around the front of the car. All the sounds of the night rose to meet him.

He could not hear his own footsteps, his own breath. He had gone only a few steps when he felt a sudden sharp pang of unease.

What's wrong? Something's wrong.

From the corner of his eye, he saw a figure rise up among the silvery palmettos. For an instant, the shape seemed composed of shadows. But it wasn't the shadows. Henry Slater was standing no more than ten feet away, and in a voice that he knew only too well, said, "Looking for me, Burris?"

Reeves turned to face him. The shotgun Slater was holding steadied, and Reeves stared into the twin black holes of the barrels, his mind racing, What're you doing with that shotgun? I know that gun. That's the gun from my office.

The twin hammers drew back. The LeFever clicked, twice, ready to fire.

Reeves was operating on automatic, all his instincts flash-feeding him. He's right-handed, he realized. If he fires, an old gun like that will likely pull to the left.

"Goddamn you, Henry," he said and he pitched to the right for the high grasses, the blast of both barrels exploding in his face. A red-hot mass ripped him open down his right side as he was thrown back across the hood of his car. He let out a long, agonized scream and slid, then fell slowly downward onto his face, lost in waves of shock and pain.

Lunging and twisting, he tried again and again to get up. He had fallen over his gun, on top of it, his hand groping weakly at his side as if trying to get at it, but he was only trying to take the pain in his hands.

Then he fell over on his back and the night closed over him.

LIKE A NIGHTMARE, Slater watched the shots disintegrate in the man's flesh. He could almost feel their incredible violence. The monstrous kick of the shotgun, the abrupt obscene touch of it, still registered in his hands and arms; the flash from the twin muzzles, the blue smoke, the smell of cordite, filled his senses. The echoes faded into themselves.

At first he couldn't bring himself to look at the body. So much blood streaked over the hood and down the side of the car that a wet heavy scent rose from its glistening surfaces. Slater clutched at a bush for support, tucking his chin in hard against his chest, dizzy and nauseated.

Slater began to shake. The worst thing had been the sheer terror. Reeves lay on his side, his arm flung up and back across his face, covering all but his forehead and the corner of his right eye—the tiny, unafraid eye that gleamed and did not close.

God, Slater thought, what if he's still alive?

It was becoming easier to bear, but not much. He

stepped around the bloody places and stooped down to examine the body. No question that he was dead. Slater reached around to the police chief's pocket and pulled out the slim leather-grain notebook.

Then it dawned on him: the noise could've carried for miles. What if someone down the beach had heard?

Slater was off, racing back to the Jeep. And as he ran what he had done grew more and more distant from him so that when, at last, he swung into the seat, Burris Reeves was as far from him as the stars above his head. He looked at his watch and understood that time no longer had a hold on him. He was free. He didn't want to think anymore, not about Reeves, not about Faith or his job, not about anything but Sheila. He wanted to let his mind fill up with the memory and sensuality of her until it had crowded out and obliterated everything that had been before her. The hot sweet relief was overpowering.

He would go to her now and take her away.

Suddenly, he was a long way from the murder scene and he was back in the city, back to who he really was. Slater turned his face toward the glittering sky world and his heart soared in triumph.

THE BRICK DRIVEWAY curved among the enchanted-looking oaks that overspread the lawn, thin dots of moonlight lying in the grass like scattered coins. Aglow at the center of the moonlit darkness, lights on in every room, was his home. Home, he thought and shook his head. It had never been his home. It was all meaningless now. He couldn't wait to leave it—to get away and start his life over with the girl he loved. Slater went up the walk, crossed the veranda, opened the door and went in. And what he saw gave him a deathly chill.

"Oh, Henry, darling, look who's here," Faith said. "Sheila was so upset I thought she should stay with us for a while."

And there they were, Sheila and Faith, sitting side by side on the sofa, their wondering eyes staring at him. But it was the way their hands were clasped together between them that seemed to defy anyone to tear them apart.

PART
FOUR

33

SILENT PATROL CARS flanking it front and rear, the ambulance rolled to the lowest shallows of the parking lot behind City Hall and the criminal justice system of Rio Del Palmos took possession of the murder case of Police Chief Burris Reeves. It was a mark of the severity of the crime that the mayor climbed out of bed and came down to police headquarters in person at four in the morning. A couple of kids looking for a place to park had come upon the body two hours earlier. Nothing even remotely like this had ever happened here. Slater hugged himself against the dampness of the dark hour and gazed down at the pellet-riddled face that would never plot its mischief again.

As the body passed into the hands of the medical examiner, Slater turned to the patrolmen standing uselessly around him. Immediately, he assigned two of them to seal off Burris Reeves's office and to await further instructions. "No one goes in there," he told them, "unless I say so." At the front desk, he put in a call to Abigail and asked if she would come in as soon as possible. "I'm sorry to wake you at this hour," he explained, carefully considering his words, "but I'm going to need you. Burris Reeves has been killed."

"Oh—" He heard the catch in her voice. "Yes, Mayor, yes, of course—I'll come right down."

"I wouldn't ask you to, if it wasn't . . . a crisis."

Then Slater returned to the trunk of his car for his briefcase.

He set up a temporary command post in the police chief's outer office. "What's the name of Burris's secretary?" he asked the two patrolmen stationed outside the door. "Maggie . . . ," they said, "Maggie Fitch." To the first of them, he said, "Give her a call, try to get her down here and then go downstairs, wait for the medical examiner's report and bring it to me."

He turned to the second officer. "Keep your position here and see that I'm not disturbed for ten minutes. I've got to try to get organized."

Left alone, Slater went into Reeves's office and locked the door. He pulled the drapes, turned on the fluorescent desk lamp and opened his briefcase. Keenly aware of the passing seconds, he picked up the LeFever shotgun. Working quickly, he tightened the wing nut at the back of the tubular-steel stock, firmly reattaching it to the gun. With the key from his pocket, he opened the credenza and put the shotgun back into the oversized gym bag. As it had been.

Methodically, he searched through the desk drawers one by one and came upon a small manila envelope with a lump of soiled tissue inside it. Is this it? he thought, undoing the metal clasp. Is this where he kept it? Inside the tissue. *My diamond. It's my diamond.* A smile spread over Slater's face. He put the diamond into the envelope and slid it into his pocket. Quickly he went through the stacks of papers on top of Reeves's desk. Finally, he located the thick file marked BUCHANAN, RACHEL, and placed it inside his briefcase. Then he had second thoughts, picked it up again and sandwiched it between two handfuls of current files.

When he had done all the things he could think to do, Slater unlocked and opened the door. In the hall, Abigail was demanding that the patrolman outside the door admit her; Slater immediately intervened. "We'll need to call the members of the city council," he told her. "What time is it now?" They looked at their watches. "All right, quarter to five. Have them here at seven, if you can, for an emergency meeting. The purpose of the meeting will be to appoint an interim chief of police." In his arm, he carried the stack of as many as a dozen files, including the file on Rachel Buchanan. "I'll need these files to brief the interim police chief. Abigail, would you take these up and then coordinate with Miss . . . Fitch."

When Reeves's secretary arrived, Slater told her, "Don't let anyone take anything from this office without signing for it. Starting with my office. My secretary has taken a number of the files, which I'll need to give the new police chief in a couple of hours. But I've instructed her to inform you what they are." He handed her the keys to Reeves's office. "It's your responsibility. I'd like to have a status report on each of the bombing investigations, if you can pull that together."

"By what time?"

"Before seven if possible," he told her. "I'll be upstairs."

In the short time he had been sequestered in the office the word of Reeves's murder had gotten around and a small crowd of reporters was already waiting for him as he made his way past the front desk toward the elevators. He ducked his head and waved off the usual crash of questions; a cameraman suddenly loomed before him, poking a television camera in his face before Slater could sidestep him into the elevator. "I'll have a statement later this morning," he said as the doors snapped shut.

Abigail updated him, handing him a stack of telephone messages as he went through to his office. He shut and locked the door. The sun was just coming up, a pale blue rim in the east, the palm trees and buildings below still in hard, black silhouette. Going to his desk, he was taken aback by the number of calls from police all up and down the coast offering their help. No, he thought, no, we don't need this. He could imagine police from everywhere in California swarming all over his city.

He got Abigail on the intercom and reminded her to tell them thanks, but no thanks, in a nice way. "We'll take care of our own," he said. Then putting the matter out of his mind for the time being, Slater carefully, laboriously, went through the Buchanan murder file.

He found his own name mentioned only twice, on two different pages. The handwriting wasn't quite the same, which he took as an indication that Reeves had been musing, perhaps doodling and thinking about him, on two different occasions. Slater was certain there had been many more times than that, but apparently Reeves had made no note of it. At least not here.

Slater removed the two pages from the file and put them among his own papers inside his notebook, to be disposed of at another time. Then he threw the file back into his briefcase, closed it, and leaned back in his chair.

It was done. At last; at last.

Everything had gone according to plan—except for Sheila. Damn it! Damn it to hell! Although Faith had explained to him about getting the phone call, he still couldn't imagine it. *Sheila!* Christ! There at the house with Faith. It was unthinkable. But he couldn't take the time to straighten it out right now. He would though, he would, just as soon as this horror was over. He had to stay alert; there were too many demands on him.

In speaking before the cameras later that same morning, Mayor Henry Lee Slater announced the appointment of Vincent P. Koehler to the post of acting police chief. Koehler, a veteran of nearly twenty-five years on the force and having the highest seniority, stood at Slater's side and was flanked by other members of the city council. After an expression of grief and a few brief comments, Slater turned the microphone over to Koehler, who in the course of answering reporters' questions, announced that he would be heading up a special task force with Mayor Slater to investigate the murder. No speculation was made as to who the killer or killers might have been. When asked if he thought this could be the work of the one remaining convict still at large, Koehler would only say that the investigation was ongoing.

He's no Reeves, Slater thought as the conference was concluded. He reached out and shook Koehler's hand. "Good man," he said. "Good man."

NEVER IN THE history of Rio Del Palmos had there been such a funeral, never such an outpouring of anger and frustration and remorse. The entire town shut down for the hour of the church service. Policemen from all along the western coast formed an honor guard to accompany the coffin. The procession from the church stretched for nearly two miles. Cars were parked three across in the cemetery lanes. By some estimates as many as three thousand mourners attended.

There were those who said Henry Slater's eulogy could not have been more inspired. Time and again his words were punctuated with angry cries for revenge from the crowd. But they were quieted by Slater's promises that the murderers would be caught and made to suffer the harshest justice.

LATER THAT AFTERNOON, Faith made herself drive down to the Reeves's house to pay her respects. She had to. She was the mayor's wife. Winding her way through the countless neighbors who were there to help, she finally found Mrs. Reeves in her bedroom, surrounded by family, hysterical with grief. Faith meant only to take the time to tell the distraught woman that she and the mayor would help in any way, but Mrs. Reeves begged her to stay, to sit with her son. And then to see the child sobbing convulsively. Faith couldn't help it—her eyes grew wet, and once she'd started she could hardly stop. Here, too, she understood well what had happened. He had done this awful thing. First Rachel, now Burris Reeves. She had known it as soon as she heard the news.

Who am I, she thought, that I can still love a man who could do these things? Who am I that I could get to this place myself? The man should be put away. But I can't, God help me, I can't.

She stayed as long as she could, loathing it but

staying. Suddenly she had to get out of there. A
great rage had overtaken her. Rage at him. All that
dignity at the funeral, all the fine pretense about
Reeves and what he'd meant to "the city." And no
one the wiser. *Only I know.* She wanted to tear him
apart.

34

IT WAS DRIVING him crazy.

He couldn't get used to it—it was like an insane joke of fate seeing them together. At the end of the day, coming in through the door to the laundry room, he would hear their laughter in the kitchen. Slater never knew what to expect, but he was surprised to see them walking around in their stocking feet, pouring some sort of drink. Sheila was too young to drink.

"Want something, Henry?" Faith asked. They appeared to be completely comfortable, infinitely relaxed with each other. How could this have happened? And so quickly? After Marjorie Sanders had given her permission for Sheila to stay with them, what could he say? He had to give in. He shook his head and went to the bedroom to change clothes. Down the hall, he could still hear their voices.

Faith and Sheila. Sheila and Faith.

Who could have known that she would have invited her to *stay* here? In my house!

It seemed he hardly had time to put out one fire before another sprang up somewhere else. I'm dying the death of a thousand leaks. If only I could talk to her alone, he thought. If I could touch her. She was in his blood, running through his veins, eating through him with a sweet burning. But Faith was always there. And so kind, so damnably kind. To Sheila. To him.

At night as he was getting ready for bed, Faith sometimes moved up close to him and for a brief moment she was familiarity itself. With Sheila two doors away. It was maddening. He didn't want to touch her, didn't want to be near his wife.

Every day dawned glassy and clear; the eucalyptus and jade plant hedges turned a deep ocean green. Every morning, dressed for the office, he went down the hall and, on the other side of the door to the guest room, he could hear the sound of water running— Sheila taking her shower. If only he could wrap her in an enormous towel and carry her back to bed.

He missed her almost more than he could bear. He was lifeless without her. He waited for a chance to see her alone in the evening and then dreaded the thought of going home because more and more they weren't there. Faith had started leaving him annoying little notes—notes that he quickly grew to hate: *Sheila and I are at the club. Why don't you join us?* Or, *We've gone shopping. Be back late.*

"God," Henry said, under his breath. "God, God, God."

Nights he spent drinking alone, trying to make some sense out of things. He saw that Sheila was changing little by little over the week, then the week and a half she had been living there. He was powerless to stop it. And the way she had begun to carry herself, her expressions. Just like Faith's. He wanted to shake her, hard, shake some sense into her. He wanted to rave at her: don't you see what she's doing to you?

They sat at the dinner table, waiting for Luisa to

serve dessert. Faith was talking; he hadn't a clue about what, and Sheila was listening attentively, toying with her hair, lifting strands first over one ear then the other. Never once stealing a glance at him. Running her fingertips inside the gold chain of her necklace, she lifted it to her mouth, drawing the bright thread slowly through her teeth. His palms were clammy.

She was getting down glasses from the wall cabinet one evening when he came in from the office. It seemed the perfect coincidence for them to be suddenly and unaccountably alone. The sight of her stretching upward lured him on. Sheila had her back turned; he needed only to be beside her for a moment, perhaps to let his hand fall over hers as she filled the glasses, when he heard Faith entering from the back balcony. "Darling," she said, both of them looking at him now, "how was your day?"

When he could bear it no longer, he went to his study and finding no peace there, he went to bed early. He lay awake, listening, following their little sounds through the house, footsteps up and down the hallway and back again to the guest room. Sheila's room. Doors opening and closing. The rustle of nightgowns, whispers, a muffled giggle. Girl talk, he thought, goddamn girl talk. Once late at night while Faith slept beside him, he woke to the click of a doorknob in the hall. He lay waiting for Sheila to appear, perhaps in the door, perhaps to beckon him, but Sheila didn't.

When he was home, he couldn't escape the thought of her. The look in her eyes was different, lovelier perhaps but different, and her makeup was different. She would smile at him, her eyes shining. Noth-

ing else. On one of those few occasions when Faith
wasn't in earshot, he said, "When can I see you?"

"You're seeing me."

"Sheila," he whispered desperately, "I don't care
what happens, as long as I can see you—as long as
we're together." He was nearly out of his mind. He
looked for that sensuality in her eyes and it was
there. Smoldering. He knew that she felt it. But she
wouldn't do anything about it.

One evening when they left him to attend a bene-
fit for the Women's Club, Sheila was wearing Faith's
simplest black sheath, and pinned at the center of it,
above her breastbone, was Faith's cameo.

Another night when Sheila brushed by him on her
way to her room, if he had closed his eyes, it might
have been Faith. It was Faith's scent, her perfume:
Ma Griffe.

It was driving him crazy.

35

SHEILA HAD BEEN living with the Slaters for nearly three weeks when Faith accepted a dinner invitation at the club for Saturday evening and invited Sheila along. "You don't mind, do you, Henry?"

"Why should I mind?"

It was after six when Slater arrived home, expecting to find them preparing to go, but Faith's car wasn't in the garage. A misty, whispering drizzle had begun. He stood under the eaves for a moment, looking out at the edge of the gray-green hazy woods, dripping with rain. Where are they? he wondered, angrily. They're never where they should be anymore.

He went inside to take his shower. He had finished shaving when Faith rushed into the bedroom. "Sorry we're late. Traffic was horrendous. How long will you be?"

"It's yours," he told her.

He was buttoning his shirt when he heard the spray of her shower. Looping his tie around the back of his neck, he needed to see what he was doing and leaned toward the triple mirrors of her vanity to complete the knot. At first he noticed nothing unusual—her vanity was a shambles, as it always was—but then he caught sight of a thin edge of paper protruding from under her silver tray. Curious, Slater pulled it out.

What's this? he thought. Some kind of letter? And why had Faith hidden it? Why was it torn in half?

Slowly a flush darkened the coppery skin across his cheekbones. Slater held the two torn pieces of paper in his hands, gazing at them as if dumbstruck. He saw that originally it had been a single sheet of notepaper folded over once—it was obvious that the two halves fit together, that it had been a letter. For a moment, the handwriting blurred before his eyes—all except for the signature: *Rachel Buchanan.*

An awful fear began to steal through him—a chill that raised gooseflesh on his arms. His world seemed suddenly as fragile as glass, full of broken cracks through which he would fall forever. In an instant everything changed.

It has to do with Henry.

The words stared up at him with simple, untouchable truth. He understood exactly what it meant. It was like the dawn of death.

Faith did this.

His hatred was a living thing. *It was Faith.* The bedroom went black before his eyes. He stood absolutely still, far beyond pain. *It was Faith! Faith's been doing these things.* But as his rage increased so did his sense of helplessness. *She knows everything!* He looked at the bathroom door, dreading the sight of his wife, blinking to clear the burning in his eyes. He had never hated anyone so much as during those ghastly first minutes.

He looked for a date on the letter but there was none. He lifted the tray and looked under it, searching for an envelope. No luck. When did Faith receive this? What did it matter? Clearly she had gotten it before he killed Rachel. If she knows about Rachel, she knows about Sheila! And probably about Reeves. Was anything more vile, more detestable?

She put that dress in my office. It must've been her. His mind reeled. For a long moment he could do nothing but strain against the impulse to tear the letter to shreds. But he didn't. He put it back quickly, as he had found it. He had stumbled onto her vicious secret and now it was hidden, the way she had intended it.

You'll never know, he thought.

He heard her returning to the bedroom and fought his way desperately to the surface of his own terror. Okay, he muttered to himself. It's okay.

He was aware of movement behind him, through the light. His throat was tight. Did you say something, you sly bitch?

"If I'd known you would disapprove, I'd never have invited them," he heard her saying.

I should have sensed the danger a long time before. What a laugh, he thought, what a goddamned laugh. He was boiling with fury. "No," he said, he had to stop his voice from trembling. "I don't want to have the Fergusons over for dinner." The stunt was to keep talking—to keep her talking.

"I don't think I can change . . ." She made things sound so normal and sane, as she always did.

He kept his eyes turned toward the window. "Why did you ask them for Wednesday . . . anyway?"

Keep talking, he thought, and pretend . . .

"I had to ask them."

"I don't know why." Swiftly and precisely, Henry picked up the wire brush from the edge of her vanity and ran it through his hair. He was packed with violence.

"I'm sorry," Faith was saying. "I kind of had to. Can I do anything for you before we go?"

He summoned self-control from somewhere deep, deep within him. He shook his head.

She said, "Will you tell me if there is anything?"

Only stay away, Henry thought. Stay away from me. If you don't, I'll hurt you. There's nothing I can do about myself anymore. This thing's going to kill me. With the back of his hand he wiped the perspiration from his forehead. "Yes," he said.

When Faith looked over her shoulder at him, Henry was standing by the bay window, his hands clasping his hips, staring at her. His face showed no emotion whatsoever. Then she noticed something happen— not a change of expression, exactly, but a flicker behind the eyes. He smiled at her and it was a smile of recognition, almost of welcome.

"Henry . . . ?"

But he abruptly turned and left the room. He had the feeling he had spent hours, not inescapable minutes, with her. He went through the living room. In the garage, he hit the electronic door opener and the wide door ratcheted to the ceiling. The rainy, humid air struck him with its dampness.

Slater was shaking so hard he had to steady his right hand with his left to light the end of his cigarette. She's the one; she's behind it all. She did everything. Reeves was for nothing. Running his hand through his hair, he paced the floor, consumed with misery and hate. This is it. This is the end, Faith.

Ten minutes later, when Faith and Sheila came out, he was standing at the open garage door. He took a deep drag on his cigarette and blew a stream of smoke into the night. "Ready?" he asked, still tasting of some primeval, unreckoning fury.

Sheila was wearing a strapless black evening dress, her hair catching the light. She was young and irresistible and fatal. But he couldn't hold her close, couldn't say the things he longed to say. Not yet. The night shut down around them as they pulled out of the garage. Cars flew past them at the bottom of the hill, chrome flashing in the rush of lights. Slater knew he had to find a way to be alone with Sheila.

The smooth running lights of passing cars lost their dimension in the swirling white layers of fog and rain. It was raining more heavily as the Cadillac rumbled over the Rialto River Bridge, the girders appearing and disappearing in endless symmetry. The wind was howling on the wires; he saw the rainy night float by his windows and knew that this was the last time the three of them would be together.

They entered the Rod and Gun Club through the flagstone lobby with its beamed and vaulted ceiling. "It's a palace," Sheila whispered. "It's fantastic!"

Slater led them through the crowd with dignity, smiling into faces he hated. He didn't want to be here. "Do you want a drink?" he asked.

Faith nodded. Sheila said she'd have a Sprite. At a table nearby, a woman laughed—a throaty giggle filled with cognac—and leaned her head against her husband's shoulder. Faith couldn't remember the last time she had laughed without artifice, in the simple joy of the moment.

Henry was thinking nothing at all, still aghast at the shock of his discovery. When the waiter brought their drinks, he picked up his glass, drank it down and ordered another. He could hardly bear to look at Faith; then, seconds later, he couldn't take his eyes off her. He hated her.

The ballroom was crowded by then. The orderly arrangement of tables and chairs soon dissolved as the guests rearranged things to suit themselves. The waiter brought a second round. Unwillingly Slater's mind kept returning to Faith and the evil she had done. It was incomprehensible to him that he could have known her all these many years, *lived with her* for so long, and yet, suddenly, not know her at all.

One of the young men asked Sheila to dance and she rose from the table. Eyes followed her when she walked. Her body had lost none of its quicksilver lightness; it was there in every movement she made. He would make no more mistakes.

With the next dance, the table emptied and as soon as they were alone, his eyes were on his wife. It was as though everything in his soul had floated to the surface of his eyes with a mingling of fascination and loathing and fear. Faith thought, He must really be at the end of his tether.

All that evening he mulled over his hatred for her. He fantasized getting away from her, flying far away with Sheila. He longed to be rid of it all: the city and his position in it, the intrigues, the hypocrisy.

The evening was almost at an end when he got up to dance with Sheila. It would be the first time he had held her since she had come to live as a guest at their house. Taking his hand tightly, she leaned against him, her golden head just below his chin. The orchestra had already begun. "Who was that," he asked, "you were dancing with?"

"A friend," she said, with all the nonchalance of a seventeen-year-old. "Just a friend. From school." On the dance floor, she lifted a hesitant hand and settled it gently on the back of his neck. "You're not very mad at me, are you?" she asked coyly, and he could only answer, "No, not now."

They lost themselves in the crowd. Once again, he was aware of her as a part of himself—even her smallest movements followed and mirrored his. How wonderful it was to let all his worries dissolve for a few minutes as he felt himself drifting away in the warmth of her arms.

"You're miles away," he said.

"No," she murmured, "I'm here."

She smelled of the rain; he was conscious of drops glistening in her white-gold hair. "Have you been outside?"

"Just for a breath of air," she said, a secret, delicious smile lurked at the corners of her mouth.

He held her, feeling the urgent pressure of wanting her. She was close after weeks of waiting, but he knew the ritual, knew he would have to let her go. He could feel the heat emanating from her skin, her breath upon his face, her faint perfume. She had kept him perched on the keen edge of desire too long. She drew back and looked into his eyes. Her lips were close; he could smell the rose petal fragrance of her lipstick. The dim light stole down her cheek and along the line of her chin. She swayed gently against him.

He wanted her. She was fully a woman now, vibrant and sexy. He bent his head and whispered it in her ear; she put her head on his shoulder. In the very air they breathed, there was a feeling of exaltation. Slater loved her body—it was so vulnerable, so open to him. He loved her willful sexuality. He wanted desperately to clutch her to him and kiss her lovely red mouth—but he couldn't risk it. He drew back. Undoubtedly someone would see and he knew he would regret it afterward. Their love had never seemed so frail or so terribly important. They were close to freedom now, closer than they had ever been before. "Meet me," he said.

"I don't know," she whispered. "I shouldn't."

"Meet me, Sheila," he said again. "You've got to."

He could feel her give over to his embrace for a long, dangerous moment. "Henry," she whispered urgently, her eyes seeking his, "do you still think you love me?"

"Yes."

"Then, say it," she murmured. "Say you love me. Tell me, tell me."

And he did as she asked. "Meet me," he pleaded.

"I don't know. When?"

"Monday. Monday evening."

"Where?" she said. "What time?" And he told her.

She didn't stay any longer than she had to; with a smile she made her promise and broke from his arms swiftly and shyly. I can't lose you, he thought.

He and Faith left the party at eleven-fifteen and Sheila stayed behind with several of her friends. This time, driving back, it wasn't just adrenaline that burned through his veins but a slow, seething anger at himself. How could he have grown so slack, how could he not have known? He who had always planned for everything with such fastidious attention. He looked at his wife. Silence hung between them like a strange truce.

The house was lit by a single living room lamp. The door latch made a little click as it closed. Here at last, here alone at last, he did not try to touch her. Faith yawned and plucked off her earrings.

"Aren't you coming, Henry?" she said, going to the bedroom.

He turned off the light, as he did every evening, and went down the hall behind her. Sitting on the edge of the bed, he began to get undressed.

When Faith came from her dressing room, her leg slipped through the overlap of her nightgown and he saw her white thigh, her skin starved for the sun. The thought of lying down beside her utterly repelled him.

At midnight, Slater was in his den, wide awake. Sheila still hadn't come home. But even if she had, he didn't dare talk to her. That would have to wait until next week. He was drinking straight from the bottle now, savoring his rage, his mind going back to Faith, again and again.

He watched the drizzling beads of rain trickle down the windowpanes. Like the drops of rain caught in Sheila's hair when they danced. I can't turn back now, he thought. I've come too far. He couldn't afford to take even the slightest risk of Faith telling what she knew.

But it would have to happen in such a way that she had no fear, no warning.

36

"MORNING, MR. SLATER. Fill it with premium?"

"Fine," Slater said. He got out of the Cadillac, took off his suit jacket and rolled up his sleeves. "Tiny, how long would it take to get an oil change and a lube?"

The mechanic squinted at him from the gas pump. "I could squeeze you in—probably in fifteen minutes or so."

"Sounds good. Got anything I can drive?"

"How long would you be, Mr. Slater?"

"Maybe half an hour, forty-five minutes."

"You can always use the shop van—if you don't care what you're seen drivin'."

"That's all right," Slater said, "I'll try to be back by ten."

"Take your time."

Half a block from the St. Pius Catholic Church, he pulled up to the curb in the borrowed van and waited. It was 9:18 on Monday. Hardly five minutes had elapsed when Faith drove past him in the red Mazda. He watched her get out of the car and enter the chancery.

When she came back outside, Slater noted the time: 9:22. Faith was accompanied, not by Father Vasquez, but by a younger priest, one Slater didn't recognize. Impatiently, drumming his fingers on the steering wheel, he watched while the two of them spoke on the church steps; then, all at once, Faith was getting into her car and driving away. It was precisely 9:25.

He let her go through the next intersection, waited for a car to pass and then, shifting gears, he followed her in the borrowed van, staying back, giving her plenty of room. With the rear of her car in sight, he determined the exact route she took. Every Friday and Monday morning. Then he let her go.

The next day, at noon, while Faith was attending a luncheon, Slater followed the route she had taken again, this time with a stopwatch. Starting at the Catholic church, going past the high school and out toward the beaches, he moved through the city, matching her previous day's movements turn for turn, up into the higher altitudes of the old coastal highway. When he reached the parking lot of Mama Emilia's restaurant and souvenir shop, he pulled in and hit the plunger on the stopwatch. 10.4 minutes. And that was allowing for traffic and stoplights. This would be the perfect place. He would have to allow another thirty seconds or so for her to drive beyond the restaurant, and then, that would be that. Altogether she would have twelve, twelve and a half minutes to live after leaving the church.

The white Karmann Ghia convertible sat half-hidden off one of the trails to Blue Mountain Lodge. Slater pulled up behind it and stopped. He remembered riding in the car with her; he remembered giving it to her and the long night that had followed. Sheila had been out walking; he saw her coming toward him through the trees.

She was wearing blue jeans and a man's white

shirt. "I'd begun to think you really didn't want to see me . . . and this weekend I've got to go back to live with Mrs. Sanders," she said. "I wanted so much to talk to you again after that night at the picnic, but . . ." Sheila hesitated, then cleared her throat. "I guess I might as well tell you—I dream about being with you," she admitted, "almost every night." She looked away from him, as if her revelation had made her self-conscious.

"I dream about you, too," he said, never for a moment taking his eyes from her face. Here was his Sheila, restored to him at last. "What would you say if I asked you to go away with me somewhere? To come live with me and leave all this behind?"

She smiled. "Oh, you asked me that before," she said. "I never know when you're kidding—especially after that night at the picnic. Would you still want me to?"

"I want you to forget about that night. Of course, I want you to."

"But where would we go?"

Her presence made him reckless, heady. "I was thinking about Mexico. Or Rio."

"I don't know. I've never been to any place like that before. What am I going to be—your mistress? I can't do that."

"No, no . . . I . . ."

"What, then?"

"Let me finish . . . that's not what I'm asking you to do, Sheila . . . nothing like that. I was thinking we should get married; God, I swear I'll marry you."

"You don't mean it."

He was mesmerized by the pulse in the hollow of her throat. "Yes," he said, "I mean it." Now there could be no possibility of turning back.

"But how could we? I'm not old enough. And besides, Henry, you're already married."

"We'll get married there ... in Rio. No one will give a damn down there."

"But what about Faith?" she asked, flushing. "I love you, Henry, but how could I do that to Faith? She's my friend." Her slender shoulders were braced. The blood rushed into her face. "Oh, I *want* you to marry me. I want it. But I can't stand to think about it."

"I do nothing but think about it," he said.

"But what about Faith?"

"I just thought if I were ever free," he said. "Would you go away with me? Would you? Or not? I've got to know right now."

"Well—yes, yes, I would." She looked at him and tried to smile. "If you were free. But you're not free. It's impossible."

"I just wanted to hear you say it. You would go away with me then?"

Sheila smiled. "Henry, I love you more than anyone. You know that."

"I know," he said. "I know these things are dangerous. I know they're only thoughts and nothing can come of them. But I am so selfish ... I want to spoil you as if you were the only girl in the world."

Slater touched her shoulder and the touch was electric. He wanted to devour her but instead his lips found hers in gentle kiss, and yet when he tried to draw away, it was Sheila who held on. Her mouth was pressed to his, hard and full, her lips parted—he could taste their succulence. She was hot and damp from the heat, her body under the white shirt firm and yielding to his touch. "Oh, Henry ..." she gasped between kisses. It came upon her, overriding everything else, how much she loved him, how she could never feel his kisses without responding helplessly, that her passion for him was still very much alive.

"Don't leave me," he said simply. "Stay here with me tonight at the lodge. I want you to."

"I can't," she said, finally.

"Why?"

"I told you, Henry. You know why. Things are different now. There's Faith."

Then she was gone.

SATURDAY PASSED.

It was Sunday night, in the middle of the night, and Faith was sound asleep when Slater left the master bedroom. In the garage, he opened the trunk of the Cadillac and removed from the hollow in the spare tire, a parcel containing two sticks of dynamite and a remote-control device. Using the 150-watt shop light, he slid under Faith's red Mazda and attached the explosives to the floor of the car with soft malleable wire.

37

"LUISA, WHEN YOU'RE through picking up here," Faith said, "you can have the day to yourself, if you'd like. I won't be back for lunch and we'll be going out to dinner this evening. The only thing I ask is that you stop by and see if Mrs. Reeves needs anything."

"Yes, Mrs. Slater."

Gathering up her bag and notebook, Faith left the house. Seconds later, she backed the red Mazda out of the garage and sped down the brick driveway. It was 9:20 on Monday.

ON THE SIXTH floor of City Hall, the small square window stood open, rotated to its full axis, and through it, the lenses of Slater's binoculars scanned the city. Slowly, he tilted the glasses upward, sweeping over the roofs of houses until, in the deep distance, he fastened upon the sleek red blur of the Mazda making its way into town. Right on time, he thought.

Faith came to a stop and proceeded across the intersection. At 9:26, he watched the small red car idle in front of the St. Pius chancery while a large basket of what appeared to be clean laundry was loaded into the trunk. Scarcely a minute later, the car pulled away and vanished from sight in the dense foliage that lined the streets.

Slater started the stopwatch. Now, he would have a twelve-minute wait before the car reached the high, curving altitudes of the old coastal highway. The door to his private washroom was locked; the water in the sink was running to mask any incidental noise. He dampened the end of a towel in the cold water, wrung it out and wiped his face, all the time listening for even the slightest movement outside his door. But there was nothing. He glanced at the stopwatch. Nine and a half minutes remained. Putting the towel on the rack, he waited. When there were three minutes remaining, he took up the transmitter with its small black button and leveled it out the opened window. And waited. The red Mazda, shooting toward incandescence, was nowhere in sight, as planned.

FAITH DIDN'T KNOW if she saved any time by taking the shortcut through Marengo Park, but it always seemed like it and she was trying to be prompt with her errands this morning. When she came to the intersection of Park and Logan Avenue and turned the corner, she thought all was lost. A backhoe was digging out one entire section of the street. "Oh, no," she groaned, slapping the steering wheel and casting about for some means of escape. Faith might have been delayed indefinitely if the policeman on duty hadn't recognized her and motioned her around the yellow barricades.

She was zipping past the high school when, to her surprise, she saw Sheila walking across the lawn with half a dozen of her friends, and she braked behind the white Karmann Ghia. "Sheila!" she called, "Sheila, over here!"

"Oh, hi, Faith!" Sheila shouted, waving good-bye to the other girls. She jogged to the side of the car. "We just got out of cheerleading practice. You know, we've got our first game in a couple weeks."

"You must've gotten out early. I thought you said you'd be tied up until noon."

"Yeah, but I've got to come back this evening," Sheila said. "So what're you doing here?"

"Just running some things out to the resettlement camp. Want to come along?" Faith scooped up an armful of things from the passenger seat and dumped them into the rear.

"But—what about my car?"

"Oh, leave it. We'll pick it up later."

As soon as Sheila had closed the gleaming red door behind her, the Mazda whipped onto the street. Faith looked around at her and smiled. "I'm glad you decided to come," she said. They drove past the sign that read TO ELLINGTON BEACH and then made a right-hand turn onto the coastal highway, heading north. "I always take the old highway," Faith told her. "There's a place you've got to see."

SLATER TRIED TO ignore the slow passage of time. He waited, poised at the small window of his private bathroom. She's got to be up there by now, he thought. The minutes continued to fall away on the stopwatch. There were two minutes left. One—

I can't do this. I can't do it again. He lost his nerve. He let the needle sweep past its mark, his hands sweating and unsteady. It still wasn't too late, not yet. He put the transmitter down and wiped his hands on the towel and took it up again. He was thirty-five seconds past the time he'd set for himself. Forty-five seconds. It was getting away from him.

Now. It had to be now.

Slater hit the button.

Far in the hills to the north, he saw the blinding splinter of light. It was followed immediately by a small, white puff of smoke that marked the sky and then, like vapor, disappeared.

It was done. In seconds, it was over.

The red Mazda and his wife were no more.

THIRTY-FIVE MINUTES had passed and still he heard nothing.

The conference room grew more crowded. The opening and closing of briefcases, the shuffling of papers, the incessant salutations and clearing of throats—it had subsided to an even, low-level hum. Slater couldn't look at his watch, for fear of someone noticing. He found it almost unbearable to sit quietly and wait—to wait for the news to arrive. No matter how absurd it was or how careful he had been, he always half-expected the police to appear at any second to place him under arrest. This morning would be yet another test of will, of poise. Just get through it, he kept thinking, then everything will take care of itself. He studied the edge of the notebook opened before him and slowly went over in his mind every move he would have to make.

The meeting got under way. Childers, the county commissioner, launched into his report. His words, his obvious concern for the problems of the city, were irrelevant to Slater. It was as if, now that he had done what had to be done, everything else had been reduced to triviality. But he couldn't let down his guard. He knew that his performance had only begun; that his life depended on how persuasive he could be.

Several minutes had gone by when he heard the door open and Abigail's rapid, secretive footsteps cross the room. Okay. Slater leaned his head toward her confidentially, as he always did in the presence of others. She put her hand on his shoulder and bent close, whispering, her lips nearly grazing his ear. "There's been an accident," she said. "Mr. Slater, it's your wife; it's her car." He drew back, searching her face only a few inches above his own. Frowning, he muttered, "But she's all right . . . isn't she?" He felt strangely distanced from his secretary, as if he were soaring above the room.

"Oh . . . I don't think they know for sure. You see—her car—it was another bomb."

He opened his mouth to speak, but to anyone who saw him, he seemed unable to make a sound. Do this right, he thought. His face reflected waves of disbelief like a man drowning in deep water.

"A bomb?"

Overhearing him, two of the men at the table pushed back hesitantly, got up and left the room. Slater knew what they were doing. They would make calls and return with up-to-the-minute details.

Abigail's hand still rested on his shoulder; her voice was beginning to break. "Oh, Mr. Slater," she said, "oh, Mr. Slater." He stood, fighting for balance, as if overwhelmed by the ominous news she was giving him about his wife.

Done. It was done! After a few seconds, he pretended to recover his voice. "But where did it happen?"

"She was on the old coastal highway. Very near the place called Mama Emilia's." Abigail gripped his shoulder in support. "Are you going to be all right?" she asked.

He nodded. Dizziness, he thought—he did, in fact, feel dizzy. "Yes," he said, his voice rising, feigning outrage and grief, "but have we all gone out of our minds?" Even to him, his voice sounded like someone else's, someone who was losing control. "But what . . . happened? How the hell could this happen?"

One of the men beside him said quietly, "Easy, Henry, take it easy. You're only making things worse."

I've got to be careful, he thought. Play it safe—one part shock, one part grief. He nodded his head. This pretense was grim work; he was now a thoroughly pale and shaken man. "I've got to go there," he muttered. "I've got to get out there."

"I've arranged for a police escort," Abigail said. "They'll be here any second." Around him was deep silence; he was surrounded by a sea of horrified, uncomprehending faces. He could tell that the men had heard it all, which, of course, was exactly how he had imagined it happening. The word that Faith Slater had been killed by a bomb had spilled throughout the meeting room. Even more important, the men accepted the grave reality of yet another bombing without a trace of suspicion; if there was any sentiment in the air, it was one of hopeless pity for a man who bravely continued to cling to hope.

The air of urgency and tension increased with the arrival of the police. Guards came in. Slater saw two uniformed policemen enter the room and take up places inside the door. Through the now-crowded doorway, he glimpsed men with cameras—the press had arrived. As expected.

He was suddenly up on his feet. He wanted to seem as if he were dazed, a little lost. He continued to act as though he couldn't absorb the news. His two colleagues, who'd left minutes before, returned with further information. "Henry, don't try to go out there. Traffic's backed up both ways, and they're having a hell of a time getting emergency crews through. The coroner had to take a helicopter—and there's a stiff head wind off those cliffs. The pilot says he won't do it again."

Slater shook his head; all he said was, "I've got to."

"But there's nothing you can do."

Abigail said, "I'd like to come with you, Mr. Slater, if you don't mind. You shouldn't be alone at a time like this." With a nod he indicated his acceptance. He saw one of the policemen approaching to escort him out, and he took up his briefcase and moved forward through the hushed room.

Quickly, they went out, Abigail at his side, patrolmen front and back, a sergeant in the lead. Slater could feel the tension in the patrolmen. Aware of the barrage of flashbulbs, Slater lowered his head and put his arm out as though to fend them off. "Clear the area," the officer called. "Clear the area." The five of them were riding down in the elevator and moving out through the lobby.

The day was flowing like a mighty river, carrying him with it. The course he had set for himself could not be altered, and it seemed to him that it would go on forever. He told himself the worst of it was over. They were outside, getting into the second of the three waiting patrol cars. Slater climbed in the backseat, where the windows were covered with heavy-duty mesh wire. "Where's my car," he asked, as if in a daze.

"Don't concern yourself, Mayor. We'll have one of the men bring it out to your house."

Church bells rang, a loud jubilation that horrified him. From the backseat, he handed his car key to the officer in charge. It was a beautiful day, still soft and warm, the sky so blue it seemed purple, a smell of orchids in the air.

"You all right, Mr. Slater?" asked the patrolman behind the wheel.

"Let's go," he said and the three cars moved forward, red lights twirling, sirens signaling their departure. Along the route, silent policemen waved them on. Slater looked back and saw two police cruisers now following along behind. Here and there, small crowds gathered—there were more people now, filling up the sidewalks as though they'd been expecting him. Among them he glimpsed a girl wearing shorts—long, beautiful legs. He thought for a moment it was Sheila, but he couldn't see her face. *Sheila.*

And Abigail was talking to him, telling him he shouldn't be going out there. "Mr. Slater, the car's in a ravine about seventy-five feet down the side of the cliff. They can't get to—can't do anything until they bring the car up. It could take all day. Besides I wonder if she would want you to see her this way."

He waited an appropriate amount of time before answering her. "All right," he said weakly. "Then take me home. I'll wait there. But will you go back to the office and take the calls?"

"Yes, of course."

A SMALL CROWD of sightseers and a camera crew were waiting at the end of Slater's driveway by the time the patrolman waved the motorcade through. He allowed Abigail to hug him before he stumbled from the patrol car. "Are you sure you don't want me to stay with you?" she asked, handing him his briefcase.

"No," he said. "I just want to be by myself."

Slater could smell decay of leaves—a resiny, sweet rottenness—as he crossed the brick driveway, went up the walk. Head bowed, he stepped up to the veranda. Then he heard what he had been waiting for—the sound of the patrol car pulling away. He could hear the telephone ringing behind the front door as he unlocked it. *Safe. I'm safe.* Inside, he kicked the door shut and flipped the lock.

The gloom at the front of the house was relieved by light pouring in from the back balconies. Seeing that a second patrol car was now parked at the far end of his drive to keep the crowd back, Slater pulled the drapes closed on the large front windows.

How do I look? he wondered.

He moved to the long pier glass and stared at his face. Okay, okay. Despite the pretense of grief, he hadn't changed at all. His gray eyes were thoughtful, serious, his eyebrows brooded forbiddingly. He told himself that he'd been under a tremendous strain. Now all that would end.

He took off his suit jacket and threw it over the back of a chair. He unbuttoned his cuffs, rolled his sleeves and cleared his throat, "Anybody here?" he called. No one answered. Sheila? But no: he knew she had gone out for the day. Still, Sheila and the evening to come lingered in his thoughts.

All at once, the telephone rang again. The noise ran jarringly through the silent rooms. Christ, he said to himself and shuddered. It's enough to give you heart failure. He didn't want to deal with all the condolences, not yet, anyhow. Slater let it ring until it stopped, then he turned on the answering machine.

His feeling of liberation was enormous. He felt at ease and unburdened, expansive, benign. The si-

lence enveloped him. He pulled off his tie and threw
it on the sofa. The peacefulness of the house, the
fulfillment of a lifetime. It's over, he thought, *I've
done it!* This is my life now . . . the life I created. For
you, Sheila. For you.

He went to the recessed bookshelves at the end of
the room and pushed the spine of *David Copperfield*.
The hydraulics wheezed while the bar rose and arranged itself before him. On the third finger of his
left hand, in place of a wedding band, he wore the
expensive, square-cut diamond ring. It gave off brilliant splinters of light. With his right-hand fingers,
he gave the ring a few twists for good luck.

With his fingertips, he pushed the side panel and
his secret cash drawer sprang open. From inside it,
he removed two airline tickets to Rio. While pouring
himself a stiff Scotch, he looked them over and put
them back. He drank quickly, gulping it down as if it
were water, and took a deep breath. "Damn that's
good," he said and poured another, taking it with
him to the master bedroom.

Before he did anything else, he closed the blinds
on the front-facing windows and opened the sliding
glass doors to the back balcony, savoring the breezes
that washed over him. Air the damned place out, he
thought. He stepped outside and looked down for
perhaps the last time, because as soon as this matter
was cleared away, he would be getting the hell out of
here. He saw the hills and trees and the city below,
but the view paled next to what he was feeling. He
started to laugh and couldn't stop. Coming back
inside, he placed his wallet on the dresser, his cigarettes and lighter and loose change, and sat down on
the bed and laughed and laughed. It had been like

nothing in this world. He knew he could do anything now, anything at all.

Slater clicked on the remote of the giant TV set and ran through the local channels with their mini-cam reports from the scene of the bombing. A milling crowd had gathered at the site—one of the cameras had zoomed in on two Mexican women with crucifixes, heads bowed in prayer. Slater leaned back on the bed and stretched out his legs. What a relief. He fished a cigarette from the pack and lit it. He laughed until there were tears in his eyes. Good, he thought. *Good!* Except for the formalities, it was behind him now.

Smoking the cigarette and drinking his Scotch, he watched the telecast. Slightly out of focus in the background, behind the announcer, Slater could see the two wreckers with their steel cables, still trying to recover Faith's Mazda from the side of the cliff. But it hadn't been brought up yet. He switched channels and turned the volume up.

". . . interrupt our normally scheduled programing to bring you this special report," said the announcer at the news desk. "It now appears that a car driven by Mrs. Henry Lee Slater, wife of the mayor of Rio Del Palmos, has been the latest target of a terrorist bombing. We are awaiting news of Mrs. Slater's condition at this time. Mayor Slater has been taken home, devastated with grief . . ."

Again Slater changed channels. ". . . it may be another twenty minutes before they're able to bring the vehicle up. But we repeat, please stay tuned for further developments . . ."

That'll come next, he thought. The morgue. I'll have to go to the damned morgue.

Humming to himself, he took off his shirt, then

his shoes and socks. He stepped out of his trousers and hung them up. Turning the volume up so the news could be heard from the bathroom, he shed his shorts and got into a hot shower. With clouds of steam coming up around him, Slater forgot his disappointments, his problems, his fears. He was happy— happier than he had ever imagined possible. How had he lived without her? he wondered. How had he possibly lived before this beautiful girl came to him, before her body keened so perfectly to his? He remembered how languid her eyes became after they made love, how she ran her hands up through her hair, its long champagne strands streaming through her fingers.

As soon as Slater was out of the shower, he finished his drink and wrapped in a towel, went to the living room for another. He roamed barefoot through the house, his own territory, utterly free.

When that was gone, he filled his glass with ice, broke open a new bottle of Johnnie Walker Black and took the bottle, the glass and the ice down the hall to the bedroom and the television.

But what was this?

The camera's angle had revealed a sickening apparition—the road crew was bringing the battered red Mazda up over the ledge. Suddenly, he felt the chill of revulsion, of horror.

"Jesus," he gasped.

He shouldn't be seeing what he was seeing. No. With a shock of recognition he saw long blond hair dangling against the flame-red side of the Mazda. What's this? he thought.

What the hell is this?

His heart was racing with such fright he felt it might explode in his chest.

"Oh, Jesus!"

The thing he saw was inconceivable: radiantly pale hair. But Faith has dark hair. It's someone else, he thought.   ut who? No one had hair like that—no one but Sheila. *Sheila?* Something's wrong with this, he told himself. There's some kind of mistake.

That part of his mind still in touch with the possibilities told him that the girl—whoever she was—was dead. *Dead.* He couldn't believe it. Any of it. He grabbed up the remote control and began flicking through the stations two and three at a time.

On the screen, Slater watched aghast as the battered rear end of the Mazda, dangling from the wrecker's chain, shifted; the car jostled, the girl's face lolled against the frame of the blasted window.

"No—no, I didn't, I couldn't—" He felt a vast, delirious unreality. For an instant, he saw her lips rising to meet his, a memory of hallucinatory vividness, but ever-fading, an experience that melted before his eyes. He said it out loud, "Oh, Jesus God, it's Sheila!"

What was she doing? She shouldn't be there. Bile flew to the back of his throat. *It's her! It's Sheila!* He said, "Oh, God! Oh, my God! *I killed her! I killed her, too!*"

He didn't know from one minute to the next where he was or what was happening. The announcer said, "The body has now been identified as that of Sheila M. Bonner, seventeen . . ."

No.

Slater grabbed the remote control and hit the buttons.

". . . the body of Sheila Bonner . . ."

No!

He changed the channels; he strained for one last glimpse of her.

". . . the victim is Sheila Bonner . . ."

No! No! No!

He hit the button faster and faster, always the chance that he might see her again lured him on, deeper and deeper. *I killed her, too.* Slater could feel the pain everywhere, even to the ends of his fingers. His will to happiness, his self-control, everything crumbled.

All the voices were saying, ". . . the body of Sheila Bonner . . ."

I killed her, too.

He couldn't get the sight of her lifeless face out of his mind.

Suddenly he was sobbing. He heard the despairing cry that rose in his throat—the sound of devastation and of grief. He could no longer bear to watch; he reached out and hit the button and the large screen faded to black.

Instantaneously, reflected on the black screen, a shape materialized before him.

An insane terror ripped through his mind. He realized there had to be someone behind him, but he was too terrified to turn around. And the more he stared at its pale image, the less clear the outlines became—it was like staring into the sun. Summoning his strength, he slowly turned.

Faith!

Slater thought he might be going mad. *It's Faith! But how could it be?*

Framed against the shimmering sky, she stood there on the balcony straight and pale and slender, her cold fanatical eyes boring into him. Had she been here all along? Her hair had slipped free of its aus-

tere arrangement, it streamed over the whiteness of
her face. Her slim arms hung at her sides—a statue
carved of flesh.

Faith.

A deep, dead cold spread through him. There was
no thought, only the massive shock in the gut. He
leaned back against the wall, closed his eyes and
tried to grip his nerves back into control. The room
seemed too small for the both of them. He saw that
she wore bracelets, and with her every step, the
sound of them, like the clatter of bones, grated viciously on his nerves.

He saw her coming for him, straight as a slab,
bloodless, ghostly, she seemed. But Slater couldn't
move. She seemed furious, capable of anything, and
at the same time, fearful of him, almost in tears. Her
mouth was trembling so much she couldn't speak.
He stepped back in horror.

Slater had never before lost consciousness in his
life—not from drink, not from a blow—but he thought
he might be going to now. His legs doubled up
under him. Everything became a sickening whirl of
ice-colored silver light.

Her face looked hard and parched as bone. "You
killed her," she said. She sounded delirious with
hatred. "But you didn't mean it to be her, did you,
god damn you! You meant it to be me."

He recoiled, trying to back away from her, but he
was against the wall. The hand he held out to defend
himself could not stop the force of the words. "You
didn't know I picked her up before I stopped at
Mama Emilia's, did you? I went to get empanadas
for us. I was coming back to the car when it blew
up." He started to sob again, his hands covering his
eyes. "No, Henry, I want you to listen to this." She

grabbed his hands away from his face. "You've got to hear what you did. I wish I could make you feel what it was like, Henry—to see her die!"

And he knew what had happened to Sheila out there. "I left her in the car," Faith said, "while I went inside. You did it! You did it! You killed her!"

Every word was like a nail in him.

"And you meant it to be me."

Slater wept. He heaved for breath; tears ran silently down his face.

Faith got up and straightened her clothes. "Don't stay down there, Henry," she said, at last. "Come, I'll help you up."

He rose like someone in a trance, only realizing what he had done after he had taken her hand.

She had him steady on his feet. "Don't worry," she said. "Everything's under control. I won't tell anyone." She opened the bedroom door and led him through it, her voice calm. "I'll take care of you."

Music was coming from somewhere. Faith was leading him down the hallway toward the dining room. He was coming around slowly.

"You want romance," she said, and Slater could smell something cooking.

At the end of the hall, at the end of all he could see, the walls of the dining room shimmered with a fiery amber light, a light that gleamed from their china and silver and crystal.

"I'll give you romance," she said.

Then he saw the lighted candles. She had fixed lunch. Had she been expecting guests?

"When you're alone . . . the magic moonlight dies. At break of dawn . . . there is no sunrise . . . when your lover has gone."

Sinatra.

He turned his head toward the closed study door, where the music was coming from. It was unimaginable that Faith was expecting guests, so why had she set out the silver?

"... *like faded flowers ... life can't mean anything ...*" Faith moved close and put her arm around his waist. And through his numbness and despair, he heard her say, "I loved you, Henry, God knows why." Then in a flash of comprehension, he understood. She hadn't been expecting anyone but him.

He looked around at her and there were tears gathered in her eyes, tears that rolled down her cheeks. "Henry, Henry, did you hate me so much?"

Suddenly the spell was broken. And here it was, his uncontrollable hatred, his threat. She could see it in his eyes.

"No," she told him. "No, my darling, never again. You won't ever do those things again."

The fire went out of him. And he looked around, at the table set for two, at the shut door through which the music came, and from his depths, he said, "My God, Faith, what've you done to me?"

EPILOGUE

ALL WAS CALM in Rio Del Palmos, all serene.

There were those, of course, who wondered at the tragedies that befell Rachel Buchanan and her granddaughter. How could such terrible things happen, they asked, to just one family? And yet as suddenly as the bombings and murders descended on the city, they ceased. The trouble washed away like rain.

Most people said that if it wasn't for Mayor Slater and his wife, Faith, the feeling of renewal might not have happened so thoroughly or so quickly. But what an inspiration they were and how brave. Those who attended Sheila Bonner's funeral would never forget Mrs. Slater's eloquent and uplifting eulogy. No one who stood in the crowd while Henry Lee Slater dedicated the plaque commemorating Chief Burris Reeves at police headquarters could help but feel better for it afterward. And the women of the town were especially moved by how attentive the mayor was to his wife, Faith, after so many years of marriage. Whenever he had to go away on business, he took her along. And no matter how busy he was, he always made it a point to be home on time, for her romantic candlelight dinners.

From time to time, the two of them could be seen sitting across from each other outside on the veranda in the evening. How soft the breezes were that made the branches sway and the leaves tremble. Soft as a sigh. No one noticed the play of shadows across the front of the old brick, the streamers of shadows that were like a vast, twilit spider's web.

Perhaps if you stayed long enough and watched carefully, you would see its larger design—that the web was there every evening.

And would be forever and ever.

ABOUT THE AUTHOR

GARY DEVON was born and grew up on the banks of the Ohio River, a part of the country to which he has since returned with his wife and son. Educated in Indiana and Iowa, he is the author of the critically acclaimed first novel *Lost*, which was nominated for an Edgar Award.